The Mazovia
Legacy

The Mazovia Legacy

The snow in a Montreal winter covers a multitude of sins...

MICHAEL E. ROSE

McArthur & Company
Toronto

This paperback edition published in 2004 by McArthur & Company

First published in 2003 by
McArthur & Company
322 King St. West, Suite 402
Toronto, Ontario M5V 1J2
www.mcarthur-co.com

National Library of Canada Cataloguing in Publication

    Rose, Michael E. (Michael Edward)
    The Mazovia legacy : the snow in a Montreal winter covers
    a multitude of sins— / Michael E. Rose. — Mass market ed.

    ISBN 1-55278-406-1

    I. Title. II. Series: Rose, Michael E. (Michael Edward).
    Frank Delaney mystery series.

    PS8585.O729M39 2004   C813'.6   C2003-906282-1

Jacket + Composition: *Mad Dog Design*
Author photo: *Matt Dunham*
Printed and bound in Canada by: *Webcom*

The publisher would like to acknowledge the financial support of the
Government of Canada through the book Publishing Industry Development
Program (BPIDP) and the Canada Council for our publishing activities.
The publisher further wishes to acknowledge the financial support of the
Ontario Arts Council and the Government of Ontario through the Ontario
Media Development Corporation's Ontario Book Initiative for our
publishing program.

10 9 8 7 6 5 4 3 2 1

I do not like being moved: for the will is excited
and action is a most dangerous thing.
I tremble for something factitious,
some malpractice of heart and illegitimate process.
We're so prone to these things,
with our terrible notions of duty.

A.H. CLOUGH

Sound, sound the clarion, fill the fife,
Throughout the sensual world proclaim,
One crowded hour of glorious life
Is worth an age without a name.

T.O. MORDAUNT

PART I

Montreal, Quebec — Winter 1995

Chapter 1

The snow in an overlong Montreal winter covers a multitude of sins. It covers the dirty pavement and gives the more rundown of the city's houses and apartments a postcard appearance that they don't always deserve. A heavy snowfall muffles sounds, blanketing busy streets in eerie silence at unexpected times of the day or night. Cars and buses glide noiselessly by. The sky takes on a leaden hue and the sun is just a circle of slight, white light somewhere above the bare black branches of trees.

People take no pleasure in their winter walking in Montreal. In a heavy snowfall, they move quickly, bundled up against the wet flakes and the cold. The colour of their clothing is muted by the weak light. Collars and scarves are held up against faces that rarely look left or right. The walkers wish only to hurry forward, careful not to slip on icy sidewalks or stumble over banked-up snow, the sooner to remove their heavy coats and boots in the warmth of office, shop, or home.

It was on a January day like this that Stanislaw Janovski, a very old but still very sturdy Polish émigré, got off the Number 24 bus at the corner of Sherbrooke and Claremont streets in a neighbourhood called Westmount. It was midweek, a Tuesday, and getting on to late afternoon. The light was fading even faster than normal because of the thickness of the grey clouds overhead and the snowflakes falling steadily. Claremont begins to rise sharply north of the Sherbrooke Street shops, and Stanislaw faced a treacherous, slippery uphill walk under a row of aging elms to Chesterfield Street and then left to his solid red-brick house on the quiet cul de sac.

He paused before beginning the climb and looked around. Many men in their eighties, as he was, might have done the same after the long bus ride he had just finished, needing a breather and taking their bearings before attempting the final few hundred snowy metres toward home. But Stanislaw was not stopping to catch his breath. Instead, he intently scanned the crowds and the cars.

That brief survey of the terrain appeared to satisfy him somehow and he adjusted his scarf and his old-fashioned Russian-style fur hat. *Coast clear,* he said to himself as a former military man might. His long tweed overcoat added to his somewhat military bearing, even though he was far too short to fit the quintessential image of the soldier, the Polish soldier. He turned his attention to the way ahead.

He carried no walking stick, but clutched a small, scuffed leather briefcase with no handle, as he always did on his excursions, inside which could be found the latest edition of *Le Devoir*. He always carried newspapers with him to read while riding on buses or the Métro, or while waiting for the few old acquaintances who were still alive to join him for their now infrequent lunchtime reunions.

It was from one of these lunches that he was returning on that January day. He thought about it as he trudged up Claremont Street, with the snowflakes gathering as they always did on his bushy grey eyebrows. The meeting place, as usual, had been the *Brasserie des Sources* in the city's east end across from the tower that housed the CBC. All the Canadian Broadcasting Corporation services were in that tower, in both an English and a French incarnation, like so much of Canadian life.

Stanislaw had spent many years working for the Polish short-wave service in that tower of broadcast babble. He had loved the highly charged atmosphere at Radio Canada International — an atmosphere created whenever expatriates from dozens of political and social backgrounds are thrown together somewhere in the world and required to broadcast information to their former homelands.

In those years, the short-wave service had been hungry for speakers of foreign languages who were literate, reasonably sane, and could at least make a good pretence of objectivity in their broadcasts. Not that any except the most naive of the Canadian producers expected the Polish Service, for example, to be sympathetic to the Communist regime installed in Warsaw after the war. Nor did they expect the broadcasters to be able to forget their grievances and their family histories and their dashed personal hopes.

Stanislaw had met many expatriate Poles at the

CBC, many with stories more or less like his own —
a hurried exit from Poland when the Germans
attacked in 1939, refugee status, and family tragedy
as they made their way to France and eventually to
Britain to join the Polish forces assembling there.
Parents and other loved ones left behind. Comrades
killed along the way. Stanislaw's story was not
unique. But to be around people who could even
begin to imagine such stories was a small comfort
for him in the lonely days of his Montreal exile. And
those lonely days were frequent with his wife now
gone for almost fifteen years.

The lunches at *Brasserie des Sources* were invari-
ably surrounded by the hubbub of dozens of journalists and technicians who hurried over from the
tower each day to eat and drink and argue and
scheme. Until recently, there would have been three
or four other Poles of émigré vintage with whom
Stanislaw could have had a sensible conversation.
They would have talked of the war or the betrayal at
the Yalta peace conference after the fighting ended
and the recognition of the Communist regime that
followed. They would certainly have argued about
that Solidarity peasant electrician Lech Walesa who
had proved such a disappointment as president since
the Communists were thrown from power in 1989.
But most of Stanislaw's older colleagues no longer
came for lunch.

There were, of course, the younger Polish broadcasters, who had not been born when the war began
and who had grown up under the Communists and

somehow ended up in Montreal. These young men wore their Solidarity lapel pins like war decorations. They found it amusing to bait the older ones who had fought with rifles or bomber planes for their country, rather than having marched with the pickets in Gdansk or Warsaw. But the young ones could never really know what Stanislaw and his comrades-in-arms had done for Poland from many miles away, in France, in Britain and, yes, even in Canada.

Even the young ones, though, shared Stanislaw's deep concern for the way things were now going in Poland — the repeated changes of prime minister, the financial crises, the persistent rumours of Walesa's authoritarian bent and of his shady advisers, the worries about the second post-Communist presidential election that was to come later in the year. Walesa looked certain to lose that election, they all agreed. But what might befall Poland if a Communist president took power once again?

Stanislaw was drawing nearer to his house now and his breathing was heavier, not because of the climb, although this had been more of a challenge in recent months, but because these thoughts weighed heavily on him. The lunch today had ended on a jolly note as usual, with young Kwiencinski or someone else laughing off all the unkind or unthinking things that had been said, with another round of draft beer, with more steaming plates of Quebecois food brought to the table, with no one, apparently, meaning any harm.

"All friends here, Stanislaw," Kwiencinski had said. "Good loyal Poles one and all."

But now, as he approached his house, Stanislaw felt his cheeks heat up with regret. He wished that his oldest friend, his brother-in-arms F.O. Navigator Zbigniew Tomaszewski, were here to talk to, rather than old and alone in Paris. Letters and brief telephone calls were now their only connection. How could young fools like Jerzy Kwiencinski or, for that matter, drunken fools of retirement age like Pawel Bazlyko ever know, while they ate their lunches and drank their beer, the truth of what he, Stanislaw, had done for his country? Zbigniew, his friend and his navigator, knew. He knew all that Stanislaw had allowed him or anyone else to know.

An intense memory of a freezing bombing run over Europe, as the Mazovia Squadron headed out once more from Scotland to pound smoking German cities, filled Stanislaw's mind and grasped at his heart. Zbigniew, not thirty, and Stanislaw, just as young, together on a Wellington, fighting from the air for Poland. The Polish Air Force, regrouped and reborn.

Tears threatened, when in the past such memories only brought pride or adrenalin. *Not to cry in this cold*, Stanislaw ordered himself. *You are becoming an old fool. Soft and full of tears.*

This ambush by emotion stirred other feelings as he paused for a moment in the falling snow. He looked apprehensively over his shoulder once again, as he had done when getting off the bus. He remembered why he had to remain vigilant and he wished even more fervently that Zbigniew were closer, that someone could help him now in this very difficult matter. He wished even for his dear wife to be back on this earth — poor Margot who had always longed so desperately for Poland, who could never accustom herself to Montreal or to the French Canadians. Though he would never have involved her, never have put her in the way of anything like this, he wished she could be inside the house this afternoon, turning on lamps and putting on the kettle.

Even his niece, Natalia, so dear to him she was like the daughter he and Margot had never had, was not in the city today for at least a coffee and some small cakes to cheer him up. *Natalia will be shortly back,* he thought as he turned into Chesterfield Street. As he walked the final few paces home, he thought: *We will talk then, a little, I think. Maybe Natalia and I will talk of these matters a little.*

At his doorway Stanislaw paused again. The snow had covered his black fur hat and the old tweed on his shoulders. He shook white flakes from his briefcase and then unzipped it to find his key. The light was failing quickly now and the storm showed no sign of stopping. He sighed heavily and put the key into the heavy brass lock. As he stood on the snow-swept stairs he suddenly looked very much the old, lonely, and frightened man of eighty-three that he was.

As he stepped inside he was careful not to tread with his wet boots on a scattering of mail on the vestibule carpet. Without taking off his boots or hat or coat, he stooped to gather the envelopes and eagerly checked them all.

"Nothing," he said out loud.

He tossed the sheaf of mail onto a small, white shelf that held a variety of gloves and hats and an old wooden-handled clothes brush, and he sat down on a stool to remove his boots. He carefully shook and hung up his coat and lovingly brushed the black sable of his hat before placing it on a rack in the corner. As he always did on such days, he warmed his hands briefly on the hot-water radiator just inside the door and then put his feet into a pair of maroon corduroy slippers before moving on into his house.

It was a solid comfortable place, with high, white ceilings, carved wooden banisters, and stained glass in the windows. Stanislaw and Margot had bought the house many years ago, when displaced people like themselves could still afford homes in this part of lower Westmount. Even though Margot had been gone for many years, Stanislaw still kept the house in the spotless, obsessively tidy condition she had preferred, and which, if the truth were known, he too had always preferred despite his protests at the hours she spent cleaning and polishing.

Stanislaw moved to the living-room window and looked out furtively between the heavy brown drapes and white curtains his wife had made with her own hands. Then he pulled the drapes all the way across, and he went back to the front door to make sure it was securely locked.

It was too early for supper and, in any case, he was not going to be hungry after the large meal he had eaten at lunch. So he wandered, as he often did, enjoying the quiet of the house and examining the bits and pieces from his past that were set out lovingly on tables, mantels, and shelves. Later, he thought, he would listen to his old short-wave radio and then read and smoke a little.

It was the pictures he liked to examine the most in these wanderings inside his own home — pictures in shiny frames that lent the images the respect and attention they deserved. There was the one of himself and Margot with his brother and his wife at some lakeside beach in the 1950s, soon after they had married. There was their wedding picture, taken outside the stone church in Saint-Sauveur, the Laurentian village north of Montreal where they had all had so much joy skiing and hiking.

Beside the wedding picture was the one of Stanislaw and some Radio Canada International colleagues standing in front of the newly opened tower on Dorchester Boulevard. And beside that was a much older photo of him and some comrades in the Mazovia Squadron, a very faded 1940s image in shades of grey and burnished yellow. It showed them in Scotland, all standing near a large bomb on a wooden roller before it was loaded onto an aircraft. One of the squadron was crouching to write some Polish threat or vow in chalk on the side of the bomb and the others were smiling and clasping each other around the shoulders or making V-for-victory signs.

Not such a good photo to have had perhaps in our peaceful living room all these years, he thought. *War photos*. There was another picture of himself in a leather flying helmet, sticking his head out the small pilot's window of a Wellington, with the red-and-white-checkered square of the Mazovia Squadron painted on the side just above the images of bombs that indicated how many runs the plane had survived. In this photo there were twenty-three such little images.

Then there were the photos of Natalia — many photos, large and small, everywhere. Natalia as a baby with her parents, Stanislaw's brother and his wife; others of her as a lovely young woman just before her parents died, suddenly and together; still more photos of her as a university graduate with Stanislaw and Margot standing beside her as proud as her parents would have been. The most recent photograph showed Natalia now, when she was almost forty and a psychologist, a very good one, an intellectual — Dr. Janovski, just as Stanislaw's own father had been Dr. Janovski at the University of Krakow before the Nazis killed him.

She must marry very soon, time is passing, Stanislaw thought as he replaced the picture among the cluster of other frames. *When she gets back to Montreal I will tell her this again.*

When the telephone rang, Stanislaw was startled and his heart began to pound in his chest.

Natalia? he thought. *From Zurich?* He moved to the phone table and stared apprehensively at the receiver before picking it up.

"Janovski," he said in English. "This is Janovski."

The male voice at the other end was deep, and Stanislaw had heard it before. *No*, Stanislaw thought. *Not this.*

"Ah, Janovski, you are back at last," the Polish-accented voice said in English. "We have been wishing very much to talk to you again."

"And I've told you I have no wish to speak to you until you can explain to me better your business and who you represent," Stanislaw said, the irritation in his voice masking fear.

"We think, Janovski, that you should meet us," the voice said. "The telephone is unsatisfactory in these matters."

"No. I have told you no," Stanislaw said. "Not before I know more about who has sent you and what you want exactly."

"We can explain this, Janovski, do not fear. We will explain it all in private when we meet. The telephone is not good."

"No meeting," Stanislaw said. "You must first send me some sign I will recognize. I've told you this."

"In time, my friend. In time," the voice said. "Why would we have contacted you at all if our intentions were not good, if we did not represent those you yourself have been seeking to contact? How would we know of you at all?"

"This is not good enough," Stanislaw said. "These are serious matters. I have told you I do not like all of these phone calls. I didn't think it would be like this. I need some indication of your credentials."

"Our credentials," the voice said. A bitter laugh came down the line. "Yes, well, our credentials can be had easily enough. But the telephone is not for this sort of thing, Janovski, not for credentials. We must come to see you and then all will become clear."

"No. Impossible," Stanislaw said. He hung up and stood breathing heavily.

This is becoming too much for me, he thought. *These are surely not the ones. It has been too long now since I first tried.*

He walked to the window and peered out carefully. The car was back. Exactly the same car, with two men in it like the other days. It must have just arrived, but already the snow was beginning to build on the hood, the roof, the trunk. The warmth from inside was clearing the windshield and moisture ran in rivulets down the outside of the glass. Stanislaw could see a dark figure on the driver's side dialling a mobile telephone.

Then his own telephone rang again. Stanislaw thought: *They are calling from just outside my own house.*

He rushed to the door to check the lock once more and then grabbed the telephone receiver.

"No," he shouted into it. "You must give me a sign before I speak to you again."

He slammed the receiver down. *Calmly, calmly,* he told himself. *You are a soldier. This can be managed.*

His breathing slowed. *They will not come in*, he thought. *I will not allow them to come in. I have nothing to say to them.* He looked at the old clock ticking slowly on the mantelpiece — 4:10 p.m. *It will be dark soon*, he thought. *Not good.*

He sat in his armchair and considered the situation.

They have been outside before, he thought. *But if they are telephoning from outside, is this not an important change? Perhaps they have now decided that they will see me whether I wish to see them or not.*

This thought troubled him. But then his old face slowly took on an expression of resignation.

I have had troubles before, he thought. *Much worse trouble than this.*

He sat very still in his chair, doing nothing. As he had sometimes sat alone before a mission during the war. Then, with something decided, he moved to the telephone and sat at the small stool near the table on which it stood. He dialled a number, waited, and then began to speak slowly and at length.

"Ah, Natalia," he said in English. "Your famous answering machine. You know how much I despise these machines. But this time I will leave you a message. At last you will be happy. It is your Uncle Stanislaw speaking."

Fool, he thought, *she knows this. She would know this.*

"I am sorry you are still away," he continued. "There is something very important I need to speak to you about when you return. I wanted to tell you there is something, so you would know as soon as you get back."

This is not making sense, he thought. *You will alarm the girl unnecessarily. You cannot make changes in these recordings once they are started. Say exactly what needs to be said.*

"I have been worrying about some important matters these past months and you yourself remarked on this, I know, before you left. So perhaps we could speak just as soon as you get in, please, if that is all right. Could you call me immediately? There are matters you should now perhaps know a little about. Yes. And, yes, I should also say, even though you know this, that I love you very much, Natalia, my dear. But you know that, I suppose. I do hope I have never hurt you with my foolish bad temper or my old-fashioned way."

Tears came, and he found it difficult to continue.

"I am sorry, Natalia, for this call," he said. "But you will understand better when we see each other at last and I can talk to you face to face. So goodbye, darling. Stanislaw."

He stood up. He wished he had not left his name at the end of the message, as if it had been a letter. *It is a tape-recorded message, old fool, not a letter,* he thought. And why call her and then tell her nothing? He wished there was some way to call again and erase the message he had left. He thought: *I have mishandled this. All of this.*

Suddenly he felt very tired and very old. He was sleepy from the afternoon's heavy meal and the beer and the warmth of his house after the cold of the streets outside. Suddenly he wished only to doze for a time on his sofa and then listen to a program on his radio before going to bed for the night. He wished for a night with no troubles.

The telephone rang again. This time Stanislaw only sat and stared at it. It stopped ringing eventually and he waited quietly, listening to the ticking of the clock.

When he eventually heard the sound of footsteps on the verandah and the knock that came at the door, he did not jump, he was not surprised, because he had suspected that the men outside would come. He waited, and the knock was repeated, louder this time but muffled by the glove that covered the knocking hand. He knew that the knock would come again. He had known in his heart that the events he set in motion, so long ago it seemed now, would somehow come to something like this.

He stood up and faced the door. He thought: *The war is never over.*

Chapter 2

The pilot's voice when it came over the speakers was businesslike, ever-so-slightly military, and jovial, all at the same time. It sounded like all pilots' voices do when the destination airport is almost in sight after a long international trip over water. The flight from Geneva to Montreal had gone well, the voice told the passengers, and good tailwinds meant that they would be coming into Montreal Mirabel just a few minutes ahead of schedule at 8:46 p.m. The city had been suffering under a heavy snowfall and strong winds for the past three days, the voice said, and the bad weather had cleared just a few hours ago. So they were in luck. And would they all please have a pleasant weekend in Montreal, and thanks for flying Air Canada.

Natalia Janovski was not awakened by this announcement because she rarely slept on airplanes. Instead, she enjoyed the dark mystery of narrow, silent cabins littered with bundled sleeping shapes and illuminated here and there by intense shafts of light from overhead reading lamps. She was one of those introverted people who sat for hours in darkened airplane cabins, as if under a spotlight, reading quietly, perhaps writing, perhaps just lost in the musings that enforced stillness and the presence of many strangers inspire.

In fact, this flight, more than many in Natalia's recent memory, had been unusually dreamlike. It had been like a long dream of travel. The dreaminess was partly to do with her fatigue, but also partly because in recent days she had been devoting all her energy to intensifying and deepening exactly this sort of introversion.

Just as her fellow passengers were now stirring and stretching and smiling wanly to one another as the cabin lights were brightened and cabin crew began to bustle around for the final few minutes of the flight, so Natalia was beginning to come back in a more general way to her waking state, her daytime persona of a young professional woman, single and thirty-seven years old, a consulting psychologist with a life in Montreal and responsibilities to clients and to everyday matters in the world.

For the past several weeks since Christmas, she had been able to ignore all that and to delve, with the guidance and encouragement of like-minded colleagues at the Jung Institute in Zurich, into the world of dreams. These visits to Zurich were, of course, part of the long, daylight road to certification as a Jungian analyst; but Natalia liked to think that she would have made pilgrimages there anyway, that alone in small hotel rooms she would have scribbled each night and morning in dream journals anyway. Because this inner world was where Natalia felt she was most at home.

Each trip like this, each time she dipped further into Jung's treasure chest of ideas, she felt her affinity for his thinking increase: that there are archetypal ways of experiencing all that is grave and constant in human life, that these archetypes manifest themselves across cultures and across history as symbols and dreams from the collective unconscious for those attentive to them. Such Jungian precepts had by now become articles of faith for her. The "inner work," as the Jungians liked to call what they did, had been productive for her once again. Natalia was coming home, as always after such trips to Zurich, feeling replenished.

But the time had been intense and so she was pleased that the journey home was a long one. Even Jungians do not always find it comfortable looking deep into their own psyches, do not always like all of what they see there. Natalia always needed something to act as a punctuation mark between the work at the institute and the resumption of her life and duties in Montreal. To move quickly, like some of the European participants in the sessions, from the rarefied atmosphere of the villa beside Lake Zurich back into their waking lives would be too much for her. She had been happy, therefore, to be able to sit dreamily in the near dark for the entire flight, turning thoughts and dream fragments and new perceptions around in her mind like treasured objects picked up on a beach holiday.

The long journey, too, had had the effect of bringing her in touch, sometimes more sharply than she would have preferred, with the real world. *No*, she chided herself, as the Jungians in Zurich would most certainly have done. *Not the real world, because the world of dreams and imagination is every bit as real. Not the real world but the waking world, the exterior world.*

That world had thrust itself upon her almost as soon as she had checked out of her *pension* in Zurich so many hours ago on that same day. The train journey to Geneva was a bracing tonic of Swiss efficiency and also, she thought with a smile, a metaphor. It forced her to sit face-to-face with a row of other human beings in the second-class carriage. She had to decide consciously whether to make eye contact, to make conversation, to make acquaintance. This dose of reality continued at the Geneva airport. Incessant public announcements of real events and necessities were forcefully delivered in several languages from loudspeakers throughout the gleaming terminal building.

The reality therapy continued soon after the flight took off, when she was obliged to endure the mating behaviour of her neighbour in seat 46-B. A corpulent businessman of some European origin or other, tightly bound into his shirt, tie, and jacket, inquired with an oleaginous smile, which revealed a gold tooth, whether she was travelling alone, business or pleasure, been away long my dear, how wonderfully you speak German and French, and English too? My dear, would you like to have an aperitif with me after takeoff?

Despite her psychologist's detachment from such behaviour, despite her professional judgments and insights — this was obviously a man with low self-esteem, unconsciously projecting his anima archetype onto the first available young female in his line of psychic vision — she could not help but find such textbook zoology boring and unsettling at the same time.

She resented, so soon after her quiet dreamy days in Zurich, the man's intrusive gaping at her hair, her breasts, her thighs. Despite her professional training, she could not stop herself from feeling a surge of anger at this vulgar intrusion. By the time Natalia had been able to convince her would-be suitor with unmistakable facial, body, and finally, spoken messages that she had absolutely no interest in anything more than a brief pre-flight conversation with him, and by the time she had endured his petulant silence before he haughtily asked the flight attendant somewhere over Iceland if he might change seats, the spell of the days in Zurich had been badly shaken, though not entirely broken. Natalia had still been able to commune privately with her thoughts for the remainder of the flight.

Now that the aircraft was banking and making its final descent into Montreal, those thoughts at last had to be turned fully outward, to see not just psychic phenomena, but also events in the world as they truly were. As a psychologist, she was coming to recognize the origins of her habitual reluctance to do that. Overcoming that reluctance was another matter.

Her first thought as the plane descended slowly over the flat, white fields of rural Quebec was that she preferred to land at the city airport, at Dorval, because she could then peer out like a child and try to see her apartment building near Mount Royal or perhaps glimpse Uncle Stanislaw's snug little house in Westmount. She had never, in fact, been able to see these places in all her landings on the domestic flights that were routed into the city airport, but she liked the game.

Mirabel airport was far from the city centre. It was a massive, underused, and overquiet cavern of a place, and landing there required a long taxi or bus journey into the city. It was lucky, she had to agree with the pilot, that the weather had recently cleared. The endless flat fields of expropriated farmland that surrounded the airport were deeply covered in snow. In the winter darkness they glowed feebly under roadside lights and farm lights and, now, under the lights of the aircraft itself. The sudden bump back to earth of the landing was a metaphor too, she thought, for being well and truly home again.

And so it was a woman of this personality and this set of recent experiences who paid the tired Haitian taxi driver on deserted Esplanade Street sometime nearing 11:30 p.m. this Friday evening in Montreal. She climbed alone up the steep, exterior staircase to her home in a small, renovated block of apartments across a park and playing field from Mount Royal. At least two generations of immigrants would have lived in, and been in a hurry to leave, this workers' neighbourhood northeast of the mountain that dominates the Montreal skyline. But Natalia and many others like her had moved into these rambling places with their floors of Canadian hardwood, their high ceilings, and their fireplaces, and they had made them into inner-city homes for themselves.

The apartment always gave her pleasure when she came into it on a cold night, especially if she had been away for some time, and it gave her this pleasure again that night. The place was warm and the radiators were cracking and groaning quietly as they did all winter. She dropped her two small bags inside the door, removed her boots, and went in. In the hall mirror she saw an angular face, somewhat pale and tired, framed by long and very black hair. She saw that the face was wearing little makeup and that the nose was somewhat thin in the bridge. She saw intensely green eyes, small ears, and skin that had never been burned by the sun. She thought: *There I am. There I am at home.*

She saw the neat pile of letters and magazines that her neighbour, Gustavo, the Chilean refugee social-worker soccer-player ladies' man, had so carefully left for her on the little umbrella stand as yet another unrequited gesture of his esteem for her. She sniffed the air of a place that had been closed for many more hours than usual. She turned on lamps. She sat in a favourite chair.

This is what she did and what she thought just before all the calm, all the pleasure, and all the refined thoughts and memories of the previous weeks were suddenly and totally ripped away from her by the events of the next few hours.

The shock had not come in its full intensity right away, although she had soon had an intuition that something was enormously wrong. She later began to imagine that she had known even before pressing the replay button on her answering machine that it would contain bad news of some sort and that the news would have something to do with Stanislaw. But in the blur and the pain of the days that followed her return home she could not be really sure of the origin of any feeling about the series of experiences that unfolded.

The sound of her uncle's voice in the apartment startled her. It gave her a brief moment of pleasure, which was quickly followed by perplexity and then by fear. *What is this?* she thought. *What is this? Uncle Stanislaw? On my tape? In English?*

She stood and listened to his rambling message and to something else that lurked below the words, far below, something she could not until much later even begin to label. She listened to the message again and then a third time, too frightened to be touched by some of the soft things the old man had said. Then she dialled his house in Westmount in dread, despite the late hour.

No need to panic, Natalia, she counselled herself as

the telephone rang, rang, rang. *He is an old man, getting sentimental. There is no reason to believe anything is wrong.*

But when the sentimental old man failed to answer his phone in the minutes before midnight on a freezing Montreal winter night, Natalia allowed herself the indulgence of fear, if not panic. And when the taxi pulled up to the old house on Chesterfield Street perhaps 30 minutes after that and Natalia saw many lights blazing in the windows, she knew that her first reactions would be more than justified.

The path to the house was deeply covered in snow. There were no footprints on the verandah. *But the lights are all on inside,* she thought. Of course there was no answer at the door. Of course she felt trepidation as she fumbled in her bag for the key that she always carried for emergencies. The house, when she opened the door, was not silent. It was filled with the metallic voice of the BBC World Service coming from Stanislaw's old short-wave set on the table near the fireplace. *Too loud, too loud, too loud,* she thought as she hurried to turn it off.

The house was filled as well with a disturbing smell. Not, she would learn from the police later, the full-blown smell of an unattended corpse. It had been too few days for that, they said. But not the odour of life and vitality either. It was the hint of a smell of death, the smell of a hint of death. So as she called out for Stanislaw and looked for him, and as she hurried around the ground floor and then up the stairs to the bedrooms, she knew, as if she had already dreamed it so, that when she found him he would be dead.

She could not say that the police had not been kind or empathetic or understanding in their way. But they could not know what the sight of her dead uncle had done to her, how the sight had seared itself into her psyche. To them it was all too routine. An old man, obviously too old to be living alone, had slipped while getting into his bath and drowned.

C'est dommage, madame, they had said. *C'est vraiment dommage,* but these things happen. The two young officers in their insulated blue windbreakers and their too-shiny black police boots had come quickly enough and had made the appropriate secondary radio calls and phone calls. They had even urged her to go back downstairs while they did what needed to be done and wrote things in their small leather-covered notebooks as their walkie-talkies crackled in Quebecois French.

The red flashers on their van had pulsed endlessly into the house through all the windows that overlooked the street. The lights had also pulsed blood-red onto the snow and onto the shoulders of the few neighbours who peered out from their chilly verandahs to see what could possibly have happened at Number 12.

But the police had not been the first there, as Natalia had been. They had not been first to see the frail old body face down in the water, in the ghastly blood-reddened water. They had not seen one old weathered foot askew over the edge of the tub.

They had not waited as the men from the morgue, in cheap business suits and rubber galoshes, loaded Uncle Stanislaw's body into a zippered plastic bag and into their discreetly marked silver-grey van to be taken away somewhere far from his home. They could not feel what she felt, sitting afterward in the silence of her dead uncle's house, silent except for the ticking of his beloved old clock. There was nothing in her psychologist's training or her personal history to prepare her for this.

Psychologists are good at enduring other people's pain. Despite her having been the child of immigrants who had suffered in the war, she herself had not had to face down much grief in her lifetime. Once only, one other tragedy before this — when her parents had died in an accident. But she had been still only a girl when that tragedy happened. She experienced grief then, of course, but it was a child's grief and over the years it had transformed itself into a compact burden that she now simply carried with her everywhere. That burden of grief did not interfere with her life anymore, not her conscious life in any case.

And that time there had been Uncle Stanislaw and Aunt Margot to run to. They soaked up her girl's tears and grief and helped her through to the other side. This time, that little surrogate family was gone. Now she was left with only her own psychic resources to deal with the shock of what she had seen. She knew that this would take her, as all things psychic took her, a very long time. So now she merely sat quietly in her uncle's favourite chair doing nothing, to let her mind examine all the images she had just been forced to witness, to think all the thoughts that went rushing through, and to feel all the feelings that erupted from somewhere deep.

Perhaps most troubling for her, as she sat trying to collect herself, was the intense, persistent intuition that her uncle had been murdered.

She knew that this was irrational. She believed that nothing in Stanislaw's personal story, nothing in his recent personal story in any case, would make this thought an appropriate response to what the police had assured her was an all too common accident for old people living alone. The intuition came from somewhere else and was also, she suspected, a result of things her conscious mind had perceived, but which her unconscious was only now putting together into different, alarming, patterns.

The complexity of the intuition built slowly as she sat there. It continued to build as she later sleepwalked through the waking world's requirements for funeral arrangements, administrative arrangements, and financial arrangements. It continued as she resumed her work, tried to pick up her caseload once again at the clinic, tried to listen to tales of other people's pain and confusion. But she found herself unable to give that work her full attention. Her capacity for empathy had been diminished.

Fragments of thoughts about the scene in that Chesterfield Street bathroom began as early as the first night to assail her as somehow, subtly, wrong. She saw in her mind's eye, for example, the pile of clothes tossed beside the bath, their extremely rumpled condition, the scattered socks and slippers.

He never threw his clothes on the floor like that, she thought. *He was too tidy and proud a man for that.* She thought: *He never listened to the short wave while he was in the bath. Never.* She thought: *How could he fall face down into the bath like that?* She thought: *Why was there blood in the water?*

Of course, the police, when she contacted them later to ask about such matters, had convenient and, on one level, perfectly sensible answers to such questions. They were even willing after the funeral to send two detectives out to her apartment to discuss her concerns — Detective Mario Tremblay and Detective Jean-François Létourneau of the Montreal Urban Community Police Department Homicide Unit. They wore identical clothes, bought, apparently, from identical suppliers of detectives' suits, overcoats, and scarves. They were a team, their clothes and demeanour said, and this team had seen, *madame,* some very distressing things in this city over the years.

Ah oui, c'est vrai, madame, la ville n'est pas comme autrefois, c'est maintenant exactement comme une ville

30

américaine. But *madame,* they insisted, you must not jump to conclusions about your uncle's unfortunate death. He was a good man, he lived a long and blameless life, and he slipped and fell one night while getting into his bath.

Why, then, the blood? she wondered. The two detectives looked at each other sagely as they reassured her. Well, *madame,* it is something most people never see, blood. But we have seen many such cases and when people fall in the bathtub they often hit their heads as they fall and it is this blood that you saw in the water that night. And, they added, as they folded their notebooks and adjusted their splendid silk scarves, the coroner's report and the autopsy report said that there was nothing at all *louche,* nothing unusual, nothing that was inconsistent with an unfortunate household accident. The old gentleman had indeed had some cuts and bruises on his head, but consistent with such a fall. And besides, *madame,* who would have wanted to kill Monsieur Janovski in any case?

She watched them through the window as they carefully made their way down her slippery staircase and got into a shiny, oversized, unmarked car that even to her untrained eye was a ludicrously obvious police vehicle. They had looked expectantly around as they got into their car in the snowy street, perhaps behaviour learned from too many years of hoping to be photographed for the Montreal crime tabloids. But this case, they knew, would not be one to attract *les journalistes.*

Natalia knew, however, as she watched them drive away that they were wrong. *How can they ever know what happened to him that night?* she thought. *How can they know what madness may have resulted in a murderer entering his house?*

Other intuitions came to her as the days progressed. Nothing has been stolen, *madame*, you are quite sure? the police had asked. But then one night she sat bolt upright in bed, not long after the funeral, and thought: *his address book.* It was not beside the telephone where he always kept it. She had dressed and taken a taxi back to the dark, chilly, and too-empty house and searched madly through his papers and his clothes drawers, everywhere, until she was satisfied that it was gone.

Perdu perhaps, *madame,* the police had said. Lost. Perhaps Monsieur Janovski was getting forgetful at his age.

And then there was the phone message, which she listened to over and over again, so many times that she began to worry in the psychologist's part of her brain that she was displaying compulsive behaviour, that the grief and anxiety were manifesting themselves as obsessional symptoms. But still she listened to it, again and again, even going to the trouble of buying another blank tape for her machine to avoid the risk of this one being erased by mistake.

"Ah, Natalia. Your famous answering machine," Stanislaw's voice said. "You know how much I despise these machines. But this time I will leave you a message. At last you will be happy."

How could I be happy, she thought as she listened yet again. *How could I ever be happy now?*

"I am sorry you are still away. There is something very important I need to speak to you about when you return. I wanted to tell you there is something, so you would know as soon as you get back." *But what? What did you want to say so badly that you could not have waited until I get back? Why did you not just say what it was?*

"I have been worrying about some important matters these past months and you yourself remarked on this, I know, before you left." *Yes, poor Uncle, yes, you did seem worried about something and I didn't insist enough that you tell me what it was. I was too busy thinking about the worries of others rather than of you.*

"So perhaps we could speak just as soon as you get in, please, if that is all right. Could you call me immediately?" *He never would say I should call him immediately. Never. That is a word for emergencies.*

"There are matters you should now perhaps know a little about." *What matters? What? What secrets did his heart hold after all those years of life?* she wondered. *What are these things that I should know a little about? How seldom did I ask him to tell me his story.*

And then there was the most distressing part of all, the part that pierced her to the depths of her soul.

"And, yes, I should also say, even though you know this, that I love you very much, Natalia, my dear. But you know that, I suppose. I do hope I have never hurt you with my foolish bad temper or my old-fashioned way." *Poor, poor old man, she thought. Poor dear old man. Alone, and speaking into machines instead of to someone he loved and could trust.*

"So good-bye, darling. Stanislaw." *Good-bye, darling Stanislaw. Good-bye.*

The funeral helped her to say good-bye, but the scene itself was full of sorrow and metaphors of sorrow. No funeral in Montreal in midwinter can ever be anything else. The light on the snow was brilliant, but the trees were black and leafless. Lifeless. The headstones at Côte des Neiges Cemetery were dark and the roadways were dark and the coats and hats of the people were dark. And it was very, very cold.

Puffs of frozen breath came from the mouths of the few mourners who attended. Most of them were from the CBC, some neighbours, and a few old émigré faces she did not readily recognize. The earth from the frozen gravesite had come away in rock-hard brown and black clods, and these were piled beside the black rectangle in the snow where her uncle's body was to go.

The priest, in black cassock and overcoat and a pair of black rubber boots that showed below the hems, said the service in French. After the coffin had been lowered, it was impossible to find a few loose grains of earth to toss into the grave, and no one wanted to throw frozen clods noisily against the coffin lid. This is not done at midwinter funerals in Montreal. So the few mourners walked with some difficulty through the snow in their dress-up shoes and boots and stood beside the black cars idling on the roadway. Great plumes of steam trailed out behind the limousines into the clear cold air.

Natalia had said good-bye to Stanislaw at the funeral, had been glad of the ritual, but she had not said good-bye to her growing certainty that there was more to this death than anyone might ever know.

Some days after the funeral, she had a dream that confirmed this to her in the way only a Jungian and an introvert can accept that an intuition is correct. It was this dream that convinced her that she must take steps to discover the truth of the matter, the daylight truth as well as the psychic truth.

She is running alone in a snow-covered field somewhere in rural Quebec. She is not sure whether she is running urgently to find something or running away from some danger. It is possibly both at once, as is the case in dreams of this nature. The sky is grey, the snow is wet and deep, and the scene is colourless, black and white, as winter days in Quebec can appear to be. She reaches the exact centre of the field and the centre is marked formally, symbolically, by a small rock cairn. She knows that the secret of Stanislaw's life and of his death lie under that

35

small pile of rocks, but before she begins to dismantle it to see what is underneath, she feels a pressure building in her head, a strangely intense pressure which, she fears as she sleeps and dreams this dream, might cause her head to explode. She links her hands over her head, pressing hard against the skull and squeezing her eyes shut, and she feels the cool strands of her hair against her ungloved palms. And in the dream she thinks: I already know what this is about. I have always known what this is about.

When she woke up she was shivering, badly chilled by the sweat cooling on her skin. Even the extra blanket she pulled over herself before going back to sleep had not taken away that chill when morning came.

Chapter 3

n the end, it was the beginning that was important. And the beginning for Francis Delaney came on a damp February day in Montreal in the form of an unexpected telephone call from Natalia Janovski. It would be fair to say that a call from Natalia Janovski was among the last things he was expecting at that stage of his life. Not that there had been no connection between them in the past. His unease when she called was in the forced recollection that there had been any connection between them in the first place, and that he had been the one to seek it.

Delaney leaned back in his swivel chair after he hung up the telephone and put his feet up on the giant uncluttered desk where he had been doing far too little real work of late. He looked out through the sheet of plate glass that was all that separated him from the ice fog that had covered Montreal for the past several days. Normally, the view from the apartment on the twenty-sixth floor of the stark highrise where he made his home and his office would have been spectacular: sweeping from the slope near McGill University south to the St. Lawrence River and across flat Quebec farmland almost, it seemed, to the U.S. border. Today there was no such view to distract him.

More than two years after he had made what for him was an astonishingly uncharacteristic move to seek Natalia Janovski's professional services, she was for some reason now telephoning him. Delaney still felt that his decision to indulge ever so briefly in what Natalia had insisted then on calling an "exploration" of his troubled sleep and his intense, chaotic dreams was simply a bit of mid-life foolishness, best forgotten. But now, as he sat thinking about her telephone call, all of the feelings from that time came flooding back.

The truth of the matter was that Delaney still felt embarrassed by his decision to cast aside for a time the public persona of no-nonsense investigative journalist and seek the services of a psychologist, and a Jungian at that.

Something urgent to discuss, Natalia had said, in the ever so slight accent of a daughter of European immigrants. Nothing whatever to do with their previous professional relationship. Could they perhaps meet soon? Her reticence reminded him a little of how he had sounded when he first called her. Wondering if he might come in to see her, to talk over a few things. Aware of her reputation, highly recommended. Had always had an intellectual interest in Jung, in that sort of psychology. Could they perhaps meet soon?

He had stopped short, at the time, of staking out the journalist's best-loved escape route — that of making contact under the pretext of preparing an article, or seeking background information. The fact of the matter was that he had wanted to talk to her as a therapist and he didn't try to conceal that from her in their first conversation.

His choice of a Jungian had seemed natural, given the unlikely premise that he would seek out a psychologist at all. He had, even though he did not play this journalist's card in his first call to Natalia, done some feature stories many years before, when he was still in the mainstream of daily journalism, about competing schools of psychology and the therapy industry in Montreal. He had found Jung's ideas attractive, for reasons perhaps best known only to his unconscious.

The articles he had eventually produced, however, did not betray that aspect of himself. His stories in that period rarely did. They were typical of the sorts of short, sharp stories that ambitious young feature writers early in their careers might put together. Thankfully, all that angling for big play in the newspapers, the scrambling for position in the media game, was no longer required. Delaney was assured now of prominent play no matter what he wrote, and for the subjects of his own choosing. He was no longer making a name for himself. That work was done.

Jungian psychology had also come up occasionally in his days, an even longer time ago, at Loyola College. It seemed a natural thing for some of the younger lecturers and the hip Jesuits at the university in those days at the very end of the 1960s to be reading such work and to be sharing their excitement about this Swiss psychologist who had taken religion and the spirit and their manifestation in dreams so seriously. They had found Jung's notion of the Shadow archetype particularly useful, it seemed, in imagining causes for the evil that Catholics worried about so often.

Any interest in matters of the spirit and in things irrational, however, had been quickly beaten from Delaney's consciousness by the work he started to do after leaving the university and that he still did, some twenty years later. But as he turned forty and found himself in the state of psychic confusion that plagues so many men at that unfortunate age, he allowed himself to slip ever so briefly back into the openness for such things which pre-dated the intensely extraverted work he had done on the streets of Montreal as a police reporter, then as a feature writer, then covering the intricacies of Quebec, Canadian, and eventually international politics.

His career had built itself, in Delaney's view. He took no credit for what he saw as accidental successes in his political reporting, or as a war correspondent, or, most recently, as a so-called investigative journalist. Exposer of secrets, so-called. Writer of weighty, worldly books on corruption and political intrigue. So-called. He was not deluded by such labels.

In the course of his work the opportunities for

introversion had slowly but steadily receded. Hard, he thought as he sat and considered Natalia's call and all that it had stirred up, to be an introvert while trying to avoid Contra bullets in Nicaragua or dodging mortar fire in Grenada. Still, that fortieth birthday had forced introversion and doubt and depression upon him and, in what was not quite panic but perhaps its precursor, he had contacted the talented and highly recommended and, as it turned out, the strikingly beautiful Dr. Janovski.

He had seen her name sometime earlier in a newspaper article about her work with torture victims, victims of war trauma, and he had clipped the piece for future reference. But it had been his dreams that had sent him, in the end, to her. Deeply unsettling dreams and the overwhelming sense of dread he began to feel — the sense that somehow, somewhere, he had made a terribly wrong turn and could never hope to turn back.

Or perhaps it was that he felt he had made no turn at all, that all the important turns had been made for him, that he had made no real commitments to any issue, task, or person, and that this was somehow about to catch up with him. Catch up with him, he thought in his less lucid moments in that period, and destroy him. The episode had turned him almost overnight — though Natalia would insist later that there are no sudden psychic turnings, that all such turnings stem from seeds sown years before — from a man with his feet planted firmly on the ground to one completely at sea.

The episode had not lasted long. He had not allowed it to last long and the number of sessions he had had with Natalia was relatively small. Smaller, he liked to think, than more self-indulgent people would have allowed themselves. Were the sessions useful? Perhaps a little. He allowed himself to admit this. Perhaps he had found it useful to tell someone his story, to try to see the patterns that it presented, to try, for a time, to see what his dreams and intuitions could tell him. But these were not things he wished to be detained by for very long.

The problem now, when he allowed himself to acknowledge it, was that two years later he found himself not in a state of confusion or panic but quite simply numb.

His career, of course, had never been in better shape. His latest book, on CIA surveillance of Quebec separatist groups in the 1960s and 1970s, was selling well. His earlier book, on the diplomatic conflict between Canada and the U.S. over Cuban policy and the secret American pressures being applied to Canada at high levels, had been an unexpected big seller in the U.S. market, and he had made more money than he ever thought possible from a piece of journalism.

His designation as investigative journalist, however, amused him. He had only used what came easily to him: the ability to ask the right questions to the right people, to know what to look for and where to look for it, to link complex scenarios in his mind, to make people trust him, and, most important of all, to sense when people were lying or had reason to lie. He knew that these skills were highly valued, by others if not by himself.

He was now on a vaguely defined leave of absence from *Forum* magazine, enjoying a cashing in of sorts, of all the stock he had built up while on difficult assignments for them in Cuba, Grenada, Haiti, and Central America. So far he had resisted the editors' repeated requests that he do the same thing again for them in Bosnia. Research grants from a high-minded foundation, another book advance, and freelance bits of this and that meant that he could now work at home, not troubled by daily or even weekly deadlines. He was able and encouraged to produce more articles on any subject, more books on any subject, more media babble on any subject.

But as he stared at the too-tidy, too-empty desk before him, he knew, as he had known when he crept away two years earlier from the commitment that Natalia had demanded if their sessions were to continue, that it was all becoming a very elaborate and very empty charade. He knew that he had spent all of his adult life observing and recording the misfortunes and weaknesses and strivings of others without ever having to decide what side he was on, or if any side were worth joining, or if there were really any sides at all.

He was a professional observer who no longer wished to observe. As he observed his own thoughts on that cold grey Montreal afternoon he knew that he did not very much care anymore, if indeed he had ever cared, about journalism, about career, about politics, about corruption, or even, if he really let such thoughts take their dangerous course, about himself.

He dreams he is a soldier or a commander making a long trek back from a difficult campaign. He walks exhausted across a blasted, smoking landscape with other soldiers and refugees who are also trailing home from the wars. His assignment in this dream is to find his former headquarters and his comrades-in-arms to regroup for a new assignment in peacetime. He finally locates the bomb-pocked old building in a ruined city and enters a cavernous hall of aging desks and office equipment. He sees an old schoolmate, whose name he cannot remember. This man, too, is in a tattered uniform and returned from the wars. Delaney begins taking stock — looking in desk drawers, examining the contents of storage lockers. He sees several uniforms on hangers, and military hats of various sorts on shelves. There is a dunce cap there as well. Then he finds some personal items he left behind years before: mementoes, and some books he had treasured before the wars. He gathers up various items and takes them back to where he is now to resume work. It is a large newsroom. He feels an overwhelming sense of loss, boredom, and emptiness, and dreads the pointless drudgery ahead of him. He renews acquaintances but is repulsed by all the tired, dejected faces. He is resigned, however, to settling back into his old routine because

there is nothing else. He has been away for twenty years.

Natalia was nervous when she arrived the next day, more nervous than Delaney imagined she could have any reason to be. She was dressed in a long, down-filled overcoat in a fashionable purple shade and a yellow scarf and beret. When she took off her outdoor clothes, he saw that she wore the same sort of soft wool outfit in earth tones that she had generally worn when he first knew her, the cut and texture accentuating her dancer's body and her fine smooth skin. As she had always done, she wore heavy, vaguely Latin American silver jewellery on her ears, neck, wrists, fingers.

Delaney felt again the alternating current of sexual attraction he had felt for her when she sat across from him in her office during their short-lived attempts, many months before, to delve into the depths of his personality. Those feelings of sexual attraction for a therapist, she assured him in an early session, were common, should he find himself having them. She had been correct.

Now, he watched her as she wandered a little around his nearly empty, white living room, remarking as everyone did about the view, which on that day was sunny and spectacular. She remarked, as everyone did, on the spareness of the apartment, on its extreme order, its obsessive neatness, on the austere furnishings, on the bare wood floors. She looked briefly at the titles on his bookshelf and then sat down suddenly on his black leather sofa. She declined his offer of coffee, cold drinks, whisky, wine. He knew before she started that she would be telling him a long and involved story.

"Thank-you for agreeing to see me, Francis," she said — quiet, tentative, too formal.

"It's no problem," Delaney said, feeling awkward himself.

"You were surprised to hear from me, I suppose."

"You could say that. But I surprised myself by calling you a couple of years ago, so there you go. I'm used to surprises in my line of work."

"How are you now?" she asked, professional for a moment.

"How was I then?" he asked.

"Well, you would know that better than I."

Delaney paused.

"You'll be pleased to know that the patient has made a miraculous recovery," he said. "Back on the job, pumping out high-quality rubbish for the media just as before."

"Miraculous," she said. "And after so few sessions. I'm flattered. But what did you recover from?"

Delaney didn't want to talk further about his glimpse into the abyss, so like all good interviewers, he simply didn't answer. He let the silence build for a moment. She knew this trick as well, however. They looked at each other intently. Two profession-al questioners, silently duelling.

"I shouldn't really be bringing personal business

into a professional relationship," Natalia said finally.

"We no longer have a professional relationship," he reminded her.

"No, of course we don't," she said.

"Look," Delaney said. "I'm not going to turn you over to the Canadian Psychological Association for giving me a call. How can I help you? You said you wanted to talk about something."

"I do," she said. "It's a family matter. It's complicated."

He let the silence build again, knowing she would fill it.

"My uncle died a few weeks ago, about a month ago," she said.

"I'm sorry."

"He was a very old man, and the police say he drowned one night while getting into the bath."

Delaney knew from her eyes and from the ever so slight tremor around her lips that this was hard for her. He watched how she handled it.

"The police say," he repeated.

"Yes."

"And you don't buy that."

"No, I don't."

"I see. And you would like me to help you find out what really happened to your uncle. Is that it? Investigative journalist, knows his way around the police stations, that sort of thing?"

Delaney was surprised at how hard that sounded.

"Do you think I might get a story out of it, is that it?" he asked.

This sounded even worse. He didn't bother trying to correct the impression he must be giving.

"No, I don't think so," Natalia said. "That would depend. But, no, I was wondering if you would perhaps just help me find out what happened."

"Why would I do that?" he said, for some reason still wanting to appear cruel and uncaring. "Especially if there is no story in it."

"Oh, I think there is a story in it," she said. "But maybe not the kind you are used to. Not the kind you would use for your magazine. Or, no. Maybe not the kind I would want you to use for your magazine."

"So why would I bother?"

He wondered whether she would still want such a person to help her now.

"Because, and I know I shouldn't mix my professional knowledge of you . . ."

"Such as it is."

". . . mix my professional knowledge of you with my own needs, but I know that you are experienced in these things, that you've travelled a lot, and you've been in difficult and complicated situations, and that despite all your defence mechanisms and your attempts this morning to make me think the contrary, I think you still have a curiosity . . ."

"Curiosity," Delaney repeated, smiling bitterly.

"Well, perhaps that's too silly a word. You have a desire to understand things and I think you are a kind person and, again I am being unprofessional in saying this because of what I learned about you some time ago, I think you may simply decide to help me because the opportunity presents itself and you are that sort of person and you are at that stage of your life."

"Oh, please," he said. "Do reasons for things have to be always complicated by all of that?"

"Well, I don't know then," Natalia said. "I was just hoping you would be able to help me. That's really all there is to say."

They sat quietly for a moment, considering the situation, several situations. For a moment, Delaney thought she might be about to get up and leave. But she continued to sit quietly on his couch, watching him watch her. He observed that the tremor was gone from her mouth, that her hands did not move at all as they lay in her lap. Whatever she was feeling was now not betrayed by her body movements. *She is probably thinking the same thing about me*, he thought.

"Why would anyone want to kill your uncle?" Delaney said suddenly.

"That's what the police have asked me," she said.

"It's a natural question," he replied. "The police ask the natural questions. Reporters may stay around to ask other ones."

"I don't know who would want to murder him," she said. "I have an intuition that someone did. And besides that, some things didn't seem right at his house on the night I found him.

"It was you who found him," Delaney said.

"Yes."

He considered this for a moment, knowing how hard that must have been for her, knowing what a drowned body looks like. He remembered watching a couple of distraught Nicaraguan mothers finding their sons floating in the river near the border with Honduras, in Contra country, when that particular war was in an especially nasty phase. He hoped that Natalia's uncle was not long dead when she found him.

"And someone is following me now, I think," she said suddenly. "Since he died. I don't think anymore that I'm imagining this. I'm getting to be a little afraid. At first I thought I was just anxious. Grieving and displacing this onto something. But now I really do think someone is following me. Or maybe I need a therapist."

She smiled a little.

"Look," Delaney said. "I really hate to stay with the obvious here, but it's the way to start. Why would anyone want to kill your uncle? Why would anyone be following you?"

"I just don't know."

"How long have you thought someone was following you?"

"Since a short time after Stanislaw died. I started to see a couple of men regularly. I thought I started to see them in places I went. On my street, near my office. I don't think I imagine such things."

"Have they approached you?"

"No."

"You think they are connected with your uncle in some way?"

"Possibly. I really couldn't say at this point. I don't know."

"Did your uncle ever say people were following him?"

"No. But he wasn't the sort of man who would say these things even if they were true. I have no idea, really, what his thoughts were. I've realized that since he died."

"Well, let's try this then," Delaney said. "What's the most interesting thing about your uncle? What would reporters want to write about if they met him?"

"So you are going to help me?" Natalia asked.

"Apparently. For now."

She began to tell him things, much as they came into her mind. Delaney listened, as he had listened to so many hundreds of people before, and helped her along with questions and suggestions and requests for clarification. It was an interview, but she did not seem to mind being interviewed. He did not take notes, and she didn't seem to mind that either.

The story she told was, in some ways, not extraordinary. Young Polish man, Jesuit trained, then Polish Air Force officer, about twenty-six when the Nazis invaded. Father a professor at the University of Krakow, mother a musician. Both killed. But not until after young Stanislaw had left with the first wave of refugees to Romania. Then into France, then England and distinguished service with the Mazovia Squadron: Polish aces flying Wellingtons out of Scotland. But as always in such stories there was also an angle, the lead for a possible good feature item. Not that a feature lead was necessarily a clue to a possible murder, but Delaney knew that the unusual in a life often led to the even more unusual, often years later. He had untangled too many complicated stories by following up on the smallest of oddities to think otherwise.

In this case, Natalia provided two elements that an alert reporter would underline in a notebook. Young Flight Lieutenant Stanislaw Janovski had been aide-de-camp, or one of several, to the Polish president after the headlong rush by citizens, soldiers, and senior officials out of Poland to Romania in September 1939. Possibly interesting. And he had been assigned by the Polish government-in-exile, before being allowed to throw himself into the air war over Europe, to travel with some Polish officials to Canada to accompany the famous shipment of national treasures that were to be placed there for safekeeping. Tens of millions of dollars' worth of artworks, jewels, ancient armour and weapons, rare books, manuscripts, and tapestries hurriedly loaded into crates as the Nazis attacked and then onto trucks for the escape. All later to go by sea to Canada. Another possibly interesting angle in the old man's life, Delaney thought.

After the war, however, there seemed nothing out of the ordinary in Stanislaw Janovski's story. Reasonably predictable émigré experience. Never returned to Poland after the Communists took over. Montreal to resettle. A bit of bush pilot work right after the war, and then a stab at running a small bookstore. Then a sort of career at Radio Canada International. Marriage, no children, life in a solid little house in a solid little neighbourhood. Then retirement and an even quieter life. *He probably had enough excitement as a young man to last him a while,* Delaney thought.

The apartment was warm now, as the late-morning sun beat through the glass in the windows that were everywhere. Natalia did not seem tired out by her storytelling, nor by the long sit. Sessions like this would be her stock-in-trade.

"How did he get chosen to be one of the president's aides-de-camp?" Delaney asked her.

"I never really thought to ask him. A family connection, I suppose. His father, my grandfather, was a prominent academic. Stanislaw was in the Air Force as an officer. I suppose someone in the president's entourage was given his name. They needed someone who could fly, I think my uncle said, in case they could get a plane in Romania."

"The same would go, I guess, for his being chosen to travel to Canada with the art treasures. His connections."

"Probably," she said.

Delaney, as a reporter, knew more about the Polish art treasures story than Natalia was able to tell him that morning, except for the points where the story touched her uncle's. He had heard nothing about it for years, of course, and he was still a boy when it all came to a head in the late 1950s. But it was the sort of story that the older editors at the *Montreal Tribune* would know and love, and they had talked about it occasionally when Delaney was a young newspaperman. They loved the cloak-and-dagger elements in particular.

Treasures being moved out of Ottawa in the dead of night, after the Communists took over in Poland and demanded that Canada send them back. Hiding places in convents and monasteries. Secret passwords. Disputes among custodians. Then the fiercely anti-Communist premier of Quebec, Maurice Duplessis, sending his provincial police force to help agents of the government-in-exile hide the treasures somewhere else in the province. And Duplessis refusing for years to send them back. The Warsaw regime outraged and the Canadian government no longer willing, or no longer able, to step in against Quebec.

Delaney himself had later been in the thick of Quebec political reporting in the seventies and eighties, and had had to learn all too much about the Duplessis era and the battles for constitutional turf that the man they called "*le chef*" had waged with the federal government. It would be natural for Duplessis to seize on the art treasures issue to make a stand against Ottawa when the federal government formally recognized the new Polish government after the war, and to vent his spleen at the Communists at the same time. Some of the details were hazy in Delaney's mind, but he knew the outlines and they still intrigued him.

"Did your uncle talk a lot about the art treasures story to you? Was he involved in the negotiations at the end to send them back?" Delaney asked.

"He would sometimes mention bits of that business, but never really in detail," Natalia said. "I was just a baby when the things were eventually sent back, in 1959, or 1960, I think it was. And later I suppose I didn't take enough of an interest. They were just war stories to me, really."

"But war stories that had a chapter in Quebec with your uncle as a player," Delaney said.

"Yes," she said. "He was a man who would say a little bit once in a while about something like that, and then smile and stop, as if to tease people or maybe because he didn't want to say more. Maybe both. He would always hint that he knew a lot about the government-in-exile and the secret diplomatic things they did in London during the war, and the secrets he was entrusted with in Romania, and I guess in coming here too with the treasures. But I suppose my father had heard all this too many times and probably thought Stanislaw was just exaggerating. And I was just a child. My uncle liked to tickle me and say, 'Ah, Natalia, there are secrets within secrets. Secrets within secrets.' But that's the sort of nonsense things old uncles and grandfathers say to children."

"I don't know," Delaney said. "Would your parents remember more about this?"

"They're both dead. For many years now."

"I see."

Delaney thought he had said he was sorry enough for one morning so he went straight to the next question.

"Did he keep in touch with any of the art treasures people?"

"Which people do you mean?" she asked.

"Well, the people who came over here with them. Or the ones who argued about where they should go. Or the London Poles. Anyone really. Did he want to see the treasures go back or stay here?"

"I think he thought they should stay. He had fought in the war and he didn't think they should be just handed over to the Communists afterward."

"Just like Duplessis," Delaney said.

"I suppose," Natalia said. "Stanislaw was close to Jozef Kozlowski, I remember. And Kozlowski was the man who argued with the other official custodian I mentioned to you, this Piotr Zdunek, about whether the treasures should be sent back to Poland. Kozlowski didn't want them to go back. I remember my uncle telling us that. But Kozlowski has been dead for a very long time now, since not long after I was born if I remember."

"Was he a friend of your uncle, as well as someone he had to work with on this during the war?"

"I don't really know. I suppose so, yes. He was much older than Stanislaw, of course. But they were friends. My uncle's closest friend was not in Montreal in those days. He was in Paris. Zbigniew

Tomaszewski. That was his closest friend. Zbigniew was Stanislaw's navigator on the bombers. But he settled in Paris after the war and they didn't see each other much. They wrote to each other often, for many years."

"He's still alive?"

"Yes."

"Did your uncle have a lot of friends at Radio Canada International?"

"Not really," Natalia said. "I think they were just acquaintances, Polish work acquaintances. I think he didn't like many of them but he would have drinks with them and they would argue about politics. For fun, though, I think. But they were not really his close friends."

"And you say your uncle was worried toward the end," Delaney said. "Troubled about something."

"Yes. It seemed so. I thought he was worried about how things were going in Poland, mainly, with all the changes of government in the last few years, and the splits and the infighting and the old Solidarity people turning on Walesa after he became president. I thought he was just fretting about what would happen in the elections this year. Things like that."

"Did he keep in touch with people in Poland or in London?"

"I don't really know. Possibly."

"But he watched things closely over there."

"He was a newsman, a sort of newsman. A radio announcer. And even Poles who never went back after the war never forgot they were Polish."

"You're sure they never went back? Not even after Walesa became president in 1990? A lot of the old émigrés and government-in-exile people in London went back at that point, apparently. To hand over the official insignia they'd been holding, I think it was. Or just to see Walesa sworn in."

"No, he didn't go," Natalia said. "I know it infuriated him when some of the younger ones at Radio Canada International used to mock him and say he and the old ones were too scared to go over when Solidarity was taking on the government. But he never went. He said he had done enough in the war."

Delaney said nothing for a moment. Natalia was again the one who eventually broke the silence.

"You think it might have something to do with the war?" she asked.

"I'm not even sure yet there's anything here at all, whether to do with the war or not. But if there is something, it's helpful to know at what points your uncle's life was out of the ordinary. If there is something going on."

"Something is going on, Francis," Natalia said. "Even if you don't accept that he was killed, there is someone watching me, I'm almost sure of that."

"Almost sure," Delaney said.

"There is someone following me," she said.

"Did they follow you here?"

"I think so. Yes. That's one thing. I've told you about the address book. That's gone. And there's the priest."

"Tell me again about the priest," Delaney said. "More details."

"My uncle was a Catholic, a good one, as I've said. Maybe a little bit of a critical one sometimes, but a good Catholic. When he first came here he lived in Lachine and his priest there was this Father Bernard I've told you about. He became almost like a friend to my uncle. I'm not sure why. So much so that Stanislaw apparently stopped going to him for confession, or so my mother told me when I was a girl. That was the family story in any case. My uncle and aunt moved in closer to the city around then anyway, and started going to the Catholic church in Westmount, but I know that my uncle would still see Father Bernard as a friend, eventually as a very old and close friend."

"And tell me again why this is a problem."

"Because he was not at the funeral," Natalia said. "Father Bernard was not at the funeral and he would most certainly have wanted to be there. I called the church in Lachine after Stanislaw died, to tell him, and they said he was ill and couldn't come, and then after the funeral I still couldn't reach him and I can't reach him now. It's impossible he would not have come to the funeral or at least call me now to ask what happened, to pay his respects. I left the messages with his people. It's a big church, with a convent and a school and a lot of priests and nuns and brothers. This is another strange thing that's happening."

"Could this Father Bernard really be as close as

you say to your uncle?"

"Yes. I think so. Very close."

"A priest."

"Why can't someone have a priest for a friend, Francis?"

"I don't know. I just don't know many people who do, I suppose," he said.

Delaney felt a familiar stirring of interest beginning to grow in him now. He had felt it from early in this long conversation. He knew the signs and knew that he would want to know more about this story than Natalia had told him. He would want to know if her uncle had indeed been killed, whether someone was following her, and more about this Father Bernard. He knew that he would want to know more, but in this case he did not yet understand why. That, too, intrigued him.

He went down to the lobby of the building with her, to see for himself if someone was following her around the city as she suspected. They had talked for a very long time and then they came to a point at which it was clear to both of them that they should stop. Delaney wanted to consider what she had told him and to make absolutely sure that he wanted to get involved. But the answer to the question was already reasonably clear in his mind, if he were honest about it.

They rode the elevator looking silently up at the

numbers changing over the doors. The lobby was not busy at that time on a weekday. It was overdecorated, with smoked mirrors and chandeliers, and a doorman named George in a vaguely military uniform. George opened the door for them onto University Street and a cold blast of air rushed in.

"You'll need more than a sweater if you're going out today, Mr. Delaney," he said. George was the eyes and ears of the building, but absolutely discreet if matters involved people he liked.

"We're just going to get a taxi for my guest here, George," Delaney said. "Back in a second."

They stood for a moment on the windy sidewalk, looking around them. Cars rushed by, and a couple of Volkswagen Jetta taxis idled at the curb. The Haitian drivers looked expectantly through the watery glass, hoping for a fare.

"See anyone familiar?" Delaney asked.

"No. I don't," Natalia said. "I'm sorry. I don't see anyone now."

"OK. I'll get you a cab."

He motioned to the first Jetta and the driver leaned over the back seat to open the rear passenger door.

"You better get in before this guy freezes to death," Delaney said.

"What have you . . ." she stopped before finishing the obvious question.

"I'll call you," he said. "Give me a little while."

"You know, Francis, even I realize that not all problems are solved by therapy and dreams," she said. "Sometimes even a good Jungian thinks action in the world is required."

"Give me a little while," he said again.

Natalia climbed into the back seat of the taxi and told the driver in French her address on the Plateau Mount Royal.

"Better lock up when you get home," Delaney said. "Call me if there's a problem."

"You sound like a doctor," she said. "Or a policeman."

She looked resigned to something as she sat back in the seat. Or perhaps it was a trace of fear he saw in her face. He watched the taxi roar off up University Street, trailing steam.

It's been a long time since I put a woman into a cab down here, Delaney thought. *And the doorman will think so too.* Chilled by the icy wind, he turned back into the building.

"Nice-looking woman," George said. He had thick ginger eyelashes like the spines of tiny sea animals, and these flicked higher as his eyes widened and he gave Delaney his toothiest grin.

"Business, George," Delaney said.

"Not your ex-wife anyhow, eh?" George said. George knew the story of every tenant's life by the people who came in and out to see them, and by those who suddenly did not. Delaney had lived in the building for a long time.

God damn these doormen, Delaney thought.

"You see anybody strange around here when we were upstairs, George?" he said.

"Couple of foreign guys came in just after that lady, in fact," George said. "They looked at the bell panel for a long time, but when I asked them who they were looking for they said they had the wrong building."

"They ask you where she went?"

"Nope. Not sure they were looking for her anyway. Went back out, that was it."

"In a car?"

"Nope. Walking."

"How did you know they were foreign?"

"They sure didn't sound like you and me." George was a big grinner, and he grinned again. A sea creature descended briefly over one eye as he winked. "They weren't Anglos like ourselves, an endangered species around here these days, and they sure as hell weren't Quebecois, so what does that leave us?"

"What nationality?"

"Christ knows. Europe somewhere, probably. You know this neighbourhood. Could be from anywhere."

"Thanks."

"What's up?"

"Nothing really."

"Working on a story?"

"I'm always working on a story, George. You know that. Why should today be any different?"

After Natalia had left, Delaney found it hard to do much except sit and ponder what he had been told that morning. Her perfume had left a new scent in his apartment and he looked for a long time at the empty couch where she had sat and talked for so long. He moved over to his desk and looked at the notebooks and the pens and the cassette tapes and the laptop computer that lay there. The tools of his trade, lately untouched.

Why would I bother with this? he thought. *There is no story in this for me and if there is she won't want me to run it anyway. So why would I bother?*

But Delaney already sensed that in this case getting a story would perhaps not matter very much. And perhaps he knew already that in the end this was precisely why he would bother.

Chapter 4

They drove out to Lachine in Delaney's car. Natalia had said she didn't drive in winter and that her car was covered in a season's worth of snow in the alley behind her apartment. Delaney didn't drive his gracefully aging Mercedes much either, especially in winter, but he parked it in the underground garage in his building, it would be clear of snow and he knew it would start, so he agreed to pick her up on Esplanade Street.

She was waiting at the top of the old staircase that led to her door on the second floor, and she was dressed in the same purple overcoat she had worn to his place two days earlier. She moved down right away when he pulled up, as if she had known his car. When she got inside she gave him a very brief smile and didn't seem to want to talk much, so Delaney pulled off immediately and did not try to fill the silence.

They hadn't talked since the night of their first meeting. Delaney had surprised himself by phoning her that night, ostensibly to tell her he would help her make some inquiries. Only for a while, he heard himself insisting. He was, he told her, very busy with other projects, with his book. But he had also wanted to make sure she was all right, though he didn't tell her that. Something about her story had touched an alarm somewhere inside him and he wanted to know she was safely back in her place. They had ended up talking again for a long time on the phone about the circumstances of Stanislaw's death and about what was to be done first. It seemed to both of them that the natural place to start was Lachine, with the priest who had been Stanislaw's friend. A priest who didn't go to funerals.

Delaney looked often in his rear-view mirror to see if anyone appeared to be following them, but if someone was, he wasn't able to tell. It was a brilliant winter day, unusually warm, and the sun had melted all the snow on the roads. The glistening black asphalt contrasted starkly with the piles of wet, white snow that still covered everything else. The heavy snow tires on the car hummed loudly on the wet road surface. For Montrealers this was one of the sounds of spring, but it was not yet spring. Delaney glanced over at Natalia and saw she was looking intently into the mirror on the passenger side. When she caught him looking at her as they stopped at a traffic light, she smiled somewhat guiltily. Delaney smiled back, but didn't bother trying to reassure her that he thought no one was behind them.

He was feeling intensely pleased that morning. He had not realized just how much he was looking for a reason not to continue the charade of his next book, not to sit all day and fail to achieve anything at his desk, not to have to write anything. He felt an unmistakable sense of liberation at not having to do anything at all except what he wished to do. That meant not having to look at things like a journalist today — although that was why Natalia had asked for his help — and not, unless he wished to do so, writing or reporting anything about what they might discover.

It had been a long time since he had been in that position. It was like the infrequent times when he and his first wife had taken a vacation together and he quite deliberately failed to bring along a camera or a notebook so that for a short time he could just look at things and not record or interpret them for anyone. Today he was also enjoying the feeling, less intense and slightly more difficult to identify, of simply having a woman beside him in his elegant old car. He drove slowly: motoring, basking in the proximity of this pensive, attractive being.

He took the long route out to Lachine. On the highway, the trip from the inner city to the old industrial suburb would have been no more than fifteen minutes. His route, through Westmount, Notre-Dame-de-Grâce, and Montreal West would take almost twice that long. It took him past the corner where Stanislaw had gotten off the bus the day he died.

"My uncle lived just up there," Natalia said without apparent emotion, pointing up Claremont Street north of Sherbrooke. "Just off that street there."

Delaney said nothing. He continued along Sherbrooke, making good progress with the clear roads and the light traffic. The route took him past Loyola College, but he didn't bother to point out to Natalia that this was where he had studied, where he had worked on the university newspaper, where he had been infected with the not-yet-fatal journalism virus two decades earlier.

When they pulled onto St. Joseph Boulevard in what was coming to be known as Old Lachine by the young professional couples now moving in to renovate the old Quebecois houses, they had still exchanged few words. Lachine was a place as full of memories for him as he ever wanted Montreal neighbourhoods to be. He had always considered it the no man's land between the city's two solitudes of English and French, and of working class and bourgeoisie. In the west of Lachine, the streets were predominantly for the English-speaking and the middle class. Eastward toward the Montreal city centre they became much more heavily French-speaking and blue collar. About midway through Lachine the two worlds met uneasily, as they always did in Montreal.

The place was as old as Montreal itself. French explorers had mistakenly thought when they sailed up the St. Lawrence River to the rapids that began here that they had reached China through the long-sought Northwest Passage. They were wrong but made a settlement nonetheless — an outpost for the fur trade, and, later, when the English had conquered the French and taken the colony away from them, the beginnings of an industrial centre.

For Delaney, there was also family history. The Catholic Irish workers who had flocked to Quebec in the 1800s settled in large numbers around the Lachine Canal. His own Irish ancestors had not ever actually lived in Lachine; they had ended up in another workingman's suburb nearby called Point Saint-Charles. But he had heard the stories and knew the lore.

He knew, for example, as he and Natalia drove past the rough-hewn stonework of the canal, that English soldiers had fired on some of the Irish workmen who had built it so many years ago, when they rioted for better pay and rations. It had always annoyed him that most French Canadians insisted that English-speaking Montrealers were all descended from the wealthy English or Scot merchants who had dominated the city's finances until only a couple of decades ago. Delaney, when he bothered to express it, had taken pride in his Irish workingman ancestors, if only because he thought they absolved him of any blame in the bitter stand-off between the French and the English that still existed in the city.

Lachine had also been where his ex-wife grew up. She, of course, was from the eastern side, the French side, and he had ventured into that zone to visit her parents first with a young man's trepidation and then with a growing confidence. His French had been good, as was the case with many Irish-

Quebecers, and this, along with his Catholic background, made him more or less acceptable to
Denise's family, if a somewhat odd specimen for her
to have brought home. His role as a hustling young
journalist also made him a bit of a specimen as well,
but eventually he was accepted simply as "*l'Anglais.*"

Denise's parents, he guessed, had also likely
thought that as a social worker she was in the habit
of bringing home strays. He hadn't been to Lachine
for years, however, since long before his marriage
had suddenly, unceremoniously, ended. He preferred
to think that the main reason for that had been that
his wife simply tired of playing social worker to
himself and the crowd of maladjusted media people
he ran with in those days. There were other reasons.
But he didn't want to think of those today.

The Church of the Resurrection of Our Lord,
and its convent and school, stood on a giant walled
parcel of land granted to the Catholic Church by
the French colonial administration in the seven-
teenth century when land like this was next to
worthless. Its venerable hewn-granite buildings
showed no signs of having been allowed to decay,
and Delaney observed that parts of the green copper
roofing glowed with burnished sheets of new metal
where they had been recently repaired. The paint-
work was gleaming, if uniformly grey. The drives
and walkways were all carefully plowed and shovelled. The church, like most French-Canadian
Catholic churches of the era, was massive, too large,
built in the hope that pious Quebec habitant farm-

ers would do their duty and produce the hundreds of parishioners required to fill it.

The convent building was equally imposing: four stories of straight grey walls, surrounded on all sides and all levels by high wide balconies. Long lines of heavy wooden rocking chairs, the only recreation of generations of French-Canadian nuns, were marshalled on each balcony to take in the view of St. Joseph Boulevard, the abandoned canal, and the wide stretch of the St. Lawrence River that separated this part of Montreal island from the rich plain of farmland on the south shore.

The heavy bronze gate was not shut, and Delaney drove into the main courtyard. A more-than-life-sized crucified Jesus regarded them balefully from a cross in the centre. His halo and crown of thorns featured an array of small electric light bulbs, now not illuminated. There was no one around. Delaney paused for a moment and then made for a smaller stone house that was almost certainly the priests' residence. He pulled into the one space marked "*Visiteurs*," shut off the engine, and sat for a moment listening to it tick as it cooled. In the deep shade beside the house the air was still winter cold. Natalia, too, sat quietly and made no move to get out.

"Thank-you," she said for some reason. She seemed distracted, lost in her thoughts.

"Thank-you for what?"

"For agreeing to help me out," she said.

Delaney looked at her closely. She appeared

nervous, uncomfortable. He realized, more clearly than before, just what position she was in: here in the car of a near stranger, about to go into an old church building to question other strangers about matters of which she knew little and of which she might wish to know even less. He realized how major had been her recent loss, that the old man who apparently constituted her entire family was now dead, that she was still grieving for that loss, that she was more than likely intensely lonely and afraid. He saw a sort of desperation about her.

She would not have come to me unless she were desperate for someone to help her along in this, Delaney thought. *This sort of thing is the last thing she would normally want to do.*

He wondered, as she smiled wanly at him, what she might be thinking about why he was sitting in the car with her in this chilly place, what she saw as she looked and waited for some sign from him that they should go in.

Someone calling himself a journalist, early forties, somewhat disreputable beard and indifferently cut brown hair, wrinkles around the eyes, not from laughing, aviator sunglasses, battered parka. What else? A former patient — *client* was the politically correct word now — a man who had come to her complaining of unease, inability to sleep, something close to depression. A man who had started to tell her a little about his life, about his own sense of loss, about his newly vivid dreams, and who had then just as quickly retreated, hurried back to his waking life, never, she had probably thought at the time, to be seen again. And now here they were together on some unlikely excursion that was leading, he realized, God knows where.

"Let's go in. See what we can find out," he said, the no-nonsense reporter once again.

The door of his old car creaked extravagantly as he opened it and this seemed to end the awkwardness that had descended on them. They walked up the few steps onto a broad porch and Delaney banged loudly on the door with the black lion's-head knocker. They waited a long time before a severe nun, perhaps in her sixties and wearing the full grey habit of the Ursulines, opened the door. She regarded them with suspicion through her convent-issue steel spectacles. The overheated foyer smelled strongly of furniture oil and floor wax.

"*Oui?*" she said, unsmiling, not welcoming.

"We're here to see Father Bernard Dérôme, please," Natalia said in French. "We are friends of his friend and we would like to speak to him about something important."

The nun was taken aback. She started to say something and then did not. Her expression of surprise turned, Delaney thought, to annoyance. She stood with her hand on the inside door handle, and then said: "*Moment.*"

She left the door slightly ajar and as they stood on the porch they heard her hard heels snapping at the hard wood of the hallway. She was gone a long time. Delaney and Natalia moved to the edge of the porch and looked silently out over the vast property. An old man in blue overalls and a faded red lumberjack shirt walked slowly up the driveway in the distance, a large shovel hoisted over his shoulder. The buckles on his rubber boots jangled faintly as he walked.

"*Puis je vous aider?*"

The priest who now stood in the doorway was as severe as his housekeeper, in the oldest of Quebecois clerical styles. He wore robes of intense, slightly iridescent black, as if they had caught him preparing to say a Mass. A large crucifix and chain in what looked liked chrome steel glinted at his chest. He, too, was wearing unfashionable steel eyeglasses and his face was ruddy and chapped from years of shaving too close and living in cold rooms. His very thick old man's ears were also ruddy red. His lips, however, were pursed thin and bloodless. Delaney knew *visiteurs* were not at all welcome here.

"Yes, we are friends of Father Bernard and we have been trying to reach him to tell him some important news and we have been unable to do this," Natalia said, a little breathlessly. "I have called many times and left messages and he does not reply. We would like to speak to him if possible."

The priest did not give them his name or invite them inside. His irritation appeared to increase.

"I'm afraid that will not be possible," he said.

"Why not?" Delaney asked, then realized this was perhaps not quite the moment for that tone, for journalistic proddings. He sensed that Natalia wished he would stay quiet. The priest looked intently at him. Something about the quality of Delaney's French made him switch, in the baroque logic of Quebec social relations, to English.

"*Monsieur,* Father Bernard has unfortunately died," the priest said.

He had delivered the bad news to the other male in the group, as would have been his practice, but now he turned his gaze to Natalia to gauge her woman's reaction. She was shaken, and looked it. The priest offered no further information or explanation. He did not ask any more about their connection to the dead man. The death, apparently, was all the news he was willing to give, the end of the story he was willing to tell.

"He's dead," Natalia repeated.

"*Oui, madame.*"

"When did he die?"

"Some time ago, *madame.*"

"But when exactly?" she insisted, looking over at Delaney with fear in her eyes. *Stay cool,* Delaney told her wordlessly. *Stay on it.*

The priest stood silently, angrily, for a few moments before speaking.

"You are friends of Father Bernard?" he asked.

"Well, my uncle was his friend," Natalia said. "Stanislaw Janovski. And my uncle has died too and I know he would have wanted Father Bernard to come to his funeral and when he did not come I telephoned to find out why."

"Was Father Bernard your uncle's confessor?"

"No. A very old friend."

"He did not come because he was dead, *madame*," the priest repeated.

"But when did he die? What happened to him?" Natalia asked again.

"Why does that matter to you? He was an old man. As your uncle was probably an old man. *Le bon Dieu* called them both and now they are gone," the priest said.

He looked over their shoulders into the parking lot and then back over his own shoulder into the dark hallway behind him. Delaney thought he could make out the dim form of the Ursuline housekeeper deep in the shadows.

"Look," Delaney said. "My friend here just wants a little information about what happened to Father Bernard. Her uncle was very close to him and she would like to know a little about the circumstances of his death. Why would that be a problem?"

The priest had clearly decided he did not like this tall anglophone with a beard.

"I did not say it was a problem, *monsieur*."

"Then why not just tell us what happened?"

It was apparently easier for the priest to give them the information than to tell them why doing so might be a problem.

"Father Bernard met with an unfortunate accident," he said.

"What kind of accident?" Delaney suspected that the news was not going to be good, that somehow the news would be very, very significant, for

Natalia and, by extension now, for himself.

"He drowned, *monsieur*."

"Drowned," Delaney repeated. "He drowned."

"Oui, monsieur."

"In the wintertime."

"When? When did he drown?" Natalia seemed very alarmed now. Her eyes had widened and she looked over at Delaney briefly.

"It was in January. About four weeks ago."

"What date? What date was it, please?" she asked.

"The date? Well, *madame*, that is hard for me to remember."

"What week? What week? The second week?"

"Yes. I think that would be correct. Yes, the second week of January."

"What date? What day?"

The priest looked intently at her and then at Delaney. He could clearly see her distress, but he just as clearly did not want to know why she was distressed. Delaney knew that a priest of this vintage would be unused to being questioned. There would be far too much questioning going on nowadays, in his view. This priest would prefer the days when the Catholic Church in Quebec was above question, when the authority of priests was unquestioned, when two young people, who were not French Canadians and possibly not even Catholics, would not dare to stand on his doorstep and demand information.

He would be wishing for a return to the old days,

before the Quiet Revolution when the new Liberal government after Premier Duplessis's death had changed everything, had taken control of the schools and the hospitals and the charities away from the Church and made it their own. He would not like the changes of the last thirty-five years in Quebec very much at all.

"I believe it was a Friday, *madame*," he said at last. "A Thursday or a Friday in the second week in January.

This news alarmed Natalia even further.

"Friday is the day I got back from Zurich," she said to Delaney. "That's the day I found my uncle. He had been dead for maybe one or two days, the police said."

At the mention of the word *police* the old priest moved to conclude their interview.

"I'm afraid I must go," he said. "I have other duties this morning."

He made as if to close the door but Delaney stopped him with a hard look and a question.

"How did Father Bernard drown?" Delaney asked. "What happened to him?"

The priest saw this as the line these impertinent visitors should not be allowed to cross.

"That is a private matter, *monsieur*. I have tried to help you with some information, and now I must go. *Bonjour, merci.*"

He moved again to close the door but Delaney took a step forward and that stopped him.

"No," Delaney said. "It's important for us to

know how he died. You must tell us. How did he drown?"

"Yes, how did he drown? Did he drown in the bath?" Natalia asked. Her voice was higher, insistent now. She looked over at Delaney to see if he thought she was making the situation worse.

The priest's anger, displeasure, and frustration were intense. He stood and waited, but then seemed to realize that his unwanted guests might now create a scene on the porch of his retreat. He would want that even less.

"Father Bernard died on the ice, *monsieur*. He was a fisherman, an ice fisherman, and the ice under his fishing shack gave away."

"He would fish," Delaney said.

"*Oui*. It was his hobby, *monsieur*. He liked the quiet of it."

"He went into the river? Through the ice?" Delaney recalled seeing as they drove through the gates a couple of ice-fishing shacks out where the river widened into what was known as Lac-Saint-Louis. He wondered how anyone living in a place like this would crave a quiet refuge.

"*Oui*."

"Did they find his body?"

"Why do you want to know so much?" the priest asked. "Yes, they found his body. He was able to climb back onto the ice."

"He climbed out of the water and died on the ice," Delaney said.

"*Oui, monsieur*."

"He drowned, but they found him on the ice."

"*Oui, monsieur.*"

"That's not possible," Delaney said.

"How would *monsieur* know what is possible and what is not?" the priest demanded. "I have tried to help you and that it is all for today. *Bonjour*. I must go."

"Look, people do not drown like that," Delaney insisted. "If he could get back onto the ice he was not drowned. He would have frozen to death maybe, but not drowned."

"*Monsieur,* I have told you it was an unfortunate accident. It was very cold. His head must have rolled back into the water and he drowned. This is what the police said. The police have been here and they have said it was like this. And now I go."

The door slammed shut and Delaney and Natalia were left alone on the silent porch. Natalia stood looking shell-shocked. She said nothing. Delaney said nothing either. An intense feeling began to build, however, in Delaney's guts, a feeling he had had just a few times in his life before.

It was not fear, though he had felt intense fear many times before. Fear was what you feel when rebels point their AK-47s at you and grin the toothy grin they grin when they are thinking about killing a *gringo periodista* in the rain. Fear is what you feel when border guards somewhere else take away your passport and throw you in the back of a dank armoured personnel carrier and argue loudly in Spanish about whether you may be a Yankee spy.

Fear was what you felt interviewing a Cuban dissident at his rundown Havana home and suddenly hearing military boots kicking down the front door and the howls of the Neighbourhood Brigades urging soldiers on.

No, the feeling Delaney felt just then was not fear. It was a deep sense of dread. Dread of entanglement, of ensnarement. It was not at all the same as fear. He remembered clearly the first time he had this feeling. He was sixteen, and intensely, hormonally, involved with a buxom young high school sweetheart. They had been kissing and fondling each other with teenage ferocity for weeks and in her ardour the girl had one night whispered: "Oh Francis, I love you." His reaction had been unmistakable and it had not been joy. He had thought, instead: *How will I ever get out of this now?*

Delaney felt that dread of entanglement once again as he stood with Natalia on the old wooden porch. He knew that what they had learned that morning was important, that the facts they had uncovered meant there was much more to the death of Stanislaw Janovski than he had suspected. The coincidence in the timing and nature of the second death was simply too great. So far, he had been simply taking a journalist's interest in what Natalia had told him of her uncle's story. But he knew that he was now also personally implicated in this increasingly complex affair, that he was connected to this other human being because he had said that he would help her. He was becoming involved in a way in which he, the professional passive observer, had spent a lifetime trying to avoid.

They walked the short distance out the gates and across St. Joseph Boulevard to the canal. They strolled for a short while along the bicycle path that ran beside it and then stood looking out over the frozen lake to the group of three ice-fishing huts sitting brown-black against the brilliant white expanse. Delaney had left the car where it was parked, apparently not caring that it would trouble and annoy the priest if he saw it still there. They did not talk much immediately after the encounter on the porch. Natalia walked with her hands in her pockets, and felt the fear that Delaney had not felt. *The priest has been murdered too,* she thought. She looked over at Delaney, but he also was deep in thought. *Francis thinks so too.*

"He was murdered too," she said.

"We can't be sure of that, Natalia," Delaney said slowly. "We don't even know if your uncle was murdered."

But she knew he was not stupid, that he had been around the world. She knew that he, too, found it a most disturbing coincidence.

"I would like to know if my uncle came out here to visit Father Bernard around the time they died," she said.

"I wouldn't count on our friend across the street

to help us out on that," Delaney said. "I could possibly make some inquiries about this so-called drowning through the ice, though. I know some reporters who find that sort of thing interesting. It might have hit the French police tabloids."

They had stopped, and were leaning against the old iron railing that separated the path from the frozen water in the canal. The municipal authorities had spent a lot of money fixing up the area. There were benches and picnic tables, now heaped with a season's fall of snow, beside the bike path. Small bronze plaques here and there described the history of the place. A squat building of ancient stones to their right was the main trading post of the early fur trade, one such plaque said. It was now a museum, and brightly dressed schoolchildren were filing inside behind an impossibly young teacher.

Natalia looked across the street and saw on the second story of the main convent building a solitary nun rocking slowly on the balcony, bundled up against the cold air. Perhaps, Natalia thought, she had been there the whole time they had been with the priest. Perhaps she was often there, watching the street below.

"I'm going to talk to that nun," Natalia announced suddenly. She hitched her purse up higher on her shoulder and moved toward the sidewalk to cross the street back to the gate. Delaney was startled, looked up to where she had pointed, and then moved to go with her.

"What do you mean?" he said. "What would she

have had to do with anything? Hold on."

But Natalia was determined to go on and to do so quickly. Something about the situation suddenly made her want to act, to move beyond the precipice where the old priest's news had left them. She had been moving, she realized, as if in a dream since the night she discovered Stanislaw's body. She was tired of introspection. She yearned quite uncharacteristically for movement, action, definite answers, some promise of resolution.

"No," said Natalia. "I want to ask someone else about all this. Anyone else. You stay here. They won't like men going in there anyway. I might be able to get her to tell me something."

"Tell you what? What could an old nun possibly know about any of this?" Delaney asked impatiently. "Wait."

"No. I'm going in."

Natalia dashed across the road. There was no traffic. As she went back through the gate, she turned and saw Delaney standing on the sidewalk, looking perturbed.

Perhaps he will be angry with me now. But surely he of all people can understand this need for answers, she thought.

For the first time in many weeks she was clear in her mind about what she was doing and why. She carried on up the driveway and into the main convent building. The worn wooden stairs inside were broad, gleaming with wax and the effort of many Ursuline arms. No one was around. She ran lightly up, and on the first dark landing saw the pale light from outside coming in a long row of windows that gave onto the shaded verandah. Through the spotless but very old glass she could see the back of a nun's veil — rocking, slowly rocking.

Natalia went through the door and apologized immediately to the old woman for the intrusion.

"Please, I'm so sorry to startle you," she said. "I need to talk to you."

The nun, easily past her seventieth birthday, stopped her rocking and sat up very straight in the high-backed chair. She had small, dark eyes that stared. She did not, however, seem afraid. Perhaps that was because she had seen Natalia coming across the road. Or perhaps it was because she had expected someone, eventually, to come.

Delaney watched from across the street as Natalia disappeared into the convent building. He felt the unpleasant sense of entanglement grow.

I'll have to wait for her now, he thought, surprised at how annoyed this small inconvenience made him. He was used to being the one to make the moves, to seek the information, to plan a strategy. He expected that Natalia would be discovered by someone, reported to the priest, and that there would be a scene in which he would have to intervene.

He saw Natalia appear on the high, wide balcony, saw the old nun stop her rocking and sit bolt upright in her chair. Natalia pulled another rocker close to the old nun and sat facing her directly, lean-ing forward, and talking intently. The two women sat like this and talked for a long time. *Psychologist with client*, Delaney thought.

It was impossible for him to guess from their movements whether Natalia was having any success. He did not like being kept in the dark like this. He did not like depending on someone else to gather information for him. Then it occurred to him that not since they had driven in the gate that morning had he thought to check whether they were being followed. He did not like that very much either.

As he looked carefully around him now he could see no one watching, no car waiting, nothing unto-ward. He felt nonetheless that he was somehow losing control of the situation. He turned, crossed a small footbridge over the canal, and began trudging through deep snow down an embankment and out across the frozen lake toward the fishing shacks.

Sister Marie Alpha Gilberte Huberdeau, ever-devoted, ever-obedient member of the Blessed Order of the Ursulines, watched quietly as the pret-ty young woman who had spoken such excellent French moved slowly back down the driveway to the street. At the gate, the young woman turned briefly back and gave a furtive wave up to the balcony. Sister Gilberte did not wave back. Nor did she yet rock, for the moment, in her favourite old oak chair. She watched as the tall young man, older than the woman, crossed the street to join her. He stamped snow from his boots and his trouser legs. They spoke for a few moments, and then the young man looked briefly up in the direction of the balcony before they walked together to get into a fine old car that was parked near the priests' residence. She waited until the car had sped off in a plume of steam in the direction of the city before she resumed her rocking once again.

Ah, the nun thought, *ah, mon bon Dieu seigneur. The things one sees, the things one must endure in this life.* She rocked, and felt the chill of the coming afternoon in her nostrils. She smelled the vaguest hint of a Quebec spring, too, however, and that gave her spirit some repose. *After the winter comes spring,* she thought.

She thought, calmer now, of all of the winters and springs she had seen unfold from this very balcony and this very chair. She thought of other winters and springs she had seen in other convents and churches in other parts of this snowbound province. *Quelques arpents de neige,* she thought. *A few acres of snow. That is what the French kings called this place.*

She was calmer now, after the surprise visit, and after the questions about things she might have seen. The girl's questions had been from the heart, Sister Gilberte had thought. Some things about Père Bernard, God save him, some things about the girl's uncle who had also recently been taken. Sister Gilberte had listened quietly and said very little, as was her custom, the way she and thousands of young Quebec farm girls had been trained to do as their duty to God and the Catholic Church. She felt that she had not sinned by telling the girl that, *oui,* sometimes she saw visitors come in the courtyard, and that, *oui,* she remembered seeing Père Bernard walking in the grounds and along the canal with another old man, not a priest, who would come by bus to visit from time to time. Even not so long ago, *mademoiselle,* yes that is true.

And, *oui,* she had seen other visitors. Of course, people came from time to time for the priests and for deliveries and to make repairs and remove the snow. *Oui,* people came in from time to time. It would be impossible, however, to remember all such visitors and so she really could not say who else might have come to see Père Bernard. That would be impossible to say. Sister Gilberte had preferred to listen to the girl's story of how her uncle had suddenly been taken, that he had been a good Catholic man who had fought bravely in Europe's War — the one which *les Canadiens français* had not wanted very much to fight — and that she missed him very much.

Sister Gilberte had listened and had not told the young woman about those she herself missed, about her own family she had left so long ago, about all that she had seen these past fifty or more years wearing the habit of the Ursulines.

She did not tell her about the day very much like this one, so many years ago, when she thought God had called her for her sinful thoughts and her disobedience, when the trickle of blood ran down inside her thigh and she ran and ran and ran to a rushing icy stream between the hard frozen farms and sat with her skirts billowing up in the freezing water to wash that sinner's blood from her body. She did not tell the girl how the pains each month had been intense, excruciating punishment after that first time in the cold, cold water, how no matter how much she tried to wash away the sinful, sinful blood it still came, and how there was no one she could ever tell. There were things that must be kept strictly between a Catholic girl and her *Dieu seigneur*.

Sister Gilberte did not describe to the girl how proud her family was when she had been the first child to enter the convent, how they had waved and waved at the train the day she left for Saint-Jérôme. They had waved that way when her older sisters had left the village to work in the textile mills of New England and the shoe factories in the east end of Montreal. She did not describe all the convents and schoolrooms and hospitals and *presbytères* where she had done her duty to God and the Catholic Church. All of the things she had seen, and heard, and some she wished she had not seen and heard, things she was not supposed to see and hear.

Sister Gilberte shuddered. The wind from the river was getting colder as the sun moved. She did not wish to think this afternoon about some of the things she had seen and heard as an Ursuline.

The sounds in the night in the wide dark wooden convent halls. The sounds of weeping, the sounds of punishments, and the sounds of secret footsteps. The sounds, in those years when she was house-keeper to a priest far from here, of protesting, whimpering, groaning altar boys who had been summoned to consult with him behind closed doors. What did they do in that room those after-noons? What on earth could make the small boys whimper so?

There were things even here in Lachine that she wished she had not seen, wished she had not heard. And so she could not tell the young woman of that darkening late afternoon not so very long ago, when as she sat and rocked she saw two men in suits and fancy coats come and knock at the door of the priests' house much as the young woman herself and her friend had done this very day.

She thought it would not be right to tell how Père Bernard had answered, how the men had gone inside, how they had stayed for a very long time, only the three of them there that day. She did not tell how in the early evening dark the two men had come out to carry a long, dark bundle to their car, how they had driven it across the small canal bridge and past the boatsheds and down onto the thick hard ice and out to the fishing shacks.

She did not say how she saw them unload their bundle into one of the shacks and then drive away in their fine new car. She had not even told Père Carpentier when he returned that night from his duties in Montreal. It was not for her to tell all that she had seen and heard.

Chapter 5

Hilferty loved being a spy. He loved it even though he was the Canadian version of a spy, a sanitized and civilized version of what he secretly called "world class spies" like the CIA guys or the Brits or the Israelis. Still, he was as much a spy as you could get in this great northern outpost and he loved it. He really did.

He was particularly content on days like this. A classic late-winter or springlike morning — the choice of descriptions said a lot about your personality, the Service psychologists would no doubt claim — filled with February sunlight, the snow brilliant, the air not too cold. Alone in a shiny, oversized, and very comfortable government car, driving down the highway from Ottawa to Montreal. His snug little house in the charming New Edinburgh district, his charming assistant deputy minister bureaucrat wife, his charming perfect daughters behind him for a day or so.

He was fresh from a secret Saturday briefing with his supervisors — he just as secretly called them his masters — confirmed in the assignment he had been on for many weeks now, knowing exactly what his next moves would be, the issues of back-up and resources and manpower all sorted out, the way clear, for once, to carry on with what he was trained to do, what he suspected he had been born to do, for Canada.

Days like this, assignments like this, clear-cut situations like this, he knew, as he adjusted the balance control on the car radio so as not to miss a nuance of the baroque concert playing on the CBC, were becoming harder to arrange. His masters were lately far too worried about parliamentary committee submissions and staffing cuts and the cost of surveillance overtime and their own pensions, too frightened by the budget cuts to all federal government departments and services to keep clearly in their minds what the Canadian Security Intelligence Service had been set up to do and why minor issues of money and bureaucracy and mandate and accountability had to be pushed into the second tier of things to consider.

The meeting had gone exceptionally well. Hilferty had picked his most unspooklike suit for the occasion, since he knew Smithson did not like people flaunting their spy status on the arch-conservative streets of Ottawa, and Rawson was jealous of those who dressed better than he did. Hilferty's briefing was a classic. The adrenalin flowed directly to the speech centres of his brain and the words flowed out just as they had to in order to reassure his masters that all was well with this operation, that it was worth every penny and every operative who had been assigned to it, that no minister or journalist would get wind of it, that if they did there could be no hint of scandal or waste or violation of procedures or of the Canadian Criminal Code or, God forbid, of the constitutionally enshrined Charter of Rights and Freedoms.

And, of course, as was always the case when Quebec turf was involved, they had wanted endless reassurances that the operation would not flare up into another in the decades-long series of federal-provincial jurisdictional battles, that CSIS agents, and in particular Smithson and Rawson themselves, would not find their pictures on the front of the *Globe and Mail* or, God forbid, *Le Devoir,* in a year when the separatist government in Quebec City was planning to hold yet another referendum about whether people in the province had finally decided that, yes, this time they really had had enough of Canadian federalism. Everything was fine, just fine, Hilferty had assured them. Everything was going exactly according to plan, no chance of a fuck-up — Smithson liked briefings to have a few bits of profanity in them, as this made him feel more like the hard-bitten spymaster he would never prove to be — all going exactly according to plan.

Quite routine, really. Just carrying on, gentlemen, with our tracking of two Polish agents who have been in the country for some time. Monitoring their activities before kicking up a fuss at the Polish Embassy or approaching anyone in the band of reprobates and paranoiacs and malcontents and thugs who now made up Walesa's sorry excuse for a presidential team and the chaotic remains of a security apparatus in Warsaw. And most definitely, gentlemen, this high-priced journalist in Montreal could turn out be a help to them in their investigations. Yes.

It was a shame, Hilferty thought as he drove, how the whole CSIS thing had turned out, how cautious and apologetic Smithson and Rawson and those like them had had to become in carrying out what Hilferty, in secret, liked to call Their Important Mission. He hated having to make such earnest pitches for support for operations, having to go cap in hand to the Smithsons and the Rawsons of this world for permission to do what he knew was best.

It was true, he acknowledged this, that CSIS had never been set up to rival the American agencies in its work or its style, that it could never hope to anyway. And it was true that the official mandate for this civilian security agency, which had replaced the RCMP security service in 1984 when the Mounties had been caught doing un-Canadian things like breaking into offices and burning down separatists' property and stealing dynamite and other spooklike things, was domestic only. He was embarrassed to say to the American agents he came into contact with that, no, CSIS had no mandate to undertake covert operations abroad, and no mandate for its agents to carry weapons, and, no, he didn't think that was like running around without a dick.

In secret, however, Hilferty yearned for the

wide-open spaces of Yank or even British spook-dom, for the overseas intrigue and the high-tech toys and the deadly weaponry and the life-and-death nature of some of the assignments the Langley, Virginia, cowboys told him about in hotel bars over expensive CIA-issue bourbons. He wanted a piece of all that. He was tired of the endless, earnest debates in Canada about "security intelligence" as opposed to "foreign intelligence," about when something posed a threat to the security interests of Canada and when it did not. He was tired of all this precious bullshit about Canada being a respected middle power and therefore, somehow, above the need for a bit of dirty old-fashioned overseas spying from time to time.

What other decent-sized country in the world would stick with such a ridiculous line besides dear old Canada? Not one. The world was changing fast, in Hilferty's humble opinion, and Canada had to change along with it. For all he knew, the powers-that-be in Ottawa would never be able to come to a decision about whether to set up a real foreign intelligence service in Canada. They had been dithering about it since the last war and they were dithering about it still. But he didn't give a damn about any of that bureaucratic bullshit. Never had. He knew what his real job was and he just got on with it.

Hilferty nursed the secret thought that he would have been a highly successful and valued CIA man, given the chance and the accident of birth in the U.S. of A. He had all the credentials, in his reckoning. A conspiratorial mind — chess was his game from about the age of ten — a nice little degree in military history, an even nicer law degree from McGill. Then varied experience defending scumbags as a young criminal lawyer, then prosecutions in Montreal and the makings of a very nice little career in the Ministère de Justice. Another Montreal Anglo boy makes good.

But then, thankfully — there being no possibility of his ever playing in the American Spook League and his having no taste for becoming a Mountie spook — had come the McDonald Commission, the Commission of Inquiry Concerning Certain Activities of the Royal Canadian Mounted Police. With that came the decision to take spookery away from the Mounties, because they had been naughty boys, and give it to bright young non-policemen just like, Hilferty thought happily as he drove, his very self. His pleasure in having won the right to serve Canada as a CSIS agent had not been marred by the fact that, fair-minded Canadians all, the bureaucrats in Ottawa assigned to set up the new agency had sought applicants through large display ads in the careers sections of the major newspapers of the day. That didn't make the job any less special, any less important, in Hilferty's view.

So now, ten years in, he found himself driving down the almost empty highway toward his former hometown to continue his Important Mission to keep Canada a safe haven from nastiness of all sorts.

He had been doing his bit to push the envelope a bit, to do on the ground all he could to move CSIS along a little farther down the road to real agency status. He was sick of relying on those smug liaison officers from other services for the real dope on things that were important to Canada. Sick to death of it. So he pushed the envelope a bit whenever he could. He and some other like-minded CSIS men. Even if it meant keeping a few things to themselves, or occasionally breaking a few of the more vexatious rules and regulations that constrained them.

He had been doing his bit these ten years and, he liked to think in secret, the country was a little better for it. Those simple families in the little red-brick farmhouses he saw out the window of his car could have no idea just how fucked up a place the world was becoming, how very lucky they all were. They really had no idea.

And it was a very fucked-up place. This latest assignment showed that clearly. Hilferty guessed that when all was said and done he would probably just find that the Polish guys were here to watch Borowski, so they could report to Walesa what this loose cannon of a Polish-Canadian entrepreneur, so-called entrepreneur, was up to in Poland's election year. Hilferty guessed that was what they were doing here, but, then again, you could just never be sure anymore, with the Soviet Union completely fucked, and amateurs like Walesa running the store in places like Warsaw. It seemed to his logical military-historian's mind and his lawyerly training and his CSIS experience that it would be a natural thing for Walesa to want to watch Borowski, because the guy had scared the shit out of everybody in the last presidential election in Poland by suddenly going over and winning almost 25 percent of the vote.

Borowski, with his dubious, his really very dubious, biography, was worth watching. Even if you weren't Walesa and scared shitless about this mysterious millionaire who claimed he had made his wad in Canada in refrigerators after exiting Poland via Sweden in 1969. Who then acquired Argentine citizenship while running a restaurant in Buenos Aires, for Christ's sake, and then decided during the 1990 election that he'd go over from Toronto and stir the Polish pot with some statesmanlike rhetoric.

"Poles need a unifying goal and one such goal that can unite Poles is war." That was one of his good ones. "The most effective weapon for Poland today is an intelligent medium-range missile with a nuclear warhead of about one megatonne." Hilferty and the lads at CSIS had particularly liked that one as they sat in Ottawa and monitored coverage of Borowski's progress in the campaign.

So, OK. It's natural Walesa and his merry men would want to watch Borowski a bit this time around, especially since good King Lech had thrown the guy in jail for a few days after the 1990 campaign was over and had him charged with defamation before squeezing him for $100,000 bail money and kicking him out of the country.

But Hilferty had a sense there was perhaps more to it than that. He had never bought the rumours in 1990 that Borowski was KGB, or even CIA, for Christ's sake; the rumours had gone that far. He never bought that stuff at all. But, and God knows he would never say this to Smithson and Rawson, maybe he was dead wrong about the Borowski connection in the first place. Why would the Polish agents be spending so much of their time in Montreal? As far as he had been able to gather, they hadn't even gone up to Toronto or anywhere near Borowski's turf. Why was that?

And why would they bother with an old guy like Janovski? Where did an old World War II–vintage émigré like that figure in this? Hilferty had been able to make no connection between Janovski and Borowski, no matter how many keywords and cross-references he fed into the CSIS computer late at night when all the little secretary foxes had gone home. And why would these guys be bothering with Janovski's niece now that the old man had bought it?

The questions troubled him, despite the soothing baroque music that filled the warm sanctuary of his large automobile. It also troubled him, though God knows he wasn't about to tell Smithson and Rawson this either, not yet anyway, that maybe the Poles had snuffed old Janovski, that maybe the little coincidence of his drowning was too hard to fathom any other way. It troubled him that if it turned out they were the ones who had done the old guy in, maybe the Smithsons and Rawsons of this world would wonder why someone on Hilferty's team had not been around the night it happened, seeing as they were costing the Canadian government such big bucks in surveillance overtime.

Hilferty sat up a little straighter now and began to concentrate on the heavy traffic that always built up on the western approaches to Montreal. He'd have to ponder all of that a little later, after he'd finished talking to Delaney. Yes, Hilferty thought, Delaney might just be able to shed some light on this for them, after he'd heard the little proposition that the fine young undercover representative of the Canadian Security Intelligence Service was driving to Montreal to deliver personally. Hilferty would ponder all of that later, and then he would take little Ronika — racy little Ronika of the tight jeans and the university textbooks clutched so fetchingly against Danskin ballet tops — out for a bit of dinner and a bang later at the hotel, to console himself, in secret, about what a complex and possibly dangerous place Canada had become.

The tires on Delaney's Mercedes crunched wetly on the treacherous mixture of gravel and slush that passed for Brian O'Keefe's driveway in wintertime. He hadn't bothered to call first. In fact, he had had the most fleeting of intuitions that he had perhaps better start limiting what he said about all of this over the telephone. It was a Saturday morning, the day after his trip out to Lachine with Natalia, and he knew that O'Keefe would be home. Whenever he wasn't at the *Tribune* these days, and even on some days when he was supposed to be at the newspaper, O'Keefe retreated to his few hectares of land at Saint-Jean-sur-Richelieu and played out his strange role as part gentleman farmer, part survivalist.

It was a game that annoyed his wife, Karen, unspeakably. Delaney could only just remember the days when he and O'Keefe were young reporters together on the *Tribune*, and O'Keefe's marriage had not yet deteriorated to a tense stand-off. The O'Keefes had still lived in the inner city in those days, and even with Brian racing around on his beloved police beat for the newspaper and Karen working hard at university courses, they still had time for some semblance of a life together. Karen even smiled a little in those days and consented from time to time to having a few people over from the paper for bad pasta and cheap wine.

Now, a few unsuccessful separations later, she and O'Keefe still shared the same space, far though it was from the inner-city media life they had once shared, but she did not share her smiles very much at all. Karen had grown tired, in a way that Delaney knew all too well, of the raucous reporter's life O'Keefe loved so much. Tired of the boozing and the late nights and the shoptalk and the occasional indiscretions on the road, on assignment. Even the very late addition of a son, an enormous surprise to all O'Keefe's colleagues at the paper as well as to himself, had not improved matters much. The boy, Seamus, was now five years old. O'Keefe and Karen were five years older and five more years into their disastrous marriage, but there was still no end in sight.

Karen was underemployed as a nurse in a local community centre. Treating the cuts and scrapes of farm boys after their brawls in local taverns was not quite what she had imagined for herself when she was somehow won over to O'Keefe's mad scheme to escape the city. O'Keefe, for his part, contented himself in his time off with his gun collection, his two mongrel dogs, and tramping the overgrown fields around his house like some mad Irish lord, shooting at any bird or small animal that moved and dreaming of the day when an intruder might venture onto his precious sod.

Journalism had ruined O'Keefe in not quite the same way it had ruined Delaney. Delaney had moved around a lot in the business, worked here and there in a variety of media, thereby postponing the inevitable realization that 90 percent of journalism is repulsive, venal, mendacious, and cheap — a killer of souls and a graveyard of talent. O'Keefe hadn't gone the parliamentary correspondent, foreign correspondent route. Airplane and chopper rides and good hotels and expense accounts and glamour assignments hadn't spared him from the inevitable for as long as they had for Delaney. O'Keefe had stayed for almost his entire career at the *Tribune* and had taken on the persona of the loud, brash, terminally cynical city reporter so completely and so early that he could now hardly take the mask off, even with his oldest friends.

His inability to see any redeeming feature in any human endeavour, any public figure, in just about anything at all, had made him a very hard man, at forty-six or forty-seven years of age, to be with for very long. That, and his not terribly well disguised alcoholism were exhausting for those who dared spend time with him. Even Delaney did not come out to the farm very much anymore, though there was a period after his wife left him that he had spent more than a few nights with the O'Keefes, drinking the house whisky and fighting hounds for space on the couch. Karen had endured this for a while and then it became clear that Delaney had best begin passing his time some other way, inflicting his grief on someone else for a while.

O'Keefe, though, would have let his old friend, a fellow Irish Quebecer scribe of the bilingual kind, stay on forever. He would do anything for those he considered his friends and Delaney was counting on this for some help in the Janovski killing. For he had now decided that it, like the priest's death, was murder. O'Keefe's contacts in the police and the coroner's office and the more disreputable of the crime tabloids were up-to-date and first rate. And O'Keefe spoke the sort of raw French *joual* of the streets to which Montreal cops and coroners responded well. Delaney's French was simply wrong for this sort of work. It made him suspect, an *Anglais*.

Karen appeared more sullen than usual as she opened the door to the O'Keefe kitchen. She had gained a lot of weight and her hair was dry and not well combed. She was busy heating soup on the stove for young Seamus, even though it was mid-morning. The heir to the O'Keefe land holdings sat at the plastic-covered table with a foolish grin on his face.

"Hi, Uncle Francis," Seamus said. "I'm having soup."

"Brian's out in the barn," Karen said. "Hunting pigeons." She was not one for small talk anymore. But she paused, and then asked: "You doing OK, Francis?"

"Yeah, good. You?"

"Terrific." She ladled steaming soup into Seamus's bowl. "Had lunch?"

"Bit early for me," Delaney said.

Karen looked relieved. There was a burst of gunfire from the direction of the outbuildings and she looked sharply at Delaney, as if this was somehow his fault.

"That'll be Rambo in the barn," she said.

Delaney heard several more blasts from inside the dilapidated grey barn as he crunched through old snow toward it. He was careful to call out loudly before going in, lest O'Keefe think he had at last found some human target for his rage.

The firing stopped and Brian appeared, wearing what looked like a Crimean War greatcoat, a tweed cap, and a pair of grotesquely soiled rubber boots.

He stood well over six feet tall. In one hand he carried a short-barrel pump-action shotgun, of the sort used by riot squads the world over. In the other, a quart bottle of Molson's Export Ale. The murderous gun had come from a friend in the Quebec Police Force; the beer was from the battered Kelvinator fridge O'Keefe kept in the barn.

"Oh fuck me, it's Delaney," O'Keefe said. "What do you want now? Don't come whimpering to me about your girl troubles again, whatever you do."

O'Keefe somehow managed to grasp Delaney in a bear hug without spilling any of his beer or killing either of them with the shotgun. Delaney always felt like a frail boy in one of O'Keefe's extravagantly rough embraces.

"Have a beer, young man, and we shall eliminate this pigeon problem together," O'Keefe said.

They went into the dim stinking barn. A couple of frightened cattle, the sum total of O'Keefe's herd, looked without hope at the new arrival, aware that nothing would save them from this madman with a riot gun. High in the rafters sat a line of pigeons, equally terrified, at whom O'Keefe had been launching fusillades.

"These fucking pigeons are driving me crazy, Francis. They shit everywhere." O'Keefe managed to open the fridge door, retrieve a bottle from inside, open it, and hand it to Delaney, again without putting down his own burdens. "I'll get my double-barrel from the house for you."

"Never mind, Brian. I'll just watch."

This was O'Keefe's cue. He put down his beer, loaded three shells into the chamber, and fired them in quick succession in the general direction of the rafters. He pulled expertly at the wooden stock between shots to reload.

"Bastards, bastards," he shouted with each explosion. "Sons of bitches."

Birds fell. The hunt and the beer and the too-warm coat had reddened O'Keefe's face. He grinned wildly at Delaney.

"Want to have a go?" he asked.

"No thanks," Delaney said.

"Faggot."

"Look, Brian, I'm not going to keep you long. I need a favour." Delaney found himself unable to be charmed by O'Keefe today, or anytime lately.

"What's up?" Brian asked as he reloaded.

Delaney explained as little as he could about his interest in the death of Stanislaw Janovski and Father Bernard Dérôme. Could O'Keefe possibly help him out by making some inquiries about actual times and causes of death, coroner's reports, autopsies, police investigations, if any?

"Your police contacts have always been better than mine," Delaney said. "And I've been out of the front lines for a long while now."

"Yeah, I know," O'Keefe said. "Too cerebral for the police beat now. Let your old pals deal with the pigs now. I know that little game."

"So what do you think?"

"I'll check it out for you. When do you need it?"

"I don't know. Soon. Monday?"

"I'll try," O'Keefe said. "What are you working on exactly?"

"Oh, just a little sniffing around for a longer piece."

"And you don't want to tell your old pal Brian O'Keefe too much about it just yet."

"Not for the moment, Brian, that's true. You know the scene."

"Yeah," O'Keefe said. "Investigative bullshit. So what have we got here? Old Polish guy, drowned. Old French priest, drowned. Don't tell me, let me guess. A couple of old faggots, and young Delaney figures he's got the Catholic Church in his sights at last. Any choir boys involved?"

"Not so far."

"Or no, I've got it. Old Polish guy wishes to leave his vast riches to the Church, but a jealous relative, no, his wife, finds out and kills the fucker first. Then does the same to the priest who had the idea in the first place."

"It's good, Brian. Very good."

"'Two Dead in Catholic Sex Romp. Pope Implicated.'"

"That's it exactly."

"Sounds exciting. I can't wait to see it. Joint byline if I help you out, of course."

"Of course."

They both took manly pulls at their beer. Delaney realized, somewhat sadly, that there was not much more to say.

"Here. Take a shot," O'Keefe said. "You'll need some practice if you're taking on the Quebec Catholic Church hierarchy, my lad."

For some reason, Delaney took the offered shotgun. He loaded it with one shell. He'd been around guns often in his reportorial travels over the years, but had not fired many. He sighted up to the rafters and then out at the bright rectangle of snow that shone through the doorway. He felt a growing urge to fire, to unleash what was contained, to see the effects of this powerful tool he now held close to his face. He smelled the polish on the stock and the light oil on the barrel.

"Go ahead," O'Keefe said as he drank from his bottle and watched Delaney's hesitation. "Shoot."

Delaney turned and sighted along to a cluster of empty brown beer bottles that O'Keefe had placed on a wooden crate near a support beam. Delaney suddenly wanted to effect change in this target, to transform it, if not necessarily to destroy it. All other stimuli momentarily fell away.

He sighted down the barrel for what seemed to him a long time. Then he slowly squeezed the trigger, remembering how a Sandinista soldier had once shown him to keep a gunstock tight against his shoulder. The explosion of sound was deafening, so close to his ear. The target burst into a brief cascade of brown glass and droplets of beer and bits of shattered wood. Pigeons poured from the rafters and the cattle lowed in terror. O'Keefe's maniacal laughter frightened them even further.

"You're a natural, Delaney," O'Keefe roared as he danced briefly in the muck and straw of the barn floor. "You're a fucking natural."

As Delaney drove away down O'Keefe's driveway, he heard more gunfire coming from the barn. His right ear was still ringing from the single shot he had fired. He felt a dangerous exhilaration.

Delaney knew Hilferty slightly. They'd had a couple of extremely off-the-record conversations when Delaney was researching his book on the CIA and Quebec separatist groups. Hilferty, Delaney had decided then, should be placed in the category of not-terribly-reliable source. Close enough to information of interest but either unwilling or unable to share the truly interesting bits with anyone, least of all an investigative reporter.

Still, some of the things Hilferty had passed along proved useful, if only in leading Delaney to people who really knew what was going on in those days and were willing to say. Hilferty was also to be placed in the category of those police officers and not-so-secret agents who get a thrill out of journalistic interest in their work and their lifestyles, those who have to restrain themselves from telling more than they know should be told, or from telling more than they realize they are telling.

After all his years as a reporter, Delaney was not surprised when Hilferty called unexpectedly from his car phone and said he wanted to meet. He'd had dozens of unexpected calls from people over the years, and dozens of unexpected meetings. The only surprise was that Hilferty was already parked downstairs on University Street and wanted to come up right away. As usual lately, Delaney had not much work he wanted to do and the call he wanted to make to Natalia after his morning session with O'Keefe could wait. He told Hilferty to come up. He didn't try to guess whether this could have anything to do with the Janovski thing. Hilferty was the type who would tell him soon enough.

Of course Hilferty took Delaney up on his offer of a drink, even though it was early afternoon. *He reads too many thrillers,* Delaney thought as he poured a Jameson's for his guest and a mineral water and lemon for himself. Hilferty had taken off his black cashmere overcoat and placed it carefully down on the sofa, label out, so it would be clear it was from Holt Renfrew. The silk scarf, he left on. It actually looked quite good with his Holt's houndstooth jacket and his bright yellow V-neck sweater, which was also in cashmere. He took the clinking glass from Delaney and wandered around the living room a little, talking as he went.

"Still got no money for furniture in here I see," Hilferty said, grinning like a college boy.

"It's the minimalist style, John. Understated."

Delaney had no taste for empty chatter today. His time with O'Keefe had left him in an odd mood.

"Working on another blockbuster exposé book, I hear," Hilferty said.

"Yeah."

"Anything we'd be interested in?"

"I doubt it, John."

"Sure?"

"Yeah." Delaney waited a bit while Hilferty admired the view of the St. Lawrence and then he asked the obvious, "What's up?"

"Oh, you know how we like to keep up with what the media's doing."

"Spare me, John."

"What you working on, really? Got an article going?"

"Not at the moment."

"Not having a look at the Polish community in Montreal by any chance are you?"

"I'm not a feature writer anymore, I'm afraid. I leave that sort of thing to ambitious young cadets."

"I see. Been interviewing any Jungian psychologists, then? Any foxy little second-generation Polish numbers? Hmm? Or have we simply developed a taste for young women of East European stock?"

Hilferty's grin was getting on Delaney's nerves badly today.

"Look, John," he said. "Let's not piss around like this, OK? What can I do for you?"

Hilferty paused to put his drink down on the glass coffee table, looking around unsuccessfully for a coaster. He put it on top of a stack of magazines, and then sat on the edge of the sofa looking intently at Delaney. The no-nonsense spy now.

"We're really quite interested in why Natalia Janovski might have been in touch with you, Francis," he said.

Delaney didn't bother pretending he didn't recognize the name.

"Lots of people contact me, John. You know that as well as anyone. Why should it be unusual to have someone give me a call and come around to see me? The question, really, is why you'd be interested, and why you would be in a position to know what Natalia's doing on any given day."

It didn't surprise Delaney that this meeting was going to be about Poles.

"Can we go way off the record here, Francis?"

"I suppose."

"Not sure whether this will give you a story or not. Not sure we'd want this to give you a story anyway, if you get my drift."

Delaney said nothing.

"We're sort of interested in an old guy named Stanislaw Janovski."

"Why would that be?" Delaney watched Hilferty watching him to see if he knew that Janovski was dead.

"Well, it's really because some other people we are quite interested in . . ."

"As opposed to sort of interested . . ."

"Yeah. Some people we are quite interested in have been taking an interest in the old guy."

Again, Delaney said nothing.

"Well, unfortunately old Janovski has passed on," Hilferty said, "and we couldn't help but notice that his niece, this Natalia woman, has been round to see you and we were wondering if you could help us out a bit on what she might have said about why anybody would have been watching her uncle."

"Why don't you ask her yourself?"

"To be really honest with you, Francis, we don't want her to know we're interested just yet. Best she doesn't know just yet. Just carry on with your story for a bit, nothing fancy. You've got a much more trustworthy face than my guys and you'll get more from her than we will, I would imagine. You know how these things work. Cloak-and-dagger."

"I see. And what happened to this Stanislaw Janovski then? Just so I know how these things work."

"Well, of course the lovely and talented Natalia would have told you all about how he slipped in the bath last month and croaked."

"What do you figure?"

"Well, a lot of accidents happen in bathrooms, Francis. You know, with bath oil or bubble bath or whatever, it can get pretty slippery in there sometimes. Maybe he was a bubble bath sort of guy."

"So CSIS is working with the Canadian Safety Council now on this sort of thing, is that right?"

Hilferty always hated it, Delaney knew, when anyone suggested his employers were anything other than a band of good, hard men. Even in jest.

"OK, Francis," Hilferty said. "Let's not fuck around. It would be really helpful to us if we could find out a bit about why a couple of Polish spooks would be watching a boring old fart like Janovski, and why his niece would come a little while after he dies to approach Canada's foremost, ahem, investigative journalist and why you guys would then take a little car trip out to Lachine to go to confession at a lovely old seminary by the canal."

His people must be getting better, Delaney thought. "I hope you had more luck with the priest than I did," he said.

"Well, to be honest, we haven't actually made the approach yet," Hilferty said. "We thought you might be able to save us the trouble."

Delaney wasn't sure he bought that. He very much wished he knew whether Hilferty's people had found out about the other priest yet, the dead one. The drowned one.

"If you're calling in old markers, John, I'd have to say with all due respect that you haven't exactly filled my ear with state secrets over the years."

"True. But we do what we can."

"What is it you want exactly?"

"Well, it's just like I said. Help us out on this thing for a little while. Have a sniff around on our behalf, sort of, and then give us an idea what young Natalia knows, for example. Maybe you'd even turn up something interesting about her old Uncle Stanislaw."

"Do I look like a spook to you, John?"

"If you bought yourself some clothes you might pass."

Delaney thought about the few other times he had had such an approach. It happened to people like him from time to time, but generally overseas, if they were going in to somewhere unstable or strategically interesting. Sometimes an embassy type would make a gentle suggestion about a "possibly fruitful" line of questioning for an interview, that sort of thing. Maybe with a civilized little debriefing later over drinks.

It had happened to Delaney in Cuba, and in Malta when he was doing up a piece on Libyan terrorism. In Malta, though, it wasn't even the Canadians making the approach. This was the first time CSIS had pitched something like this to him overtly, and he was intrigued that it was on home ground.

"And what do I get out of this?" Delaney asked. "A nice little feature story?"

"Maybe not this time, Francis. Hard to say."

"So why would I bother?"

"Just to help out. Future considerations. 'Cause you're a nice guy. Out of a heartfelt passion for this great country of ours. Because there's nothing on TV tonight."

"Let me get this right," Delaney said. "Are you actually recruiting me to work on something for you?"

"No. No, not at all. Recruiting is absolutely the wrong word. Asking you to give us a hand here for a little while. You know there's a hiring freeze in the civil service anyway."

There was that boyish grin again. *He loves this stuff,* Delaney thought.

"So, what do you figure?" Hilferty asked. "Depending on what comes up, maybe you could even get a story out of it in the end. Depending."

"Maybe I would get a story out of it whether you guys are involved or not. Maybe I could even get a story about you making this approach, John."

"Now you know, I figured you would joke around about that," Hilferty said. "But we simply don't think you'd do that to us. It's not your style. You are known in high places for your discretion, Francis. Even though there were a few people pissed off by that last book of yours, nobody in my shop got burned. Or nobody you named anyway."

They both paused to study each other. Delaney remembered now why they had wordlessly agreed after their last encounters to hold each other in polite mutual disregard. Hilferty because Delaney was committed to nothing. Delaney because Hilferty was committed to anything. Anything his people in Ottawa might tell him to commit to.

The ice had by now melted in Hilferty's drink. Delaney also remembered he was one of those people who talked much more about drinking than he actually drank. He was one of those people who generally talked much tougher than they actually were.

"What have you got on Janovski?" Delaney asked. "Anything stand out?"

"Not a lot, Francis. Pretty basic story of a war vet

who settles down in Canada after it's over. He was a flyer. Parents killed over there. Brother here for a bit but dead now. Nothing special. Worked as a broadcaster in the Polish Service at RCI for quite a while. Maybe there'd be something there. I don't know."

"Who do you figure sent the agents over here?" Delaney asked.

"We're not sure."

"You mean all of the best CSIS minds in this country can't get a fix on who sends a couple of agents over from Warsaw these days?"

"It's not our fault, Francis. Really. You can't imagine how fucked up things are getting in Warsaw. There are factions and counterfactions and plots and intrigues like you wouldn't believe. Walesa's gone paranoid because he thinks he might lose the election this year. There was even talk he was thinking of a coup at some point a while back. Like that crazy fucker Yeltsin in Moscow. Parliament doesn't hop to it and you send in a couple of tanks. Walesa's been getting a wee bit cozy with the army lately, for our money. And his office is full of very nasty people ever since his old Solidarity pals decided he was an asshole. Then you've got the Commies freaking him out by taking so many seats in the Sejm that last time. The right hand doesn't know what the left hand is doing over there anymore, if you'll pardon the political science jargon."

"But you figure it's State Protection Office agents over here?" Delaney asked.

"Yeah, maybe UOP. But you can't figure who the State Protection guys are working for on any given day anymore, if you get my drift. Probably even Walesa doesn't know anymore. They seem like professionals, however."

"What makes you say that?"

"Oh, just a gut feeling," Hilferty said.

"Because they did in the old man?"

"I didn't say that."

"The UOP still like to duck heads in bathtubs when they question people?" Delaney asked. "Like the old days?"

"We haven't inquired," Hilferty said.

Delaney knew this would be about the extent of what Hilferty would be saying today. On cue, the CSIS man looked briefly at his stylish Swiss Army watch.

"Tell you what, John," Delaney said. "Why don't you let me think this over for a bit. You wouldn't want me to throw away my journalistic integrity just on a whim, now would you?"

"No, not a bit. No. Just take your time, and see what you might be able to do for us, that's all we're asking. No strings."

"I'll hold you to that."

"Hey, no problem." Hilferty was taking a small package out of the inner pocket of his overcoat. It was wrapped in black cloth. "I'm going to leave you something, in case you decide to have a go. Nothing special. You just may find this stuff handy. You know, in the trade."

He put the package down on the coffee table with a thud.

"That sounds suspiciously like a gun in there," Delaney said.

"Could be," Hilferty said.

"Unless I've got my facts wrong on this, you guys still don't carry guns."

"Reporters quite often get their facts wrong, Francis. Not plugged in to the real story."

"My readers would love to know about this sudden shift in CSIS policy, I'm sure," Delaney said.

"Not a policy matter, this one. For some among us, anyway. You get my drift. No comment."

Hilferty stood up, and for reasons known only to himself very formally offered his hand for Delaney to shake. They did so awkwardly.

"You thinking this makes a non-verbal agreement?" Delaney asked.

"God, you're suspicious. Reporters are all the same." Hilferty pulled on his splendid black coat. "Perhaps I should say, on behalf of the Dominion of Canada and of all her departments and services and all of the ships at sea that you should perhaps watch your ass a little bit in this one, Francis. Really. And the lovely Natalia's ass too. Whether you help us out or not."

"Cloak-and-dagger stuff."

"You got it."

Delaney peered down twenty-six floors to the street, and watched the tiny perfect spy get into his tiny perfect car and drive off. He realized suddenly that this would be an excellent vantage from which to watch whether anyone pulled out to follow. No one seemed to, however. Delaney also realized suddenly that he had been very bad at remembering to watch if anyone was now following him. This morning, for example. Then he sat at the coffee table and slowly unwrapped the package Hilferty had left behind.

Inside the cloth wrapping was a neat stack of Canadian hundred dollar bills, with a paper band around them on which was marked "$5,000." And a black, very new semi-automatic pistol. On the side was inscribed "Browning-FN9mmHP. Inglis Canada." There was an extra clip of nine-millimetre bullets, and a small booklet explaining how to load and care for the gun. A Quebec government firearms acquisition certificate in Delaney's name. A membership card, also in his name, for a gun club and target range on the North Shore: "*Club de Tir de Laval, Inc.*" Another little booklet, a government publication this time, explained who and in what circumstances citizens, including *bona fide* members of registered shooting clubs, were allowed to own and transport handguns in Canada. There was also a brief unsigned note:

> *"Thought this stuff might be of some use to you. Cash for expenses and the like. No receipts*

required. Weapon for show, mainly. Not sure if you've ever used one of these. Doubt you'll need to, but people can calm down nicely if you wave one of these around under certain circumstances. Watch where you point it, and mind the safety catch. The certificate and the membership card are not bogus. I've still got a few pals in useful places. Like-minded men — you know the drill. Have a go on the target range if you like. Practice makes perfect. And remember, even with the permit we've given you it's a serious offence if the cops stop you in your car and the gun isn't in the trunk."

How very Canadian, Delaney thought.

Chapter 6

On Sunday, February 19, 1995, some time just before midnight, consulting psychologist Natalia Janovski sat at a desk in a silent apartment before a school notebook that she used to record her most private thoughts. She wrote:

"Inability to sleep continues, classic symptoms of anxiety continue — restlessness, fantasies, mildly obsessional behaviour. Dream images vivid, disturbing. Various patterns can be seen to be emerging. Grieving process apparently unresolved. How I wish I could get this monkey off my back. How I wish for a clear psychic space, so I can just sleep for a while, forget about all of this for a while. Surely there is nothing in what I am experiencing that many, many people do not experience all the time when they lose someone they love. I have seen elements of it in many of my own clients. But how many of them become convinced that their missing Other has been murdered? It is natural that such a loss would provoke a psychic disturbance. But where does this perception of murder come from? Is there any basis in reality or is it just an unresolved neurosis?"

Natalia paused for a moment and looked around her intensely silent apartment. The air was pleasantly warm, the radiators ticked reassuringly, and the small desk light made a cozy circle in the otherwise winter-dark room. She wrote:

"There is no fear in here tonight, nothing to fear. So where does this anxiety come from? Perhaps it is simply, and this is what I would likely say to a client, that this death has taken from me a target for the projection of my animus complex, and this release of psychic energy is disturbing my equilibrium. Is this maybe why I have sought out Francis now? Another male figure on which to project my animus? Surely not."

Surely not, she thought as she looked at the entry in her lined schoolgirl's notebook. Surely I am more self-aware than that. There is surely more to this than a rather mundane unconscious projection. I asked him to help because he is experienced in these things.

"Why can't I accept what I see before me? Why can I never just accept that some things are real, that events are real events, that perceptions are to be trusted and not always just projections from the unconscious. My uncle has died. He left me a disturbing message. He seemed troubled before he died. I don't see how he could have drowned the way they say he drowned. His close friend has also drowned, at about the same time. I don't accept the explanation for that death either. I think that the old nun in Lachine did see something, just as I suspected she might. I could sense it in her eyes, her body language, her speech pattern. I have considered a situation, acted on it, sought information, found new information. So why do I always feel that I must apologize for my perceptions? Why would I always feel that the actions I have undertaken in the world are just symptoms, rather than reasonable responses to the facts? Why am I always so uncomfortable with action in the world?"

She became impatient with the tone of her journal entries now. How many years, she wondered, had she spent time like this, alone, recording her thoughts in journals exactly like this one? How many times had the entries sounded quite like this one? Enough scanning of the contents of her psyche for clues to her behaviour. Enough self-castigation. Tomorrow she would simply continue what she had started, no matter where it might lead. Any good Jungian analyst would agree, she thought, that intuitions, any elements scooped from the unconscious, are to effect change in a personality or to help accomplish some other useful work, in addition to merely being interesting in themselves.

She decided that she would try once again to sleep. But she could not resist the impulse to write one more line in her precious journal, her introvert's journal. She wrote:

"What is archetypal about all of this?"

The call from O'Keefe didn't come until very late on Monday, but Delaney had had no doubt that it would come. O'Keefe was many things, but he was surely a reporter who never missed a deadline. Delaney had asked for the information by Monday and O'Keefe delivered it.

"I got a bit for you on the old dead guys," O'Keefe said on the telephone. He was calling from the *Tribune* newsroom, and Delaney had to marvel, as he regularly did, at how quiet such places had become. No more than ten years ago, O'Keefe would have had to shout down the line over the din of typewriters and braying editors and ringing phones. Nowadays, there was an eerie stillness to the computerized, carpeted places where the news was processed. Phones no longer rang: they warbled politely. Editors no longer shouted: they hissed threats and whispered plots.

"Good man," Delaney said. "I'll come over. You on deadline?"

"Yeah, but I don't give a fuck. But why don't you just take it over the phone? You want me to type it up nice and neat for you or what?"

"Ah, the phones. You know."

"No, I fucking don't know," O'Keefe said. His swearing increased as deadlines approached. "Someone tapping your phone? Your story that big? Hello, hello, RCMP? This is Brian O'Keefe. Get off the line this instant. You leave my friend Delaney alone now, you hear?"

Delaney recognized this manic behaviour in O'Keefe. He knew it would be a mistake to say anything more. Not just because he did wonder if his phone was indeed being tapped, now that CSIS had made an approach, but also because he didn't want to wind his friend up any further. *He must have had a fight with Karen or a long lunch,* Delaney thought. *Probably both.*

It was the lunch, and a few other things. When Delaney arrived at the *Tribune* newsroom a short time later, O'Keefe was as pumped up as he could get and still function before a computer screen. It wasn't just the alcohol, although O'Keefe's red face told part of the tale. It was the rage. The newsroom was full of people half his age who dressed in smart clothes and whose careers were ahead of them, and this enraged him. The paper had less and less space for the kind of cop-and-robber material O'Keefe had made his reputation on, and this enraged him. He was finishing a bitter conversation with the assistant city editor when Delaney walked up to his workstation and this, clearly, had enraged him too.

The assistant city editor's name was Fiona Williams. She had an Honours degree in Mass Communications from Concordia University. She hadn't had her thirtieth birthday yet, but she wore an expensive female-editorial-executive outfit in the requisite creams and white. Word at the Press Club, according to O'Keefe, was that her meteoric rise at the paper had more to do with the managing editor's extramarital appetites than young Ms. Fiona's news judgment. Delaney had heard many such rumours, most of them unfounded, from enraged male journalists of a certain age.

"If you'd give me a few more fucking minutes without interrupting me, I would give you the motherfucking story," O'Keefe was hissing to her.

"OK, Brian. You file by five p.m. or we fill that hole with Canadian Press copy," Ms. Fiona said.

"Fuck that. Those CP idiots wouldn't know a lead if it bit them on the ass."

"Five p.m.," Ms. Fiona said. She looked at Delaney, who knew her slightly. "Don't distract him, Francis."

"Fuck you, Fiona," O'Keefe said.

She walked back to her office, her many strands of amber beads swinging rhythmically against an ever-so-slightly transparent blouse. "Yuppie scum," O'Keefe said as she disappeared.

"Another rewarding day in the news boutique, Brian?"

"Yuppie scum. This paper's completely fucked."

"I better not keep you away from it too long, then. You got a second to give me what you got?"

"I got all goddamn night. I'll file when I fucking want." O'Keefe reached into his very battered shoulder bag and retrieved a notebook that had served many times as a coaster for sweating mugs of draft beer. He flipped it open to the back page. "This looks more interesting than you said it was, dearie."

"What have you got?"

"My extensive contacts in the police and court system, which as you know have made me what I am today in the Canadian media, tell me that your man Janovski the Wonder Pole slipped and killed himself while taking a bath."

"That's yesterday's news, I'm afraid, Brian."

"Some tiny questions in the autopsy report about the amount of bruising around the head but nothing really inconsistent with an old guy falling around in a slippery bath and buying it. They were a little bit troubled by the hair, however. Some little question marks, I'm told, about what seemed to be a few bits of hair missing on the back of his head and neck, but nothing the rocket scientist down at the coroner's office could figure out or gives a fuck about. Figures it's one less vote against independence in the referendum."

"Hair missing," Delaney said.

"Yeah. A few bits. Maybe the guy was a bit rough with the old comb. Maybe he missed you so much he was pulling his hair out. You know this guy?"

"No. What do the cops say?"

"Ah, you know. Nothing, as usual. They couldn't give a shit about this one."

"What do you figure?"

"If they gave a shit, my guy tells me, they might have wondered a little more energetically about whether someone pulled out his hair for him."

"What do you mean?"

O'Keefe sprang up and grabbed a large handful of hair on the back of Delaney's neck, and began to force his head down onto the computer keyboard and then pull it up sharply. He did this a few times. No one in the newsroom appeared to find this unusual, and the reporters in the area around O'Keefe just continued their work. A neatly dressed young man at the next desk polished a pair of steel spectacles as he held the phone receiver with his shoulder and said: "Gee, Stewart, I'll have to get that lawyered and it's almost deadline. My editor won't want another darn defamation suit."

O'Keefe finished his little demonstration and let Delaney up for air.

"You know, a bit rough while they were helping the guy into the water. Ducking his face in to make sure the temperature was right. Just how he liked it."

"Ducking his head in?"

"Maybe," O'Keefe said. "If they gave a shit, the cops could have asked a little more about that. But they don't, and they didn't. They just figure the old bastard slipped and drowned. Or that's what they want to figure. Pathologist just probably put in a little note about that in case it blows up some day and somebody asks why he missed it. If it was anything at all in the first place, which is not at all sure anyway. They've got a lot of other worse cases than this these days and the guy was, what, eighty or so. So they don't give a shit. Nothing stolen, no motive, no suggestions from his daughter or his niece, or whoever she is, about why anyone would want to bump the guy off, so case *fermé*."

"What about the old priest?"

"Ah, now that one is much more interesting."

"I'm ready." Delaney was taking notes in his ersatz shorthand.

"Well, for one thing, it's fucking hard to drown in an ice-fishing shack as you know from bitter experience. But he managed it. That's fine. Took a fair bit of water in his lungs, apparently, after falling down inside and slipping partway into the fishing hole. You know. The usual household accident."

"What was he doing out there?"

"Don't ask me. Cops figure he was humping some local kid up the ass. Bit of a cold place to get your rocks off but who am I to say? Maybe the boy was big enough to get pissed off and he snuffed the old faggot. Maybe the kid's father got wind of it and did him in himself."

"Is that what the police are saying?"

"Not really. Not explicitly. I think that's what my pals are thinking as they proceed methodically to get to the bottom of this murder most horrid."

"There's a murder investigation?"

"Ah, now there is where it gets interesting. There should be one. How's this for a little human interest item? The autopsy shows the water in his lungs was chlorinated, fluoridated, all ready for drinking, and even had some small traces, very small, of soap and cleanser and a few other things."

"Bath water?"

"Nope. The Province of Quebec has gone to such lengths to clean up the St. Lawrence River that it flows down now from Ontario all ready to drink, and with a little soap mixed in for bathing."

The two journalists looked at each other in the way that only journalists look when they know they have a story, or the beginnings of one.

"Guy drowns in his bath, and then brings himself out to the ice-fishing shack so as not to upset the housekeepers," O'Keefe said. "You know the drill, Francis. A man of the cloth."

"So it's a murder investigation."

"Well, not exactly. The cops tell me there's a go-slow order on this one. Check it out, but don't solve it too fast. Not that these dumb fucks have a hope in hell anyway of solving it, but never mind."

"A go-slow order? Who from?"

"My guess is the Pope. He doesn't like it when his guys fuck little boys, or big boys for that matter. Bad for business."

"Seriously."

"The guys I spoke to say they don't know. Not from their level. They're guessing someone in the Montreal Church hierarchy has got to one of the senior officers. A good Catholic probably."

"They going to go along with something like that?"

"For a while, probably. They're busy, and they figure it's just another faggot priest anyway. They'll get around to it eventually. They weren't told to drop it, just to go slow for a while."

"I see." Delaney felt a small spurt of adrenalin go through him. He wasn't sure if it was the journalist in him who was excited by this, or someone else.

"What's the connection between the priest and this Janovski guy?" O'Keefe asked. "Was he gay?"

"No. Don't think so."

"Can you use this stuff?"

"Absolutely," Delaney said. "Eventually. I owe you one."

"If you don't use it, I can use it. Let me know. Christ knows I need a front-page hit about now. Throw the editors a bone."

Delaney called Natalia that night. There were two messages from her on his answering machine, along with the usual string of requests and queries from editors, colleagues, producers, and publishers' representatives. He should, he knew, check in more often with his magazine and with his publisher but he knew also that he would not. He realized as he dialled Natalia's number, however, that he had checked in with her, or she with him, every night since that first afternoon when she came to his apartment. *My hot new assignment,* he thought as the telephone rang.

She was agitated, but also guarded.

"Oh Francis, I've been trying to get you," she said. "Someone has been in my apartment."

"When?"

"Sometime today. While I was at the clinic. I know someone's been in here."

"What did they take?"

"Nothing I can see. But things are moved around a bit. Papers, books. I can sense someone was in here."

"Want me to come over?"

"Well, actually, someone is here with me now. A neighbour."

"We should talk over a few things. I've got some information."

"Would tomorrow be OK?"

"Yeah, I guess."

"Maybe you could come here."

"OK. What time?"

"In the morning?" she said. " Midmorning? Late morning? I'm still only back at work part-time."

"OK," he said. "Midmorning. Lock your door. When your neighbour goes."

"I will."

A neighbour, Delaney thought.

Delaney took a cab to Natalia's place the next day. The snow had returned so he decided to leave the

Mercedes where it was. It was also harder to follow someone in Montreal in a cab, if indeed someone was going to try to follow him today.

The cabbies all seemed to drive the same sort of Volkswagen Jettas. Fleets of them swarmed up and down the main streets these days. By the time the particular Jetta he had chosen pulled onto Esplanade Street, Delaney had looked out the back window a number of times and seen nothing unusual. The gaunt black driver in a Montreal *Canadiens* hockey sweater had asked him in Creole if he had left something back at his apartment; did the *gen-ti'hom* want to go back?

No, he did not want to go back. No, he thought, what he really wanted to do was see if some Polish agents were following him. He wanted to see if some CSIS agents were following him, he wanted to see if his editors or his readers or his accountant or his ex-wife's lawyers were following him. In fact, he now thought he saw a large car with two men in the front pull over on Mount Royal Street as his taxi turned down Esplanade, but he couldn't be sure. How could you be sure? But Delaney had to stop his thoughts from wandering. The cab driver wanted his money.

Gustavo, the Chilean refugee social-worker soccer-player ladies' man, was with Natalia when Delaney arrived. Very tall, very thin, very balding, but with what hair he had left fashionably gathered in a long grey ponytail. Despite the weather, Gustavo wore only a light denim jacket, replete with

pins declaring his various social and political allegiances. He worked with Natalia, apparently, doing
Good Works with refugees, torture victims, coup
victims. Art therapy, or some such thing.

Gustavo was just leaving, he said. No, no, he told
Natalia, he wouldn't stay for coffee with them. No,
gracias, no. Delaney and Gustavo eyed each other as
male primates do. *Been here all night, amigo?*
Delaney asked wordlessly. *Going to be staying the
night, gringo?* Gustavo was likely asking wordlessly
back. He was gone after a brief hug and a light kiss
on both cheeks from Natalia. He showed no desire
to be embraced by Delaney.

"Don't tell me, let me guess. He's in love with
you," Delaney for some reason thought it necessary
to say.

"He thinks he is," Natalia said.

"Therefore he is. That's how it worked when I
was a boy."

"He's projecting. He's in love with the idea of
being in love with me."

"Oh, please," Delaney said. "No wonder I
stopped paying you for therapy."

"Learning to withdraw your projections, Francis,
that's the hardest thing. All the psychic figures you
need for completeness are with-in. Any good
Jungian will tell you that."

Was that a wicked smile he saw on her face, or
just a smile?

"Makes it a bit hard to connect with real people
then, doesn't it?" Delaney said. *Not that I'm any*

authority, he thought.

Natalia seemed taken aback by this remark.

"I've had my small successes making connections, Francis," she said quietly. "Not as many as most, of course. Perhaps not as many as you. But I have always preferred to live alone in any case."

"It's none of my business anyway," Delaney said quickly. He didn't bother correcting her version of his prowess at making connections, especially recently. "It's none of my business."

She spared him her explicit agreement. They let the proddings about love lives go at that.

Natalia's explanation of the supposed break-in was vague at best, in Delaney's view. She *thought* she noticed things slightly rearranged. She had a *strong intuition* someone had been inside. There was even a *different smell* about the place when she got back the day before. The whole thing had made her *very anxious.* Still, he had a good look around for himself.

It was his first time in her apartment. He had always very much enjoyed looking around an attractive woman's apartment. The little things — the pictures and the books and the mementoes — told you a lot about a woman, and there was a pleasant element of voyeurism about it. In Delaney's experience, being allowed to look at a woman's things, or doing it surreptitiously, was a prelude to further intimacy. Maybe.

He examined the heavy inner-city door lock and could see nothing amiss. He suddenly felt very foolish doing so. *I'm no detective, for Christ's sake,* he thought as he straightened up. Perhaps the tiny scratches he thought he saw on the brass key cylinder were normal. He wasn't able to say. Natalia showed him how books appeared to have been moved and replaced on her many bookcases.

There were scores, hundreds, of books. Jung, of course. *The Collected Works* and just about everything else written about Jung's work. Jungians by the bushel. Emma Jung, Marie-Louise von Franz, Hillman, Progov, Campbell, O'Connor. The titles on these shelves were intriguing. *The Death and Rebirth of Psychology. Synchronicity and Human Destiny. The Discovery of the Unconscious. The Psychology of Romantic Love. Care of the Soul. The Soul's Code.* Others on other shelves equally intriguing. *The Varieties of Religious Experience. The Idea of the Holy. Tristan and Iseult: A Study of the Sources of the Romance.* Delaney very much enjoyed looking at a woman's books and wished he could linger over these for a long while.

"Why did you get into this sort of work?" he asked, pulling a volume from a shelf.

"Oh, some broken part of my own personality that needed fixing, I suppose," she said, smiling.

"Seriously," he said.

"I'm serious," she said. "Almost serious."

"Why Jung?"

"Because he links everything together for me. Behaviour, and the unconscious reasons for it. Human experience and symbolic representation. Rational, irrational. Inside, outside. Light and shadow."

"All right, all right," Delaney said, laughing as he put the book away.

"You asked for it," she said, laughing too.

She showed him her neat consulting-psychologist's desk and he wondered how anyone would dare meddle with the ordered stacks of papers and journal articles and notebooks. Here and there, however, a scrap of paper or a brightly coloured note was slightly out of place, or tucked roughly in amongst other pages. Her pens were fantastic shades of purple, green, and pink. Many crumpled balls of paper, too many, sat discarded in a wastebasket. A very small flash of exuberance, of disorder, hereby betrayed. *Of course she would deny this is a hint of some kind of inner chaos,* Delaney thought.

She brought him to the kitchen and the bedroom and the bathroom, as if to complete the tour, as if he were thinking about renting the apartment. The kitchen was somewhat New Age for his taste, but it was a true cook's kitchen. Meals were actually prepared here. Stainless steel, and open shelving, and serious knives, and eggs in wire baskets. Tall glass jars of pasta and politically correct Third World lentils and peas and beans. *I bet Gustavo enjoys that,* Delaney thought.

The bathroom was woman-fragrant; stirringly so. Oils, powders, creams. One toothbrush only. The bedroom was dim, secret, the bed surprisingly large, its cover a deep maroon. A comfortable reading chair with a serious spotlight beside it told of many bookish nights. He sensed that this was where she hid herself from things she had heard in sessions with clients, from things that had happened to her, from deaths of parents, deaths of uncles, war stories, torture victims; the usual household accidents. He stood at the threshold of the bedroom, looking in.

"So nothing has been taken?"

"No. I don't think so," she said.

"Well, I'm not sure what we can do. Unless you want to call your friends in the Montreal Police."

"No, thank-you."

They were standing by her desk. Delaney wanted to tell her about what O'Keefe had discovered, but his paranoia was increasing daily so he suggested a walk. She looked surprised, but something in his look made her simply put on coat and boots and go with him. They walked across Esplanade and past the hockey rink using a path that had recently been plowed. A few kids had wisely stayed home from school to scrape around on the hard Quebec ice instead. Their shouts echoed off the apartment buildings that lined the street.

There was a dangerous race against the traffic on l'avenue Parc and then they were in Mount Royal Park, just below the giant electric cross on the hill whose light had for years dominated the Montreal skyline. Delaney suddenly hailed a cab. Again, Natalia looked surprised, but she said nothing. In a couple of minutes, after a risky U-turn in the cascade of traffic, they were up what passed for Montreal's mountain and under the snow-laden trees around Beaver Lake. If they were being followed, their pursuers would surely now be dead in traffic behind them. They watched more kids skating on the man-made lake for a while, and then walked and talked.

Delaney told Natalia what O'Keefe had told him, or almost all of it. He spared her, however, the image of intruders possibly forcing her old uncle's head into a bathful of water, of a possible interrogation. Her eyes told him she was frightened enough with this near-confirmation that someone had killed him, no matter what means they may have chosen. Her eyes also told him, if he had not already known, that he was now irretrievably implicated in this affair with her and that she very much wanted him to be.

He told her he had been able to ascertain there was at least the possibility of Polish agents being in the city. He told her that he thought it best if they limited their conversations on the phone from now on, and kept a sharp eye out for people who might be watching their movements.

He did not, however, tell her about Hilferty, or about the CSIS proposition, and he did not tell her about the gun that he had put carefully away in his filing cabinet for safekeeping. He did not tell her about the $5,000 being offered, in advance, for "expenses." He decided that he didn't want to know why he did or did not do things today. He just wanted to trust his intuitions, as Natalia might, under other circumstances, have advised.

She stopped suddenly in the path and brushed

snowflakes from her eyelashes. He thought she was going to ask about why Polish agents might want anything from her uncle and he was ready with precisely the same question for her. But she had something else on her mind.

"Francis," she said, "I think you may be angry about this, but I may have done a silly thing."

"What did you do?" he asked.

"Sunday night, I called my uncle's friend in Paris. This Zbigniew I told you about when I first came to see you. The man who flew with Stanislaw in the war."

"What did you tell him?"

"Well, I had already phoned him just after Stanislaw died, but of course he couldn't come to the funeral. He is too old, and he hasn't got much money. I just told him his old friend had died and that the funeral was on such and such a date and that I would be in touch afterward maybe to tell him how it all went. I was in a sort of dream state then anyway. He sent me a card soon after that, asking for news of how it went."

"Did you tell him how your uncle died?"

"Yes, I told him he had drowned in the bath."

"The first time you called?"

"Yes."

"How did he react to that?"

"I don't really remember. Of course he was sad. It's a sad story."

"Did he ask you for details?"

"Like what?"

"Did he seem to think it was an odd way for his friend to die?"

"It is an odd way for anyone to die, Francis."

Delaney could not debate that.

"But when I talked to him on Sunday night," Natalia continued, "I asked him things. I asked him whether he knew why anyone would hate my uncle enough to do him some harm. I asked him if when Stanislaw had spoken to him last he had thought maybe something was wrong. I needed to know something, Francis. After we found out about the priest in Lachine."

"Did he tell you anything?"

"No. Nothing. I was going to tell you anyway except I was distracted by the break-in. Zbigniew went very silent on the telephone and then, this is a little odd, he said what you have just now said. That maybe we'd best not talk about these things on the phone. He said perhaps a letter was best, seeing we lived so far apart and there was so much to tell and phone calls were so expensive and so on. And then he seemed to be upset. I thought because I had stirred memories about his friend, and so we hung up. I told him I would write to him."

"Did you tell him about me?"

"No."

"Did you tell him about the dead priest?"

"No."

"What does he do over there?"

"He doesn't work anymore. He was a printer, after the war. Now he owns a little shop of some kind I think. For posters, antique posters, or something like that. Someone runs it for him now, I think. He was my uncle's navigator, in Scotland. His best friend."

Silence was what they now needed for a few minutes. For pondering things. The snow crunched and squeaked under their boots as they continued their circuit around the lake. No more snow was falling, and the sun now scattered diamonds on the morning's fresh fall. They came eventually to a kiosk where an old man in a battered watchman's hat rented skates. He had also been assigned the never-ending task of keeping the rink clear of snow.

"*Vous allez patiner, mes amis?*" the old man asked. "*C't'une belle journée maintenant pour ça.*" His hat said "*Moniteur – Parcs Montréal.*" He clearly thought they were lovers.

"*Oui,*" said Natalia, looking only briefly at Delaney. "*On va patiner.*"

Delaney somehow found it perfectly natural for people with their preoccupations to suddenly decide to rent skates and slide around Beaver Lake with ruddy-faced French kids in the middle of the day. They spent a long time fussing about the right fit and then signing little blue rental agreement cards. The *Ville de Montréal* wished to inform them that no responsibility could be taken for accident or injury while on the rink. They took the risk, and then added to it by both borrowing heavy socks from a wooden box of very suspect hosiery the watchman kept for the impulsive.

Their first glide out onto the ice was wobbly, but then, like all skaters young and not so young, they did their best to be elegant. They spoke very little. The smiles and the fine curved lines their skates etched behind them in the ice said what needed to be said. They hardly fell at all.

Chapter 7

On Tuesday, February 21, 1995, sometime just before midnight, investigative journalist Francis Delaney sat at a desk in a silent apartment before a flickering screen of the type he used to record his most public thoughts. He scanned databases. Not inner, like Natalia's, but outer. Worldly databases, electronic libraries, endless repositories of news, analysis, opinion. All available instantly now, even at home, for the sleepless.

He had been searching for a long time. The online charges tonight to his magazine would be excessive, ridiculous, and he expected a stiff note to come eventually from an angry editorial comptroller with whom he had had much conflict in the past. But he did not log off just yet. He had been browsing through years of newspapers without, he thought happily, having to go into foul newsrooms and convince surly librarians and researchers to pull out old clipping files. There was not much reason, he thought with satisfaction, to go into foul newsrooms at all anymore.

In some ways, this was what he did best. Working alone and letting his journalist's mind wander through dozens of stories and thousands of words, making connections, making linkages, cross-checking, cross-referencing, following leads down information corridors. Some of these corridors, of course, would always be dead ends. Others, he knew from previous journalistic successes, could help earn someone who still cared for such things a reputation as a reporter who knew where to look and what to look for.

Tonight, however, he wasn't certain what to look for. The keywords *Janovski* and *Dérôme* turned up nothing, except the brief announcement in the Births and Deaths columns of the *Tribune* of Stanislaw Janovski's death. *Natalia couldn't have been absolutely overwhelmed if she was organized enough to put an announcement in the paper,* Delaney thought. *Or maybe that's how she deals with things like that. Just like I would.* Father Bernard's people, on the other hand, had wisely decided to let his death go unrecorded in the media, as far as Delaney could tell. The dead priest received no newspaper entry to mark his passing.

Delaney's review of recent items out of Poland added important details to what he and Hilferty had talked about briefly the week before. Walesa was in deep trouble in Warsaw, behaving erratically, fearful he would lose the presidential elections at the end of the year. Lots of changes of government, prime ministers dismissed, forced out, resentful.

Some of the Warsaw newspaper correspondents had filed particularly good material about the small group of advisers Walesa had recently gathered around him. In particular, one Mieczylaw Wozniak, the director of the president's private office. A peasant, a small-time fixer from Gdansk, formerly Walesa's chauffeur and bag carrier, and now his right-hand man and gatekeeper. Brainless, vulgar, and powerful, by all accounts. A man who liked to help the president of Poland decide foreign and domestic policy over daily games of ping-pong. Impatient, like Walesa, with the intellectuals in Solidarity who helped topple the Communists in 1989. Impatient with the inconveniences of parliamentary democracy. Likes to play with army toys. Both he and Walesa spending a lot of time, apparently, with the crowd of old generals who used to order up the water cannons, and worse, against the Solidarity crowd in the bad old days.

Some good reporting also on the wave of ex-Communists now filling the Sejm. And on this young Kwasniewski, the ex-Communist technocrat who looked very like he was going to beat out Walesa and become the next president. There was further good material on the infighting over how fast to reform the creaky Polish economy, how capitalist to make it, how much to kowtow to the International Monetary Fund. Over who should get hurt most by the reforms, and when. And there were reports about bitter conflict over toughened abortion laws in the country. The Polish Catholic Church and Walesa on one side in this, and a lot of others on the other. The Communists had made it too easy, apparently, for women to get abortions, and Walesa was determined to do something about that for his friends in the Vatican.

There was a lot of news indeed to be had about Poland. The crowd of reporters in Warsaw right now knew a good story when they saw one. It was all very interesting. But where was the connection with an old Polish flyer in Montreal?

A very small news agency item from April 1993 caught Delaney's eye. It was about the UOP foiling a plot, apparently, to kill Walesa.

"Sources close to Mr. Walesa," the item noted, "said a man had reported that he had been offered money to assassinate the Polish leader. This could not be independently confirmed." But there were no follow-up items that Delaney could find, as if the story had fizzled, couldn't be properly checked out, or was found to be false. Or had been planted, perhaps, in the international media by Walesa's own people.

More good material, news agency copy again, from August 1994, under the headline "Former Polish Spy Resigns."

"A former Communist master spy who was put in charge of Poland's civil intelligence service last week," the piece said, "resigned yesterday after complaints that his nomination could endanger the nation's relations with the West. Mr. Marian Zacharski, who was given a life sentence by a U.S. court in 1981 for spying, and later released in a spy swap, said he was quitting because he did not want to enflame the situation. . . . Some analysts suggested that Mr. Walesa, who technically is in charge of the Interior Ministry, first approved the nomination but then changed his mind after suggestions it was a sign the ruling left-wing parties were bringing back the old system. Walesa's officials were not available to respond to the allegations yesterday."

Vanguard had a good analysis piece in October 1994 about Walesa's election chances.

"Mr. Walesa has never been very easy to understand," the magazine said. "If he had been, then it's a safe bet the Solidarity revolution would never have happened. But his offbeat behaviour has made many Poles doubt he can win a second time around in the 1995 presidential race. . . . His recent behaviour is probably designed to kick off his campaign and to enhance presidential authority just as Parliament starts to examine various drafts of a new constitution. The drafts — there are seven of them — differ mainly over the divisions of power between the president and Parliament."

The Borowski articles were good too. Polish-Canadian millionaire takes 25 percent of the vote in last presidential election. Rumours fly thick and fast in that period about who he really is, whom he represents, where he really wants to take Poland if he wins. Defamation charges, bail, and a post-election retreat to Toronto. Will he run again this time? No indication about that in the reporting. Something to check out.

Delaney wrote a note to himself on a yellow, lined legal pad. *Double-check Borowski angle. Toronto.*

Ottawa? Hilferty? But, again, where was the possibility of any connection to Stanislaw Janovski in Montreal?

The information on Poland's gangsters was also good. Too many ex-security service people and secret police and army types and released prisoners and unemployables and malcontents now had dangerous amounts of time on their hands, with alarming results. Idle hands, as always, being the devil's workshop. Protection rackets were thriving in Warsaw and in cities all over the country. Fraud, prostitution, drugs, construction kickbacks, white-collar crime, insider trading. Things getting so bad there had even been a shopkeeper's strike in Warsaw recently, demanding protection from racketeers and extortion gangs. The wild, wild East.

Delaney wrote on his yellow pad: *Janovski somehow in rackets? Friends in rackets?* Then he wrote: *Natalia in rackets?? Just back from Europe.* After a moment's thought, however, he carefully crossed the last items out.

Delaney even went back to the 1950s and '60s in his browsing, at great cost to his magazine. The notes he had made for himself after Natalia left on that first day in his apartment had underlinings in the section about Janovski's World War II service, his connection to the government-in-exile and to the Polish art treasures story. A long shot where Janovski was concerned, maybe. But still the makings of a good feature item, if nothing else, and Delaney could not resist having a look.

There was not much at all in the Canadian data-bases about the treasures angle, however, because not much newspaper material from that era had been entered into the system. But the *Montreal Tribune* had a fair amount. The scribbles on Delaney's legal pad multiplied.

The *Tribune* headline writers in the 1950s, Delaney decided, were not at peak form. "Poles Bid Canada Return Treasure." "Warsaw Hankers for Kingly Sword." "Canada to Yield Polish Treasure." "Polish Treasures Leave Ottawa." "Gutenberg Bible Off to Poland After Wartime Stay In Ottawa."

But Delaney noted with interest that old Max Cohen, who later became a respected columnist with the paper, was in the late 1950s paying his dues as a foreign correspondent in Warsaw and had covered the return of the so-called "Ottawa treasures." Cohen had filed some very nice colour pieces. Trunks opened in an Ottawa bank vault and the Polish coronation sword, Chopin musical scores, a Gutenberg Bible, and some other priceless little baubles found safe and sound inside. Insured by nervous officials for US$100 million. A secret train shipment to the United States under cover of snow and winter dark. Worries that Duplessis might order his provincial police to seize the goods as they passed through Quebec. But they are safely loaded onto a Swedish vessel in New York, bound for Poland. Crowds in the streets to greet the arrival.

Young Cohen was in fine form.

"Krakow, Feb. 16, 1959 — The joy here in

Poland at the return of the treasures is matched by Canada's relief at having been able to solve at least part of the problem. But officials say a lot more treasure still lies in a Quebec museum, including a priceless collection of ancient tapestries. They hope that negotiations to persuade the Quebec premier, Mr. Duplessis, to change his mind and release the booty still under his control will work out, and that they can further defuse this dramatic situation."

There was another flurry of articles in the *Tribune* in 1961, after Duplessis had died and his successor finally agreed to send the Quebec treasures back to the Communist government in Poland. "Quebec Sends Back Poland's Treasures." "Quebec Yielding Polish Treasure." "Poles Hail Return of National Relics."

There had been more secret machinations to head off angry diehards from the government-in-exile. A final deal signed just before the dead time of a New Year's holiday. Heavy crates loaded onto a convoy of trucks for another secret winter journey under police guard, this time to Boston. Onto a Polish freighter, then special train cars are laid on from Gydnia docks to Warsaw. More cheering crowds, and lots of Communist officials cheering a small Cold War propaganda victory. Now all but forgotten.

"Warsaw, Jan. 18, 1961 — Polish art historians said today that the Wawel treasures returned from Quebec appeared to be in relatively good shape, miraculously good shape. The twenty-four crates were opened in the National Museum here yesterday for a preliminary examination."

The only recent item on the art treasures that Delaney was able to track down in the late-night extravagance of his electronic roamings was a feature in the *Toronto Herald* from 1984, when Pope John Paul II — the Polish Pope, Delaney duly noted on his pad — made an official visit to Canada. The *Herald's* Ben Kingson, whom Delaney had worked with when they were both Parliamentary correspondents in Ottawa, had had the dream assignment of following the Pope around Canada and filing colour pieces. Kingson had stumbled onto the Polish art treasures story, apparently, and thought it well worth telling again, if only because of the Catholic Church angle and the Pope's Polish background.

Kingson ended his *Herald* piece on a conspiratorial note, as any good colour man would.

"No one can say for sure whether Pope John Paul II, then Father Karol Wojtyla of Krakow diocese, played any direct role in the treasures dispute. And no one is ever likely to know. But it's hard for anyone to believe that he knew nothing at all about the story and even harder to believe that he wouldn't have been aware of the controversy. In the mid-1950s, Wojtyla was a professor at the Catholic University of Lublin when some staff and students started to put pressure on the government of Canada to send the goods back. And then in 1958, Wojtyla was an assistant bishop of Krakow, at the very time that his mentor, Cardinal Wyszynski, was pressing Catholic Church officials in Canada to intervene and do all they could to get the treasures sent back to Poland."

All, Delaney decided as he at last switched off his computer and modem, very, very interesting. Wartime Europe, Nazis, governments-in-exile, treasures, Catholic Church intrigue, secret passwords, Quebec politics, anti-Communism. Stir in a bit of Solidarity, a bit of revolution, an unstable post-Communist government, underemployed army generals, rumours of coups and assassination plots, hordes of former Communists back in Parliament, a paranoid and erratic Lech Walesa, cliques of shadowy advisers Walesa might not be able to keep under control, a shaky Polish economy, the IMF, the UOP, the RCMP, CSIS, maybe CIA, maybe former KGB. Add a band of gangsters terrorizing Warsaw, and a Polish-Canadian millionaire with designs on the presidency. Fold in church-state tensions, the abortion question, and a papal connection that might go back fifty years. Top it all with a couple of Polish agents operating in Canada. It was a very rich mixture indeed.

But what, exactly, do you get? Somehow you get a dead Polish bomber pilot in Montreal and a dead Quebecois priest.

Delaney wondered what consulting psychologist Natalia Janovski would make of all these conspiracy theories, of all these conspirator figures.

What projections of inner psychic content would she

blame this on? Delaney thought wearily. *What would she find archetypal about all of this?*

Delaney at the shooting range. *Club de Tir de Laval, Inc.* Weapon transported, as per instructions and regulations, in trunk of car. Said weapon, nine-millimetre semi-automatic pistol, Browning brand, now held tightly in right hand, at end of outstretched right arm. Left hand bracing right wrist. Orange safety goggles, provided by club management, to protect eyes. Ear covers, provided by club management, to protect hearing. Box of bullets on small table.

Target some distance away. The familiar semiotic target in concentric circles of red and white. No human silhouettes here. This is not America, this is Canada, where targets are in the abstract, not in the shape of human beings. Canada, where targets are concentric circles of red and white, not enemies in the shapes of men.

The sound of rapid gunfire close by, loud even through the ear covers. Other club members practising their aim. What brings them here? Are Polish agents killing uncles of their friends too? What secrets, what secret fear, brings them to *Club de Tir de Laval, Inc.* to aim and shoot at red-and-white circles some distance away?

Delaney, in jeans, sweatshirt, ball cap; fires, fires, fires. No stranger to weapons he. But, until now, an observer of weapons. Not always from afar. A taker of notes, a notetaker of weapon types, brands, calibres, numbers. Reporter, colour man, describer of conflict and carnage, of armed commitments he has not himself been forced to make. Now, however, he fires, fires, fires.

A clever system brings the targets whizzing on wires back down the range to shooters for perusal. The little holes Delaney's bullets have made form no particular pattern around the centre. Some are far from it, some closer. No shooting champion he. But he has not completely missed the target this session. There is improvement.

A few minutes of instruction from young Jean-Yves Pelletier, club coach, two-time Quebec and one-time Canadian rapid-fire pistol-shooting champion, explains again the theory and practice of shooting pistols. The champion shooter fires, fires, fires. The competition badges on his windbreaker quiver slightly with each shot. Target whizzes back to the two men. They peer at it together. Indoor warriors, in baseball caps.

The holes this time are soldier-close, crowded around the all-important centre. More words of instruction, encouragement. Then Delaney's turn again.

His right arm jumps up slightly with each shot, left hand steadying. This is the opposite of observation. Stand many metres away, pull a trigger, and a target is transformed. Something has actually happened; something is changed. A shell empties itself of its bullet, right arm jumps up, left hand steadies, a hole appears in a cardboard target. Ears ring, nostrils sniff explosive smells.

Delaney fires, fires, fires. This is the ultimate projection, the ultimate interaction of subject and object. This has it all: perception, implication, decision, action, consequence, change. Squint down the barrel, look for the clever little sight, fix target in said sight: fire, fire, fire. And target is changed. Holes appear in cardboard. Elsewhere, in other circumstances, something may fall over. Man-shaped cardboard silhouette. Man.

A target can be changed by this action. By action. A target can be something sought, desired, or something hated, feared. A target can be sought, aimed at, because it is where one wants to be, what one wants to be, or it can be destroyed because it is a threat. In Canada, at *Club de Tir de Laval, Inc.*, targets are sought, not feared and destruction is, mostly, s ymbolic.

Delaney will not write about his target practice, will not report. There is no story here. Only targets, desired or feared. Changed through desire; destroyed through fear.

Before departure, Francis Delaney dreamed this:

He is moving through dense rainforest undergrowth in an unknown troubled country with some local guides and translators and soldiers. Their mission is to find a foreign hostage who is being held by rebel forces somewhere in the hills. They know that the task is a dangerous one. His companions are in battle fatigues and heavily armed, but he himself carries no weapon — only a notebook in his breast pocket. He is to cover the ambush for a newspaper in a far-off place. He feels absurdly vulnerable to sniper fire, to any attack. The birdsong is intense, as is the screech and click and flutter of insects. The sun and the salt from his own sweat burn his eyes and it becomes increasingly difficult to see. Then, for some absurd reason, he finds himself pushing a battered old baby carriage along the narrow, ill-defined mud track, as a refugee might. He realizes as he looks inside the carriage that the baby is missing, that it has been dropped somehow along the way and is now surely dead. He knows that his wife will be angry, but then remembers that he no longer has a wife. Then the scene shifts suddenly to Europe and he is both in the jungle and in a major city at the same time, in the impossible logic of dreams. His sense of disorientation and impending doom increases. Then snow begins to fall heavily on all that is before him. Then the realization presents itself to him as clearly as anything he has ever known that he will never be able to find the hostage, because the hostage is himself.

Before departure, Natalia Janovski dreamed this:

She is in the company of familiar, welcoming women. The meeting is in Emma Jung's house. They have been

*invited to help Mrs. Jung complete her famous research-
es into the legend of the Holy Grail. Natalia is guest of
honour at this gathering. They are on the shores of Lake
Zurich. Jung himself is not there. He defers to his wife
on Grail research; he always has. Natalia gives a brilliant paper about her latest work on the Grail legend.
Emma Jung is delighted. There is polite, though enthu-
siastic, applause. Natalia is given an important new
research assignment. The party then lunches on the most
delicious foods imaginable, gathered from the far reaches of the globe. They move outside into the brilliant
Swiss winter sunshine. The lake is frozen solid but the
ice is black, not white. It looks like a chill expanse of
black marble. Everyone skates elegantly, their skate
blades describing mysterious arcs and symbols on the ice.
Then Natalia is skating alone, ever alert for the Grail.
It is somewhere close; she knows this in her dreaming
heart. Then she begins to skate figure eights, over and
over and over again. The inscriptions on the marble ice
are exquisitely chiselled. Then the figures of eight become
symbols of eternity, the numerals turned on their sides.
Natalia skates and skates eternity signs, chiselling them
deeper and deeper into the lake's hard surface. The ice is
finally pierced by her sharp blades and she sinks elegantly in. Below the surface, though, is not water but
ash, the blackest ash. She disappears without a trace.*

Delaney stood alone in his quiet apartment, looking
appreciatively around, as he always did before

leaving on a long trip or a new assignment. It was his personal style of meditation. He noted with small private pleasure the order, the neatness, the cleanliness of it all. Books and papers stacked properly in their places, pens and pencils ranged in rows. Paintings and photographs straightened. On the kitchen counter a polished drinking glass upturned on a fresh, folded dishcloth, so as to leave no ring on the shiny surface. No chaos here.

Delaney stood in the quiet of his own space, knowing too well its stark contrast with the world outside, the world he knew almost against his will of teeming cities, mazes of streets, taxis jostling for position, airports, customs officers, baggage, hotels, strangers. The world, sometimes, of risk, violence, sudden change. This space he called his home, however, his own and only space, with its austere order, was one of the few things that never changed, never posed a threat, never betrayed him. And to which, therefore, his commitment never wavered.

PART II
Europe — Late Winter 1995

Chapter 8

t seemed perfectly natural for them to be in Paris together. Delaney had been there many times before, of course: on assignment, or en route to various ex-colonies of France in Africa, or with ex-lovers, ex-wives. One ex-wife. Long ago, there had been holidays here, and in Provence, but that was another lifetime. Paris was still a city Delaney liked very much, however. He was comfortable there and it was just seven hours from Montreal so it never seemed like a major journey.

Natalia had been there often as well, or so she told him on the way over in the droning stillness of the night flight. As a student, as a backpacker, on holidays, as a pilgrim en route to her Zurich mecca. He did not ask her if she, too, had been to Paris with a lover. He knew that she would simply smile her wry psychologist's smile and be thinking of the subtext of a question like that. So he did not ask it and she did not volunteer any information on the subject.

It was becoming perfectly natural for them to be doing any number of things together, Delaney thought as they made their way in a taxi through the snarled traffic on the *périphérique* to the hotel.

Natalia had not seemed terribly surprised when

he said he thought they should go to Paris to visit this Polish comrade-in-arms of her uncle's and see what he might know, or not know, or not wish to know. Especially since she had already phoned old Zbigniew Tomaszewski and given him more information than perhaps she should have. Delaney had become convinced that the way to the answer to the question of Stanislaw's death would be through those who knew him best. The old man's priestly friend was dead. That left the comrade in Paris.

Natalia had simply thought quietly about the idea for a few moments, and then agreed to go without much further discussion. She could see the logic, she said, and anything that might shed some light on the death of her uncle was attractive to her at this stage.

So they had set about tying up the few, the surprisingly few, loose ends in each of their lives before leaving. Natalia had prevailed on colleagues at work to indulge her grieving process a little longer and take over her cases. She had seen to some of her most distressed clients for a day or two, cancelled some evenings with her victims of torture and some other evenings of good psychological works, and then she was free to go. Gustavo, apparently, was not a factor in any of this. If there were other lovers in her life, she didn't appear broken-hearted to leave them for a while, at least as far as Delaney could see.

Delaney had likewise prevailed upon his editors at the magazine, but with much less difficulty for anyone concerned. Technically he was on leave anyway, technically hard at work on another book and chasing a few wisps of investigative possibilities. But he did check in with the desk, as a courtesy in an increasingly discourteous media business. And then he, too, was free. For all of his smart talk to Natalia a few days earlier about connections with people, he recognized that he had very few.

Delaney made a point of buying his airline ticket with CSIS money, for reasons, Natalia would probably say if she had known about it, deep in his unconscious. To Delaney it seemed somehow appropriate and amusing to be counting out his spy cash at the Air Canada office. Natalia, however, would not hear of his paying for her ticket, even when he explained that the money would not be from his pocket, that it was "expense account money," that his magazine was accustomed to him spending money to go off here and there on short notice. She insisted that Stanislaw had left her some money and his house in his will. She said she did not want to be a burden on this journey for tickets, hotels, or anything else.

Or, Delaney suspected, to be under any obligation to anyone. She would have been looking after herself for too long to want that.

Late February and early March in Paris are often grey and damp, the price paid for the April that follows. The streets in front of the Hotel Méridien were slick with late-winter rain as the cab pulled up. It was still very early, 7:30 a.m., and the traffic had thinned after they passed the Porte Maillot.

Delaney reached over the taxi driver's small sleeping dog on the passenger side to pay and to have the usual debate about the impossibility of being issued a proper receipt. The driver made no move to help with their bags, although they had both brought only small ones, and the hotel doorman was hurrying to help the arriving occupants of a gleaming Jaguar with Swiss licence plates, so they went into the lobby unassisted and unheralded.

It was busy, as always, but with the subdued sound of all large first-class hotels. Delaney knew many other smaller hotels in Paris far more charming than this highrise establishment on the edge of the city and far closer to the parts of Paris he liked better than this. But he knew from experience that hotels of this size and quality were places where you could be anonymous to a certain extent, where people could be met in lobbies, where staff asked few questions, and where taxis congregated outside.

The desk clerk was supercilious, naturally — a caricature. He pretended, as all Parisian desk clerks are apparently trained to do, to have trouble with Delaney's Anglo-Quebecois accent. In years past this had angered Delaney, but now he simply continued such conversations in his own brand of French without apology or any change in accent. Clerks, drivers, and waiters all eventually abandoned their little post-colonial charade.

As a punishment, however, this particular clerk then attempted to make it seem an impossibility that there would be any adjoining rooms. He argued that they would have to stay on separate floors, that it was all too impossibly complicated a matter to arrange for this bearded Canadian in a disreputable hooded parka. Natalia stood quietly as this transpired, neither amused nor embarrassed — in the sort of dreamlike state Delaney had by now observed as her usual response to any number of situations. She looked tired from the flight and tired from the events of the past few weeks.

"*Il va falloir que vous prenez ou un chambre double, avec deux lits, ou deux chambres sur deux étages,*" the clerk said, daring Delaney to declare publicly the nature of his relationship with Natalia and the importance of the request for separate but adjoining rooms.

Delaney had been to hundreds of hotels, with hundreds of unhelpful desk clerks, and had learned that in such situations the best strategy was to simply stand his ground. A small line of impatient people began to form behind them and, suddenly, a solution was found. The clerk produced two keys for rooms on the fifteenth floor. Near the elevator, *malheureusement,* and rather small, but nothing else could possibly, *monsieur,* be arranged. The desk clerk, too, failed to ask them if they needed help with their bags.

"The City of Paris bids you welcome," Delaney said to Natalia as they moved across the lobby.

"Not a very happy young man," she said.

Delaney had stopped to peer again at the number on the keys when Hilferty came up to them with a very natty young man at his side. Quite clearly French secret service, Delaney thought, or at the very least Quai d'Orsay.

"Welcome to Paris, Monsieur Delaney," Hilferty said, pleased to have startled Delaney in this way. "Fancy meeting you here."

Delaney could not say that he was terribly surprised that Hilferty would now be in Paris. The surprise was only that he had found their hotel so quickly and had been there, apparently, even before they arrived.

"Hilferty," Delaney said. "*Quel grand plaisir.*"

They eyed each other for a moment, each waiting for the other to provide a clue about how to play this scene. Hilferty was in one of his mischievous moods and offered no help. Delaney was tired and in the somewhat nihilistic state of those who have just gotten off a long overnight plane flight, so he let the silence build until Hilferty's White Anglo-Saxon Protestant embarrassment forced him to fill it.

"Let me introduce my colleague, Jean Stoufflet, from the French Ministry of Foreign Affairs," Hilferty said eventually. "Jean, this is Francis Joseph Delaney, one of Canada's foremost scribes. A righter of wrongs, defender of the weak, teller of tall media tales."

Hilferty had adopted his CSIS-operative-on-foreign-soil look: dark suit, no yellow cashmere sweater this time, Gucci loafers, olive-green Aquascutum trench coat.

Stoufflet was wearing a quite splendid dark-green suit, very European in cut, and he had a magnificent camel-hair topcoat slung over his thin shoulders. He carried one of the regulation, tiny, purse-cum-briefcases that an upwardly mobile young Quai d'Orsay–type must always have on his person.

Delaney figured him to be about thirty-five, from one of the old, monied Parisian families. *Ecole Nationale d'Administration,* a couple of years volunteer service in Chad or Côte d'Ivoire or some former French colony as a *coopérant* to avoid his compulsory military service, and then into the Quai and moving up through French Intelligence. Delaney had seen his type many times. Sometimes, perhaps those a little less advanced on the career path than this one or with slightly less promising family connections, to be seen paying their dues in one of the many Irish pubs of Paris, trying to look relaxed as they forced down pints of Guinness and listened for evidence of IRA plottings.

"*Enchanté,*" Stoufflet said. He seemed reluctant to offer Delaney his hand. "I'm afraid I do not know your work."

Stoufflet looked immediately to Natalia. For her, a hand was extended.

"*Et vous, madame?* You are a journalist, as well?"

"No, I'm not," Natalia said.

Delaney was pleased to see she did not bother offering Stoufflet any other information, at least for the moment.

"You should introduce us to your lovely lady

friend," Hilferty said.

"This is Natalia Janovski, from Montreal," Delaney said. "Natalia, this is John Hilferty, someone I know from my Ottawa days." Delaney could see Hilferty waiting to hear how much Delaney would not say in front of Natalia. "He's with External Affairs."

"A bureaucrat," Hilferty said modestly. "A humble civil servant."

Natalia had already made it clear with her body language that she did not wish to make small talk in hotel lobbies today and said she would go upstairs. The three of them watched as she got into the brass-doored elevator. Delaney saw Hilferty looking at the number lights go on and off over the door, out of habit only, as he would almost certainly soon know what rooms they were in without any of this rather old-fashioned detective work being required.

"Our lovely young Polish friend is not aware, I take it, that you keep the company of spies," Hilferty said, with an elaborate sideways glance at Stoufflet to see how this stylish gambit would be received by the French. "And you, old buddy, you don't seem at all surprised to see us."

"I don't know what you could be talking about, John," Delaney said. He had no wish to talk over with Hilferty how much or how little he had told Natalia about anything at this stage.

"Ah, a natural. Just as we suspected," Hilferty said.

"A natural."

"Yeah. Our newest little Maple Leaf spook. Keep up the good work."

"I'm a freelance journalist."

"Exactly."

"I wouldn't presume too much, if I were you Hilferty," Delaney said, suddenly impatient with the game.

"Well, I've presumed five thousand dollars of Canadian government funds on you Delaney. A first instalment only, of course. But handy for those little extra expenses. Business class is always such a treat, isn't it."

"What five thousand dollars are you talking about?"

"Very good."

"I hope you haven't mislaid any of our government's precious money," Delaney said. "That would be a very bad career move these days. They'll take it out of your pension."

Stoufflet gave a little snort, and opened up a pack of *Disque Bleu*. He threw the cellophane wrapper on the floor and stared malevolently at the bellboy who had noticed.

"Well, do let us know if you need anything further, Francis," Hilferty said. "We'll be around and about."

"*Le gouvernement de la République Française* is at your service, Monsieur Delaney," Stoufflet said as he lit his cigarette. The match, too, went onto the marble floor.

"*Je vous en prie,*" Delaney said.

"Why don't we meet tonight for a quiet drink somewhere?" Hilferty asked. "Do some plotting and scheming. Cloak-and-dagger stuff."

Natalia took a long while to answer when Delaney knocked later on the panelled door that separated their rooms. Her room was the mirror image of his. It was dim with the drapes half closed. She had been resting on the bed. *Le Monde* was in sections on the bedspread and a bottle of Badoit water was open on the night table. She was still in her travelling clothes, waiting, probably, for Delaney to appear before she showered and changed or went to bed or whatever was her pattern after a long flight. She looked even more tired than before, but also somehow troubled now. It was a look he had seen before, a faraway look that came over her when she was worried or suspicious or, more likely these days, grieving.

"You all right?" Delaney asked.

"Yes. A bit tired."

Natalia stood awkwardly at the door.

"I'll let you be, then," Delaney said. "No rush to do anything. We can see this Zbigniew tomorrow."

"This is feeling a bit strange all of a sudden, Francis," she said.

"What, exactly?"

"Being in Paris. Why we're here. This hotel. Being here with you."

"Just relax for a bit," he said lamely.

"You're very used to this, aren't you?"

"What?"

"Plane flights, assignments, hotels, getting information, meeting strangers."

"I guess I am."

She looked at him even more directly than usual.

"Who were those men downstairs?" she asked.

Delaney had to decide in the space of a moment whether to explain about Hilferty, to add this variable to the equation just then. He decided against it. He was not sure why.

"I think they might be agents," he said.

"What do you mean, agents?"

"Agents. Spies. Security Intelligence Service, the Canadian guy, and French Intelligence, probably, the other one."

"You know them?"

"Hilferty I know. I worked in the Press Gallery in Ottawa for a long time. I knew a lot of External Affairs guys and CSIS guys in those days."

"Is he here because of us?" she asked.

"I don't know. Maybe."

Delaney knew that these lies could create a problem for him eventually but it was already too late, even if he had had second thoughts about the tack he was taking and that he had been taking for some time with her on this. *She's getting more frightened now*, Delaney thought. *She is afraid of her fear.*

"What would they have to do with Stanislaw, Francis?"

"Maybe nothing. Most likely nothing," he said quietly. "But that's sort of what we're here to find out, don't you think?"

"How would they know we were here?"

"That's not really that hard these days, Natalia."

"Would they know what we're doing?"

"They don't. I can't see how they would. I think they might just like to know."

"Should we tell them?"

"I don't think so, Natalia."

"Why not?"

"Because it can get very complicated when people like that get pulled into something like this," Delaney said. "Let's just have a look around ourselves and see what we can dig up. We'll just have to play it a little close, that's all. For a while anyway."

Natalia looked neither more troubled, nor satisfied.

"Things are already very complicated, Francis," she said.

This, he knew, was all too true. He knew that it would get even more complicated the more he allowed himself to become involved. And the more Natalia allowed herself to become obsessed with finding out the truth about her uncle's murder.

They decided they would rest for a while and then shower and meet for a late lunch in the lobby restaurant. After they had eaten, Delaney said they should get word to Zbigniew that they were in Paris and that they wanted to see him the next day. He felt that the phones were no longer wise, particularly if Hilferty and Company were staying at the Méridien too. So he had a quiet word with the concierge, asking, as he passed him a hundred-franc note, if he could recommend a courier service *très fiable, très discret*. This was arranged, while Natalia wrote Zbigniew a note on hotel letterhead at a table in the lobby.

The courier, a Parisian motorcycle cowboy dressed head to toe in black leather, also became unusually cooperative with an extra hundred-franc note and a word from Delaney in the lobby. The address on the envelope was for the 20th arrondissement, far from the tourist track, where North African Jews and Arabs and a dwindling community of vintage Parisians lived in somewhat rundown apartments in the northeast of the city.

Oui, the courier said, he would be quick and, *non*, it did not bother him in the slightest if the address on the bill of lading was not exactly the same as on the envelope. *Ca fait absolument rien, monsieur*. Zbigniew was to send a note back by courier, collect. *Pas de problème*.

Delaney watched as the young man roared off into the afternoon Paris traffic faster than anyone could possibly have imagined a motorcycle could go in such streets. He saw no sign of anyone watching and no one appeared to have taken on the dangerous job of chasing the courier's bike. Hilferty, it appeared, had gone to ground. Or to a large expense account lunch with Stoufflet. But Delaney was not altogether reassured.

The evening was, again, just as dozens of

evenings after long flights had been for Delaney over the years. He and Natalia took the requisite long stroll of the jet-lagged and the unhurried. They made small talk about Paris as they walked and they remarked on how little it ever changed. Teams of tall black Africans in lime-green overalls swept and sprayed gutters as they passed. Then a return to rooms, with no energy or desire or necessity to do anything at all until the next day. Each in their separate spaces to read newspapers, magazines, watch newscasts, eat light room service suppers, and sleep.

Delaney had been wrong about Hilferty going to ground. He called on the house phone at about eight o'clock.

"So, what about that drink?"

"Tied up tonight, John," Delaney decided to say. "Sorry."

"Seriously. We should talk. And I've got a *petit paquet* for you."

Hilferty was in the bar when Delaney came down. Sports-jacketed this time and no Quai d'Orsay escort. He was drinking what looked like a double Scotch and eating pistachio nuts from a silver bowl on the bar. A small pile of shells was accumulating in the ashtray. Delaney ordered a beer and sat waiting for Hilferty to play spy.

"So, what's the plan?" Hilferty asked eventually.

"I have no plan, John."

"Just over here to visit a family friend, are we? A pleasure trip?"

"Yeah. Like you, I would imagine. As CSIS does not indulge in intelligence-gathering operations overseas."

"We are here simply to help our French colleagues. At their invitation, and so on and so forth."

"I see."

Delaney could see Hilferty was in a bit of a sour mood and would not stand for idle banter much longer.

"Look Francis, this thing is getting a bit more delicate than we thought. We don't want to fuck up on this one."

"What have you got?"

"What have *you* got?"

"You're the civil servant, John. So serve."

"Well, it looks like maybe UOP. Polish State Security."

"We knew that, I thought."

"Yeah, well the signals traffic is a bit unclear on this one, Francis. Their embassy in Ottawa is making a lot of weird sounds. We're not sure exactly who's who, who's working for whom anymore."

"You better hope an investigative reporter doesn't get wind of the Communications Security Establishment guys listening in on supposedly friendly embassies again, my friend," Delaney said.

He had often wanted to do up a long article about what exactly went on lately inside that four-story CSE building in an Ottawa suburb, but had never gotten round to it. The Canadians had for years, ever since the war, dined out among friendly spy agencies on their signals-intelligence prowess. They had been able to trade important information with the Americans and the British for years thanks to their CSE intercepts and thereby avoid having to make the hard decision to set up a foreign intelligence capability of their own. But Delaney knew that couldn't last much longer. The world was changing too fast.

Hilferty ignored Delaney's reporter games.

"My guys are getting a little edgy about the possibility of some of Walesa's people snuffing old pensioners on Canadian soil," he said.

"Is it Walesa's people?" Delaney said.

"Can't be sure. He probably doesn't even know anymore, the dumb fuck. But if it is his people, and it possibly is, my people want to know."

"Communists, maybe? Maybe not Walesa's guys at all."

"What would they want with an old guy in Montreal?" Hilferty said.

"What would Walesa's people want with him?" Delaney asked.

"Fucked if I know."

"Was he murdered?"

"Yeah," Hilferty said. "Looks like it now."

"By Poles? You sure?"

"Yeah. Looks like it. Some faction or other." Hilferty paused. "Of course, we're way off the record here, as you hacks like to say."

Delaney was still reluctant to ask about the dead priest in Lachine, in case CSIS was by some incredible inefficiency or oversight still unaware of that death. But he had to think that one was murder too, and murder by the same people.

"What about Borowski?" Delaney asked.

"Nah," Hilferty said. "Not involved. Doesn't wash anymore. He looks clean as a whistle. But it looks like he may have another try at the presidency in November, for what that's worth. He's trying to drum up nomination signatures on the fucking Internet from Toronto as we speak. Or so I'm told."

They drank in silence for a while. Then Hilferty said: "Look Francis. We don't want to lose control of this thing, OK? Maybe it's not really the place for an amateur anymore. Never was, probably. But who would have figured."

"This morning I'm a Maple Leaf spook. Tonight I'm an amateur."

"Yeah well, I've been on the phone to Ottawa this afternoon. We don't want a fuck-up is all I'm saying. My people get nervous. So watch your ass and don't get us all into trouble at home. Or over here. Get my drift?"

Hilferty pushed a small *Boutiques de l'Aéroport de Paris* duty-free bag over Delaney's way. Through the clear plastic Delaney could see what looked like a box for a small appliance.

"Travel iron," Hilferty said, smiling at his wit. "Presuming you didn't carry yours over on the plane with you."

Delaney had thought very briefly in Montreal of packing the CSIS-issue Browning in his checked bags but had decided it was not worth the risk. He could not see himself using it in France, or anywhere else for that matter. Needing it maybe, but not using it.

"Another gun. From the gunless Canadian spy service," Delaney said. "You seem to have a healthy supply."

"Some of us, that way inclined," Hilferty said. "Don't get caught with it over here. We don't know you over here."

"Check."

"Don't use it. Just wave it at someone if you get into a jam and get into a cab. *Comprenez?*"

"Check."

"You're a pain in the ass tonight, Delaney, you know that?" Hilferty said. He pushed the bar tab over, before getting up to go. "Here. Your round."

Delaney knocked lightly on Natalia's door when he got back to the fifteenth floor. He chose the hall door this time, not the one that separated their rooms. There was light shining through the peep-hole.

She let him in and went straight back over to the desk where she'd been writing in what looked like a ledger. She was in the Méridien bathrobe. It was very white and far too large. She did not ask him about his duty-free bag.

"You all right?" he said. The room smelled like bath oils and creams.

She finished what she was writing and closed the

book before turning to him. In felt-tip pen across the leather cover was written "Commonplace."

"I'm doing up my journal," she said.

"Your diary?"

"More than that. It's a dream book and a place to record interior dialogues and some other things. It's called Intensive Journal Therapy. Or it is when it's used in therapy."

"Is this your therapy?"

"No. Not really. For me, it's just my Commonplace book. I've had one for years."

"Don't let it fall into the wrong hands," Delaney said. "Now that it contains state secrets."

"None of those so far."

They looked quietly at each other for a moment in the still room and then said their good-nights. Now was still not the time.

Delaney fell asleep thinking, ever so slightly amused, of Natalia at her secret work next door, carefully recording dreams and interior dialogues and possibly some other things in a language he did not yet understand.

They indulged in a little cloak-and-dagger activity the next morning. Delaney knew it would infuriate Hilferty and would likely bring whatever relationship they had to a head, if not to an end, but he didn't want to lead the Canadians or the Poles or anyone else to Zbigniew if they didn't already know where he lived.

The concierge beamed in Pavlovian pleasure

when he saw Delaney approaching him in the lobby. Could he possibly arrange, Delaney asked him, for a *Taxi Bleu* to be waiting out in the laneway behind the hotel in a few minutes' time? A little matter of a young lady, a family matter. One must be *très, très discret* in hotels these days, *n'est-ce pas?*

The concierge protested only briefly before putting the first of this day's crop of banknotes into his waistcoat.

"A *pourboire* is really not necessary for this service, *monsieur,*" he said.

Delaney then went out on the street to the line of cabs waiting at the curbside. It was busy on the streets now, the beginning of a weekday in Paris, and a wan sunlight was shining on the bustle. He leaned over into one of the Peugeots and asked various inane tourist questions in English before straightening up and looking ostentatiously at his watch. Then he went back in to call Natalia from the house phone.

"The cabbie said it was about a two-minute drive from here," he said. "There are a lot of them out front. You ready?"

"I'm ready," Natalia said, as arranged. "I'll meet you out front."

Delaney went back up to the fifteenth floor to pick up the battered old equipment bag that had been with him on so many assignments. It had carried many things over the years but never a Browning semi-automatic pistol. He wrapped the gun in a hotel facecloth and placed it under his reporter's notebook. Tools of the trade.

They got off the elevator not on the main floor but at the mezzanine level and walked quickly down a flight of service stairs into the banquet kitchen. Some of the chefs and underlings looked annoyed at the intrusion but Delaney and Natalia walked on through in the French way: never apologize, never explain. Out the delivery entrance at the back of the hotel and into a waiting Volvo station wagon. The driver had been smoking heavily and the car stank of *Gauloises*. He threw away his cigarette when they got in and told them that rue Julien Lacroix could be as much as half an hour away, depending on traffic, depending on where *les boutillages* might be.

"Go," Delaney said.

No one seemed to be behind them. *A natural,* Delaney thought, as he settled in for the ride.

Zbigniew Tomaszewski lived in a somewhat disreputable building off rue de Belleville. It was an area of Paris Delaney didn't know well. The side of the building had a giant mural of a black face smoking a cigarette in a pair of ruby-red lips. The street was so narrow that the taxi blocked traffic as they paid the fare. The sound of the car horns echoed off old brick walls and windows. Some African and Arab kids were noisily playing soccer in the small square under the giant smoker's gaze. They did not ease up their game even as Delaney and Natalia walked through it.

Natalia had the exterior security code for the

building. The heavy door gave a small electric click after she punched the code into a small keypad outside, and the lock opened for them. The hallway was damp, dark, and not terribly clean. Bright green garbage bins were haphazardly pushed into a small alcove to their left. There didn't seem to be a concierge. They were a dying breed in the new Paris. But if there was still to be a concierge this would be the neighbourhood for it. She would be Portuguese, more than likely, with a tiny cluttered apartment at the back of the building and canaries in a cage.

The ground floor apartment behind Zbigniew's battered door, however, was a revelation. It was gigantic, by Paris standards, with magnificent gigantic furniture and it was blessed with its own garden courtyard. The apartment walls formed two sides of the garden, and the stone back wall and high fence of a small church the other two. The old man led them out there immediately and stood proudly while they admired the flowers and trees. He explained to them that he had bought this oasis many years ago before prices went skyward even in this unfashionable neighbourhood. It was something no retired lithographer could ever hope to afford these days, he told them, and he himself could barely keep up with the building charges and taxes anymore.

Zbigniew was well past seventy, with an intensely white thatch of thick hair and equally thick thatched eyebrows. He walked with a slight limp and his arms were thin, their skin loosening, but he looked reasonably robust for a man of his age. His face was well tanned, probably from hours spent out in the garden. Today Zbigniew was wearing an old tweed jacket, cravat, flannels, and a pair of deep-blue velvet slippers with gold brocade. A pair of half-frame glasses hung on his chest from a gold chain. He offered them coffee.

"To think, Natalia, that we have never met but once before," he said as he prepared espresso cups. He spoke English better than Delaney had expected. "You were one of those backpacks, backpackers, then."

"Yes. But I'm no longer a backpacker of nineteen, I'm afraid."

"Still lovely, however."

"Thank-you."

"And Mr. Delaney, you are a not a backpacker anymore either, I would assume."

"No. I'm a writer," Delaney said.

He did not wish to set off alarms with the word *journalist*. Natalia did that for him

"A journalist," she said.

Zbigniew looked at her for some sign as to why she would bring a journalist along with her.

"Francis is my friend," she said. "He's been a help to me in many ways since Stanislaw died."

"But some stories are not to be written, Mr. Delaney. Not all stories are for the press, would you not agree?" Zbigniew said.

"Of course," Delaney said. "I'm not working today."

"But tomorrow perhaps."

"I'm Natalia's friend."

"I see," Zbigniew said. "A friend and a journalist. An unusual combination."

Delaney said nothing. He took his cup of excellent espresso and looked calmly at them both. *I will be asked to exit shortly*, he thought.

They drank coffee and they chatted about the apartment and the neighbourhood and about the changes in Paris since the war. Stanislaw's name was not raised again. Eventually, Zbigniew turned to Delaney; very formal, very Old World.

"I wonder, Mr. Delaney, if now, after our little coffees, you would mind if I had some time with my friend's niece alone," he said.

Zbigniew did not consult Natalia about this. He would not have been in the habit of asking younger people permission for what he wanted to do.

"Please do not be offended," Zbigniew said, "but there are some family matters that bring Natalia here to me as well. In addition to my abilities as a *raconteur*."

It would have been impossible not to agree. Delaney had not anticipated this when he and Natalia were making their plan. He had expected, foolishly, as he now realized, that this old Polish gentleman would simply open up to them both, sharing quite possibly dark secrets of various sorts without hesitation, without giving a thought to the presence of a stranger, and a journalist at that.

Delaney got to his feet. Natalia looked flustered

but made no attempt to intervene on his behalf. It would be difficult to make any sort of new plan with her in this situation or to warn her to be careful, to be discreet, to look behind her as she left. Delaney felt annoyed, worried, and cornered. Not in control.

"I'll meet you back at the hotel, Francis," Natalia said.

"I could come back to meet you here," he said, looking at Zbigniew.

"It is difficult to say how long we might be," the old man said. "I might even prepare Natalia some lunch. We have not seen each other for so many years."

"All right," Delaney said. "Thank-you for the coffee."

"A pleasure," Zbigniew said. "Enjoy your day." He added, as he smoothed one of his unruly eyebrows with the back of an index finger: "What does a journalist do in Paris when he is not working, Mr. Delaney?"

It was a question Delaney would have at one time found difficult to answer.

Chapter 9

Natalia could see immediately why her uncle had loved his old comrade so much. After Delaney left, she and Zbigniew cried together a little in the silent old apartment about Stanislaw and about the way he had died, alone. They had told each other stories in Polish about Stanislaw and the family and the past, and had cried at some of them until they began to laugh at some of them, and suddenly it was a little easier.

Then Natalia told Zbigniew more about what the police in Montreal had said and about what Delaney had said and about what they now thought might be behind Stanislaw's murder. For she called it murder, and Zbigniew made no attempt to debate this with her.

"He told me there were things he wanted to talk about just before he died," Natalia said finally. "He said there were things that I should know." She felt the tears coming again. "But he said this on my answering machine, Zbigniew, a foolish, foolish machine, on a night when I was not there for him to talk to."

"There are indeed some things you should know, Natalia," Zbigniew said. "Very definitely. Now that

Stanislaw is gone. And I think he would want me to tell them to you. It is good you have made the effort to come here."

As he spoke, he got up to go to a massive mahogany sideboard that sat in the living room. He reached inside and pulled out a leather briefcase stuffed with what looked like letters and papers. The briefcase was so full it could not be closed and properly fastened. Zbigniew brought this over to where they sat.

"I have letters here from your uncle from twenty, thirty, forty years ago, my dear Natalia," he said. "Letters, newspaper cuttings, and other papers he sent to me over the years. And I also know things that were best not written down. I will tell you what I know, and then you and I will decide together what is to be done. And who else should be allowed to know."

Natalia felt a strong urge to check that the door to the apartment was locked, to draw the curtains, to indulge in what Francis liked to call "cloak-and-dagger stuff." She wished he had stayed to help her sort out what she would now discover — to take notes in his reporter's notebook. She looked toward the door.

"This can be done safely here, I think, Natalia," Zbigniew said quietly. "There is nothing to fear in here."

"All right," she said. She thought, however: *This time my fear is not irrational.*

Zbigniew began pulling papers and letters from

his briefcase as he talked. The larger bundles of envelopes were carefully secured with string or elastic bands. Some had notes in tiny Polish script attached.

"I am the archivist, it would appear, Natalia," he said with a small smile. "The keeper of a secret history."

"So it seems."

"You are lucky to have been born in Canada," he said. "And after the war. Old men like me and Stanislaw, we are like all the Poles of our generation. We lived with the entire burden of our history on our shoulders. Or so we thought."

He seemed to have organized the papers to his satisfaction.

"You young ones can never imagine, no matter how much you read about it or hear about it from old men like me, just what it was like to have been in Warsaw or somewhere else in Poland in the First World War and, then, after that one, the second war," he said. "It is unimaginable for young ones like you. The Nazis cannot be described. They simply cannot be adequately described."

It seemed to Natalia as if he had waited a long time to be able to say this to someone who wanted to listen.

"We knew they would come in 1939, your uncle and I," Zbigniew continued. "We were soldiers, Air Force officers, and we knew that when they came, they would be animals and try to destroy our country totally, to wipe it from the map. And when they came it was like that. Worse than that."

He looked at her, as if wondering whether any-one young or old could ever know how to reply to a description of the events of 1939.

"Your uncle was one of the lucky ones, really. He became aide-de-camp to Raczkiewicz when Raczkiewicz was made president in Romania after their group escaped. Stanislaw had gotten out right away and then he got out of Romania right away too, into France with the government-in-exile. Some of us had to creep away and live like animals in the forest before we could get to France or Britain to regroup."

Zbigniew paused.

"Did he ever tell you about our squadron? The Mazovia Squadron in Scotland?" he asked.

"A little," Natalia said. "He didn't really like to talk about the war."

"A wise policy," Zbigniew said. "But you knew about our squadron, how we flew Wellingtons together to bomb Berlin and Mannheim and Essen and Dortmund and other places many of us had been to, places we actually knew? Poles bombing their own Europe."

"I knew some of it."

"But did he ever tell you about his little secret, about how he was assigned before any of our adven-tures on Wellington bombers together to travel with the treasures of our country from Wawel Castle, to bring these to safety before the Nazis could steal them or destroy them? Did he tell you that Hitler was not just a madman with people, that he was a madman with art, that he wanted to destroy all of what he called decadent art in Europe and bring the rest back to Germany for his super museums, his *über* museums, in Berlin and Linz? Did he ever tell you, Natalia, about what the Nazis were trying to do to the art of Europe?"

Zbigniew did not wait for Natalia to reply because he had long ago decided there was no adequate reply.

"Your uncle was one of the lucky ones, Natalia. He was given the important task of trying to save our country's treasures before he was asked to try to destroy the Germans from an aircraft. He told me a great deal about his adventures with those art treasures, my dear, on the back roads of Romania in trucks, and on boats to Malta, and then France and then England and Canada. Your country now. He was entrusted with a great secret, Natalia, he and some others, and he, at least, never betrayed that trust. Even until he died. He was a soldier. I watched him in the fighting and he was not one who would give up or betray."

Natalia said nothing. Today she would listen more than she would talk.

"We were betrayed, of course, Natalia," Zbigniew continued. "All of us. And you and your generation of Poles, too, when you consider it. At Yalta, when the so-called great powers betrayed us all to the Communists and recognized their bad joke of a government, their outrage of an illegitimate government in Warsaw and withdrew recognition of the government-in-exile, it felt to all of us as though our fighting had been for nothing, that we had fought for years and still lost our beloved country to those who had been our enemies. And in the end it was through the betrayal of those who had been our friends. The Allies, so-called.

"So, you see, those trunks and crates hidden in Canada were worth more than gold and silver to us, Natalia. Those treasures were something we had snatched from the Nazis and then the Russians and, yes, even from Churchill and Roosevelt, and they were made safe in your country until we could win back our own country from those who took it from us.

"After the war, your uncle thought it was his duty to carry on looking after those precious things he had helped bring to Canada. So he went there to live and be close to the comrades he had worked with on that secret mission and to wait for the right moment."

Zbigniew looked intently at Natalia now, waiting for some sign she was understanding the significance of all this.

"Why didn't you go to Canada as well, Zbigniew?" Natalia asked.

"Because I am a European, Natalia. Because I had no duty to go. Because I felt that it was too far, too new, too cold." He laughed a little at this. "Paris was my choice, my dear. I love this city and I always felt that when things changed I could simply get on a train and go back to Warsaw. But of course I never did. And now, even though there is no impediment to my going back, I cannot. I have lost my Warsaw, Natalia, and I am at home here now. But for your uncle it was different."

Zbigniew began to pull packets of letters apart and extract aging sheets from envelopes before continuing.

"Your uncle used to write to me, of course. He was a great writer of letters, your uncle. Perhaps too many letters. Perhaps, as it turns out, some letters to the wrong people, telling them too much."

Zbigniew selected a letter from a small pile he had assembled. He handed it to Natalia. It was on old, drying, flimsy paper. It was headed "Montreal, September 1945" and written in Polish. Natalia could immediately recognize her uncle's spidery handwriting:

"My dear Zbigniew:

I am so sorry for the delay in writing to you, my friend, but I have been busy these days trying to get the treasures into a safer place. The Communists are coming, my friend. They have named a new man for the embassy in Ottawa, Florkiewicz, and Krukowska is out. But Krukowska has ordered that Zdunek and Kozlowski move the goods from the Experimental Farm to somewhere safer, before they can be stolen from us.

What a ridiculous place to have hidden them

anyway, Zbigniew. A ridiculous farm in the sub-urbs, with no decent locks and dozens of scientists and civil servants in and out every day. I was the driver, the pilot, once again, and now we think the goods are safe. But we needed you for a navigator that night, Zbigniew, I can tell you. Two trunks, with some of the most rare items, are in the Bank of Montreal in Ottawa, in their vault. Only Zdunek and Kozlowski can sign jointly to have them removed from there. And the rest, many cases, are in a convent in Ottawa and another in Quebec, at Sainte-Anne-de-Beaupré. Thank goodness for the Quebec Catholics. They are on our side in this fight, you may be sure of that. And passwords, Zbigniew. We have passwords . . ."

Natalia looked up, enthralled by what she had read.

"He sounds like an excited schoolboy," she said.

"He was, what, perhaps thirty-two then, Natalia. Not a schoolboy, a soldier, and a bomber pilot, who knew his duty to Poland."

Zbigniew handed her another letter.

*"Montreal
23 August 1946*

My dear friend:

Oh the intrigue, Zbigniew. The intrigue. It is like Romania in 1939 all over again. I hardly know where to begin. Zdunek has been co-opted by the Communists, the swine. He will tell them where we have hidden things, if he has not already. So again I was the driver. Kozlowski and Krukowska and I rented a large truck and went to the convents brandishing our little receipts and mouthing passwords, and the treasures are still ours.

'The Holy Virgin of Czestochowa' — that is all the nuns needed to hear, my friend, and they would have given us the Pope's ring if they had it. When you come, and you must come to visit me here one day, I will take you to these places and tell you the story properly. The Ottawa Convent of the Precious Blood, Zbigniew — only the French Canadians still have convent names like that — then a long night drive to Quebec City, to the Redemptorist Fathers at Sainte-Anne-de-Beaupré. The password was magic for them as well, and now the crates are well hidden once again.

Zdunek can never know where they are again. Perhaps it is best if I do not tell you either, my friend. Perhaps best for you not to know. But thank God for the Quebec Catholics, Zbigniew. And for Duplessis. He doesn't want the Communists to get them any more than we do.

Our major problem now is that it is still only Zdunek and Kozlowski who together can get the other two trunks from the bank in Ottawa. They will clearly not be able to agree on a course of action anymore . . ."

Zbigniew handed Natalia a small sheaf of clippings from Ottawa and Montreal newspapers that Stanislaw had obviously sent his friend over the years. The articles reported that the movement of the treasures was being called theft by the new Polish ambassador to Canada. He and his colleagues had arrived only hours later than Stanislaw and his co-conspirators, and found the crates removed. They had spent hours combing the back roads of Quebec looking for the rented truck, one newspaper account said. Florkiewicz was demanding action: from the Canadian government, the Quebec government, the Catholic Church, the RCMP, from anyone who would listen.

The Canadian prime minister, however, clearly did not wish to be pulled into a diplomatic battle between the Communists in Warsaw and the Polish government-in-exile in London. Even less, the reports said, did he want to take on Premier Maurice Duplessis in Quebec in what could be another major jurisdictional battle. It was a matter for the courts to decide, the prime minister said, but he would as a courtesy allow the RCMP to try to trace the missing crates, if this would be of any assistance to the embassy of Poland.

Zbigniew had lit a dark Sobranie cigarette, and smoked quietly as Natalia read.

"Your uncle was in the thick of it in those years, my dear," he said.

Natalia suspected that Zbigniew knew every one of the letters by heart and every twist and turn of the story his old comrade had told him in such detail. It would have been a duty to his old friend to know and remember this story in case he was ever needed.

"The Communists would have killed him, and the others, if they dared do so in Canada," Zbigniew said.

"But of course they couldn't until they knew where the treasures were as well," Natalia said.

"Precisely. But that became a somewhat academic point, you see, because Maurice Duplessis stepped in a couple of years after that. He was angry that the RCMP had been investigating on Quebec soil and apparently going in to convents and questioning Mothers Superior and so on, you see, and he saw this as a way to assert himself against Ottawa and consolidate his position with the Quebec Catholics as a fighter of Communism. So he took the treasures himself."

"He took them?"

"Not for himself, my dear," Zbigniew said with a slight smile. "He took them from the Hôtel Dieu Convent in Quebec City where they were in a sort of cavern in the cellars and he locked them up in vaults in the basement of the provincial museum. And he made sure he embarrassed the federal government as much as he could in doing so. The RCMP were supposed to be standing guard outside of the Hôtel Dieu, but he sent the chief of the Quebec police and some other officers in plain clothes and they lifted the crates right from under the noses of the federal police. Using food delivery vans. And, my dear, Duplessis said he would never, ever release the treasures to the godless Communists. Can you imagine how that would have been received at the Polish Embassy in Ottawa? In 1948? Imagine that if you can."

"And he never did release them, did he?" Natalia said.

"No. Not in his lifetime."

Zbigniew handed her some more newspaper clippings. One was a news agency dispatch from March 1948:

"'When it is a question of the Communist and atheist government of Poland, satellite of Stalin, the federal government communicates with this government through the intermediary of an ambassador and with all the protocol and respectful consideration which these proceedings involve,' Premier Duplessis told a press conference in Quebec City.

"'When it is a question of one of our most noble religious communities, Mr. St. Laurent and the federal authorities communicate with them through the intermediary of the federal mounted police, whose mission it is to seek and arrest criminals in the domain of federal jurisdiction,' the premier said."

Zbigniew re-read the clipping himself, chuckling quietly, before continuing.

"Kozlowski was allowed to visit the vaults at the museum in Quebec City every six months or so to see that the goods were all right and to air the tapestries and so on, but they were never to be removed or sent back until the Communists had been ousted from Poland," he said. "Your uncle would be the one to drive Kozlowski to Quebec City sometimes for this. He and Kozlowski got to know Duplessis very well, and some of his senior police and officials, as of course they would. Because they were partners in a big joke on Canada and on the Communists. A deadly serious diplomatic joke."

"It's a very long time to keep a joke going," Natalia said.

"I agree. A very long time. And some people are not able to keep faith with comrades forever. Your uncle was one of the rare ones who could. But Kozlowski, I'm afraid, could not."

"He gave up?" Natalia asked.

"Yes," Zbigniew said. "He came under intense pressure over the years to give the treasures back. From Poland, from some factions in the government-in-exile — for there were factions, Natalia, many factions — and eventually from the Catholic Church as well. There was a loosening of things in Poland in the late 1950s, a sort of loosening. The worst of the Stalinists were removed and the Catholic Church there thought it politic to try to cooperate with the regime for a time.

"And of course Kozlowski was getting old. He was about seventy or so by then. Krukowska was dead;

Zdunek was dead. But Zdunek had said in his will that he thought the treasures should go back. Kozlowski was working in his little delicatessen in Ottawa by then, a strange fate for an architect who had moved treasures from Wawel Castle. And he was, Stanislaw said, becoming worried about the condition of some of the things that had been hidden.

"Kozlowski said that if he got word from the government-in-exile, he would gladly sign the papers and allow the treasures in the Ottawa bank to go. But he said he had given an oath and he felt he should keep it until he received an official signal. The decision about the Quebec treasures, of course, was no longer his to make."

"I know some of this story," Natalia said. "My uncle told us once about how the Ottawa treasures went back."

"Yes, they went back. Poland sent a new man to be joint custodian with Kozlowski, and a faction in the government-in-exile used go-betweens, prominent people, émigrés, to work on him over the years. Even Malcuzynski, the pianist, became involved. As a sort of envoy, from Switzerland, where he lived after the war. Eventually Kozlowski agreed to sign. He gave in to the pressure and the two Ottawa trunks went back. This was in 1959. Your uncle was outraged. I have a letter of his here from that time. He could simply not believe that Kozlowski would betray this trust."

Zbigniew began looking for the letter to show her.

"All those years," Natalia said. "I would have been just a girl when all of this started to happen. A baby. I was born in 1958. Stanislaw never talked very much about this when I had grown up."

"Well, he would not have had much to say to you about it, my dear. There were many things he could not dare to say after that. Because matters became even more complex, Natalia. Even more dangerous, I would say."

Zbigniew handed her another letter, this one clumsily typewritten. Natalia could imagine her uncle hunched over his beloved Remington Noiseless in his snug house on Chesterfield Street, writing this secret letter to his oldest friend.

"Montreal
13 March 1959

Dear friend:

Zbigniew, I am writing to entrust to you a most important secret. I no longer know whom to trust here anymore but I know that I can trust you as always.

Kozlowski is behaving erratically now. The pressure is getting to be too much for him, it seems. Sometimes he says he had no choice but to sign the papers for the Ottawa treasures. Sometimes he regrets it so much that I fear for him. I really do. But I myself have taken action to safeguard the treasures left in Quebec from any further betrayals, my friend, and I am going to tell you how. And then it will be only you and me who know this new secret, Zbigniew. I know that you would never reveal it to the wrong people or at the wrong time.

I have been to see Duplessis. I felt that I must go to discuss what is happening with Kozlowski. And Duplessis, my friend, was in a rage that the Ottawa trunks went back. He shouted in French for a long time about that and about what was happening with Kozlowski. But I knew that he was angry also because he could see the end was in sight. He is not well, Zbigniew, and he also knows that the Catholic Church is no longer on his side in this. And if that is so in Rome, then it is so in Quebec, because the Quebec Church does the Vatican's bidding, as it must.

Eventually, the Quebec treasures will go back and the premier knows this. He is an expert politician, Zbigniew, an expert. He sees things clearly and he knows when it is time to act. Or, in some cases, when to let others act. And so there have been some changes made.

I had devised a little plot of my own that would safeguard at least some of what we had been entrusted with. I told Duplessis about my fears and that I had a plan. But he did not want to hear details of my plan, Zbigniew. He is too astute a politician for that. Sometimes people do things on behalf of powerful men and these men know to turn the other way while it is being done. They know when it is better not to know all that is being done for them. Each for his own reasons, my friend, but that is often how it is with such important matters. So be very careful with this information, Zbigniew. Because no one will know it but you and me. But someone must know it in case I die.

Duplessis agreed to let me have access to the treasures alone for a time for an "inspection." He arranged this and he assigned his personal body-guard, a policeman named Tessier, to accompany me to the vaults in the museum and to help me in any way required. And then Duplessis simply went on about his business and never asked me about any of it again. I was left to do my duty as I saw it.

So I have hidden a portion of the treasure somewhere else, Zbigniew. A small portion, but a very important one. Think of it. It is extraordinary. There will still be a cache somewhere in Quebec that will never get into the wrong hands. Something that will be valuable to our side one day, Zbigniew. Duplessis would want this too, if only as his last joke on Ottawa and on the Vatican. And so it was done.

There are 24 crates in the provincial museum. Kozlowski and Zdunek were the ones to pack them so many years ago in Krakow and they have been opened only a few times since then. Zdunek is now dead, Krukowska is dead, everyone in this matter is dying. But even here,

Zbigniew, there have been secrets known only to a small circle. Secrets within secrets.

Inside each of the 24 crates, my friend, they hid some things that never got onto the bills of lading back in Krakow in those last few days before the Nazis came. Hidden, from everyone, you see — everyone. Not visible even when the crates were opened for inspection. Eventually, the story of whether there might be hidden portions became a mystery, Zbigniew, a kind of legend in the months after the invasion and the escape. It was a chaotic time when those goods were loaded and transported so long ago, my friend, as you well know. There were any number of places along the route through Malta to France and England and then to Canada where crates were opened and bills of lading examined, stamped, even altered. The government-in-exile was grateful anything was salvaged from that shipment at all. You remember how it was, Zbigniew. So there were only a few of us who ever knew eventually of the secret cache. And then fewer still who believed it had not been taken somewhere en route, or lost, or perhaps hidden again or sold by the London Poles.

But it did survive, Zbigniew, and I decided that it was my task to now hide these things and to never return them to a Communist government. Never. Two items from each crate, my friend, all exactly the same. And very valuable they are. Perhaps you can guess what I am talking about. Something that would have been terribly useful in wartime, that all warring parties would want. But I wanted also that something else be hidden along with these things, something very rare and special. Something religious. Duplessis would have wanted that too, I am certain.

So I chose for all of us. And it is something magnificent that I chose. Truly. Duplessis would have liked very much the idea of hiding something like that away from the Vatican, you see. He, too, feels he is to be betrayed. For this item, Zbigniew, I had to alter the Quebec government's lists, their museum receipts, in my own hand. But that was a simple matter after Duplessis had ordered that I not be interfered with.

And so it was for me to hide these items somewhere else, Zbigniew. With the help of Duplessis's bodyguard only, a policeman who has been with him for many years. He can be trusted. But even he cannot betray me because it was only I who eventually hid them away and only I have the new password. Only I can ever get these goods out from where they are now hidden. Not Duplessis, not his man, not Kozlowski. Only myself. And now I must tell you, my friend. Forgive me for giving you such dangerous information, but if I do not these things may be lost forever . . ."

Natalia paused in her reading. Zbigniew was watching her closely.

"What a responsibility, for you both," she said.

"For him, my dear. I was safely in this apartment, reading letters and drinking coffee."

"You know where these things are?"

"Approximately, my dear. Your uncle had become too wise and too suspicious to put such things as passwords and exact locations on paper. But with me, between comrades who had such a history together, sometimes a hint would suffice."

"Do you know what he hid?"

"Read, my dear."

"... *If ever it becomes necessary to find these things, Zbigniew, and I am gone, remember what we used to talk about in the old days in the Wellingtons on our way over the North Sea to make a run. Remember the places we talked about and the things we said we would do. Not in Warsaw, of course, as things turned out, but in Canada. Marriage, children — no children for me, as things turned out — but marriage in special places, to special women.*

And passwords, Zbigniew. In Scotland there were always passwords for the squadron. Wartime and passwords. These things go together. One could never be too careful on the watch or when we were about to take our Wellingtons up for a run. You remember of course. Always, a password."

"And you know what he means by this?" Natalia asked.

"Yes, my dear. I think I do.

He will tell me now, and then I will be the keeper of my uncle's secret, she thought. *The one he died for.*

She put the letter back on the table.

"I can tell you, Natalia, if you wish to know," Zbigniew said. But you should know the rest of the story first and then we must decide who killed your uncle, if we can, before you make up your mind what more you wish to know and what is to be done next."

"All right."

"You see, Natalia, it really did turn out that your uncle became the custodian of these last few treasures. Duplessis died later that year. Your uncle sent me press cuttings about the funeral. And almost as soon as Duplessis was gone, the Catholic Church and the new government and premier in Quebec betrayed him. Just as your uncle and Duplessis himself had suspected.

"The treasures in the museum vaults went back to the Communists in 1961. January. There were celebrations in Warsaw and Krakow. Some of the last hold-outs of the government-in-exile, a certain faction at least, could not believe that it was over. But for your uncle it was not over. He would never tell his secret to anyone. He would no longer have known whom to trust anyway. Kozlowski had died. Duplessis had died. It was for Stanislaw alone to watch and wait and at the right time he would see that the goods went back to the right people."

"How could he ever know when that was? Or who were the right people?" Natalia asked.

"That, my dear, was precisely his burden. Because as you know, the events in Poland never became any simpler, did they? They are not simple as we speak. This was your uncle's burden."

"And he was killed because of this?"

"I believe that he was."

"But who?"

"Any number of people, any number of groups, Natalia. These goods he hid away have everything that people are ever killed for. There is money involved, a great deal apparently. There is power, potentially. And there are symbols. I think you will find that people are often killed for just one of these things. Your uncle was a custodian of all three."

"But how would anyone ever have found out?" Natalia asked.

For one cold, dark second she thought: *Because you betrayed him.* But immediately she realized that this man, her uncle's comrade from the war, would never have betrayed his friend.

Zbigniew read her thoughts.

"Do you think I could possibly betray him, Natalia?"

"No. No, I don't. I don't think that you could."

"Thank-you, my dear. He was like my brother. He was my brother. And the simple fact of the matter, Natalia, is that as it turned out, your uncle betrayed himself."

"What do you mean?"

"I mean that he waited and he watched and he picked his moment to reveal his secret because he thought the time was right, and he was, unfortunately, mistaken."

"Who did he tell?"

Zbigniew handed her another letter, this one on modern bright blue airmail paper.

"Montreal,
July 3, 1992

Ah Zbigniew, I am tired. I am a tired old man, and a foolish one. All these years of watching and waiting and now I realize I have made a very foolish error, my friend. Like a young man I have been impatient and I have made an error. But perhaps you of all people will understand and will be able to forgive me this sin of impatience after all these years.

We have been seduced, I think, Zbigniew, all of us old ones who were in the War. Were we not all seduced by that peasant Walesa, with his smiles and his promises? Did we not all rejoice to see, at last, at last, at last, the insignia given back to him that day when he was sworn in as president of Poland? Our old comrades, Zbigniew, some of them anyway, travelling to Warsaw at long last to give him back the insignia and the documents they said would only go to a legitimate government of Poland.

But, you know, I did wait a little, my friend. Perhaps I was not as impatient as all that. For those like us who saw Poland clearly, knew her history, nothing would ever be quick or simple. Is that not true, my friend? I waited, as I knew I should. I decided to wait one more year. As you know, not a long time in the history of our struggle. But now it is clear that this was not long enough.

By the beginning of this year, I thought it was enough. Walesa was in power, there had been parliamentary elections, the Communists were being removed from their posts, all seemed in order. Surely you would agree with that, Zbigniew. All seemed to be in order. And so I sent word to Walesa's office and told a little, not all, of what I knew. But now, Zbigniew, it is clear that I moved too quickly.

Walesa is no friend of democracy, Zbigniew. He is a little tyrant who knows nothing of statesmanship and respect for others. The place is in an uproar again, my friend, and I can only hope that they continue to ignore my foolish old man's letters from a few months ago and that I can watch and wait for much, much longer before I decide what is to be done. I don't even know who might have seen it or how far up the line of command they may have gone. I seem to have been dismissed for an old madman, in any case, Zbigniew, and that is a blessing."

"He wrote a letter to Walesa about the treasures," Natalia said.

"Yes, my dear," Zbigniew said. "To Walesa's office, in any case. Several letters. I have never been clear on how many. Early in 1992. Nothing too detailed, as he says in that letter you are holding now. But enough to indicate to them that he had some very important information about a matter from the war, concerning the Wawel treasures and Canada.

"Anyone with a knowledge of those times could not have failed to be intrigued. But you see Walesa and his people are fools, amateurs, frauds. The place was in turmoil again soon after Walesa became president, as I'm sure you know. He could not cope with the transition from Solidarity hero to president. He was impatient with democracy, he was impatient with economics and planning and gradual transformation, and it all began to go to his head. And, of course, there was Wozniak, that fool of a chauffeur he used for a personal adviser.

"Can you imagine, Natalia, Walesa and other such people in Belvedere Palace, planning the future of our country, drafting constitutions, negotiating with the International Monetary Fund? It is unimaginable."

Zbigniew opened his tin of cigarettes to find a fresh one to light.

"Stanislaw picked the wrong time to involve Walesa," Natalia said.

"Yes," Zbigniew said. "Or Walesa's people, in any

case. Stanislaw was never clear about who in Walesa's office actually got this information he sent to Warsaw. But he soon realized his mistake. He became very worried when prime ministers began to be ousted and governments started to collapse one after another. Then the files started to emerge from the secret police offices about who had been the informers and which MPs in the new Sejm might have been KGB spies in the old days, about infiltration of the new regime by secret police, Communists, and the old guard KGB.

"Walesa even started playing up to the army in that period, my dear. The buffoon started wearing battle fatigues at about that time and was photographed with generals on top of tanks. There was talk that he might lead a coup against the Parliament — you will remember that too, I would imagine."

Natalia was ashamed at how little she had cared for the intricacies of Polish politics, any politics. The stories were not unknown to her but as always she had been more receptive to other things. Too introverted, she thought, ruefully, to pay much attention to what Delaney liked to call "the real world."

"And so your uncle regretted alerting Walesa's office that an old man in Montreal had important information for them," Zbigniew said. "But quite some time after that letter you have just read, many months after, he allowed himself to believe that things would be all right, that his few letters had been ignored, that they had been lost in the bedlam of what was going on in Warsaw then. There was not much detail in what he had told them. And the letters would have been among thousands of letters going to Walesa's office in that period in any case. So he thought the information had been ignored."

"But it wasn't, was it?" Natalia asked.

"No. Eventually, they responded. Someone in Walesa's office, or claiming to be in Walesa's office — we must be careful here — sometime in 1993 when things were getting even more crazy and when it was becoming clear that Walesa would probably lose power in the next presidential election. Someone close to him, or maybe the intelligence service, or God only knows who in a situation like that, decided that, yes, perhaps this odd bit of correspondence from Montreal should be followed up.

"So they began to write letters to Stanislaw, asking for more information. Then, when he ignored them, there were apparently some phone calls and telegrams. All of that took time, as these things do. Then there was a polite visit from some people claiming to be officers of the embassy in Ottawa. That sort of thing. Of course, at no point did your uncle tell them anything more. But you see, Natalia, their appetites were whetted, and he could not stop what he had started.

"They checked his name, I would imagine, and found out what he had done in the war. Any simpleton, even among Walesa's people, could have found out Stanislaw had been a presidential aide-de-camp, that he had been involved in the movement of the Wawel Castle goods, that there had been this long battle in Canada to get them back. It would not take long for a greedy treacherous bunch like those in Warsaw to put a scenario together."

"But if he didn't tell them what they wanted, what could they do?" Natalia said. "Surely they would just conclude it was a prank, a joke, not to be taken seriously."

She knew as soon as she spoke the words how foolish they were. Zbigniew looked at her sadly.

"Natalia, you surprise me with your naïveté," he said. "Have you no idea what the stakes are for people like Walesa or for those around him or even for his enemies? Everyone in Warsaw is looking for advantage, my dear. Governments have been collapsing one after the other, the future of the country is at stake. There will be an election for president this November and everyone is saying that Walesa will lose, as he so richly deserves to lose. Even the slightest chance of some political advantage or the chance of some money would be too attractive to ignore these days, my dear. For any number of players."

"But why would they kill him?" Natalia asked. "Who would have killed him?"

"Natalia, for almost two years they harassed him, various people, from God knows which faction. Eventually, I believe, they became tired or angry and they killed him."

"But who, Zbigniew?"

"That is the question. It could have been any one

of a number of people or groups of people."

"But with him dead, they could no longer hope to find what he was talking about," Natalia said.

"Perhaps they made him tell them something before he died. Perhaps they might have found something after he was dead, my dear. In his house, perhaps?"

Or they could decide they might find it here, Natalia thought suddenly.

"Why would they then kill that priest?" she asked.

"We are not sure that priest was murdered, Natalia," Zbigniew said.

"I'm sure," she said.

"All right, let us assume that he was. We must assume then that they thought he also knew something about what Stanislaw knew. It is not impossible that your uncle might have confided in him. Perhaps they interrogated him."

"But he was a priest."

Zbigniew laughed ruefully.

"There are a lot of dead priests in Poland who could have told that poor old Quebecois how dangerous it is to assume anyone is untouchable," he said. "And there are still many people in Warsaw with the skills to make people tell them things, my dear. I regret to have to tell you that."

"Please. Don't."

Natalia was becoming exhausted by all she had learned so far that day. Outside, the boys were still playing soccer in the square. The sun was fading as the day grew overcast and the afternoon progressed.

"You are tired Natalia, but there are important decisions to be made," Zbigniew said. "For your uncle's sake."

And for yours, she thought. *He must know what danger he is in. We are all in.*

They went out into the garden and looked at flowers and the old church walls for a moment, to clear their heads. Zbigniew then made them rough sandwiches of heavy bread, sausage, and some excellent Dijon mustard. They ate quietly at a long table, seated on square wooden stools. Zbigniew had a large glass of Côtes du Rhône. Natalia had no taste that afternoon for wine.

"It's obvious that I have to find the treasures," Natalia said eventually. "It sounds so ridiculously dramatic, doesn't it? The treasures. The goods. The materials. The cache."

"Yes," said Zbigniew. "That is obvious to me as well."

"And then, I suppose, I will have to decide what is to be done with them."

"As the new custodian."

"The reluctant custodian," she said.

"We do not choose our fate, my dear. That is our fate."

Zbigniew sat looking directly at her from across his battered old table. He reached for his tin of Sobranies and his matches.

"I have to say this, Zbigniew," Natalia said. "I think you're in danger. And now I am as well."

"You are correct."

He did not seem troubled by this. He smoked quietly, watching her.

Natalia realized there was little use in discussing the dangers, now that they were both so deeply implicated. *Francis is in danger now too,* she thought, wondering where he might be. *Playing spook, he would probably say.*

"Where do you think the things are?" Natalia said suddenly. "And what is the password?"

It was late afternoon when Natalia left the apartment. Her head was full of this new information, this fantastical story she had been told that day. So she did not see Hilferty and Stoufflet climbing out of their silver-grey Renault as the exterior door of Zbigniew's building closed behind her.

"Fancy meeting you here, Ms. Janovski," Hilferty said. "You will remember us, I assume?"

Natalia was more frightened than she suspected she yet had reason to be. It was difficult for her to calm herself when she saw them.

"Yes, from the hotel," she said.

"John Hilferty, Canadian Security Intelligence Service. And, Jean Stoufflet, from the French side."

"Civil servants," she said, looking past him for a taxi. The soccer players had gone home.

"That was a nice little arabesque this morning, Natalia," Hilferty said. "May I call you Natalia? It delayed us for a few moments, I must admit. Our little Francis. Such a mischief-maker."

Natalia said nothing.

"Visiting family, are we?" Hilferty said.

"A friend," she said. "I really must get back to the hotel."

"Of course you can guess why we're here, can't you?" Hilferty said, serious now. Playing stern, when charm failed. Stoufflet, for some reason, looked annoyed and impatient.

"No. I can't."

"Delaney still inside?"

"He's gone. He hasn't been here. This was something private."

Hilferty looked surprised that Delaney was not there.

"And what could young Francis be up to, I wonder?" he said.

"No idea," she said. "I'm going to get a cab."

"We'll drive you back," Hilferty said. "Have a chat on the way."

"No thanks," she said.

"*Mais, oui, madame,*" Stoufflet said. "*Allez-y.* Get in, we will drive you back."

Natalia spotted a taxi coming up rue de Belleville and hurried to the curb to hail it. Hilferty and Stoufflet came alongside her, but she got in the cab quickly and slammed the door.

"*L'hôtel Méridien, s'il vous plaît.*" she said to the driver. "*Vite.*"

The taxi pulled off quickly. The two spies walked slowly back to their car, slowly lest Natalia look back and see them in any inelegant haste. Stoufflet pulled

a stylish forest-green mobile phone from his overcoat and began to dial.

"Bitch," Hilferty said.

Chapter 10

The last day of Zbigniew Tomaszewski's life turned cold, with a threat of winter rain. Zbigniew did not mind the late February dampness, however, as he hurried up rue de Belleville to do his evening's shopping. He never minded anything about the winter weather in Paris because no matter how bad it got it was not as bad as winter in Warsaw, and no matter how bad it got it was still Paris and he could enjoy the streets, the people, and the shops.

He carried his old man's string shopping bag with him. He nodded to Parisians as he laboured up the hill to his *boucherie*, his *boulangerie*, his cheese shop, and his wine shop. He had planned a hearty *pot-au-feu* for this cold evening, but Natalia had stayed longer than even he had expected and now he thought he might prepare something quick: *paupiettes*, potatoes, some of the excellent French *haricots verts*. And perhaps a special Médoc to ward off the chill and to celebrate a little. Now that his burden had been shared, if not lifted. If not to celebrate, then to mark this day in some way. For he had a feeling it would be somehow very important, in ways he could not foresee.

The singsong of the women in the *boucheries* and *boulangeries* of Paris always cheered him: *Et avec ça, monsieur? Avec ça?* Like so many of the thousands of old men and women of Paris who live alone, he chose to always cook himself a full meal in the evenings. This allowed him the small pleasure of doing the shopping each afternoon, *de faire ses courses,* to smile at passersby and shop assistants, and then to have an evening's cooking task to accomplish before turning to his books and recordings, to the radio and his letters. He no longer had the money or the inclination for the cafés or bistros for his evening meals. Home was where he belonged, where he felt most at ease these days. Home, and out on his beloved rue de Belleville.

When he got back to the apartment, his telephone was ringing. He let it ring, as he unpacked his shopping in the dim warm kitchen. It rang for a long while, and then it stopped. He was not a man who ever rushed for telephones, but tonight he was even less inclined than usual to respond. Natalia had said she would not use the telephones in this matter and there was no one else who might call him or with whom he would wish to speak on this late-winter afternoon. So when the telephone sounded again as he was slicing *haricots* and scrubbing small potatoes, he only counted the rings: *onze, douze, treize.* .... Someone very much wanted to speak with him, it seemed.

The telephone rang again as his dinner cooked. Zbigniew was calm, content, at peace, as he did his small jobs and even as the sense began to build that the incessant ringing was an alarm of some kind that he should perhaps not ignore. But he was a soldier, still, so he was not afraid. He merely became aware of a situation that was, if not a threat, then one to be carefully observed in case action might be required. *This would be a night for it,* he thought. *They might choose this night for it, now that Natalia has been here.*

He pulled open the drawer of his desk and rummaged inside for an object wrapped in velvet cloth. It was the revolver he had kept from the war days; old, but carefully, lovingly, maintained. *Stanislaw had one precisely like this,* Zbigniew thought. *Stanislaw my old comrade.* He went briefly into the garden to check something in his tool locker, and then back into the kitchen to check on his dinner.

Zbigniew enjoyed his last meal, sitting alone at his long table in the early Paris evening. The *Appellation Haute Médoc Controlée* that he had selected was excellent. He needed no one around him to tell him how fortunate he had been to be able to spend so many evenings like this since the war: in private, at peace, enjoying the wines of France and simple, well-cooked meals in his warm and comfortable kitchen. He was never truly lonely, although he enjoyed the company of others, as well.

He had enjoyed Natalia's company this afternoon, for example. He felt confident she would be a trustworthy new custodian of Stanislaw's secret. He thought, as he wiped his mouth with an aging linen napkin and began to clear up, that he, and she, had done the proper thing. Later, when he heard the ever so slight commotion outside his double entrance doors, he was not surprised. He was simply too old and too experienced to be surprised. But he knew immediately when he heard the noises that he must act quickly. He stood only for a moment beside the stout oak boards, listening to the muffled conversation on the other side, seeing the door heave slightly as a shoulder was pressed against it, seeing the handle move as it was tested, pressed, prodded, picked.

Old Paris apartments rarely have doorbells on the street, perhaps because Parisians in the days when the apartments were being built had never expected or wanted unplanned visits. But Zbigniew knew it was too easy now for unwanted callers to wait until someone entered or left these buildings and then slip through exterior doors to deserted warrens of hallways inside. And his apartment, the only one on the ground floor, was down a particularly long and silent corridor, far from any other doors.

They could have come in here while I was out this afternoon, Zbigniew thought. *And so they wish to speak to me directly*. He knew, therefore, this was danger calling at his door and he knew that he must act quickly.

Zbigniew had never imagined he would call the police if it ever came to something like this. The police could never, in the end, fully settle such matters. So he hurried to the sideboard in the living room, as he had imagined so many times he would do. He pulled out his old briefcase full of letters and hurried through the French doors into the garden, where it was now dark and cold. His cardigan did not ward off the chill, but he would not be there long. He stood listening intently, in his slippers, until he was sure his entrance door in that deserted corner of the silent building would yield to the intruders. Then he got an old can from the tool shed and sloshed kerosene from it onto Stanislaw's precious papers. He lit them with a wooden match.

His heart ached and pounded in his chest as the fire shot up with a muted roar. A plume of acrid black smoke wafted from the tips of the orange flames. His heart ached and pounded not just because he knew he was in danger, but also because this was the end of his friend's papers, of the recorded history of their friendship and their shared secrets. He felt that somehow there should be a better end to all this than a sudden splash of kerosene and a match.

He sat down in a straight-backed chair in the living room, positioned so he could watch through the glass doors as the smoky flames ate away at paper and leather in the garden. He could also see the entrance door to the apartment finally give way to the pressure and proddings from those in the hallway who wanted so urgently to get in. He simply waited quietly and held his old revolver in his lap. He suspected, however, that he would not be using his revolver that night or ever again. He had never killed anyone with it before. He had killed with bombs, yes, many times. But not with revolvers.

He did not recognize the two men when they finally crashed through his door, cursing in peasant's Polish, but they were not at all unfamiliar. He had seen their type too many times in the past. He knew that they would be rough, angry, unreflective men; stinking of wine or vodka or the cheeses they had had for lunch. He knew that when they saw the flames in his garden and their bovine minds understood that what they were seeking was quickly being turned to black ash, they would be angry and they would beat him and hurt him and then, more than likely, they would kill him. He thought, as he waited: *The war is never over.*

Zbigniew Tomaszewski watches as if in a dream the two burly men race through his living room to the garden. He does not lift his revolver to shoot, because he knows that they are two, and to kill only one before being killed himself makes no sense. The taller of the two takes the time as they pass to deliver a mighty blow with his pistol to the side of Zbigniew's old head. Then he falls as if in a dream to his familiar carpet. He watches them from where he lies on the floor, a hot suspicion of blood emerging from his wound and oozing into his eyebrows, eyes, and mouth.

He does not move his aching head from the floor as he watches through the glass their frantic kicking and stamping at the briefcase as it flares in the night. There is not much left for them, but they pick angrily at scraps of paper in the flames and ash. They curse and bark commands to each other as they rush for sticks and rakes to beat the flames into submission. Zbigniew is wavering close to sleep, in a dream, when the tall man comes back into the room to deliver two, three, four mighty kicks of frustration to the body of the old man lying there in the carpet. His colleague is flicking bits of scorched paper into a bucket he has found on the grass.

Zbigniew is in a dream when his hair is pulled roughly, when his old head is pulled roughly back, when Polish curses are hissed into his face. He barely hears the far-off sirens of the fire trucks as they labour up rue de Belleville. He does not hear the horns and commotion of the traffic as trucks and police cars block the narrow Paris street corner where he has lived until this day.

He does not feel the final blows from pistol and rake, does not feel the heavy shoes of his murderers stomp into his ribs and back and head. He does not hear the pops of silenced pistols as bullets tear into his old man's body. He does not, cannot, see the two intruders race through apartment hallways, firing at chrome-helmeted firemen as they go. He does not see them force their way through startled shouting crowds of police, *pompiers,* passersby to disappear in the rain-slick Paris night. Because he is dead.

Delaney had been playing reporter, or spy, depending on one's point of view. Delaney himself couldn't quite make up his mind. There hadn't been a great deal of difference between the two vocations for him lately, nor, he realized, had there been in the last few years of his life. The information he had been seeking in his professional life for his articles and his books had often been information in which intelligence services would also take a keen interest. Some along the way, in fact, had made their interest in his professional activities discreetly known.

Zbigniew's decision to consult with Natalia alone had left Delaney at a loose end. He went out of the apartment building on rue Julien Lacroix and looked carefully around to see if anyone appeared to be watching the building. He could see no one, but knew that meant nothing. He decided that before making another move he would do what he often did on difficult assignments, ones in which the angle was buried in a mass of events, facts, and suppositions. He would simply sit for a while and quietly examine scenes, scenarios.

He hailed a taxi and surprised the driver by asking to be taken on only a short circular trip around several of the narrow streets in the neighbourhood and let off about three hundred metres down the slope of rue de Belleville. He then walked slowly back up the street, pausing to look in windows and to buy a copy of *Libération* before going into a café that would allow him a good view of rue Julien Lacroix.

From inside the smoky café, crowded even at midmorning with tradesmen in Paris-issue blue overalls and caps, he nursed an espresso and waited. He had found in his years as a reporter that simply staring at a scene sometimes brings interesting details into focus. So while his mind moved pieces of his current journalist's puzzle around, his eyes took in the scene on the street outside Zbigniew's faded building. His mental observations yielded no new insights. But his observation of the street bore fruit after half an hour.

Far down rue Julien Lacroix, he saw a burly man climb out of a small car parked somehow in one of the absurdly tiny spaces that occasionally present themselves on the crammed streets of Paris. The man was too far away for Delaney to see his face, but he very clearly stretched himself and looked around with the air of someone who is waiting for a long time. The man then leaned down to speak to someone through the window of the car. The many other parked vehicles did not allow Delaney any view of the other figure. After lighting and smoking a cigarette, the first man then climbed back into the car. But the car did not pull off and was still there when Delaney caught the attention of the waiter to bring his bill. He thought for a moment that he would walk down rue Julien Lacroix to see them more closely, but then decided that this would be unwise.

He wished he could call Zbigniew's house to warn Natalia that the building was being watched, but they had agreed to avoid telephones and he had not written down the exterior door code to go back inside. He worried for a moment that these watchers, if they were indeed watchers, might be wanting to go inside as well. His indecision about whether to leave or to stay ended, however, as he was paying the café's cashier at her small booth near the entrance.

He saw Hilferty and Stoufflet sweep up very conspicuously in a silver-grey car. Stoufflet was driving. He pulled two wheels up onto the curb at the corner as only the French know how to do. He was not blocking traffic, but what passed for a pedestrian crossing was blocked and a series of aging Parisians took turns glaring inside the car as they tried to reach the sidewalk from it.

Delaney decided that the combined forces of these two intrepid spies from two intelligence agencies would be enough to dissuade their competitors, if that is what they were, far down the street from doing anything untoward. He was also reassured by signs that Hilferty and Stoufflet were settling in for a long stay. The Canadian was reading what looked like the *International Herald Tribune* and the Frenchman was coming back to the car carrying two newly purchased packets of *Disque Bleu*.

They did not see Delaney leave the café and walk quickly up the hill to Métro Pyrénées. He had decided that the Métro was a safe bet today and would in fact be faster for where he wanted to go. The Maison de la Radio, headquarters of Radio France, was in the 16th arrondissement, a long way away, and traffic was at a crawl. He took one last look around him and walked down the grimy stairs to the subway.

The station was dirtier than he remembered the Paris Métro ever to be, with bits of litter and discarded yellow tickets strewn everywhere. Already a small group of *clochards* had gathered on the moulded seats of the station, waiting not for the next train but the next plastic bottle of cheap *vin rouge*. One of them was asleep on a bed of cardboard behind the row of seats. The others grumbled and debated in low, rough bursts of French. A couple of policemen on the opposite platform were demanding identity papers from a bewildered African in a long thread-bare coat.

Delaney transferred at République station to another line and then it was a direct run to Ranelagh station. Then there was a ten-minute walk down rue du Ranelagh through a much more salubrious *quartier* to Radio France. Delaney didn't mind the walk. He liked this part of Paris too, despite its *bourgeois* airs. He was in no hurry now, because he suspected Natalia would stay a long time with Zbigniew, and because Lawrence Keating, the Irish journalist he was on his way to see, had said on the phone that he would be free anytime that day.

Keating was an old acquaintance, if not an old friend, and well briefed on the European story. He was gay, a refugee from Ireland's institutionalized distaste for homosexuals. He had no more desire to be in London or among the British than any other of the thousands of expatriate Irish who chose Paris instead of London for their lives in exile.

Keating was splicing bits of audiotape on an aging console when Delaney arrived at the English Service on the fifth floor of the giant glass-and-steel fortress that dominated the bank of the Seine where it had been so incongruously placed. He was smoking an American cigarette, powdering the tape machine with fine grey ash. The console had been due for replacement a decade earlier. So, too, if the truth were known, had Keating. He had been at this job far too long, had become far too comfortable with something too unchallenging for a journalist of his skills and experience. But it was Paris, he was forty-four years old, in exile, and the options for him were limited.

"As I live and breathe, it is Francis Delaney," Keating said, coughing briefly as he stubbed out his cigarette in the sardine tin he used for an ashtray.

The No Smoking sign in the newsroom was there for appearances only, apparently. The newsroom generally was in a much more disreputable state than Delaney remembered it. Scripts and carbon paper were scattered everywhere. Small reels of quarter-inch tape had been hurled onto tables and into cardboard boxes. There were far too many desks, chairs, and journalists for the space available. Only a few of the reporters there actually seemed to be working, however. Most smoked cigarettes and chatted to each other, or read French and British newspapers at their desks.

"Hello, Lawrence," Delaney said. "Got time for a coffee?"

"Always. There is always time for coffee and a cigarette," Keating said.

He called over to a haggard young man hammering away at a grubby typewriter nearby.

"Denton, my lad, I'm off for a fag with my old mate Delaney here," he said. "Not off with a fag, mind. For a fag. You've twelve minutes to news time, boyo, so no rush whatsoever. Look after things for me, would you?"

Keating always affected a thick Irish brogue, overladen with the standard ironic tone of a certain kind of homosexual. He did not wait for an answer from his colleague, but simply picked up his cigarettes and matches and led Delaney out.

"Young Denton is yet another fucking Brit waiting for his turn at the BBC," Keating said as they waited for the elevator to the staff canteen on the top floor. "Straight as an arrow, the poor dear. He's still pretending that rewriting the Agence-France-Presse wire and beaming it out across the world to the impoverished millions is his own and only sacred short-wave calling and God's gift to French foreign policy."

They ordered small strong coffees when they got to the canteen. Delaney listened while Keating explained who among the current staff of English Service was gay, who was not, and who could not truly say.

Delaney was prepared for the tart mix of gossip,

vitriol, and information Keating would, as always, provide. But he knew that on arcane matters of European Union business, Keating was a force to be reckoned with. Delaney also knew that he was an old East Europe hand who had been many times to Poland, Czechoslovakia, and Hungary, before and after their Communist regimes fell. Delaney needed an informed, dispassionate, journalist's view of what was going on in Warsaw, and Keating could provide it. And so he did, without asking Delaney why such a briefing might be required.

"That little prick Walesa's ruining the whole damned country, you know," Keating said as he smoked. "No democrat he. Solidarity be damned. Continual war at the top, that's me boyo's motto."

Keating's skin was a bad colour and his face around the eyes was deeply lined. Delaney wondered how long before he would be brought down by AIDS.

"If they don't sew up a new constitution for that place quick smart, Walesa's going to take over everything for himself," Keating said. "He's now just about finished pushing out another prime minister, Pawlak this time, from the Peasant Party, and it looks like it'll be Oleksy to replace him. A bald little moon-faced prick who's been Speaker for a while. One of the old-line Communists who got into Parliament in that wave in '93. SLD Party, he is, Democratic Left, or so they call themselves now."

"He any improvement?" Delaney asked.

"Over who? Pawlak or Walesa?"

"Either."

"Oleksy has a bunch of bad friends, dear Francis. Or so they say. Likes to go hunting and drinking with highly suspect Russians. At lodges in the deep dark woods."

"You sure? He's KGB?" Delaney asked.

"FSB now actually. They've changed their name now, as a man such as yourself must certainly know. We realize that KGB is a name from the bad old days, don't we Francis? Of course we do. Well, everybody may be reinventing themselves at the moment over there, but it's the same old shitfight. Oleksy does run with KGB people or FSB people, or used to, that's sure no matter what name you call them. Now of course you yourself run with faggots, don't you now, and that doesn't mean you're queer. But this one stinks, Francis. Oleksy stinks, the whole fucking lot of them stink over in Warsaw at the moment, I'm sorry to say."

"Walesa's people too, of course."

"Of course. The whole lot. Everyone after the main chance at present. Walesa, can you believe this one, now being pursued by what passes for a tax office over there for non-payment of tax on the sum of one million dollars, one million U.S. he got in advance from some Hollywood producer with shit for brains who wants to make a movie about his life. A million dollars, my friend. For the little electrician from Gdansk. Spent most of it already, probably."

"What on? What's for sale in Warsaw these days?"

"God only knows. Everything's for sale. But he's

told the tax office he's broke, our Lechie has. Maybe he spent it all on altar boys, or altar girls in his case, as he doesn't seem to be gay. Or some nice new fax machines or ping-pong tables or tanks maybe, or maybe some dirty tricks to get re-elected. God only knows what he might spend his money on. But he's going to go down in November no matter what he spends."

"No chance at all?"

"Oh, a small one maybe. If they keep digging up dirt on the Communists. There's a couple of groups formed over there now to embarrass the other side when they can — the Three Quarter Initiative, so-called, can't remember three-quarters of what. And the Committee of One Hundred. Right wing, centre rights, Christ knows what. A couple of others. God knows where their funding comes from. Vatican probably. Or CIA. Keeping Poland out of the hands of the Communists and safe for Lech and his band of pals."

Keating paused to watch a thin young man in a ribbed pullover sweater walk by them with a tray of food. Smiles were exchanged.

"He's cute," Keating said. "A technician. I must seduce him at his earliest possible convenience."

Delaney waited for the briefing to continue at Keating's idiosyncratic pace.

"The Vatican is upset, by the way, Francis, very seriously upset these days that the Commies would like to soften up the abortion laws again over there," Keating said. "And that the Commie Parliament won't pass a new Concordat for them, if you can imagine that. What a medieval notion that is. Jesus, Mary, and Joseph, a Concordat, so-called, to spell out relations between Church and State. We are talking here about the fucking Dark Ages all over again, Francis."

Keating's face reddened and he coughed and spat into a tissue before lighting yet another cigarette.

"Before you know it, they'll have it all shipshape again over there, Lech and the Pope will, just like fucking Ireland," he said. "Burn queers at the stake. After Communists, abortionists, and Canadians."

Keating didn't mind if Delaney sat for a while afterward at a terminal in the newsroom to scan the news agency wires for the latest out of Warsaw and Canada. Nor did he did mind letting Delaney send a fax to O'Keefe in Montreal and make some transatlantic calls for his messages. Keating didn't care anymore, if he had ever cared, what anyone did in that cramped airless newsroom.

Delaney then called the Méridien to see if Natalia was back. She wasn't, but he felt a small secret pleasure, after so long, at calling somewhere, anywhere, to see if a woman might have left him a message. Keating's eyes twinkled from across his desk as Delaney hung up.

"Getting any, Francis?" he asked.

"Your mind is in the gutter, Keating."

"Yes. Oh yes."

Delaney was about to order his third Heineken at

the Méridien's little ground-floor bar when he finally saw Natalia rush in. The hotel lobby was crammed with new arrivals, departures, doormen, bellboys, and concierges. He stepped out into the milling throng and pulled her into the bar. She looked flushed and worried. Delaney did not tell her he, too, had been worried: about her, about the growing complexity of the situation, about what she might have discovered that afternoon.

"You all right?" he asked.

"Yes," she said. "The traffic is just unbelievable. It's taken me forever to get back here."

She sat down at the bar with him.

"I've had quite a session with Zbigniew, Francis," she said. "It was exhausting. Fascinating, but really exhausting. But I'm mostly worried right now about your friend from Canada, this civil servant. He was waiting outside the apartment when I left. With that Frenchman who was with him yesterday. But today he was a little more forthcoming about his job, Francis. He said he was with the Canadian Security Service or whatever it's called."

"Security Intelligence Service. He told you that?" Delaney knew this meant the rules of the game were changing, that Hilferty was in a hurry now to move things along, or was angry, or both.

"Yes. But you knew that all along, didn't you?" Natalia looked intently at him, psychologist with client, looking for deceptions.

"Yes. I suppose I did," Delaney said, leaving it at that.

"He wanted me to ride back here with him," Natalia said. "I told him no."

"Well, he won't be far behind you. Let's go somewhere else and talk things over."

They went quickly to the mezzanine level, then down stairs and through the kitchen to the back street as they had that morning. There was a small bistro just at the corner, jammed with after-work drinkers of coffee and coloured liqueurs. They lost themselves at a small copper-covered table near the back. Coffees came, and their conversation was drowned by the Gallic hubbub all around them.

Natalia told Delaney what he needed to know. It took her a long time, but he was impressed at her reporting skills, her attention to detail. He couldn't help thinking, as he listened, about what a superb story this all was, what it could become in the hands of a sharp feature writer. But today he did not have the luxury of journalistic interest. He was a participant in a story breaking fast.

"And you think you know where this stuff is hidden?" he asked her again.

They had ordered some plates of food and were picking at it as they talked. Natalia was now on to her second glass of Côtes du Rhône.

"Yes, Francis. I do."

She did not fill the pause that followed with passwords or place-names. Delaney decided not to press her on it. He didn't try to imagine why she would choose not to tell him. *Do I really need to know this now?* he thought. *Yes. Probably*.

"And you want to go ahead and locate this, this whatever-it-is?" he said.

"Yes," she said firmly.

"I see." He did not have to ask why.

"Do you?" she asked. Again the psychologist's look.

"I suppose I do, yes," Delaney said. "Now, after all of this."

"Why would you?" she asked. "Who knows what we will find, what's going to happen. It could get really dangerous now. Why would you bother with this?"

He knew she would ask him something like that. But he was not in the mood, in this crowded Paris bistro, to start baring his soul.

"I said I would help you."

"You've already helped me," she said.

"I like to finish things."

"Why else?"

"What are you trying to get me to say, Natalia? I'm not used to reading from other people's scripts." Delaney felt suddenly annoyed, or unnerved.

She looked down into her glass of wine.

"I'm sorry," she said.

"You're really going to need some help on this thing now," Delaney said. "This could get very wild about now."

"I know that," she said. "Zbigniew said as much this afternoon."

Delaney looked at his watch and then looked around the bistro. There was no reason to expect

Hilferty's face to appear, but luck, bad luck, often played a part in such situations.

"In fact, Natalia, I think before we do anything else we'd better get back over to Zbigniew's place and figure out what to do with those papers," Delaney said. "I don't think it's a good plan to leave them with him anymore. We've been in here much too long as it is."

"Oh, I don't think he'll want to let them go, Francis."

"He'd better think that one over again. Let's see what he says."

"Maybe you shouldn't come," Natalia said. "He doesn't trust journalists."

"Well, I don't trust spies. And some of them know where he lives. So let's go see what he says. I don't need to tell you that this could get ugly for him now, too. Not just for us."

He could see she had already addressed that issue.

"All right," she said.

They used the back entrance of the hotel again. There was still no sign of Hilferty. This worried Delaney more than a confrontation. Still, Hilferty would only delay them now and Delaney was worried about the papers and about the old man, not necessarily in that order. He went up to his room to get his equipment bag with the Browning in it. There was a Méridien envelope pushed under his door. Natalia watched as he read the note inside.

It said: "We're going to have to have a little chat, Francis. The minute you get back. You are really and truly starting to piss a lot of people off."

Hilferty hadn't bothered to sign it. Either he was too angry or too rushed or too sure Delaney would know who had sent it.

"Hilferty," Delaney said. "Not very happy at the moment. He wants to know what's going on. Badly."

"Let's go," Natalia said, realizing now the urgency.

They did not risk going through the lobby. By now the kitchen staff appeared used to the two foreigners rushing in and out. A chef in a ridiculously tall white hat tossed flaming bits of this and that in a blackened pan.

It was hard to get a taxi at the back. They had to walk to a cross street and wait some minutes before flagging an empty one. Then there was the Paris traffic. So it was only some considerable time later that they rolled up to the police barricades that had been set up at the bottom of rue de Belleville.

They both knew it would be bad news, the worst of news, as they climbed out of the cab to rush up the street to rue Julien Lacroix. The fire trucks and Police Nationale trucks and the marked and unmarked police cars had absolutely blocked the streets. Radio reporters sat on motorcycles sending stories by cellular phone back to their newsrooms, and crowds of passersby and café types craned their necks to see.

"*Qu'est-ce qui ce passe?*" Delaney asked a woman holding a small nervous dog.

"*Incendie, monsieur. Rue Julien Lacroix. Quelques morts. Un pompier, quelqu'un d'autre.*"

She was marvellously concise and well informed. A policeman with a crackling walkie-talkie confirmed the woman's version for them when Delaney showed his international press pass. Two dead, including a fireman. Shot apparently, not hurt in the fire. Someone else injured. *Très compliqué.*

A young radio reporter sporting a leather bomber jacket and impossibly tiny wire spectacles told them a bit more. Robbery, apparently, and then a small fire. Or something like that. An old man, living alone. Bandits who shot their way out. *Très cool, très professionnelle.*

Delaney knew it would be useless to try to get more information there that night and unwise to indicate any involvement. The French police always panicked when one of their own got killed and usually arrested everyone in sight. And there was the small matter of the gun in his equipment bag. Natalia did not see the logic of this at first, however, and the crowd watched with interest as she wept quietly on the street and insisted that they should try to go in. They were far too late for that. Eventually, reason prevailed.

Chapter 11

They should have been on an Air Canada shuttle back to Montreal, in the company of Quebecois tourists and businessmen and arts types who'd made their various pilgrimages to Paris. Instead, they were on Alitalia Flight 18, non-stop Paris to Rome, surrounded by stylish Italians and young French travellers on other sorts of pilgrimages.

Natalia sat quietly beside Delaney in the business-class section, reading the in-flight magazine. She was still not talking much, still deep and dark as she had been in the few days since Zbigniew was killed. She didn't bother with post-takeoff drinks or the lunch or the headphones. She didn't seem to want to bother with very much at all. At least, as far as Delaney was able to make out, she no longer seemed afraid.

Things were moving very fast now, even for a journalist of Delaney's experience. A day earlier, Hilferty had been extremely terse with him on the phone at the Méridien.

"Look Francis, this is getting very hot now," Hilferty had said. "The fucking Vatican's coming in on this and I don't want any fucking around. They want you and Natalia in Rome. Like right now."

"The Vatican," Delaney said.

"You got it, baby. The Pope's own regiment. They've got wind of this now, and they're in."

They met in the hotel bar, neither wanting to say more on the phone.

"What's the deal?" Delaney asked.

"Look, the way you've been jerking us around I wouldn't tell you another goddamn thing if I didn't have to," Hilferty said. "But I'm fucked on this thing now and haven't got much of a choice. Our friends in the Holy See would like to have a polite discussion with you and your lady friend about what the hell you've been up to. A matter of some Church property? Something you can give them a hand with? Not that we'd know anything where you're concerned. So my betters in Ottawa think we should afford the Vatican every respect and courtesy and help them along on this. Or you should. Tomorrow."

Hilferty pushed two Alitalia tickets over on the bar.

How would they know? Delaney thought. *And how much do they know?* "What brings them into this?" he asked.

"Oh please," Hilferty said. "I should be asking you this stuff. You're lucky I'm CSIS, and not with some other fucking organization, Francis, or it would be cigarette burns until you come clean. It might come to that yet."

Hilferty was manic, knowing clearly that this operation was out of his hands, possibly out of control altogether and heading for the abyss. Delaney could see that in the way he munched his way through too many pistachios and picked labels off bottles of beer. This was not going to look good on a résumé.

"Walesa ask them to come in?" Delaney asked.

He was determined to get what he could from Hilferty. He was guessing that Walesa's people felt they could no longer trust their own secret service and may have called in some people they did trust in the Vatican. Maybe. On the other hand, an indiscreet priest in Montreal might have captured the Vatican's attention as well. Or a murdered priest.

"If he did, and I knew, I wouldn't tell you, Francis," Hilferty said. "Who says Walesa's a player anyway? Just who's asking who for help on this one is no longer very clear. Let's just leave it at that. The Vatican's interested, and my people know they're interested, and when the Vatican says jump, the Dominion of Canada, apparently, asks how high."

Bits of beer label continued to fall from his fingers.

"Let me tell you this, hotshot," Hilferty continued. "This is now very much the big time. You get it? There's now a lot more riding on this than you can imagine and we don't want any fuck-ups. If it were up to me I'd deport your ass back to Canada and get on with the job at hand. But we're stuck with you and that Polish shrink, and that's that. So no more bullshit, you get it? The Vatican intelligence people do not like to fuck around. They're like the goddamn Mossad. A little less money, maybe a little bit less, and a lot fewer toys, but they've got a thousand or so years of experience and God and the Pope on their side. That's two big backers to the Israelis' one."

Hilferty drank the rest of his beer and pushed the bill over to Delaney — at this point still only passive aggressive.

"We'll have a car out front tomorrow morning," Hilferty said. "Better bring your gun. Our gun. And not in your carry-on." He walked out, muttering darkly. "Fucking amateurs."

Delaney wondered again if Hilferty's handlers back home knew he was in the habit of arming journalists with very large handguns, and overseas at that. Journalists who had made it very clear they were freelancers and on nobody's staff. The gun, clearly, was Hilferty's accident insurance policy: Canadians in general and now this worried spy in particular being the biggest buyers of insurance in the Western world.

Hilferty had also been agitated a few days before that, on the night Zbigniew died. When Delaney and Natalia had come back to the Méridien, he and Stoufflet were watching out for them from the lobby bar.

"We better have a little talk, Francis," Hilferty said. "Right now."

Natalia looked bad. Her eyes were red-rimmed and tired. She said nothing and tried to go around them but Stoufflet moved to block her way. As he did he locked his eyes on Delaney, enjoying the little testosterone dance, inviting him to be offended by the move.

"*S'il vous plaît, madame,*" Stoufflet said. "Stay with us for a little instant, would you please?"

Delaney decided that Stoufflet had no redeeming qualities.

"Let the lady go up," he said. "She wants to go up to her room."

"*Ah, oui?* A little early, *non?* In Paris?"

"Hilferty," Delaney said, "I've had a very trying day; we have all had a trying day. Now get that French asshole out of Natalia's way or we'll have a scene right here in the lobby."

Natalia looked up gratefully at Delaney, ignoring, this time, the psychosocial implications of his behaviour.

"Let her go up, Jean," Hilferty said. "We can speak to her later if we need to."

"Don't count on that," Delaney said.

Natalia went into the open elevator without saying anything at all. They all watched as the doors slid silently closed and then they went into the bar for spy talk.

"Look Francis, we're going to have to get a few things straightened out right now," Hilferty said. "We've got one dead old guy over there in Belleville and one dead fireman and people are very soon going to go apeshit on both sides of the Atlantic. Now are you going to brief us on what's going on here, or what?"

"No. I don't think so, John. This is private business at the moment."

Delaney saw a smile creep onto Stoufflet's face. *He's just hoping for a chance to play the heavy,* Delaney thought. *As we're on his turf.*

"Are you working with us on this thing anymore or not?" Hilferty asked.

"I never was," Delaney said.

"Bullshit. I say you fucking were, and I say you are right now. Don't push me too far, Francis. I can mess you up pretty bad back in Canada now, you know that. Our friend from the *Quai* here can find a weapon on you, and maybe there's some CSIS cash still back in your apartment in Montreal. That wouldn't look too good for a distinguished journalist, now would it?"

"I don't think it would look too good for a CSIS agent to be found to be on a covert operation overseas either," Delaney said. "Or attempting to coerce journalists who are on an investigative assignment."

"No one will buy that, Delaney," Hilferty said.

"Let's see then, shall we? I have a bit of a way with words, and some very indulgent editors."

Hilferty looked over at Stoufflet, who now had gone Gallic impassive. The Frenchman motioned for the bartender to come over to serve them drinks.

"*Cinquante-et-un,*" Stoufflet said. "*Un double.* For you, *mes amis?*"

"Johnnie Walker Black. Double," Hilferty said.

"I'm not staying," Delaney said.

"You fucking are," Hilferty said. "Bring him a beer."

When the drinks had come, Hilferty said: "Well, we've got ourselves a little situation here, Jean. How would your people want us to play this one, do you think? We've now got what we like to call back in the frozen wastes of Canada a reluctant operative. Thought he was onside but now he's way, way offside. Probably has some information we would find very helpful indeed and refuses to give it to us. We've got some poor fireman dead, and the police asking your people a couple of questions I would expect. We've got some dead Polish émigré, and a little bonfire in his garden, which Francis over here probably knows a bit about as well. I asked Monsieur Delaney for some help, Jean, and now that things are getting interesting, he is refusing to cooperate. What do you make of all that?"

"*Cherchez la femme, mon ami,*" Stoufflet said. "Forget this piece of shit. We talk to the girl."

There was the eye contact again.

"Not a bad idea," Hilferty said. "Although she did look a little upset tonight already. Lost a friend of the family, we understand, Francis. Sorry to hear about that."

"Look, you guys can play spy games all night, if you like, but the fact of the matter is I'm not interested in this particular scenario anymore," Delaney said. "I very much doubt you've got the balls to try to force me to do anything just at the moment, John, and if you do I'll play this so big in the media back home you'll be looking for work twenty-four hours later. So why don't we all finish our drinks and go on about our business."

"We'll be on you like a fucking rash, every minute, Francis. You've got no room to manoeuvre. What's the point?"

"That's now my business only, John. Let's just see how it all plays out, shall we?"

"We'll be on you like a rash," Hilferty said.

"Fine. But tell your friend over here to be particularly careful to stay out of my way. And Natalia's way. Could you do that for me, John?"

Delaney was surprised at the intensity of his anger and the adrenalin rush. It had been a day of intense feelings all around. He left them then sitting at the bar, nursing their options.

Natalia hadn't seemed terribly surprised when Delaney told her they had been summoned to the Vatican. Now that she had seen how these things worked and had seen that people were willing to kill for whatever it was they were all seeking, nothing much appeared to surprise her anymore. It wasn't clear to Delaney whether her beloved Jung, apparently to be trusted for insights into all sorts of complex human situations, had prepared her adequately for this sort of thing. Perhaps he had. Whatever the case, Natalia seemed to be willing to just ride it out now, wherever the darker psychic energies of others took them.

Of course she blamed herself, or herself and

Delaney in equal parts perhaps, for Zbigniew's death. She argued that they should not have gone to him so overtly, without giving him more warning or a chance to say no or a way to meet more surreptitiously. And she blamed herself for taking too long to get back to the old man's apartment the night he was murdered, to warn him of the dangers and to take away the papers he had ended up dying for.

It was all Delaney could do to talk her out of going along to the Paris morgue to volunteer information to the police, to try, somehow, to set things right for the old man. Going to the funeral, if there was to be a funeral, was also out of the question. It was too late for any of that, he had insisted, and eventually Natalia let the desire to do penance drop.

"We were too busy drinking wine and eating dinners in a bistro to care enough that he might be in danger," she had said repeatedly in the first hours. That line had stopped coming so often now, Delaney noted. Then again, not many lines of any sort were coming just at the moment.

The Alitalia jet was at cruising altitude now, droning steadily southeast from Paris toward Rome. Delaney looked over at Natalia again. This time she looked up at him and made eye contact. A small improvement, a psychologist might say. The eyes were not the same as they were before they had left Montreal. But they told him she was more determined than ever to see this thing through. For the sake of two old Polish gentlemen at least.

Their immediate worry was how much of

Zbigniew's cache of letters had survived. Hilferty had been cagey on that, trying as best he could to draw them out. All Hilferty would say was that there had been "a little bonfire." Delaney had no idea whether CSIS even knew about any letters or whether the French police had salvaged some from the apartment. They would have to assume the worst, Delaney decided: that at least some papers had been taken by the people who had broken into the apartment. How many, and which ones, were of course the more important questions.

Another question, which he and Natalia talked through endlessly in the couple of days they had spent in Paris waiting for the right time to make a next move, or waiting for the inspiration for a next move, was who might have done the killing and who else knew about it.

Delaney was still leaning toward UOP, but he was less sure this sort of action would have been ordered by Walesa himself or even by his own office. If a small CSIS operation could go badly out of control, so, quite easily, could a small Polish operation. And, as the Americans in particular could attest from bitter experience, operatives often go far beyond their brief in the heat of the moment, or when things get more interesting or more lucrative for them in their own right. As for the Vatican, Delaney was not naïve enough to think that side would take the soft option either, depending on what was at stake.

He had Natalia tell him once more, and then

again, exactly what Zbigniew had told her the day he died and what the letters indicated was in the secret Polish cache still somewhere in Quebec. And then he came no closer to even an educated guess about the content or the value of the cache or about what those seeking it would want it for.

Money? Probably a fair bit of money, or something convertible to money. But which of the possible players would need it that bad? Walesa, possibly, to finance his faltering election campaign? Or maybe a nice little retirement fund for himself? Walesa's own people, just out of greed? His security service people, for similar reasons? Polish Communists, or former Communists as they now liked to be called? Maybe the Vatican? Not penniless by any stretch of the imagination. But maybe very interested in keeping whatever it was out of the hands of those in Poland who needed it more than they did.

Or maybe, and this was the thought that troubled Delaney most, maybe everyone was desperately seeking this so-called treasure without knowing quite what it was at all.

"Zbigniew said it probably has everything that motivates people," Natalia said as they made the final approach to Rome. "Money, power, and symbolism."

"What if it's none of the above?" Delaney said.

"Then it is still a symbol. Then the joke is on us," Natalia said with a dark laugh. "Then the joke's on us."

This thought seemed to cheer her in some way. She gave another little manic laugh. Delaney wondered if she really was all right.

"You know, I've never been to Rome," she said suddenly. "Jungians have a thing about Rome."

"How do you mean?"

"Jung himself never even made it to Rome. He was probably the best psychologist of religion ever. He travelled all over the world to speak to holy people and see sacred sites, but he could never get himself to Rome. Every time he went to the Zurich train station to buy a ticket he'd have an anxiety attack and faint dead away. He said the archetypal intensity of the place was just too much for his psyche to deal with."

"Really?"

"Really," she said. "The stress was just too much for him, poor dear."

This sent Natalia into another short burst of dark laughter.

The other obvious problem they now faced was how to do anything at all in Rome or anywhere else without CSIS and possibly several other intelligence services on to their every move. Hilferty was nowhere obvious at Fiumicino airport, but that didn't mean his people, and others, were not there. As Delaney and Natalia came out through the customs area, a dark-suited man with a chauffeur's cap stepped forward without hesitation and called out to them by name. They were known here, apparently.

Hilferty had told them to expect a ride.

The accent was Italian, but their man did not look much like a chauffeur to Delaney.

"I am to bring you to your hotel," the man said.

He didn't offer them a name. He picked up their small bags and walked fast to the curb outside, where a large black Lancia was idling. The driver looked quickly, expertly, from side to side as he shepherded them into the car and Delaney saw him give a sign to someone standing by another Lancia nearby.

Another dark-suited man in sunglasses was waiting in the front passenger seat of the car Delaney and Natalia were to ride in. This man only nodded, and he didn't bother talking at all.

The two cars pulled off together. This made for a very secure ride through Roman traffic to the hotel Delaney had chosen. Hilferty had wanted to book them in somewhere approved, but Delaney had insisted on making the choice: the Hotel Roma near the Spanish Steps. He had been there many times and now, more than ever, he wanted at least the semblance of familiar turf.

It was to be a late-afternoon meeting, or so the handwritten message on Vatican stationery told them after they checked in, with one Monsignor Rafael Fiorentino, Prefect of the Pontifical Household. It would be in the papal apartments themselves. A car was to come for them at four o'clock. If he had had any doubts, Delaney knew now that the Vatican was seeing this as very serious business indeed. But CSIS was still nowhere in evidence. Delaney wondered at what point Hilferty and Company would make their presence felt, if they were going to be allowed to have any presence here at all.

Natalia did not want to go out, even though it was wonderfully warm and sunny, as afternoons in Rome in early March can be. The weather was much warmer than in Paris and the streets around the hotel were full of well-dressed people enjoying the spring. Instead of going out, they ordered a room service lunch and ate together on the balcony of Natalia's room, which overlooked an elegant inner courtyard with fountains and gravel paths. It was still adjoining rooms for them on this trip. Delaney allowed himself, briefly, to wonder how much longer that might last.

They talked quietly about what was in store for them, squinting at each other in the bright sunlight on the balcony. Neither wanted to drink wine with lunch, to the surprise of the room service clerk: Delaney because he wanted to have wits about him for the meeting that was to come; Natalia for some complex penitent reasons of her own. But in the sunlight and the spring air even a bottle of mineral water in brilliant crystal glasses seemed a small celebration.

Delaney had thought, briefly, about contacting an American journalist he knew to be working at the local AP office, to check things out, to find out at least a little bit about Monsignor Fiorentino if he could. But he realized that his old ways of doing things, his constant checking in and checking out, his briefings and debriefings and scanning of clippings, were not useful anymore. Not on this assignment in any case. So he just let things flow, sipping his mineral water in the Roman sunlight and willing, as perhaps never before in his life, to simply see where things led. His reactions would look after themselves. They would have to.

The telephone in Delaney's room rang precisely at four o'clock. The car was downstairs. Same driver, different car. No second man in the front seat this time, but another car for back-up, as before. The desk clerks looked keenly interested. Was it so obvious that they were being ferried around Rome by agents, that they were on the way to the Vatican for a meeting with the Papal Prefect?

The ride was silent. There was nothing for any of them to say. The car eventually rolled up beside the high walls of the Vatican, past St. Peter's Square, where even on a weekday afternoon there were crowds of tourists, photographers, and hawkers of souvenirs. At a giant iron gate in a back wall they drove onto the grounds and pulled up on a cobbled parking area. A small squad of Swiss guards, ridiculous in their ballooning uniforms, marched past.

The real security here was much more discreet. The driver and a man in a dark suit, who came out to the car, politely helped them through a checkpoint just inside some double oak doors. The entrance was dim and slightly damp. There was an airport-style metal detector, and an X-ray machine for the bags.

No Browning pistols to be discovered on this visit, so they were through and following their two escorts up wide ancient stairs to a first-floor landing that was covered in what looked to Delaney like Persian carpet. Tapestries lined the walls. Yet another man in a Vatican-issue dark-blue suit rose from behind a tiny table to greet them. They would find that Monsignor Fiorentino was the first of their hosts to be in clerical robes.

Fiorentino came down the wide hallway after a few minutes. He was in a very black, very priestly cassock, with purple sash and purple skullcap. He was also wearing what looked suspiciously like a pair of Gucci loafers, but the long robe allowed just glimpses. He appeared to be in his late fifties. He was of medium height, but was clearly vigorous, with broad shoulders, leathery skin, and a very pronounced hook in his nose. It could have been broken years ago, or maybe it was just an unfortunate family trait; Delaney wasn't sure.

Fiorentino's eyes and teeth, however, were his most striking features. The eyes were grey. Not blue-grey or blue, but pearl grey, and a little too reptilian for comfort. He had a row of tiny prehistoric teeth, quite yellow, which he bared occasionally, not so much in a smile but as a display to any other predators in the immediate area. Delaney could see that he was a survivor: of Catholic Church bureaucracies, of Vatican *realpolitik,* of God knows what intrigues that had made him Prefect of the Pontifical Household for a Polish Pope.

"Thank-you, thank-you. Welcome, thank-you for coming," Fiorentino said. His English was Italian-accented but excellent. "Signora Janovski, Signore Delaney, welcome. Please. Come inside."

He ushered them into a cramped but elegant office just off the hallway. His small desk was something antique dealers in any major city would kill for, as were the fixtures and bookshelves and assorted other Vatican trappings. The effect was spoiled by the three too-large Italian telephones on his desk, with wires trailing down into too-large wall plugs. An assistant materialized with a tray of coffee and some plates of hard sugary biscuits. Fiorentino was Italian enough to fail to ask them if they drank coffee. The door was closed. Their host watched intently as they fiddled briefly with tiny cups and spoons. An intricate gilded clock ticked steadily on a sideboard. But not much time was wasted after that.

"Your government tells us that you are involved in some matters that are of interest to us," Fiorentino said. "A fascinating story, apparently, concerning the war and the country where His Holiness was born. You as a journalist, Signore Delaney. And you, Signora Janovski, because of a family connection."

Fiorentino looked at Natalia and waited for her to reply. But she had the faraway look in her eyes that Delaney now knew came when she had been listening to two conversations at once — one outer, the other inner.

"That's right," Natalia said. She looked over at Delaney.

Fiorentino could not miss this conspirator's glance. He now looked at Delaney and waited for a reply from him.

"I'm surprised, Monsignor Fiorentino," Delaney said, "that my country is taking such a keen interest in our activities."

He very much doubted Fiorentino's version of who had first told what to whom.

"Your work is well known in Canada, Mr. Delaney," Fiorentino said. "And elsewhere. Signora Janovski's, I'm afraid, somewhat less so."

"I'm also surprised that my government would go to the trouble of informing other governments what a Canadian journalist or another Canadian citizen are doing with their time," Delaney said. "Some other governments might do that, perhaps. But not ours. Not usually."

Fiorentino looked closely at Delaney, seeking signs.

"Oh, we all do little services for each other from time to time, as you know," he said. "That is what governments are supposed to do. Little services for their people, and, from time to time, for other governments. I am sure you would be familiar with all of that. I have had a look at your list of publications, Mr. Delaney. You are no stranger to international diplomacy."

International games-playing, Delaney thought.

"I take it this matter is quite important to you, Monsignor Fiorentino," Delaney said, "or you would not have flown us down here for this little conversation."

"Quite important to some of us here, yes. To me personally, perhaps not. But then we have had to put our personal interests aside, many of us here, as you can imagine. Could you do that for us as well, Signore Delaney, do you think? Signora Janovski?"

The reptilian teeth were bared briefly.

"That depends," Delaney said. "Why would we have to do that in this case?"

"You do not have to do anything, Mr. Delaney. We were simply wondering, many of us here, and people at the highest possible levels, if you understand my implication, if in the course of your investigation of what I am told is a fascinating story you may not have come across some information or some items that may be of interest to us here in the Vatican."

"What story do you think I'm working on, Monsignor Fiorentino?" Delaney asked.

"You surprise me, a little, Mr. Delaney. I was led to expect I would not have to play such games with you in our discussions. That you are experienced enough and intelligent enough to spare us this to-and-fro."

The rows of teeth.

"Well, Monsignor Fiorentino, how would this be?" Delaney said. "Why don't you ask me directly what you want to know and we will see, Ms. Janovski and I, if we can help you. How would that be?"

Delaney suspected Fiorentino was a man who was accustomed to posing very direct questions, but only among his own people. For outsiders, questions would usually be indirect.

Natalia sat quietly watching them both. She showed no sign of wanting to do anything other than observe the interaction at this point.

"In fact, Monsignor Fiorentino," Delaney continued, "I may have some questions for you of my own."

"This was not intended to be an interview, Mr. Delaney."

"Interviewing is to be from your side only, is that correct?"

"If you agree," Fiorentino said.

"I don't know what I'm willing to agree to yet," Delaney said. "What would you like to know?"

Fiorentino was clearly not happy with this situation. He would not want to show his hand; Delaney had no doubt about that. He would not be accustomed to having people throw questions his way. Few senior Catholic clerics were, in Delaney's experience. And certainly not in the Vatican *Curia*.

"Let me put this to you another way, Mr. Delaney," Fiorentino said after a pause. "Would you consider, if you come across information or items that may be of interest to us here in the Vatican, letting us know what you have discovered and giving us the opportunity to help you decide how these things are to be used?"

"How would we know what is of interest to you and what is not?"

"I think, Mr. Delaney, that in this case it will be obvious."

"I am not in the habit of having my activities as a journalist or what I make public approved by anyone," Delaney said.

"Except your editors, of course," Fiorentino said.

"Yes."

"Perhaps we should have a word with them on this."

"If you like," Delaney said.

Fiorentino was becoming less and less amused.

"Do you have a clear idea, Mr. Delaney," Fiorentino said, "how complex the European political situation is at the present moment?"

"I think I do," Delaney said. "Yes."

"The Catholic Church has always taken a keen interest in the political, how shall we say, proclivities of its people, as you no doubt already know. We continue to do this even as Europe and the world change daily before us. It seems to us that the article you are working on, if it is to be an article at all, could have ramifications for us here and for Catholics elsewhere. It could also have an effect on the outcomes of the political process in countries in which we take a very serious interest."

"Like Poland," Delaney said.

"Obviously. Like Poland."

"You flatter me, Monsignor," Delaney said, "if you are concerned that my work can affect politics in Poland."

"It is not so much that we are concerned your work can have an effect, Mr. Delaney. We would simply like to be able to gauge what those effects might be before they are allowed to manifest themselves. It is an old technique in the Vatican, which has served us well over the centuries. Intelligence-gathering, it is called these days. And, of course, we have always liked to be able retrieve any of our lost properties, if they have been scattered around the globe for one reason or another."

"I am not in the habit of influencing European politics, Monsignor, or any other politics," Delaney said. "Not intentionally, in any case."

"Are you sure of that, Mr. Delaney? Have you never taken sides?"

"No." Delaney was no longer sure that was true.

"Then you have been one of the lucky ones. Perhaps, though, Canada is one of the few places where people like yourself can say that and actually be telling the truth."

"Why would you assume that even if I were the type of journalist to take sides it would be your side, Monsignor Fiorentino?" Delaney asked.

"I did not suggest that you take our side in particular, Mr. Delaney. I suggested that you simply help us to get to some information that would be of interest to us."

"Is that not taking a side?"

"Not necessarily," Fiorentino said. "It could possibly be as simple as giving no side any advantage whatsoever."

"That would be assuming I might provide information, or, as you say, property, to some other side as well."

"Providing it to another side, yes, possibly. Or risking having it taken from you."

"By which side?"

"By any side, actually, Signore Delaney."

That was as much of a warning or a threat as a Vatican bureaucrat would ever be likely to make, Delaney knew. But Fiorentino was apparently tired of this conversational tack now. He abruptly turned his attention to Natalia.

"You are very silent, Signora Janovski," he said.

"I sometimes learn a great deal about things just by listening," she said.

"You may well learn things, but perhaps you do not share what you already know," Fiorentino said.

Natalia simply looked at him steadily without replying.

She uses silences like a professional, Delaney thought. It was now his turn to watch.

"Are you a Catholic, Signora?" Fiorentino asked.

"When I was a child I was sent to Catholic Church and Catholic schools, Monsignor," Natalia said. "Does that make me a Catholic?"

"I think you would know precisely what it means to be a Catholic, Signora Janovski. You are possibly being influenced by your journalist friend here. Did you always answer questions with questions?"

"In my work it's sometimes useful," she said.

"I wonder what your answer would be if I asked directly whether you would be willing to help us?" Fiorentino said.

"I'm afraid you haven't made it clear to me either exactly what you want," Natalia said.

"Do you consider yourself Polish, or Canadian, Signora Janovski?" Fiorentino asked.

"A difficult question," she said.

"Not so difficult. Do you care what happens in Poland now?"

"I suppose I do, yes."

"You suppose. That is a luxury. Do you think your father and your uncle would have had such a luxury, Signora Janovski? Of merely supposing that they cared?" Fiorentino was showing his hand a little now. "Or other Poles of their generation who fought and died for what they thought was just?"

Delaney worried about this low blow, but Natalia was not as fragile as he expected.

"You seem to know a little about my family, Monsignor," she said.

"What we need to know," Fiorentino said. "What it may be useful to know. But is that how you are going to answer my question, Signora Janovski?"

"Shall I apologize for having been born in Canada, Monsignor Fiorentino, or for having been lucky enough to have escaped the horrors of war?" Natalia asked.

"Do you feel no duty at all to Poland or to your

family?" Fiorentino asked. "Are we all just to be atoms floating around in a cold universe without duties or certainties?"

"That's a question not many of us have been able to settle," Natalia said.

"For some of us it is settled," Fiorentino said.

"How lucky for you," Natalia said.

Fiorentino paused for a moment, considering moves.

"I would like you both to give some serious thought to what I am asking of you," he said finally. "You do not have to answer today. At the very least we would like you to keep these matters in mind as you proceed. Because you are treading on what one would have to call quite dangerous ground."

Fiorentino let that sink in for a moment. He looked closely at Natalia, and then at Delaney. Apparently, the interview was coming to an end.

Fiorentino then asked Natalia suddenly: "Would you like to meet our Polish Pope, my dear?"

Natalia looked dumbfounded.

"And possibly you, too, Signore Delaney?" Fiorentino asked.

Delaney looked incredulously over at Natalia, willing to follow her lead on this.

"I never thought I would get the opportunity," she said, looking back over at Delaney.

"His Holiness as you know takes a keen interest in the events of his former country, his home country," Fiorentino said.

"That would be understating it somewhat,

would it not?" Delaney said.

He could not let this one go by. But he thought it might be unwise to raise the delicate matter of the Pope indulging his interest in Polish affairs to the extent of receiving regular briefings over the years from senior American officials on the situation in Poland. William Casey, for example, the former CIA director, who used to have cozy chats with His Holiness while they examined spy satellite photos of the home country. In exchange for the latest intelligence from the Pope's army of East Bloc priests. It was an open secret, in some circles, that the Pope had received advance word of the Soviet troop build-up that led to the declaration of martial law in Poland in 1981.

Fiorentino decided, apparently, to ignore Delaney's remark.

"We have informed His Holiness that you could possibly be of some assistance to us," he said. "I think he would see you for a very short time."

Fiorentino would probably never have had anyone ever refuse such an offer, so he picked up one of the telephone receivers and spoke for a moment in Italian. He put the receiver down again.

"His Holiness has been working in his private apartment on some papers this afternoon. He could see you in a few minutes' time, but only very briefly. We told him that you would be here today at about this time and he expressed an interest in an audience with you. Would you come this way with me? Yes?"

Fiorentino brought them to a drawing room far down a tapestried hallway. A Swiss guard stood outside the door. They sat on a couple of embroidered divans, drinking still more coffee that was brought in. They were suddenly like two schoolchildren on an unexpected excursion together. The high stakes were forgotten for the moment.

After about twenty minutes, Fiorentino returned with some assistants.

"His Holiness can see you for a very few minutes," he said.

They walked together down another long hallway and into a dim anteroom. It appeared that the room fully enclosed another smaller room and that any one of the tall panelled doors on any side would let them into the inner one. Various assistants and retainers sat or stood near them as they waited.

Monsignor Fiorentino picked up a telephone and spoke briefly into it in Italian. He then knocked quietly on one of the panels and let himself in. Delaney caught a glimpse of high, glass-fronted bookcases and more exquisite carpet and furniture. Then Fiorentino returned, saying quietly: "Come in now, please. Women are to curtsy. Men bow."

The Pope was standing beside his small desk. This one too had several telephones on it. He had apparently been writing letters. Paper and a fountain pen sat on a leather blotter. He was dressed in buff-coloured robes and a buff skullcap. He wore a pair of old-fashioned black buckle shoes and what looked to Delaney like linen leggings. His face was much redder than in the official photographs. Natalia curtsied. Delaney bowed.

"Welcome," the Pope said in English. He passed his hands over both of them in the ancient symbol of Christian blessing and made the sign of the cross. "Welcome."

He turned immediately to Natalia.

"You are a Catholic, I am told," he said.

"Yes," she said.

"And Polish."

"My parents were."

"Very good," he said, turning to Delaney. "And you are a Catholic, as well?"

"No. I'm afraid not," Delaney said.

"But you are both, I am told, going to be of some assistance to us on a matter of importance."

This to Natalia.

"Possibly," she said. "If we are able."

"Thank-you," the Pope said. "I thank you. It is a complicated matter, I am told."

"Yes," Natalia said.

"For too long in Poland ours was the Church of Silence," he said.

"Yes," Natalia said.

"It must not be such a church again," he said.

"No," Natalia said.

"I have been to your country, Canada," the Pope said. "I have said Mass for your Indians. In the outdoors."

"Yes," Natalia said. "That was lovely."

"Now a long time ago."

"Yes."

The Pope stood silently for a moment. Fiorentino gave a sign, and a grim-faced photographer with severely slicked-down hair came in carrying a Hasselblad and took two quick shots of them standing together. There was another blessing, some smiles all around, a little more polite conversation, and then they were ushered out. In the anteroom another assistant came up to them with a tray covered in small pouches.

"Choose one," the man said.

"What are these?" Delaney asked.

"These are rosaries, blessed by His Holiness. Choose one."

They each selected a small leather pouch. Fiorentino brought them back into the hallway where still other assistants stood and waited.

"That is how it usually is," he said. "Not long and not much said."

"That was fine," Natalia said.

"You have been blessed by the Pope," Fiorentino said. "Both of you. May it help you in your work. May it help you make the correct decisions about what is to be done."

"Perhaps it will," Delaney said.

He and Fiorentino eyed each other warily. It was no longer the time for *realpolitik*. That was before, and, Delaney suspected, for the future. He thought, as Fiorentino took them as far as the staircase, of all the generations of Fiorentinos and Wozniaks and Hilfertys and Stoufflets and others like them who had been in the anterooms of power over the centuries, and how many more were to come. He wondered how much, or how little, their masters would ever know of the deadly serious games played out on their behalf.

Chapter 12

The Vatican car let them off at their hotel just after 7 p.m. that evening. Tourists were milling around at the top of the Spanish Steps, and the local restaurants were gearing up for a busy night. There were no messages from Hilferty or anyone else. The desk clerk said that no one by the name of Hilferty had checked in. Delaney wondered when the Canadians would come back into play.

They couldn't agree at first on a next move. Natalia wanted to go straight back to Montreal and find the cache. Delaney was for staying on at least another day or two in Rome to see who might make a move and where that might lead them. There was no question in either of their minds, however, about cooperating with the Vatican on this. Delaney thought it likely that Monsignor Fiorentino would decide to call them in once again. The Papal Prefect had asked them how long they intended to stay in Rome, and he had not yet gotten the answers he was seeking from them that afternoon. Delaney felt that another encounter with him could provide them with more information.

In the end, they decided to stay for an extra day

at least, if only to rest a little before what they now knew could be an intense time back in Quebec.

At dinner they were almost able to forget why they had come to Rome or to Paris and play at being tourists, if not yet lovers. Natalia was wearing one of her soft black wool tops. A short rest and a bath had left her looking refreshed and more relaxed than Delaney had seen her since before Paris. Thoughts of Zbigniew, and other worries, had apparently faded a little. Delaney was beginning to sincerely want now, here, to be the right time between them at last.

"A papal blessing seems to do you good," Delaney said.

They were in a trattoria not far from the hotel. It had bright white walls and honey-stained wooden window frames, door panels, and shelves. The house wine was good enough for them and they had already had several small glasses each. An excellent pasta entree had come and gone. Now they were waiting for their Veal Milanese, in one of the long pauses between courses that makes eating in Italy so civilized. Natalia snapped bread sticks and munched them absently.

"They're hoping a little blessing will change our lives," she said. "For Catholics I guess it could."

For some reason she had brought her little rosary pouch in her purse to the restaurant and she pulled it out now so they could look at the contents. Delaney had already looked at his in the privacy of his room. Something his Irish-Catholic mother would have liked very much, he thought, before tossing it into his equipment bag next to the Browning. A good luck charm. Now two good luck charms in the bag.

The rosary Natalia had picked was just like his — semi-precious stones with an ornate cross at the end. Nothing extraordinary. Except that it had been blessed by the Pope.

"Our good luck charms," she said, looking up. The waxy candle burning in the terra-cotta holder on their table made her eyes shine. "From the Church of Silence. You must carry yours."

"It's in my bag. Don't worry."

"We will need some good luck charms, won't we?"

"Yes."

"Against the political bad ones or the church bad ones?"

"There isn't much difference anymore, Natalia. There never really was where the Catholic Church was concerned. And especially where Poland is concerned nowadays."

"I just can't get my mind around a pope looking at spy photos and scheming overthrows with politicians," she said. Delaney had told her a bit more about John Paul II's espionage hobby.

"He would never admit to anything like scheming overthrows, Natalia. From where he sits he's just watching over his flock, even if it is by satellite these days. He apparently told someone once, Ronald Reagan I think it was, that he'd really had nothing to do with the fall of Communism in Europe. He said the tree was already rotten and all he did was give it a little shake once in a while. Eventually, the bad apples fell off."

"Do you think it was them?"

"Who?"

"The Vatican. Who killed my uncle."

"I think it was probably the Polish side," Delaney said. "One of the Polish sides. God knows."

"Maybe God knows," she said. "Maybe."

Natalia looked around the restaurant for a moment, choosing words.

"Are you sorry you got involved in this with me, Francis?" she asked. For a second, her eyes clouded again.

"No," he said. He didn't want to get pulled in to this line of talk. "No, not at all."

"Really?"

"Yes, really. We'll be fine, Natalia. If we keep our wits about us, we'll be fine. We just have to stay a jump ahead of everyone, that's all. And we are certainly going to have to be very clear what we want to do with this stuff when we find it. We're probably not going to have much time to decide after we do."

"I think I'll be able to decide that only after I see what it is we're looking for, Francis. I'll have to try to imagine what my uncle would want me to do."

"Fair enough."

They ate hungrily. The food was excellent and the waiter beamed at them throughout. The wine warmed them; the restaurant warmed them. Delaney began to feel the slow rush of awareness that there would very likely be further warmth later that night, a woman's touch. *She knows this too,* he thought. He liked that thought. There was no need for idle talk between them, so there was none. He liked that very much as well. They simply sat, after the meal, stirring small cups of coffee and being intensely, exactly, where they were.

Delaney held Natalia's arm as they walked up the narrow cobblestone street toward the hotel. The evening was warm, quiet. Most everyone else, apparently, was now at home or in restaurants, eating. They took no notice at first of the tiny Suzuki van that came toward them from further up the slight incline. But when the driver flashed on the bright lights and blinded them, and when Delaney heard the motor suddenly revving very fast and very near, he knew they had let their guard down much too far. His mind leapt to the gun sitting useless in his hotel room.

It was all over in an instant. The side of the van brushed hard against his right shoulder, spinning him around so that he dropped Natalia's arm, and it almost knocked them both down. It screeched to a stop and two men in leather jackets jumped out of the side door. Delaney never got a clear look at their faces. One had a moustache, he thought later. But they both had guns, large handguns. One of them smashed Delaney across the side of the face with his and he went down, hard. The blood in his left eye blinded him slightly as he tried to get back up. Natalia had already been taken; bundled into the back of the van without a sound out of her. Delaney felt a mighty kick to his chest and as he went down again there was another kick to his ribs and it was done. The van roared off in a haze of blue oil smoke down the street and out of sight.

It was suddenly very quiet again. It took a minute, not much more, for Delaney to pull himself together enough to stand up. Running after the van was useless, and impossible anyway with the intense pain in his ribs. Shouting after the van was useless. It was gone and Natalia with it.

When the very fat, very red-faced driver of an old Fiat stopped perhaps another sixty seconds later to ask him in Italian if he was all right, Delaney had recovered enough to nod his head: Yes, yes, all right, I'm all right. Two or three other people had come out of a small restaurant to see what the screeching of tires had been about and they watched as the Fiat driver helped Delaney sit on the hood of another parked car. Hit and run, hit and run, they all said in Italian. Call the police.

"No," Delaney said. "No. *Ça va.*" He knew little Italian and hoped someone spoke French. "It's all right." He tried English, and someone in the small crowd that had now gathered was able to understand him.

No one, it seemed, had seen Natalia being taken away. That was good. Delaney wanted no police for the moment. Probably not at all.

"It's fine, I'm fine. A car just knocked me down. I'm fine," he said. Someone gave him a starched white napkin and he dabbed at his eyebrow where he had been first hit. "I'm fine. There is no use calling the police."

Everyone looked astonished. In Rome, everything is reason to call the police, to make a report, to complain loudly about an outrage of one sort or another. But this foreigner did not want one, so who was to say? Delaney saw a waiter from the trattoria where he and Natalia had eaten now hurrying up the street toward them, curious about the small crowd gathering. He wanted very much to get away before anyone asked him where his dinner companion had gone.

"I'm all right now. *Grazie, grazie.* I'm fine," he kept saying.

The business of fending off these Samaritans allowed him the small luxury of not being overwhelmed by the fact that Natalia had been abducted and was in absolutely mortal danger. Those thoughts would crowd in shortly.

Still dabbing at his eyebrow with the napkin, Delaney thanked everyone profusely once again and began to hobble with as much dignity as he could manage up the street toward the hotel. They all watched him go. He walked slowly, stiff and sore already from the body blows. But his mind raced.

No police, not for this. Hilferty not in sight, and possibly sidelined on this turf anyway. Fiorentino? Would he organize something like this? Or move so quickly against them? Nothing was clear, except the pain in his body and his intense anxiety about Natalia. The only small reassuring thought that came was that the two men in the van could have killed both Natalia and himself if they had that in mind.

They took Natalia away so they wanted her alive, at least for a time, Delaney said over and over to himself. *And they didn't kill me, so they must want both of us alive, at least for a time.*

He decided he would clean himself up before going past any desk clerks at the hotel, so he went into a tiny coffee bar, a dim one, ordered an espresso and asked for the men's toilet. The waiter stared at him and then shrugged and pointed to the back. The few other patrons didn't seem to notice what he looked like, or they didn't care.

The image in the mirror was not good. The Canadian journalist who stared back at him over the grimy sink had seen better days. There was a large gash over his eye and scrapes on the cheek below. His jacket was torn, and the knees of his pants. He opened his shirt and saw a large bruise already beginning to form over his swollen side. The water from the taps helped revive him a little and he dried himself as best he could. He had no comb and tidied his hair with his fingers. "Fuck," he said to himself.

He barely tasted the coffee. He ordered himself a double brandy and drank it down, and then a second scalding espresso. The waiter asked him no questions, but the mirror behind the bar showed him looking worse, not better. His eye was beginning to swell up badly. He hoped it would not squeeze the lid shut so he could not see well. He was going to need to see things very clearly indeed.

He was only in the café for a few minutes. At the hotel, the desk clerks rushed out from behind their counter when he walked in, saying solicitous things. Whatever could have happened, whatever could have happened, Signore Delaney? Do you need a doctor, a policeman, what do you need? He managed to fend all of them off, and finally found himself in his room, where he simply lay on his bed in his filthy, torn clothes.

He breathed slowly in and out: trying to calm himself, trying to calm himself, trying to calm himself. The room was blessedly dark. The light from a street lamp outside was more than he wanted. As expected, some very unwelcome thoughts crowded into his mind. And panic lurked in the shadows.

He tried to organize his thinking as he had in difficult, dangerous situations before. But in those situations, the direct danger was to himself and any moves he made had been for himself. This time, he was worried about the danger to someone else. Who had taken her? Who, if anyone, to call? How to play this? How much time did he have?

He got up suddenly and dialled the number at the Vatican, which Fiorentino had given him, but he didn't know as he dialled if he wanted to speak to Fiorentino at all, even on the remote chance the Monsignor would be around at this late hour. There was a taped message in incomprehensible Italian. Delaney hung up. He looked in his wallet for the mobile phone number Hilferty had given him in Paris and dialled it even though he once again wasn't sure what he would say if someone answered. But another recorded message said the phone was turned off or out of range. *What could Hilferty do anyway?* Delaney thought bitterly.

When the throbbing in his head became too much, he fumbled around in his bag for some aspirin. The swelling had stopped building over his eye, but it would take days to go back down fully. He doubted very much that a rib was broken, but he was not about to have it checked out anyway. He was on a tight deadline, and his assignment was to find Natalia before things got unspeakably ugly. In a city he knew only slightly and where he hardly knew friend from foe.

The brandy had been a very bad idea. It made him sleepy and clouded his thinking. He lay down again to rest a little and gather his thoughts once more. But the brandy and the aspirin and the pain made it hard to keep his eyes open. He fought the impulse to do anything other than rest on the bed awake. Despite his best efforts, though, he slept.

It was 2:30 in the morning when he woke up, cursing his weakness. He got up stiffly, his ribs aching unbelievably, and splashed water on his face. For some reason he expected the phone to ring. He expected it to be Hilferty, with news of some sort, with a wise remark and a sign that all was well, or word that Natalia had already been found. But the phone stayed silent. This was going to be Delaney's problem to solve alone.

He absolutely ruled out calling the police. They would be no better able than he to trace a generic delivery van in this city, and he did not want to spend hours in some overbright police station at this stage in any case. He knew he had to take action but found he could not, despite all his years of experience in dangerous places and breaking situations, think of what to do next.

"If they had wanted to kill us, they would have done it right there," he said aloud again and again as he paced the room. "If they had wanted to kill just me and not her, they could have done that too. So they want us both alive. For a while."

He knew that this was possibly even worse. He knew that this meant they wanted to ask Natalia questions, and if they were Polish agents they would know how to get answers. If they were indeed Polish agents. He did not allow himself to think that the Vatican would use such tactics or that they would move so fast against them even if they did, but he knew that this was not impossible. Nothing was impossible. Every foul, ugly, dangerous thing was suddenly very possible. His imagination was threatening to run wild. The anxiety was as intense as any he had ever felt. The panic stirred in the shadows. It came close, very close, again.

Delaney began to realize, however, that he

simply had no choice in this. He would simply have to wait, for how long no one could say, until there was a sign. If they killed her, they would come for him as well, soon enough. If she was alive, they would still likely come for him because they would want to know how much he knew. Or to negotiate some deal. So he reluctantly admitted to himself that he would have to endure the agony of a wait. In Canada, when you are lost in the woods, they tell you to stay put until someone comes for you.

He repeated his calming mantra: "If they had wanted to kill us, they would have done it right there. If they had wanted to kill just me and not her, they could have done that too. So they want us both alive. They want us both alive."

The door between his room and Natalia's was not locked. He walked into the quiet, woman-smelling dimness. Natalia's bottle of mineral water was on her night table. Her small suitcase was loosely closed on its stand at the end of the too-large bed. On the desk he saw her Commonplace book. He could not resist the temptation of opening it and looking inside. He would not read it. He would just look inside.

The pages were covered with neat handwriting and dated entries, but also with arrows, diagrams, small sketches, symbols. On some pages were more elaborate sketches done in what looked like coloured pencil. Geometric patterns, mainly, or what looked like stars and planets: dreamscapes. He saw his name in a couple of entries. It leapt out at him as one's own name often does in unfamiliar texts. But this made him slam the book shut, ashamed at violating Natalia's little psychic sanctuary. He would let her tell him herself why his name was in there. He would not steal such knowledge from her. Not now.

For Natalia, at first it was like a dream. But then it became very undreamlike as she became aware of what was happening and why. The men had been incredibly rough with her. She was thrown headlong into the back of the grimy van and she hit her head on the metal hump of the left-rear tire well. As she tried to get up, the side door slid shut with a terrific bang and she fell again as the van lurched off with a squeal of tires on the cobblestones. She was stunned by the two falls and dizzy, and simply lay for a moment on the rocking floor of the van as it careened around streets she could not see and would not recognize anyway. It smelled intensely of motor oil and tire rubber and grime.

Eventually she sat up. She could see two men in the small seats up front, talking intently to each other in Polish. One was gesturing to the driver, giving him directions. They were both smoking strong cigarettes. When the van had slowed a little and the driver was apparently clear on where he was going, the mustachioed navigator looked back and spoke to her in Polish.

"Not dead? Good." He pushed the driver's shoulder and they both laughed throatily at this witty remark.

They were almost a matched pair: identical black leather jackets; similar badly cut thick black hair, with a sheen of oils or hair creams; large rings on fingers, garish gold watches. In their thirties, both of them. Both muscular, aggressive, and dangerous. The walrus moustache on one of the faces was the only thing that really set them apart.

"Your boyfriend is probably not dead either, lucky for him," the moustache said. "I'm sure he is tougher than that. He can take a little beating now and again, can't he?"

The two men laughed again.

Anxiety release, Natalia thought.

She decided she would not speak to them at all or answer any of their inane questions. She sat bracing herself on the floor of the van, holding onto the tire wells to remain upright as the vehicle swayed. She could not identify exactly what feelings she had. She was afraid, but not truly afraid, not panicked yet. Shaken, aching, waiting to see what came next. Then she might become truly afraid. She sat staring at the floor of the van, wondering if Francis was all right and what he might do next. The odd sense began to develop that somehow she had experienced all of this before, perhaps in a dream. She allowed that feeling to envelop her, to see what intuition or insight it might provide in this crisis. But no insight came.

The van roared and rattled its way through Rome streets for about twenty minutes, according to Natalia's watch, which she could only just read in the dimness. As she was beginning to feel chilled and very sore, the van slowed and pulled into a sort of covered archway. She could see only parts of the scene outside through the windshield. But the sound changed and it was clear they were now in the courtyard of a tall building, an apartment possibly. Only a small light burned somewhere.

They did not blindfold her or make any attempt to stop her from seeing where she was. It could have been the interior courtyard in any large and run-down apartment building almost anywhere in Europe. It was late. Clearly, not many people would be around to see her get out, and if they did they would see nothing mysterious. Two men and a woman climbing out of a small vehicle in a European city. Still, her captors warned her against making a scene.

"Now we go upstairs, correct? We go upstairs like we are friends, correct?" Moustache said, switching to English for some reason. "No silly, OK?"

"OK," she said.

The driver came around to open the sliding door. He grinned toothily at her as she moved to get out. Her pants and sweater were askew and dirty, but not torn. She could not see her handbag at first, but then Moustache reached in and pulled it out from a dim corner of the van. She must have held onto it instinctively, as women do. *The rosary is inside,* she thought. Good luck charm.

"We look later, yes?" Moustache said as he slung the bag on his shoulder. "Dirty secrets maybe?" More laughter.

There were steep stairs; a series of flights went up around a dark square stairwell. The staircase was wide and worn. They stopped climbing on the fifth floor, all of them panting from the ascent. On this floor, as on the others, there were two sets of double doors. Two apartments, or possibly two small lofts or warehouse spaces on each floor. The driver fumbled with keys and then pushed her, unnecessarily rough, through the doorway into an old shabbily furnished apartment. Plates and empty beer bottles sat on tables. Newspapers were strewn around the place. She saw two handguns and a long gun, what she thought might be a shotgun, sitting on an armchair. Moustache decided this was where she must be, so he moved the guns and motioned for her to sit.

"Sit, OK? Be quiet."

Driver locked the doors and put his own gun down beside the others. Moustache took off his leather jacket. Natalia saw he was wearing a shoulder holster with another gun. Still she did not feel truly afraid. This surprised her. Her captors moved into another room and had a conference in Polish there for a moment. Then Driver dialled a number on the telephone in the main room and said to someone, in Polish: "It's done."

He hung up. Both men lit cigarettes and grinned foolishly at her.

"Welcome to our humble home," Moustache said, his shoulders rising and falling slightly with laughter. Still apparently unable to resist his own wit. "Our humble little home."

Natalia sat quietly, saying nothing.

"Do you know us?" he asked, suddenly serious.

"What do you mean? How would I know you?" Natalia said.

"Do you know us, woman? You know where we are from?"

"Poland," she said, now becoming a little more afraid. *They will try to trip me up, and then be aggressive with me when I make mistakes*, she thought. *They are this type*.

"Of course, Poland. Of course. We do not have to be psychiatrists to know this when Polish words are spoken, do we?" Moustache said. Driver smoked quietly, squinting at her.

"No," Natalia said.

"Do you know us?"

"You mean who you work for?"

"Yes, yes. Who we work for."

"No."

"We think you must, dear woman. Who?"

"I don't know."

"Who?"

"The Polish government? The secret service?"

The men both howled with laughter.

"The secret service? What a clever name. We are

secrets from the secret service." Laughter, coughing through smoke.

"Here is who we are, dear woman," Moustache said. "Not who we work for, but who we are. Who we work for is not so important to you tonight. You see? We are your enemies. That's all. We need to know something that you know, and we will know it. It doesn't matter to you who we work for because you will tell us anyway. And then maybe you can go home. Maybe."

Moustache spoke very quietly to Driver in Polish so that Natalia couldn't hear. Driver nodded and left the room. They were starting to frighten her badly now.

"Are you in secret service too, dear woman?" Moustache asked her, as he lit another cigarette.

"No, I'm not."

"We know that. We know that. Do you think we would not know that already?"

Natalia said nothing.

"I have just asked you something," he said.

"I don't know what you would know about me," she said.

"You don't."

"No."

"You are sure?"

"Yes."

"About what?"

"What do you mean?"

"What are you sure about?"

Natalia realized the aggression would come

soon. With a personality like this there could be very few correct answers.

"I don't know what you mean," she said.

"You don't."

"No. I'm sorry."

He liked that. He liked women to be sorry, Natalia suspected. Her apology was like a small treat thrown to a dog. He enjoyed it privately for a moment. Then he called out to his partner: "Feliks!"

Moustache grinned at her as Feliks came down the long hallway from another room.

"We must have a witness, correct? Feliks likes to witness these things."

Again there was a low whispered conversation in Polish.

"We will start this right away, because we do not have time to frig around, like Americans say," Moustache said.

Feliks moved his head and shoulders around in small circles, as if his muscles were stiff. Moustache walked over to where Natalia sat in the overstuffed old armchair and pushed his knees up against hers as he stood over her.

"There is something we would like to know, dear woman, and you will tell us about it tonight. Then, after you have told us, your boyfriend will come here and we will get him to tell us too. Then we will see which story we like best."

Now Natalia was afraid.

"In our business of work, we have to find out many little things, always little things people know and do not wish to tell. It happens so often. I am good at this work. Feliks too, but I am better. Correct, Feliks?"

Feliks nodded, but said nothing.

"Why am I better than Feliks at this work, dear woman? Why?"

"I couldn't say." Natalia wanted now to be very careful in her phrasing of anything, as one must be when dealing with psychotic personalities.

"Why couldn't you say, dear woman? Why wouldn't you say?"

"I don't know why you are better."

"Here is why I am better. It is exactly because Feliks asks people questions and then, after a while, he hurts them and asks them some more and then eventually they tell him. But I myself like to make clear to people first what it is that is happening, and then they cannot be unclear. You see? Make things clear first, and then ask questions next, after that? You see?"

"Yes."

"No you do not, I think."

"It's clear to me," Natalia said.

"No. I think it is not. Because you are one of those people who has never had to do very much that you did not want to do. Have you?"

"No."

"No what?"

"No, I have never had to do very much that I didn't want to do. You're right."

Moustache looked over at Feliks and said: "I am right."

Then, with a large open right hand, he slapped Natalia with great force on the side of her face. His blow came from shoulder height and smashed diagonally down across her cheek. It swung her face to one side with more force than she had ever had applied to her body. It shook her neck vertebrae, made her ears ring, her skin burn. Her body started to shake with fear and pain.

Then Moustache slapped her again, from the other direction, with the back of the same hand. Shoulder height again, with great force. He made a small indescribable sound in his throat as he hit her. His knuckles and ring grazed her left check, and her neck was badly jarred again.

She began to cry immediately. She held her hands up over both of her eyes, sobbing, and dripping tears and mucus and blood from her eyes and nose and mouth. Her heart raced in her chest, and her stomach muscles were in spasm. She hoped they wouldn't do this very long. She hoped they wouldn't rape her. Now she was truly afraid. As required.

Through the ringing in her ears, amidst the other alarms of her body now, she heard Feliks say something in Polish. Then she could hear Moustache as if from a great distance: "Do you understand now what I was trying to say, dear woman? How this will work tonight?"

"Yes," she said through her hands, looking down.

She felt the texture of her eyebrows against her fingertips. This, inexplicably, was a small comfort.

"I understand," she said.

Chapter 13

Delaney had somehow managed to contain his intense anxiety about Natalia, to put it away somewhere deep inside himself. He had decided that he owed her this calm because direct and well-considered action in the world was urgently required. The best plan now, he had decided, was to make himself as conspicuous as possible. And to search, with all the skills he had acquired over the years, for the inconspicuous.

He had not slept again after waking at 2:30 a.m. He spent the remainder of the night examining the situation from every possible angle — over and over again. And in his insomnia, against his will, he also examined in minute detail his whole life to date and all the various mistakes and missteps he had made. Mistakes professional, social, and personal. Mistakes with colleagues, lovers, and wives. But he was determined that from this moment onward he would make no more mistakes. By sunrise, he knew what he must do.

He showered as best he could with his stiff side and cleaned up his scraped face. He applied creams and ointments to the most noticeable of the wounds. He put on jeans, a loose-fitting polo shirt, and some sturdy shoes. He checked the pistol in his equipment bag and then placed his aging Nikon F camera beside it, with a long lens attached. Notebook and pen. Passport and press pass. Rosary. Tools of the trade. For now, he would simply be on assignment. He had no choice.

In the lobby he told various desk clerks and the concierge and just about anyone else who would listen that he would be around the hotel that day, doing some work and waiting for delivery of an important message or package. Could they all please see to it that he was informed as soon as anyone asked for him, as soon as anything arrived?

It was still early, before 8 a.m. He paraded himself through the lobby several times and through the small dining room. He stood for a long time on the sidewalk in front of the hotel, allowing anyone watching to have a clear view of the Canadian journalist staying there. He sat for almost an hour at a sidewalk table of the café next to the hotel, drinking several cups of coffee and standing occasionally to stretch his legs and allow hotel watchers to have an unimpeded view. *Here I am.*

The watchers, if they were there at all, did not come forward. Delaney expected word from Hilferty at any moment, and became more and more concerned when it did not come. Was it possible, he wondered, that CSIS was so slow off the mark, so poorly connected, so badly informed that they would not now know what was going on? Or were they simply content to hang back and watch him watching for others?

By midmorning, Delaney was back in the lobby, explaining to patient desk clerks that he would have to go off for perhaps two hours, that he would be back at lunchtime, that messages or letters or packages were to be expected and were to be treated with care. He would be back. *Si, Signore Delaney, si.*

Now he would be the one to watch for a time, rather than allowing himself to be watched. He went outside to hail a taxi and told the driver to move off in the direction of the Colosseum. He sat half turned around to see if any cars pulled out behind him in the narrow street. None appeared to do so. *If they want me, they know where to find me already,* he thought.

After about ten minutes he had the driver circle back to the bottom of the Spanish Steps and let him off there. Still no one seemed to be behind him. To the left of the steps there was an elegant tall apartment block with entrances both at the lower level and at the top of the steps where they met the Via Sistina, the street where his hotel was. He wanted to spend some time on the roof of that apartment, watching the Via Sistina below and the entrance to his hotel.

The building's concierge, he discovered, was a Mr. Viviano, a very dark, very wiry little Sicilian who was apparently surprised by nothing in this life. His English was New York or Detroit style.

"I am a journalist and a photographer, Mr. Viviano," Delaney said, showing his red International Federation of Journalists passbook.

Viviano peered at it with interest through half-frame glasses. At midmorning he was well dressed in flannel trousers, a quality shirt in wide blue-and-white stripes, and soft leather loafers, perhaps Gucci. "I want to possibly take some pictures from the roof of this lovely building if that is no trouble to you."

Viviano peered up at Delaney over the top of his half-frames.

"Hey, but of course," he said.

Delaney marvelled at how different the Italians were from the French, or at least the Romans from the Parisians. In Paris, none of this would be possible. Everything would be impossibly complicated and viewed with suspicion, if not outright disdain.

Viviano led him to an ornate elevator door and pressed the button for him.

"Top floor. You will see the door marked so clearly with 'Exit' you do not need me to come," Viviano said. "I am busy feeding my birds, and they are hungry this morning. You come to me when you are all finished up. No problem."

"Thank-you," Delaney said as the steel-mesh door slid noisily shut.

Viviano peered at him through the mesh as he glided up and out of sight. *He will be up to check things out in a while*, Delaney thought.

The roof gave a splendid view of Rome on a brilliant late-winter morning. Delaney did not allow himself to think for very long how much Natalia would enjoy this view. He positioned himself at the corner of the roof, Nikon at the ready, but more for Viviano's benefit than to use the long lens for viewing. Then he simply watched as intently as he knew how. He was a reporter on the job. What was there to report?

The café where he had spent an hour that morning was quiet. Only a few tourists sat at the outside tables. Most of the locals were now at work. A hotel employee was sweeping the sidewalk out front, stopping whenever necessary to watch Italian women sidle by. A couple of Fiat cabs sat at the curb. The two drivers sat together in the first car, smoking and exchanging views. Another cab sat behind the first two. Its driver was not in the mood for talk, apparently.

Across the street, some upmarket clothing shops were opening. A stunning brunette in a red-and-white pantsuit that would have cost her several months' salary, if she owned it at all, was unfurling a canvas awning over the entrance and fixing the doors wide open for the very few customers who would likely come through that day. The balconies in the several buildings facing the hotel were empty, except for a Burmese cat that was stretching out on one. Above the hotel entrance, curtains billowed out of windows and a chambermaid shook a pillow in the brightness.

All appeared perfectly normal. It was a normal midmorning on Via Sistina. But Delaney had watched streets before and knew that the unusual did not always make itself known right away. Patterns take some time to be established, or disrupted.

It took almost an hour. There had been little action of any sort in front of the hotel. But then the first taxi in the line of three parked there got a fare: two men in dark business suits, carrying mobile phones and canvas laptop-computer bags. Delaney thought he remembered them from the breakfast room that morning. The second driver ended his conversation with the first man, got out of the car, and moved his own car up into position when the first car left.

The driver of what had been the third car in line did not move up. He continued to read his paper. Then another taxi pulled up. It was the one Delaney himself had taken that morning. The driver honked at Number Three to move up so he could take his place in the line. But Number Three motioned for him to park in front, which the new arrival managed to do with only some difficulty in the narrow street.

Not very concerned about a fare.

But then Number Three, still third in line after so generously letting his colleague in, got out of the car and leaned over the driver's side of the car now in front of him, suddenly craving conversation. Cigarettes were lit. The new arrival got out to lean against his car and chat to the Good Samaritan. Delaney was now sure the new arrival was the young man who had driven him around to the bottom of the Spanish Steps.

A cluster of what looked like American tourists suddenly poured out of the hotel, perhaps nine or ten in all. There were some negotiations with the two first drivers and then with the third. That one shook his head repeatedly. More negotiations. Then, most of the tourists got into the first two cars, and the final small group hailed a cab passing by on the street. Driver Three got back into his car and resumed reading his newspapers. Another car arrived and its driver, too, was waved ahead to take the better spot.

That new arrival got a fare and moved off. Still Driver Three did not start his engine or move forward. When he refused yet another fare, Delaney knew he had his man. Or one of them. Which side he was playing cab driver for, Delaney could not say.

As he was turning to go, he saw Mr. Viviano standing at the exit to the roof, watching him quietly. He had a look of grave disappointment on his face.

"No photos today, *signore?*" Viviano said.

"No. Just looking at the view."

"It is a lovely one, no?"

"It is."

"Something of particular interest for you today, maybe."

"Yes." Delaney sensed Viviano had been around. He did not struggle for explanations.

"Perhaps you have had long enough on this lovely roof of mine, *signore.*"

"I think so. Yes. Thank-you."

"I think so too." Viviano silently escorted him down in the elevator, and saw him right out to the sidewalk. He then ostentatiously unhooked the white security door that had been opened for the air and sunshine, and shut it firmly.

"I will not see you again will I, *signore?* Not here, OK?" Viviano said evenly through the iron grille.

"No. I am finished here now."

"*Bene.*"

There were no messages, no letters, and no packages when Delaney got back. He had climbed the Spanish Steps and walked back to the main entrance of the hotel along Via Sistina. His side and his head ached. The reluctant taxi driver was still there, reading the news, and missing out on fares. He looked up as Delaney walked by, and then down again at his paper.

Delaney came back onto the street after checking with the clerks at the front desk. He sat down at one of the sidewalk tables at the café next to the hotel. He sat facing the cabstand, daring Driver Three to make eye contact, watching the driver's now all-too-obvious failure to do any work that morning. After about thirty minutes, the driver was alone in the rank with his engine still off. Delaney paid for his coffee and walked quickly over, climbing in to the back seat.

"Can you take a fare?" Delaney asked in English. The driver looked coolly at him back over the seat, not at all perturbed. *A professional,* Delaney thought.

"No," the driver said in accented English. "Not at this moment."

"Why not?"

There was slight menace in the driver's eyes now.

"Not at this moment, *signore*. There will be another taxi along soon."

Delaney had the Browning out of his equipment bag now, and he held it low in his lap. The driver looked calmly down at it and then out at the passersby and the doorman on the sidewalk.

"That is not so smart I think now, Signore Delaney," the driver said.

"Go," Delaney said.

The driver started the engine and drove slowly down Via Sistina. The street ended not far past the upper entrance of the apartment where Delaney had kept watch that morning. The driver made a difficult U-turn and began driving slowly the other way. The doorman at the hotel did not look up as they passed.

"We are going where?" the driver said.

"You tell me," Delaney said. "Where do you think I might be wanting to go this morning?"

"I don't know."

"I think you do."

Delaney resisted the impulse to stick the gun up against the driver's head. A rage was building as he thought that this might be one of those responsible for taking Natalia. It was a dangerous deep-seated rage and could bubble over at any time. He was no stranger to rages of various sorts in his life but they were a long time coming. Few and blessedly far between. He generally had been able to save his rage for the right targets, but not always. He thought he might have such a target now.

"I don't know what you mean," the driver said.

"Pull over here. Now."

Delaney's hand was beginning to shake ever so slightly. It was not fear. The adrenalin was interfering. He would have to watch that. For the rest of this assignment.

The driver pulled over. They were on another of Rome's million narrow cobblestone streets. Tall balconied apartments lined it. Few people passed.

"Take me to her," Delaney said.

"To who?"

"I am not going to waste time with you, friend."

"What will you do?" the driver said, very cool. He was about thirty; stocky, with badly pockmarked skin. He wore the most fashionable of pale tortoiseshell sunglasses.

He has been in situations like this before, Delaney thought.

"I think what I might do is wound you badly, so that you bleed all over this lovely leather in here but not so badly that you can't drive to your people and tell them the Canadian is very, very pissed off and wants to see the young lady. Or I could kill you."

"Then you would never see her."

"Oh, I will see her all right."

"Signore Delaney, I am guessing that you are not professional enough at this to kill me. You are a journalist, an amateur. You should leave these matters to others."

Delaney thought he could hear echoes of Hilferty in the phrasing. But he thought: *Not CSIS. Vatican.*

"Which others?"

"Others with your best interests at heart. You would be smarter to do what you were doing this morning. Sometimes it is better to watch and wait. We were impressed by that."

"How did you know about Natalia?"

"We are good watchers too. You watch them, we watch you."

The driver reached for a package of cigarettes on the seat beside him and pushed in the lighter in the dashboard.

"Where is she?" Delaney asked.

"We don't know that."

"And I'm supposed to believe this?"

"You have no real choice, *signore*. I either truly don't know or I won't tell you. I very much doubt that you would kill me for that."

"I will kill you if I have to," Delaney said.

"I doubt you would kill me here, now. But if you did you are no further ahead in this thing."

Delaney wanted no part of logic today. He wanted action, results, maybe even revenge. Not logic.

"Well, here's the message," he said. "You tell the people you are working for that the Canadian guy is now very, very pissed off and wants to see the girl. Today. You tell them that he has a lot to say about Quebec and Poland and the Catholic Church, but he won't say it until he sees the girl. You tell them that. And if they aren't the ones who have her, you tell them they'd better find out where she is and tell me as soon as they do. Because if she dies I have some information that will make everybody in this game very, very uncomfortable and I know exactly how to use it. You understand. I will see that girl today."

"This is a big city to find one person, Signore Delaney."

"I will see her today. Or tomorrow there are no more little secrets. You understand? Now take me back to the hotel and then you go pass this message on to whoever you're working for."

The driver tossed his cigarette out the window and drove slowly back to Via Sistina. Delaney put the gun back in the bag, got out, and watched as the cab moved off. His hand was no longer shaking. He was past that now.

There was a message waiting for him this time when he went back into the lobby. On Vatican stationery; handwritten once again. The clerk told him it had arrived just minutes after he had gone off in the taxi. Delaney could not imagine that it was connected, so soon, to his excursion in the cab. It was from Fiorentino: "Greetings, Signor Delaney. Perhaps you might get in contact with me today to say what you have decided in the regard of our conversation yesterday. We would value your assistance in these matters and could possibly be as you know of assistance to you."

Ambiguous. Delaney decided an equally ambiguous reply was in order.

At a small desk in the lobby he wrote, on hotel stationery: "Monsignor Fiorentino, I am sorry to say I will be unable to speak to you today about the matters you mention in your note to me this morning. Signora Janovski is indisposed. When all is well with her I would be happy to come in to see you, and may have some useful information for you at that time. But, of course, I could not do that until I am sure Signora Janovski is well." The desk clerk seemed impressed when Delaney told him where the courier was to take the note.

Delaney went up to his room and rested on the bed for a while, the back of his right hand over his throbbing forehead, willing the telephone to ring, knowing it would ring eventually. Even so, he was badly startled when it did ring about an hour later. He was dozing in the warmth of the Roman afternoon. The voice at the other end was gruff. He could hear heavy traffic noise in the background. Screeching tires and clattering motorbikes.

"Delaney, you listen now," the voice said in English. Polish accent or some other East European. "OK? You listen now."

"All right."

"We want to see you. About the girl. And about these other things you know about."

"Is she all right?"

"You will see that."

"When?"

"In one hour. You make sure to be alone, no one after you, OK? OK? You come to the Terminal Station, the big train station. You know where?"

"Yes."

"Walk inside. Only you. Walk in, walk around, in an hour from now. Go into the crowds to the back, and then come out the front again. OK? Through a different door. At the front again. Watch for us there."

"How will I know you?"

"Just watch for us there."

The line went dead. Delaney looked at his watch. One hour. He now had a lot to do and not much time.

He quickly packed his bag and then Natalia's bag and placed them together in his room. He checked the gun again, sighted along its short barrel, hefted it, knowing he might need it soon. Placed it carefully back in his equipment bag. Zipped that shut.

He went down to the desk and told the clerk that he and Ms. Janovski would be checking out immediately and would be leaving their bags in the storage room for a few hours. He paid the bills and then went to the public telephone near the entrance. He dialled the number of another hotel he knew well, down the Spanish Steps, not far away, and reserved a room for that night, possibly for several nights. Then he had a quiet word with a bellboy in a foolish quasi-military uniform and pillbox hat with chinstrap. New York, circa 1929. The boy's English was good.

"I need a service from you today," Delaney said, pulling out a thick bundle of lire. "But discreetly, discreetly. You understand?"

"*Si*." The bellboy eyed the bundle of notes.

"I have checked out. My bill is paid," Delaney said. He nodded over to the desk clerk, who grinned and waved at them. "I am leaving my bags here for a few hours. Here is what you can do for me. It is very important."

He peeled off about fifty dollars' worth of lire. The bellboy's eyes shone.

"In an hour, perhaps two, when it's quiet here, I want you to go outside and put my bags in a taxi and get in with them and bring them to the Hotel de la Ville, just down at the bottom of the steps. You tell no one else but the people at that hotel whose bags they are and you leave them in the storeroom down there for me. You tell them I'm coming soon. You do it fast and get back here right away. You tell no one here what you've done. When I get to that hotel later today, if you've done it right, I'll give you the same amount again. I'll send it to you. But only if it has been done right."

"I will do it right," the boy said.

"I hope so," Delaney said. "It's very important. You see?"

"Yes, I can see," the bellboy said, looking conspiratorially around the lobby. "Do you not like our hotel, *signore?*"

There was no sign outside of the agent who had

been playing taxi driver that morning. He would have been replaced. Delaney loitered for a moment out front and then hurried over to the Spanish Steps and moved down as fast as his sore side would allow him. Cars could not follow on the stairs and anyone in an apartment or on a roof could not get down to the street and then down the stairs fast enough to follow him. At the bottom he hailed a cab and told the driver to hurry off.

"Vatican," he said.

No one seemed to follow them. About halfway there, Delaney got the driver to stop, paid him, and got out on a busy street. He hailed another cab going in the opposite direction.

"Terminal Station," he said this time.

Still no one seemed to be with him. It seemed too easy.

Time was short and the traffic was heavy. Delaney arrived about five minutes late, and hurried into the mammoth, echoing train station, worried he had missed his contact. He rushed to the back, through the crowds, and out onto the street again. About ten minutes later than he had been expected. Lines of taxis were ranged at the curb. Cars, trucks, and motorbikes roared this way and that. Travellers piled out of taxis with bags, baskets, boxes, pets. He recognized no one.

Then he saw the Suzuki van rolling up fast. It stopped directly in front of him. The cargo door was braced open.

"In. In. Get in," the driver shouted.

He was one of the two who had taken Natalia, Delaney could see that immediately as he got in. The man was sweating, nervous. He roared off so fast that Delaney was sent flying to the back of the van, onto the floor. As the van careened through the traffic around the station, the driver shouted: "Close door, close door, close door."

Delaney managed to slide the cargo door shut with difficulty. He sat on the wheel hump at the back. The tiny van moved with astonishing speed through the traffic with the driver looking out often into his side mirrors to see who might be with them. His driving would be a hard act to follow. Delaney had no doubt they would lose anyone who might be behind them, but he doubted very much anyone was there in any case.

Eventually, the driver slowed down.

"Sit on floor," he said, without looking back.

This made it difficult to see where they were going. Delaney did as he was told.

After about fifteen minutes the van slowed and then pulled through what looked like an archway and into a courtyard of a decaying apartment block. The driver sat for a moment with the motor off.

"You have a gun?" he asked, looking in the rear-view mirror at Delaney.

"No," Delaney said.

"We think you do. Give your gun now."

"I don't have a gun."

"My friend up there, he has your girl," the driver said. "She says you have a gun. If he hears a problem now, he will kill her right away. You see? So you give your gun now."

"I don't have a gun."

Delaney could see the driver reaching into his leather jacket, so he pulled out the Browning fast and kneeled upright on the floor of the van.

"If you touch that pocket I'll kill you right now," he said.

"If my friend hears a gun, your girl is dead," the driver said.

"And you too. Do you want to die right now?" Delaney said.

"You are stupid, man. Your girl is up there with my friend."

Delaney slid open the cargo door.

"Out," he said. "On the passenger side."

The driver climbed over the passenger seat and got out to stand in the shaft of sunlight that was burning down into the damp courtyard. He looked up but appeared to make no sign. Delaney was pointing the gun at him through the wide opening in the side of the van.

"What's your name?" Delaney asked.

"Feliks," the driver said.

"How many up there?"

"One. And me."

"Who do you work for?"

"Ourselves."

"Come on. Who."

"Poland."

"Obviously. Who in Poland?"

"Ourselves."

"Look, let's not fuck around," Delaney said. "Who in Poland do you work for? Walesa?"

Feliks laughed.

"He works for himself too. In Poland, everyone works for himself now. Like America."

"You UOP?"

"What if I said yes? What if I said no? What if I said Walesa? How do you then know what is right, what is not right? You people from the West make us laugh. I told you who we work for. Ourselves. Ourselves."

Delaney realized that it didn't really matter anymore, that this young man before him was in fact correct. Everyone was working for themselves, when all was said and done.

"OK," Delaney said, "we walk in together now, with no fuss. You understand? Then we go up. I take the girl out and it's all over. I have nothing more that's worth asking you. I won't be calling the police. It can be over today."

The driver said nothing. He simply stood with his arms at the ready by his sides. He looked up again briefly to the windows above.

"Go in," Delaney said, climbing out of the van through the cargo door.

They went in to the damp dark entrance way.

"OK, Feliks, now the jacket comes off," Delaney said.

Feliks took off the jacket and held it loosely.

"On the ground," Delaney said.

The jacket dropped with a heavy thud. Delaney kicked it and the gun in it under the stairwell.

"Up."

They climbed slowly, with Delaney far enough back to avoid a kick or another sudden move. When they got to the fifth floor, Delaney made them wait. He caught his breath. He listened. He looked at the door opposite the one where Feliks had stopped. It had a small brass plate that said "Ravena Trading." The door they would go through had nothing on it, not even a number.

"OK, here's how it works," Delaney said. "You open the door and you walk straight in, fast. I'll be with you. I will kill anybody who tries to get in my way. Right? I take the girl out; we're gone; it's over. Give me your car keys."

"They are in my jacket," Feliks said.

Fuck, Delaney thought. But he was not afraid. Not at all afraid. The rage was not far off, however.

"Pat your pockets," Delaney said.

"What?"

"Pat your pockets, pat them. I want to hear what's there."

Feliks patted his pockets. Delaney thought he could hear no keys or change.

"OK. We go in. You could be dead in a minute if you fuck up. Just go straight in."

Feliks opened the door. It had not been locked. He walked through and Delaney gave him a mighty kick to the back, which sent him reeling into the centre of the room. Feliks stumbled over a chair and fell.

Delaney saw Natalia sitting in an armchair looking very bad. Her face was pale, puffy, scraped, bruised. Her hair was damp and uncombed. She looked up and raised her hand weakly in his direction when she saw him. She looked very bad indeed. His rage came.

Then it all moved very quickly. But it was easier than Delaney had imagined it would be. Moustache saw his partner stumble through. He looked, alarmed, toward the door and saw Delaney coming in behind, bracing his gun with both hands. Moustache moved to the table where handguns lay and Delaney shot him, once, twice, three times in the centre of his chest.

Moustache fell very heavily backwards, hands grasping at ruby wounds. He made no sound as he died. He bled large amounts of bright shiny blood but made no sound. Feliks looked more surprised than afraid.

"Good," Natalia said weakly, crying now, shoulders shaking, face in her hands. "Good, good, good."

The rage was bad now. Too bad to talk to Natalia. Delaney felt no fear, no uncertainty, and no remorse. All was clear; all as clear as anything could ever be.

He went over to where Feliks lay, and pushed the barrel of the Browning up under his chin. He pushed it hard, harder than he had to, as hard as he possibly could.

"Did you hurt this woman? Did you hurt this woman?"

"No. Not me."

"I'm going to kill you for hurting this woman," Delaney said. "Do you hear me?"

"It was him. Not me."

Delaney hit him hard on the side of the face with the gun. Blood flowed. He stood up straight, panting a little now as Feliks nursed his cut face. The Browning hung by Delaney's side as he gathered his breath. He felt a dangerous exhilaration.

He backed away from Feliks a little and spoke to Natalia.

"Did they hurt you badly, Natalia?"

"Yes," she said. Her sobs were pathetic, a child's. "They put my head in the water."

Delaney suddenly understood everything: why people do things to each other and for each other, why they seek things, why they kill each other. He stood calming himself, resting on his feet, looking at Natalia crumpled in the too-large armchair. He understood now what it was to be connected, implicated, fully engaged. He did not have anything to ask anymore, did not care who worked for whom, did not want to know who this man was sitting near his feet, bleeding from the face. He just wanted to see him dead. And he wanted to take Natalia away from there and live quietly ever after.

Delaney gave no warning. He simply fired three shots, just as he had before, and Feliks never looked up. Two shots to the upper chest, one off-target slightly, near the shoulder. Feliks collapsed backward, hard, onto the floor and died.

"Good," said Natalia through her hands "That's good, Francis. That's good."

Delaney went to her and held her. Her head shook against his stomach and she cried for a long time while he stood over her. He said nothing, simply let her cry, holding the back of her head, pressing her against him.

"Good," she said again, muffled now.

Delaney felt nothing except certainty, complete certainty. His heart beat steadily in his chest. After the shots, the old apartment was silent. The Roman sunlight cast itself in dust-dancing shafts onto the worn wooden floor.

They had been given a lovely dark old room with a giant old bed and big hotel pillows. The bed was only for sleeping in, for the moment. They rested on that bed for three days, not going out at all. Natalia slept under piles of covers for most of the time. Delaney kept the drapes almost entirely drawn. He lay often on the bed beside her, holding her, stroking her hair, helping her feel safe again. He helped rub ointment onto her cuts and scrapes. He gave her glasses of water and cups of tea. They had room-service meals. Sometimes they watched TV. No one seemed to know where they were at all.

Chapter 14

They went to Como, in the north, far from Rome, to rest some more and regroup and learn how to be lovers. Delaney had not been there for a very long time. Too long, he realized as the taxi brought them in from the small train station and he saw the shimmering water of the broad blue lake and the ferries plying this way and that. The last time he had been here was soon after his marriage ended, he remembered. He was travelling alone and had felt the intense isolation of those who travel alone in places meant for lovers.

He was not alone this time. Natalia was beside him in the taxi. She was starting to look much better. She seemed to have enjoyed the train ride in from Milan, and had even had a little wine with the meal on the flight to Milan from Rome. The swelling in her face was gone. All that remained, externally, of her ordeal were some scrapes and scratches, healing quickly. They had not talked too much about all of that yet, not more than they had had to. That would come soon enough.

Natalia's only concern as they left Rome was that they not be followed, that they be allowed to continue their vacation for a little longer. Delaney had made sure of it: booking the flight from a payphone, not bothering with a hotel reservation in Como at that time of the year. He organized a private car and driver to take them to the Rome airport, so they simply had to hurry from lobby to car to terminal to plane, and they were away. He would be very surprised indeed if anyone could find them now.

They checked into the Barchetta Excelsior Hotel, which looked over the Piazza Cavour to the lake. It was almost too beautiful, with old stone staircases and balustrades outside, gravelled terraces and iron tables here and there, and willing waiters to bring drinks, lunch, anything anyone wanted. Their room overlooked the lake. The hardwood floors were spotless; the upholstered armchairs and sofas were spotless and intensely white. The huge four-poster bed — light-coloured wood with crisp white linen — dominated the room but did not intimidate. They belonged in that bed together now and they felt no unease, none.

Natalia cried when she saw the perfect room and the perfect view and the perfect way the curtains billowed in through the wide-open windows and balcony doors. She was still crying too easily but Delaney knew this would pass when she came fully out of shock. That was not far off now, he could see that. She was almost better again.

They went back out immediately and walked along the edge of the lake with the tourists. Then they took a little ride in one of the boats. The Milanese bourgeoisie and their children always seemed to be in Como in force. Troops of them, with fresh, lovely, expensive vacation clothes and nothing but time on their hands, it seemed. Not a care. Delaney saw that nothing much had changed, that people still smiled elegantly to one another on boats, that drivers and boatmen still wore proper driver and boatman caps and coats, that the biggest worry here was still a missed ferry or a missed lunch.

It was still daylight when they made love for the first time. They had come back from their excursion, and the room was warm from the sunlight that had shone in all afternoon. Natalia closed the doors and windows to seal in that warmth against the cool of the evening. They had not bothered to unpack after checking in. Their bags were just where the bellman had left them at the end of the bed. They looked silently at each other in the still of the room and knew that at last the time was right.

They lay talking for a long time afterward in the heavy starched sheets. They had lain together before, in Rome, as Natalia rested for those first few hidden days, but not like this. That was a sickbed; the lying together then was for comfort, for safety, for warmth. This new bed was a lovers' bed and the lying together now was for many other reasons, not all of them clear. But Delaney, enjoying the utter softness of Natalia's black hair as she rested her head on his chest, and the utter softness of her back and shoulder under his encircling arm, for once did not seek too much for reasons.

"Are we falling in love with each other?" she asked, unable, for her part, to resist the urge to question.

"Yes," he said.

"Is that a good thing?"

"Yes."

"Would that be a predictable thing, in our current situation?"

"Possibly."

"Is that a bad thing?"

"No," he said. He could feel the movement of her cheek and mouth on his chest as she smiled, and he knew she was laughing at herself playing psychologist.

"Even in light of our previous professional relationship?" she asked.

"Such as it was," he said. She smiled on his chest again.

"It's something you'd better take up with your therapist," Delaney said. "Do you know any good ones?"

"I used to," she said.

"Where is she now?"

"I'm not sure. On vacation somewhere. Italy, I think."

"Is she a Jungian?" he asked.

"Of course. I would have nothing to do with anyone else."

"And what would Dr. Jung say about our situation, do you think?"

"Oh, he would probably say that I'm projecting

my animus complex onto the nearest possible male figure after a period of intense anxiety."

"Are you?"

"Possibly."

"Is that a bad thing?"

"Not necessarily. Not in all cases," she said, pulling her head back to look up at him. "Not in this case."

"Correct," he said.

They lay together some more in the gathering dark, unwilling to get up.

"Francis?" she said after a long time.

"Yes?"

"Thank-you for killing those men for me."

"You're welcome."

"No. Don't play. It's such an obvious anxiety reliever. I know that you must feel, I don't know, somehow caught by what you did back there. It's something you'll never be able to leave behind and I'm sorry you had to do it. But I'm not sorry they're dead. They deserved to die. I'm not afraid to confront that feeling. The Shadow archetype."

"I've already left it behind."

"I would doubt that, Francis."

"I have. I have absolutely no feeling about those guys at all. They're dead. I killed them. They deserved to die. They were hurting you and would have hurt me. If I didn't kill them, they would probably have killed us. It doesn't get much simpler than that."

"Denial. It's a normal reaction."

"I don't think so, Natalia."

"You'll see," she said. "Later maybe. In your dreams."

"I don't think so," he said. "But what about you? What about the psychologist who is glad to see people killed?"

"I was not glad to see them killed. I'm glad they're dead."

"Denial."

"Possibly."

They pondered all of this for a while.

"Have you done something like that before, Francis?" she asked.

"No. I'm a journalist."

"Are you?"

"Yes."

"You seem to know how these things are done."

"I've seen things like that done, Natalia. From a distance. I've been around a bit on assignments. You know that. I'm no spy."

"Until now."

"Correct. But now strictly an amateur spy."

"And the gun?"

"Hilferty."

"Hilferty," she said.

"Yes. He thought I might need it one day."

"A reporter needs a gun."

"Sometimes."

"Why would you not tell me that?" she asked.

"What good would it have done for you to know? It was supposed to be just for insurance anyway."

"And spies give reporters guns."

"Sometimes."

They shared the silence as she considered this.

"Remind me why we are doing this, Francis," Natalia said suddenly. "Would you do that for me?"

"Why we are doing this or why I am doing this?"

"Both."

"I'm doing this because you asked me to help. That was at first, anyway. Now I'm doing this because I'm doing this. Because I'm in the middle of it and because it seems like the thing I should be doing. That's good enough for me now. And because of you now, too."

He felt her smile on his chest at this last item on the list.

"I won't ask you again if you're sorry you got involved," she said.

"Thank-you."

"And why am I doing this?" she asked. "Would you mind?"

"Because your uncle was killed, because you loved the old guy, because he would have asked you to help him, because you need to know why he died, because you're angry that someone killed him over this. All pretty good reasons, I think."

"Thank-you," she said.

"You're welcome. I should charge money for this."

"Yes. You seem to have a flair for it."

"Thank-you."

"And so we are to finish it, Dr. Delaney? In your

professional opinion?" she asked.

"Yes. We are. In a while."

Eating in Como is always a great pleasure, but especially when the nights are still cool. There are dozens of warm dark places with wood-fired ovens and good wine cellars that sell baked pizzas, baked fish, baked suppers for those on brief vacations. For a few days they ate too much and drank too much red wine from small pitchers and walked arm-in-arm too much. They made love too much and slept too much and, after those first few days, began to talk again too much about what was still to be done.

Natalia was stronger than Delaney would have ever expected, if he had ever been expected to imagine how she would hold up against two burly agents slapping her and punching her and pulling her hair and holding her head under water in baths. She had told them a little, she said, as little as she could, and she had made up a little. She couldn't recall some of what she had said when it got very bad and couldn't now say whether they might have had a chance to tell anyone else before they died.

She had told them that Delaney had agreed to help her, that they had visited people to ask them things, that they had looked at letters, yes. But she had made things up about what was in the letters — some parts she had been able to make up and other parts they had made her tell — but she did not think they had been able to gather too much.

They had shown her some bits of burned letters

they had managed to find in Paris, but they were small bits and she was reasonably sure they could not piece any clear story together from them. She had told them there was something hidden in Quebec, that she didn't know what it was or where it was, and they had seemed at that point willing to wait until after Delaney's turn before starting to hurt her again. Delaney had been right: they would have interrogated him too if he hadn't killed them first.

But Natalia had not, she said proudly, told them the password. She had made one up.

"You haven't told me the password either," Delaney said as they sat one morning on a bench near the main ferry dock. "Or where you think the things are hidden."

"I know that."

"Why is that?"

"At first it was because I was afraid to trust anyone fully with what I knew," she said. "And then, almost right away after that, it was because I was worried that if you knew too you might be in more danger than you already were."

"And now? Do I get to know now?"

Natalia waited a moment.

"No," she said. "Because I don't want to put you in any more danger than you are now."

"People would kill me too, Natalia, even if they thought I didn't know."

"Maybe not."

"You're wrong about that, Natalia. That's not

how these things work. Or not this one, anyway. Not anymore."

"It's not that I don't trust you, Francis," she said. "It's also that this is my task now, my secret. And my uncle's."

"All right. That's all fine. But I will need to know eventually."

"But then it will be OK. Don't you see? Because by then we will be almost there. I'm sorry. I know it's irrational."

"It is that."

Delaney in some ways, however, didn't care at all. He was willing simply to go wherever this now led and didn't need to know ahead of time anymore what that might mean.

"What password did you tell them it was?" he asked.

"Holy Virgin of Czestochowa."

"Lovely. That should have done the trick."

"It did. It made them stop. And it was a good one for my uncle, too, a long time ago. So that's twice that password's worked, isn't it?"

"I suppose. In a way. I hope the next one works as well."

Natalia said it was perfectly natural that they would be having such intense dreams at night. They shared some of them, but not all, over breakfast in the mornings. Two psyches in collision, she said. And some anxiety release.

In his dream Delaney sees himself or an image of himself on a pocked and pitted brick wall somewhere in the world. It is larger than life; a prehistoric glyph, a cave painting, a secret sign. He sees a large perfectly circular hole or an image of a hole where his stomach and other digestive organs should be. He sees instead of food some small mysterious figurines and talismans and knives and forks and spoons absurdly jumbled into this cavity. Then the circular cavity moves up higher, to where his heart and lungs should be. These organs have been surgically removed. All that remains is a large, perfectly circular emptiness.

When they were not dreaming, they slept soundly; entwined.

Natalia dreams of blackness, the idea or archetype of blackness. She cannot find the right name for it. She struggles to name it but no words come. It does not require a name. It is simply there. The black mist hovers over Lake Como and drifts toward the hotel. Then it is over Lake Zurich, then Lac-Saint-Louis in Montreal. She is sitting on the old wide balcony on the second floor of the convent in Lachine. She is a nun, a veiled sister, rocking on a rocking chair in the chill air, looking out over the lake at the black mist. She sees figures walking on the ice, across the frozen lake. She is watching them and walking with them all at the same time. The mist is very thick and about to block out the scene completely. She is rocking, rocking, rocking. She dreams this over and over again.

Delaney indulged in a bit of cloak-and-dagger eventually, the minimum possible under the circumstances. He sent a fax to Brian O'Keefe in Montreal, after typing it out carefully on an ancient Underwood in the hotel manager's office. He watched as the fax machine slowly pulled the page in and pushed it out again. He thought of O'Keefe in Montreal, standing in his muddy boots in the old farmhouse kitchen, clearing a space for the incoming fax on the cluttered counter where his machine sat, and then reading it.

The hotel manager, the elegantly rotund Mr. Salvatore, whose bulging striped waistcoat told the story of one too many excellent Como dinners, said proudly as they watched the fax machine primly hum and buzz: "Panasonic very good. Olivetti no good. You see?"

The telephone in their room had not rung often in the days they were there. Hotel staff called with news of this and that; reservations made or unmade; responses to requests. But when it rang on the Thursday afternoon of their stay, Delaney had a sense this was to be the last of the vacation calls.

"It is telephone for you from Rome, Signore Delaney," the operator said. "*Momento.*"

The connection was clear.

"Hi, Francis," Hilferty said. "How's your love life?"

Delaney could imagine Hilferty's proud grin at the other end, as he stood in an overpriced hotel room somewhere, or in a Vatican office perhaps, proud that some textbook detective work had allowed him this small victory.

Delaney looked over to where Natalia lounged happily in a large wicker chair on the balcony. She was playing with her papal rosary as if it were a set of worry beads.

"I suppose," Delaney said to Hilferty, "that if I asked you how you found us you would make some appropriately modest secret agent sounds and pretend it was nothing much at all — all in a day's work, etcetera, etcetera."

"You got it," Hilferty said. "It was nothing much at all, really. All in a day's work. Etcetera."

"I see," Delaney said.

"Nothing the combined forces of goodness and light from various Western democracies, or near democracies, or near-Western democracies, as the case may be, and Interpol and a few other bands of stout-hearted men couldn't handle. So good of the European hoteliers to insist on recording people's passport numbers at check-in, don't you think? Even if they do take their own sweet time sending them over to the local police."

"This will look good on a résumé, I would think," Delaney said.

"Oh yes," Hilferty said. "A little well-deserved boost for a sagging career. Couldn't come at a better time. You've made my superiors in Ottawa sit up and take notice of little Johnnie Hilferty, I can tell you. Thanks for all your help in making me look so good lately, by the way, Francis. But at least they haven't taken away my gold Amex card yet. As of this afternoon, anyway."

"Don't mention it, John."

"That will be the last time. I promise."

"Something I can do for you, John?" Delaney said.

"Oh, just checking in. You know. To see how you're getting on. I must say, that's a nice little place you've chosen up there, Francis. Nice place for it. Romantic. A bit upmarket for you, I would have thought, but there you go. They tell me you've been eating rather well. Liking the local cuisine, are we? *Da Angela's* I think it was last night."

"Now you're showing off, John."

"Well, it's my turn, don't you think? After your little display down here? Hmm? Three shots each, all pretty well on the mark, from point blank range? That left a wee bit of a mess for us to take care of at this end, Francis. And no one to question, really. Dead men don't tell. But we were all mightily impressed. I said all along that you were a natural. You see what a little time on the target range can do for a man. And aren't those Brownings a lovely little item? Hammer nails all day with them and they're still right on the money every time you fire. Wouldn't your pals in the National Press Club be proud?"

"And wouldn't your pals in Ottawa have been proud if you had let a couple of Canadian citizens abroad know they were in grave danger of being kidnapped and interrogated by a couple of Polish thugs?" Delaney said.

He knew anger would not be useful anymore, but the anger surfaced anyway.

"That was a fuck-up, Francis. Out of my hands."

"So you'll forgive me for taking the situation into my hands then," Delaney said.

"You did that all right."

"So what was it? The Vatican says jump and the Dominion of Canada says how high? The Vatican says sit back and watch and shut up, and that's what you do?"

"Something like that. Not my operation, at that point."

"Was this ever your operation, John?"

"Fuck you, Francis."

"You know, a paranoid type might wonder just who those Polish guys were actually working for," Delaney said. "What country, that is. We have already concluded that it's impossible to follow the Warsaw game without a program. But what about the Vatican game? They been recruiting abroad, or what? Among like-minded Poles, for example?"

"That would be a trifle paranoid, Francis, yes."

"So that's a denial."

"That's a no comment. You know these East European types. They all look alike to me."

"That's not how Natalia sees it. She would be able to tell you exactly what they looked like and what they did."

"They give her a very bad time?"

"Yes, they did."

"She OK?"

"Probably," Delaney said. "She'll survive."

Natalia was looking over at him now as he talked too long on the telephone.

"She tell them anything?" Hilferty asked.

Delaney wondered if it might be more useful for Hilferty to think that the other side, or one of the various sides, now knew more than they probably did. He couldn't decide.

"As little as she could," he said. "Considering the circumstances."

"I see," Hilferty said. "Shall I put you down for a no comment, then?"

"John, I really think you owe it to us to tell us who they were working for," Delaney said, tiring as quickly of Hilferty as he usually did. "And who else is floating around."

"You're really expecting that we will share anything at all with you at this stage?"

"I was hoping you might."

"I am no stranger myself to dashed hopes on this operation, Francis. But try not to be too disappointed. I'm sorry your sweetheart had a rough time. You'll forgive me, though, if I don't reach for a hankie when I think about your predicament. As you decided that freelancing was your thing."

"I'm not in a predicament, John," Delaney said. "Not anymore."

"Oh yes you are, my friend."

"Really?"

"Oh yes," Hilferty said. "Here's how we see it from our end anyway. You are sitting in a top-class hotel in lovely Lake Como, with two notches on your gun, my gun — still, I might add, and nowhere to go but home. They tell me you and the young lady have been thick as thieves over your fish suppers, so my well-honed powers of deduction say you're going to make a move sooner or later for whatever it is you think you're looking for. But we will be on you, all over you, don't you see, just as I told you back in Paris. Except for this slightly embarrassing little hiatus. Which is now over."

No matter how hard he tried, Hilferty could never sound convincing when he tried for subtle menace.

"I guess my line now is something like 'Well, I wouldn't be too sure about that, Hilferty,'" Delaney said.

"That would be a good line. And then I would say, 'Well, Delaney, it's your move now, hotshot.' Something like that."

"And I would say, 'Well, good luck, Hilferty. Better watch your ass on this one,' and other male-bonding-type things."

"Yes, we would probably say things like that. I would imagine," Hilferty said.

"Well, I guess it's my move now, then, isn't it," Delaney said.

"Yup."

"So, good luck, John. Better watch your ass on this one. There's some bad people out there."

"Exactamento, Francis."

"Better watch both of our asses on this one, you and me."

"Correct. And Natalia's ass, if you'll pardon the expression. There are plenty more like those two guys you took out down here, my man."

"I see. But whose side are they on, John?"

"Very good, Francis. Gee, you almost tripped me up there. Almost got me to spill the beans. My, my. You *are* good. You slay me."

"So to speak."

"So to speak."

Natalia, it seemed, had been labouring under the delusion that they would be left on their own forever, that they would be able somehow to wander back into Quebec and carry on about their secret business unimpeded. Delaney had expected interference to come, but not that it would begin again in Europe. Natalia's fears returned. Delaney's, however, had never left. They made love some more in their sturdy wooden bed, but the vacation, they both knew, was over.

Mr. Salvatore, for his part, seemed genuinely disappointed when he learned they would be leaving for Canada. But he brightened a little when Delaney asked if he could use the hotel's typewriter and its excellent Panasonic fax machine one last time that evening. They watched again in the manager's tiny office as the fax hummed and buzzed another digital message to O'Keefe in Montreal. Mr. Salvatore looked over and smiled proudly. Delaney smiled back. Conspirators.

PART III
Quebec — Late Winter 1995

Chapter 15

Hilferty had gotten himself a haircut since they last saw him, a severe one. No-nonsense CIA-operative style. This, apparently, in an effort to show the world that this Canadian spy was firmly in control of the situation, or to provide himself and others with a comforting illusion. Stoufflet was with him, but the French agent had experienced no such anxiety about the semiotic implications of his appearance. His hair was still stylishly long. He reclined beside Hilferty in seat 3-B of the business-class section of the plane, ostentatiously reading *Le Nouvel Observateur* and sipping Air Canada's pre-departure champagne.

Hilferty nodded and smiled broadly to Delaney and Natalia as they came on board, unable as always to contain his adolescent pleasure at what he thought would take an adversary by surprise. Stoufflet affected a version of Gallic indifference. He apparently saw no need for menacing eye contact at this time. Delaney was not surprised to see either of them, nor was Natalia. He had warned her when they left Como to expect Hilferty, though not necessarily Stoufflet, to escort them back to Montreal. But of course the French would never render a service on their turf to another security agency without then expecting to be involved until the bitter end. Particularly after the nastiness at Zbigniew's apartment.

Delaney's only mild surprise was that they had been left to travel unescorted from Como to Milan, and then from Milan to Paris, where they had now picked up this flight. Perhaps, in fact, they had been escorted, but if so, it had been far more discreetly than they were to be on this last leg home. Delaney could not tell if there were any other agents on board Air Canada Flight 961 with them today. For all he knew, and after all that had transpired, the entire business-class section of the plane could be teeming with agents: Canadian, French, Polish, Vatican, others. All with their own intense interest — national or otherwise — in something hidden for five decades somewhere in Quebec. Impossible, anymore, for Delaney to predict exactly who had taken an interest in this affair and now far too late to care.

Not long after takeoff, Hilferty came back to where they were sitting, until now a sufficient number of rows behind him for a modicum of privacy. Delaney had expected an intrusion eventually.

"Everything all right back here?" Hilferty asked. "Pillows? Blanket?"

"Spare us, Hilferty," Delaney said. Natalia was now tense, Delaney could see, perhaps even angry.

"Sorry to spoil your little tête-à-tête. I thought we'd better talk over how we'll play this thing when we land."

"We're not going to play at all, John. That's what I told you back in Como."

"You're lucky you're being allowed to play anymore at all, Francis," Hilferty said. "You're lucky the French are letting you leave here at all after what happened over in Belleville. We've had to call in a lot of markers on this so far, especially with the French. They are very pissed off. My people, for that matter, are very pissed off. So you're going to have to play, I'm afraid."

"I think not, John," Delaney said.

Natalia's anger flared.

"I wonder if you could possibly leave us alone," she said. "For the flight and from now on."

"Well, I'm afraid that's going to be impossible, Ms. Janovski," Hilferty said. "Terribly sorry. I know you've been through a lot."

"Do you?"

"Yes. Are you feeling better now?"

This was starting to get Delaney angry too.

"Mr. Hilferty . . ." Natalia said.

"Please call me John," he said.

"No. I think not," Natalia said. "In my experience that would indicate some kind of familiarity or an opening for some kind of connection, and I am simply not interested in any connection with you whatsoever."

"I see."

Hilferty, despite his no-nonsense new haircut, was a little taken aback.

"Let me say this to you, before you go back to

your seat, Mr. Hilferty," Natalia continued. "I'm a psychologist, as you're already aware. In my professional work I quite often come up against manipulative personalities like yours, and I find it quite easy to deal with them in that sort of setting. Here, though, I see no reason to hide my disgust at what you are and what you do. So please leave us alone."

Delaney was impressed, but surprised at the intensity of Natalia's outburst. He watched Hilferty digest what had been said.

"What is it that you think I do, Ms. Janovski?" Hilferty said.

Natalia didn't answer. She pulled the inflight magazine from the seat pocket in front of her.

"What is it that you think I do, and your friend Mr. Delaney here does, Ms. Janovski?" Hilferty asked again.

She did not answer. Delaney said nothing. The passenger in the seat across the aisle, a businessman in a regulation blue suit, smiled over at them but he had his audio headset on and apparently could not hear the exchange. Delaney could not see who was in front of them.

Hilferty leaned closer to them and spoke more quietly.

"Has Mr. Delaney told you, by any chance, that he's been one of our operatives in this little fiasco, Ms. Janovski?" he said. "A paid operative? Did he tell you where he got the money for these plane tickets, for example, and where he got the gun that he so expertly used in Rome? Has he explained all of this to you fully?"

Natalia looked up at Hilferty, and then over at Delaney. He could not read what it was her eyes were saying to him.

"I would suggest, if I may, that before we all land in Montreal you and Mr. Delaney here have a long chat about just who has been doing what to whom and what your options might be after that. I'll leave you to it, if I may."

"You are becoming pathetic, Hilferty. You know that?" Delaney said. "You are really and truly out of your league here."

Hilferty smiled calmly at them.

"When we land," he said, "I'm no longer going to play around. Do you understand? You take us where we need to go, and tell us what we need to do, or I will choose from any number of unpleasant options available to me, judicial or, as they say in the trade, extrajudicial, and then it will be over. No more games. The minute we land."

Hilferty walked somewhat stiffly to his seat.

"He's floundering. He doesn't know what to do next," Delaney said to Natalia. "He's an amateur."

"And you? Are you an amateur?" she asked.

"Of course. Of course. He's just trying to put a wedge between us, don't you see, just when we have to stay together on this. I'm no spy. I told you that. I'm not working for anybody."

"I've wondered almost from the beginning," she said.

"I know that."

"Did you take money from them?" she asked.

"Yes, at the beginning. Hilferty came to see me, and asked me to keep an eye open while you and I were looking into all of this. I didn't agree to anything. I'm a reporter. I just watched what he was trying to do and I filed it away for future reference. That's what I do. Or what I used to do."

"Every time, there's a little bit more story for me."

"We talked this all through in Como, Natalia."

"Not the money part."

"OK. All right. But it doesn't change anything."

"Did you use his money?"

"Yes," Delaney said. "Some of it. Why not? I saw it as a bit of a joke on them."

"They haven't seen it that way."

"No. They haven't. But that doesn't change anything from where I sit."

"You used their gun," she said.

"Obviously. I had too. I may have to use it again."

"And spies give reporters guns."

"Sometimes," Delaney said. "I've told you that. When they have to. I've already told you where I got the gun."

Natalia went silent. Eventually she said: "I have to trust you."

"You must trust me," Delaney said. "This is going to get difficult now. We can get through this thing but we can't have any doubts. From the minute we touch down."

"I'm frightened again," she said.

"Me too."

"I don't like these two up there."

"I don't either. But Hilferty is not dangerous. He likes to think he is, but he's not. That stuff about extrajudicial moves is bullshit. He's CSIS, not Polish State Security, or Vatican. It's the others in this we have to worry about."

"Who? Exactly."

"Whoever has heard now about what your uncle hid away," Delaney said. "Whoever badly wants whatever it is. But it will be over soon, and we can start something new together."

"What? Where?"

"Whatever we want. And wherever."

"If they let us. Any of them."

"We're in control of this now. They haven't got much room to manoeuvre, Natalia."

"Neither do we."

"There's enough. You'll see. Just trust me."

O'Keefe came through beautifully, if perhaps a little extravagantly. He would never let them down, never let any friend of his down, even if he did not know exactly what was at stake. But Delaney was a little startled nonetheless at the sort of reception O'Keefe had arranged for them in Montreal.

The customs area at Mirabel was crowded, as it always is after a big international flight lands. But it would just as quickly become quiet again, in an oversized, underused outpost of an airport far from downtown. Hilferty and Stoufflet went through quickly with their diplomatic passports and they were waiting for Delaney and Natalia at the baggage carousel. Hilferty had just finished making a call on his mobile phone. Stoufflet looked as if he wished he had someone to call. The Frenchman still had nothing to say to them as they came up. Hilferty was curt.

"We've got a car waiting outside," he said.

Delaney said nothing. He had spotted the bearish figure of O'Keefe through the glass doors, and gave him a sign. When they all walked out together, pushing their baggage carts, the media horde was upon them.

"There they are," O'Keefe said to the waiting crowd of reporters and cameramen. Delaney nodded in the direction of Hilferty and Stoufflet; O'Keefe pointed, and the scrum skewed sideways, surrounding them.

Electronic flash guns exploded; motor drives whirred and clicked. Lights from TV cameras blinded the two spies as they tried to get through.

"Why have you decided to defect?" O'Keefe shouted at Stoufflet. "Who is this escorting you to Canada?"

Reporters fired off other questions. The scrum had stopped. Two uniformed RCMP constables moved in quickly to try to restore order. Arriving and departing passengers with laden baggage carts jammed the area as the police tried to get past.

"Quick. Let's move," O'Keefe said.

He raced with Delaney and Natalia out to the arrivals parking. A blue-and-white CBC Television news van was idling in the damp March air. A young man with long hair and stylish yellow Walkman headphones was waiting in the driver's seat.

"Go!" O'Keefe said, after throwing their bags in the back amidst a jumble of cables, lights, tripods, and aluminum cases.

He was enjoying himself hugely. Delaney and Natalia had barely enough time to settle into the small bench seat behind the driver before he roared off down the ramp to the airport access road. O'Keefe leaned back over them to peer out the rear window to see what was behind them.

"Dickheads," he said happily. "Still fucking stuck there. We're away."

He settled happily into his plush high-backed seat and pulled the seat belt forward to fasten it.

"Better buckle up, kiddies. Jean-Luc here is really going to move."

Jean-Luc grinned at them in the rear-view mirror.

"I've got to get the truck back to the station for another shoot," he said happily.

"Go for it," O'Keefe said. "We're outta here."

He looked back again past Delaney and Natalia. Still, apparently, no one behind them.

Jean-Luc was driving very fast on the slick road, but he was an expert. He had put the news van's blue flasher on and did not seem to expect trouble with radar police. Natalia simply looked stunned.

"Jesus Christ, Brian, how did you manage such a crowd?" Delaney said. "I said a little distraction, but Christ . . ."

"The awesome power of the press," O'Keefe said.

"Seriously."

"You know how it works, Francis. A well-crafted little press release, some keywords and phrases here and there. Pull the right levers, make a couple of calls, send a few faxes. Plus it's a slow news day. Right, Jean-Luc?"

They both laughed beery midafternoon laughs. They had clearly waited for some time in the airport bar.

"Jean-Luc here is my main man. We've been through shit together, Jean-Luc and me. Before he put his little Nikon away and retired to work in TV."

O'Keefe passed a copy of his press release back to them.

"You going to introduce me to your lady, Francis?" he asked.

"Brian, this is Natalia Janovski. Natalia, Brian O'Keefe. I told her a bit about you."

"*Enchanté, madame,*" O'Keefe said. "*Enchanté.*"

"It's very good to meet you, Brian," she said. "Thank-you for helping us back there."

"A pleasure, *madame.* Maybe one day you will tell me a little more than your friend over there has told me about what this is all about?"

"I will tell you, Brian, I promise." Delaney said,

"Just stand by for a little while longer, OK?"

"Have I got a choice?"

"Not just now. No. Sorry."

Delaney was reading O'Keefe's ludicrously over-written and overblown press release. On quite amateurish letterhead: "The Front de Libération du Québec. Cartier Cell. For Immediate Release."

"Brian, for heaven's sake, who's going to buy something like this?"

"Only about two dozen people. You saw them. Not a bad turnout."

"'A heretofore unknown accomplice in the 1970 political kidnappings in Quebec'?" Delaney read aloud. "'Returning to Quebec after self-imposed exile in Corsica to give himself up to authorities'? 'Plans to name members of the Bourassa cabinet who may have been implicated at the time'? Brian, for Christ's sake."

"Beautiful, isn't it?"

"It doesn't say anything about a defector here."

"I know. I threw that bit in just while I was standing there. You know how the lads love a good defector story. They always happen at Mirabel."

Natalia looked incredulously over at Delaney. He wondered what a psychologist would make of O'Keefe's overheated imagination.

"You won't have a friend left in this town, Brian."

"Who's to know?"

"The fax number."

"Press Club."

O'Keefe let go another wild howl of laughter.

Jean-Luc's shoulders heaved up and down while he laughed and drove.

"Pull in, pull in," O'Keefe said suddenly.

Jean-Luc pulled in to a giant Texaco service station about fifteen kilometres from the airport. Brian's old black Jeep Cherokee was parked near the back. They all got out and transferred the bags. Jean-Luc solemnly shook all their hands and then roared back out onto the highway, leaving behind a trail of steamy exhaust.

Brian was calmer now, as he drove. But he still looked often in his rear-view mirror. After a short while, a blue unmarked police car, with a red temporary flasher stuck on the roof near the driver's door, shot past them, heading fast to Montreal. Delaney looked intently ahead but could not see who was inside.

"RCMP, I'd say," O'Keefe said.

"They'll pull Jean-Luc over," Delaney said.

"If they catch him. And if he says anything to them. It's out of their jurisdiction here. They've only got the airports in Quebec, and Jean-Luc's a separatist. We've got some time."

O'Keefe picked up speed now. In forty-five minutes they were at his farm at Saint-Jean-sur-Richelieu, south of the city. He did not ask any more questions, and Delaney was grateful. Eventually, he would explain more of this, perhaps all of this, to his old friend. But not now. Natalia sat quietly in the back seat, composing herself, aware that there was little reason for small talk.

Karen was there, with their son. The dogs barked ferociously until Brian calmed them. Seamus seemed pleased and excited by the two grown-ups arriving unexpectedly on a weekday afternoon. Karen was not, however.

"What's going on, Brian?" she asked coldly, as they all crowded in to the overheated and untidy farmhouse kitchen.

As always, there were the remains of a child's lunch on the table, sideboard, and sink. Karen made hurried moves to tidy up, to clear spaces for guests to sit.

"Karen, relax," O'Keefe said, a little too loudly. "Francis here is in a small jam and I'm giving him a hand. I'll explain everything a little later on. OK?"

"OK," Karen said, unconvinced.

"OK," Seamus said. "Uncle Francis is OK, OK, OK, OK."

"Seamus be quiet," Karen said.

"This is Natalia Janovski, Karen," Delaney said. "We're just back from France and have to get going right away on a story I'm working on. Sorry to intrude."

"If it's not you, it would be something else, Francis," Karen said. "Hello, Natalia."

"Hello, Karen," Natalia said, shaking her hand formally. "Sorry to come in like this."

"I don't suppose anyone would want a coffee," Karen said.

No one did. She seemed relieved. They left her with young Seamus and went out behind O'Keefe's barn. The sun had managed to defeat some of the grey clouds, and the air near the barn had been warmed a little by the old wood. They stood blinking together in the suddenly bright winter light.

"Your car's about three kilometres across those fields," O'Keefe said. "I parked it there last night and put some things in it you might need. You'll have to cross old man Lacroix's property, but there's a break in the fence and he doesn't shoot at people anymore. Not much anyway."

The O'Keefe smile, directed at Natalia.

"The human interest angle," he said, "is that it's snowmobile for you, I'm afraid. The snow's still deep, and wet, and my Cherokee won't make it. Better not to use it now anyway, I'd say, after the performance at the airport. Not that I'm in any position to advise you what to do, bereft as I am of any useful information about the situation."

"Brian, I'm sorry. Really," Delaney said. "I'll explain everything soon. We just haven't got time right now. We've really got to go."

"Right. So let's start this bastard up then, shall we?"

Brian heaved himself onto the bench saddle of the old yellow-and-white Ski-Doo. The electric starter groaned a little and then the engine turned over in a burst of noise and grey-blue oil smoke. The noise did not decrease as the motor warmed. O'Keefe had to shout to be heard above the din.

"It's a good one and you're not going far," he said. "Just don't stall it or you'll have a very wet walk.

Go straight toward that maple grove over there. You'll see the break in the fence. Follow the trail I used last night, and when you hit the road you'll see your car."

He handed over Delaney's keys.

"Your doorman was reluctant to part with these," he said.

"He would be," Delaney said.

"We can put your bags in the little sled."

Delaney and O'Keefe left Natalia while they went to the truck to get their bags.

"You guys going to be all right?" O'Keefe asked.

"Yeah. It's not as bad as it looks right now."

"You got serious heavies after you or just assholes?"

"Reasonably serious, Brian. Don't you mess with them, OK? If they ever track this down to you, just play dumb. A couple of them can be a wee bit dangerous, I think."

"I laugh at danger. You know me."

"You'll have to take it easy with them if they come around," Delaney said.

"Sure, sure. I got a way with words."

"Brian, I'm serious. OK?"

"Nobody fucks with the Laird of St. Jean," O'Keefe said.

Delaney knew it was useless to continue.

"Thanks for all this," he said.

"*C'est rien, mon ami.*"

They stowed the bags in the fibreglass sled

hooked up to the Ski-Doo. Delaney climbed on, revving the handlebar throttle.

"You want goggles?" O'Keefe shouted over the noise.

"No. It's not far. We'd better go."

"OK. Don't fall off."

"Thank-you so much," Natalia said.

Brian leaned forward and gave her a gallant kiss on both cheeks. The noise and oil haze from the snowmobile were overpowering.

"*Salut,*" O'Keefe said.

Delaney pulled slowly away, and then picked up speed as he headed into the snow and brush of the O'Keefe landholdings. The last glimpse he had of his friend was of him clasping both hands over his head and dancing up and down in a sort of lunatic victory jig.

"He is a madman," Delaney shouted to Natalia over his shoulder.

"Yes," she said gravely.

They roared over the wet snow to the boundary fence and saw the break in it just as O'Keefe had said they would. Natalia was behind Delaney on the bench seat and holding him tightly around the waist. He felt, very briefly, an absurd happiness to be whizzing along with her on this oversized toy. It was a feeling, he knew, that could not last. It took them about twenty minutes to reach a small snow-covered dirt road, and another few minutes to find where O'Keefe had parked the Mercedes. Delaney realized they hadn't discussed where to hide the snowmobile, so he just pulled in beside the car.

He opened the trunk to put their bags inside, and saw a black-and-white Adidas bag O'Keefe had left for them. And a rifle bag. Delaney opened that first. O'Keefe's beloved pump action shotgun was inside. A little tag dangled from it with a note: "Shells in pockets and more in the other bag. Point the small end away from you."

Inside the other bag was a selection of goods, which said as much about O'Keefe's psyche as about their current predicament. Delaney and Natalia both laughed as the contents were revealed one by one.

Carefully wrapped sandwiches in an insulated bag. A Thermos of coffee, still only very slightly warm. Chocolate. A high-tech aluminized emergency blanket. Flashlight. A bottle of Bushmills whiskey. Six freezing cans of Molson's Export Ale. A box of shotgun shells. A Gideon Bible.

"He's lovely," Natalia said, laughing in particular at the Bible. "This is a nice touch."

Inside the Bible a sticker said: "*Propriété de Motel Reine de la Rivière, Sept-Îsles, Québec.*"

"He is really lovely," she said.

"A madman," Delaney said.

The car started easily, despite being parked overnight in winter-windswept Quebec farmland. The gas tank was full. They sat for a moment while the engine warmed and the defroster cleared the glass.

"So," Delaney said. "Do I get to know where we're going now? You trust me enough?"

"Yes," Natalia said. She reached over and pulled his head down to her with a leather-gloved hand. Her lips as she kissed him were still cool from the snowmobile ride.

"Where?"

"Saint-Sauveur."

They ate some of O'Keefe's excellent sandwiches as they drove toward the Laurentian hills north of Montreal, and they ate some of his chocolate. But even if they had stayed where the car had been parked they could not have heard any sounds coming from the O'Keefe family farm. Even if they had still been on their snowmobile, hurtling toward where the car had been parked, they could not have heard the sounds — the loud and urgent sounds. They would have had to be much closer, much quieter, to hear.

They were well away from it when the noises came, many kilometres away. So they could not hear the sounds of large cars pulling slowly up the driveway to the O'Keefe farmhouse in the failing afternoon light, tires crunching on the mixture of ice and gravel that extended a long way from the main road. Quiet again, for a time. Then the crackle of a radio, possibly official. The sound of car doors closing, and voices, as men climb out. Boots on gravel and ice, then boots on wooden steps and verandah. O'Keefe's dogs barking, barking, barking. Shouted exchanges, a door slamming, silence. For a time. Then, wood splintering, gunfire, shouting, barking, gunfire. Silence again. Then urgent conversations, the sound of urgent boot-clad feet running, shouted commands, and a child crying, crying.

All of which Delaney and Natalia, as they drove, could not hear, could not have been expected to hear.

Chapter 16

They were tired. It was late in the day after a long flight in from Europe and they realized it made no sense to continue on any farther that night. The church in Saint-Sauveur where they were heading would soon be closed up tightly against the Laurentian cold; the priest, or priests, they would have to see would be easier to deal with in the light of day. So they pulled off the Laurentian Autoroute just north of the Montreal island, in Laval.

It was the same suburb where Delaney had practised his pistol shooting, so long ago now it seemed. Parts of Laval were filled with new brick suburban homes, parts were still light industrial, and parts, such as where they now stopped, were given over to shopping malls and stark, cheaply built motels. For some reason known only to cultural historians, when the Quebecois built motels in the seventies and eighties, they too often insisted on including bars and restaurants of the most garish kind. The bars, more often than not, also offered intensely vulgar strip shows *avec nonstop danseuses nues*. Thin girls, recently in from small-town Quebec, took off their cheap clothes on grimy, too-small stages and wiggled and shook for the men hiding for an evening from chills of various kinds.

It was into one of these motels that Delaney pulled the Mercedes just as it was getting dark. The giant neon sign, with the gyrating dancer in a hula skirt, threw yellow and blood-red light on the windshield and on the wet slush of the parking lot. Trucks and rundown cars filled most of the spaces. The thump of overamplified disco music reverberated from the bar.

Delaney reasoned that Hilferty and Company, and the local police if they had now been called into this, would hardly be looking for them in a place like this. He also liked the fact that the parking lot was around behind the motel, away from the main road. They would likely be undisturbed here, except for the music and whatever alcohol-induced fist fights might eventuate among the regulars. Delaney resisted the temptation to comment to Natalia how unlike Como their next hotel room was going to be. Natalia said nothing at all.

They declined the offer from an anorexic desk clerk of a *prix très spéciale* on continuous pornographic movies via satellite in their room and she seemed perturbed at their indifference to her offer of a round bed at no extra charge. Their room, when they eventually got to it, was cold, but surprisingly clean, clinical, and acceptable. Delaney turned the heat on as high as it would go, and they stood shivering in their coats as they waited for the room to warm.

"Don't say I never take you anywhere," Delaney said.

The room warmed nicely and they could not hear the noise from the bar. The bed was comfortable, and with only the dimmest of lights on they could have been anywhere. Delaney had always liked that feeling when he was in a hotel room with a woman. It did not come often, either because of the place, or because of the woman, or both. He had that feeling tonight, however, and allowed himself to enjoy it. He was allowing himself to enjoy this woman's presence more than he would have ever, in another incarnation of himself, thought wise.

He considered the implications of this as he lay beside her. They had talked for a long time after they made love, a couple of lovers in their bed in the middle of the world. They could have been any lovers, anywhere, planning together in a warm bed in the middle of the world. But they were not able to plan very far ahead. It was wise not to jump very far ahead. Delaney knew that there was too much to be done before they could hope to get to that.

The church where they were headed was Saint-Sauveur's main one. Again, like most Catholic churches in Quebec, it was enormous, grey, stone, and very old. Delaney knew the church, and he knew Saint-Sauveur well. It was a small skiing town — or had been originally — about another hour's drive north from where they were. It had been overdeveloped in recent years, however, and the church was now on a street usually jammed with traffic and surrounded by restaurants, bars, gift shops, and ski shops. Delaney hoped the congestion might help them if things got complicated.

Natalia's uncle had been married there, she said. In 1951. It had been easy for his friend Zbigniew, and for Natalia too, when she sat with Zbigniew that afternoon in Paris before he was murdered, to guess from Stanislaw's letters that this was the church where they must now go. This is where Stanislaw and his co-conspirator from Maurice Duplessis's staff had gone in 1959 when they had something they wanted to hide. A picture of Stanislaw and his wife and their small wedding party in front of that church had sat for many years on the mantelpiece of the house in Westmount where he had died, Natalia said. She had remembered that photo well, and the glimpse of the church it had provided. What Delaney and Natalia were to do when they got there, thirty-six years after the fact, and whom they would have to see, whom they could trust — this was more complicated.

Natalia seemed confident it would all become clear when they got there. Delaney was not so sure.

"We have the password, after all," she said.

"We don't know who to try it out with. How do we know there's even anyone left there who will remember it?" Delaney asked.

"We don't. But I have an intuition it will be easier than you think."

"The intuitive personality type is at work again."

"You should get more in touch with your intuitive side, Francis. I have been telling you that."

"My intuition is that when things can go wrong,

they usually do go wrong."

"You are in dire need of more therapy."

"I'm in need of more information. Like a password."

Natalia paused.

"It really bothers you that I have not given you the password yet, doesn't it?" she said.

"Not for the reasons you think."

"Why then?"

"Because on something like this it would be better for someone else to have it too."

"In case something goes wrong."

"Something like that."

"In case I get hurt."

"Something like that."

"Why? What would you do with the password if I weren't around?"

"Finish it."

"How?"

I don't know. I'd have to use my intuition," Delaney said.

"Mazovia for Poland," she said suddenly.

"What?"

"Mazovia for Poland. The password. OK?"

"Is that it?"

"Yes. It's what my uncle and his friend and all the other young flyers used for a password in Scotland during the war. In the Mazovia Squadron."

"You sure that's it?"

"Zbigniew was sure."

Natalia was looking at him intently now.

Delaney knew that despite all her best efforts there was still a lingering doubt, an intuition, that perhaps he was not what he seemed to be. She was wondering, clearly, if giving him this new information might somehow change things, be a catalyst that would turn him back into what he was before they had met or what he might subsequently have become. But then he saw the brief cloud pass, as she put the thought away somewhere deep.

"Do you expect me to get dressed quickly now and race out into the night to share this with my spy pals somehow?" he asked, unnecessarily cruel, unwilling to leave her to her private fears. "Leave you here, race up to the church, and steal something away from you?"

"No." She was embarrassed. "No."

"I'm with you on this, Natalia. I am not a spy."

"I'm not either, Francis. I don't want to be."

He had known this from the beginning. It didn't need to be said.

Father Daniel Emile Hippolyte Lessard had almost given up hope that someone would come to relieve him of his burden. Indeed, Father Daniel Emile Hippolyte Lessard, priest all these many years of L'Eglise de L'Annonciation in Saint-Sauveur, Québec, could be forgiven if from time to time he forgot entirely about his secret and his burden. There had been months, if not years, over the past three-and-a-half decades when his thoughts had not turned at all to those secret arrangements from so long ago.

He was able for months at a time to go on about the increasingly complicated and difficult business of being a good priest in a Laurentian church with parishioners, if they came at all anymore, who were more interested in skiing and real estate and shiny four-wheel-drive cars than they were with their souls and confession and the life after death. The few who came any more often than Christmas and Easter to his great echoing old church on rue Principale seemed less and less interested each year in the edicts of the Holy Roman Catholic Church on contraception, Immaculate Conception, demoniacal deception.

They did not need the Church as his rural parishioners in the past had needed the Church. It was rare now that he would be called out in a desperate Quebecois winter night to rush through snow and wind to save a soul, to perform last rites, to learn some dark habitant family secret, or to help in some terrible accident or crisis. Father Lessard was not needed by many people in Saint-Sauveur anymore. The Church and its priests were not needed much in general anymore, and these thoughts, no matter how he tried to push them away, preoccupied him, an old priest considering his fate.

So it was not surprising that he could go for months without thinking of that time three-and-a-half decades ago when the European man and the policeman from Premier Maurice Duplessis's own staff had come to ask for his assistance on an urgent matter of State. When he thought of this at all now, he realized that, yes, he was still needed, if only as custodian of that secret they had shared with him, or the part of the secret they had been willing to share. They, in those days, had known whom to trust in Quebec, who could be relied on for years, decades, forever. That is what the Catholic Church was for and what its legions of priests were for. Then, at least. Much less so now. The thought cheered Father Lessard when it came. The memory that he had been needed, trusted, in the old way cheered him when it infrequently came.

The European would have been perhaps thirty-five, no more than forty, when he first came to L'Eglise de L'Annonciation in, what was it — 1950 or 1951? A good Catholic, a Polish Catholic. They had been welcome additions to the Quebec Church, the Poles, in those years after the war. Even if some of them turned to English-Catholic parishes, the Irish parishes, and others, in Montreal. They were still welcome additions to the Quebec Catholic flock. And this one, this Pole, had very much wanted to be married in the Saint-Sauveur church, he said, because they were skiers and because the place reminded them of Poland.

So Father Lessard had married them, in 1950 or 1951, and he thought he would not see them or any among their small group of Polish friends again. Father Lessard himself had been just twenty-five or twenty-six then, too eager as a young and energetic priest to get on with his demanding parish work than to wonder about the fate of just one immigrant couple in Montreal.

But then the Polish man had returned. In 1959. Father Lessard could remember that particular date very well. The Polish man and Duplessis's policeman had carried with them official letters from the premier himself. They had said they needed help on an urgent matter. Duplessis's letter said that the Catholic Church hierarchy in Montreal was very much in favour of this undertaking. What choice could Father Lessard have possibly had? Of course he had helped them. Of course he located an even more remote church for them to hide something away from the Communists. Polish Church property, they had said it was.

Father Lessard had already been aware of the intrigue swirling around some of these Polish treasures: how Duplessis had defied the Protestants in Ottawa for many years, had himself arranged for certain things to be hidden for a time in other churches and convents around the province. So of course Father Lessard had helped them and had memorized the strange password phrase the Polish man had given him. Of course he had been able to keep this secret over all these years. He was a priest of the Catholic Church in Quebec and that was the way these things were done. In those years, in any case.

Still, Father Lessard had almost given up hope

that someone would ever come. Now that he was seventy years of age and never sure when he would say his last Mass for an ever-dwindling flock. It was a small enough burden, he supposed, among the burdens occasionally given over to priests and the Catholic Church. If he carried it to his grave, so be it. But, in the end, he was able to do his duty, to ful-fill the trust of the Polish man and of Duplessis and of his beloved, troubled church, because on that overcast late-winter day the two young people had come and asked for his help.

Father Lessard thought when he first saw them coming into his church they were a young couple wanting to be married. It was starting to happen again more often now; young modern couples deciding that it would be a good thing to be married amidst the wooden pews and the wooden saints carved by Quebecois artisans now long dead. In such beautiful surroundings, they said. They would come to him many weeks ahead to discuss their plans and set a date for weddings in beautiful sur-roundings. He did not question the motivation of such young people too much these days. As long as they were Catholics, they would be welcome.

But the young couple who hurried into this church on this March day did not wish to be mar-ried. As Father Lessard came out of the confession-al and kneeled to kiss his embroidered priestly scarf, he saw immediately from their hurried step and grave faces that there would be more to it than that.

Natalia's intuition was correct. It was easier than Delaney had thought it would be. They parked the car in front of L'Eglise de L'Annonciation, among all the other cars with ski racks and skis on their roofs. The cars were angle-parked, front wheels to curb, as they all used to be in such rural towns years ago. Rue Principale was as busy as always at this time of the year, and the intense activity made them feel safely anonymous. They went through the massive oak main doors of the church and saw an old priest coming out of the confessional. A penitent, an even older woman wearing a farmer's rubber boots and a down ski jacket, hurried past them to a pew where she knelt and began her Hail Marys. Delaney wondered what sins were being committed these days on Quebec farms in winter.

They did not discuss any further what was to be done. Natalia simply went up to the old priest and said, in French: "Father, may we speak to you for a moment?"

The old man looked at them both carefully. He had a shock of very white wavy hair, having lost none of it to baldness despite his age. He pushed his right hand over it to smooth it — a young man's gesture, impossible to unlearn after decades of use. He answered in English.

"Do you wish confession, *madame?*"

The priest looked over at Delaney, wondering, apparently, what role this older companion may have had in the young woman's sins.

"No, Father. Thank-you," Natalia said. "We have a small matter we would like to discuss with you in private somewhere, if you wouldn't mind. Are you very busy?"

"*Madame,* I very much wish I could be busier in this church. It is empty today as you can see. It is too often empty. Would you like to speak in here? The church is as private a place as you can find these days."

"Well, if you wouldn't mind, perhaps we could go somewhere else. In an office, perhaps?" Natalia said.

"*D'accord.* Come with me. I am Father Lessard."

He didn't ask for their names. They walked toward the huge wooden altar. The wall behind it had been painted a dramatic shade of mauve. Small floodlights bathed it brilliantly even during the day. A large crucified Jesus with a wooden crown of thorns was raised high on the wall. The odour of decades of incense and floor wax lay heavily everywhere. Red lamps burned dimly. The faithful had lit candles before various saints.

The priest took them through a door to the left of the altar, and they were in a much warmer hallway, painted yellow, with blond woodwork. Heated air wafted through old brass registers set in the floor. There was an office with a door of frosted glass. Natalia and Francis sat on metal folding chairs. Father Lessard leaned against the edge of the gun-metal office desk, uncomfortable, perhaps, with the formality of taking the seat behind it. A framed photograph of Pope John Paul II was in pride of place, and there was the requisite large statue of Jesus baring his ruby-red sacred heart.

"You have troubles," Father Lessard said.

"Not troubles. Not really. No," Natalia said.

Father Lessard looked ever so slightly disappointed at this news.

"How can I help you today?"

Natalia looked over at Delaney. He saw no reason for her not to continue. He shrugged and nodded slightly. Father Lessard missed very little in such interviews. He looked over at Delaney.

"It is something very grave, *monsieur?*" he asked.

"Something important," Delaney said. "To us and some others. An old man who has died. Two old men who have died."

"My uncle was married in this church," Natalia said.

"When, *madame?*"

"Many years ago. In the 1950s."

"I was priest here then," he said. "I have been here a very long time."

Natalia's glance at Delaney showed her excitement.

"Then you may be able to help us," she said. "My uncle's name was Stanislaw Janovski. He was Polish. He came to Canada after the war and he was married here to a Polish woman, Margot. They would have had a small group with them, mainly Poles. Do you remember anything like that. From the 1950s?"

"I remember it very well, *madame*."

"You do?"

"Yes. I was a young priest then, performing many marriages. But your uncle, I remember very, very well."

"Why would that be, Father? Among so many people you married then?" Delaney asked.

"Perhaps it should be you who tells me why that might be so, my friends," Father Lessard said. "Why I might remember this Polish man so well."

"He came back to see you another time after that, I think," Natalia said. "Is that correct?"

"When would that have been, *madame*?"

"In 1959."

Father Lessard said nothing at all.

"Do you remember my uncle coming back to see you in 1959, Father?"

"You will have to refresh my memory."

"He was a solider, a pilot, in the Polish Air Force. He flew with a squadron of Poles out of Scotland. Their squadron was called Mazovia, after a province in Poland. Where Warsaw is located. Did he tell you about that?"

"Possibly."

"Did he tell you about a special password they all used in those years? So no one could damage their planes?"

Delaney thought he could detect a slight reddening of Father Lessard's already ruddy face. Nothing else.

"A password?"

"Yes."

"And what would that password have been, my dear?"

"Mazovia for Poland."

There was a long pause. Father Lessard looked closely at Natalia, and then at Delaney. He crossed his arms and leaned his head back slightly, studying them. Then a broad smile broke out over his face. He looked genuinely pleased.

"It has been a very long time since I heard that phrase, my dear. It is a very unusual phrase. Mazovia for Poland."

"You've heard it before?"

"Yes. Of course. In 1959. Just as you said."

Now it was Natalia's turn to smile.

"My goodness," she said.

"You are in the right place," Father Lessard said. "I knew that someone would eventually come. After all these years."

"My goodness," Natalia said again.

"What is your name, *madame?*"

"Natalia. And Janovski like my uncle."

"And yours, *monsieur?*"

"Delaney. Francis Delaney."

"What became of your uncle, Natalia?" the priest asked. "After I married him? And after I saw him that last time."

"He worked at various things. He was a broadcaster for a long while. For Radio Canada. And this winter, he died."

"He would have been a very old man."

"Yes he was."

"And his wife?"

"She died before him. Many years before."

"Usually it is the other way, *non?*"

"I suppose."

"And he asked you to do something for him before he died?"

"Not exactly, Father. We found out after he died that there was something important that we should do for him."

This seemed to trouble the priest somewhat.

"He didn't tell you what he wanted done?"

"No," Natalia said. "But in letters he had written it was clear there was something important hidden, something that he would have wanted us to take care of for him."

"For him?"

"For whoever deserves to have it?"

"And who might that be, Natalia?" the priest asked.

"We will have to decide that when we find it."

Delaney wished Natalia could be slightly less frank. He did not want the priest to have a crisis of conscience just now. Her look in his direction told him she knew that he was thinking this.

"My uncle was murdered, Father Lessard," she said.

"Ah," the priest said.

"He was murdered because of this secret he had. And he would have wanted us to make sure these things he hid with you were made safe."

"His oldest friend was also murdered because of this, father," Delaney said. "We want to make sure that was not for nothing."

"Murder," said the priest.

"Three murders," Delaney said. "A priest as well."

"*Mon Dieu, seigneur,*" Father Lessard said.

"Where are those things you hid for him, Father?" Natalia asked.

"What will be done with them?" the priest asked again.

"We will make sure that they never fall into the wrong hands, Father Lessard," Delaney said.

"It was the Communists they were afraid of then, *monsieur.*"

"There are even more people to be afraid of these days, Father," Delaney said. "It is not as simple as it was then."

"That is true, *monsieur.*"

"You must trust us that we'll do the right thing. We can't just leave these things hidden away forever," Natalia said.

"Some things are perhaps better left hidden," the priest said.

"Not these things, Father," said Delaney. "Other people have found out there may be something valuable involved here, and they may eventually come."

"Here?"

"Possibly," Delaney said.

"With the passwords?" the priest asked.

"No," Natalia said firmly. "Only we have the password."

"Perhaps I should get advice now on this." Father Lessard said. "From the Church."

"That would be a very bad idea, Father," said Delaney. "It is Natalia's uncle who took responsibility for this. Only people who know the whole story can make the right decision."

Father Lessard was wavering.

"I will die soon too," he said suddenly. "I would have to decide myself what to do with this information."

"Yes," Delaney said. "You would."

"My uncle was the one who trusted you with this, Father," Natalia said. "I loved him very much and I know he would want you to pass these things on to me."

They waited. The priest waited, for what seemed a very long time.

"They are not here, my dear," he said eventually. "They were never here."

"What do you mean?" Natalia said. "Please."

"We thought it wiser to make them even harder to find. That afternoon when they came. So I arranged for them to be hidden in another church. They are in that church in a very small town some way from here. In Saint-Jean-de-Mantha."

"I know where that is," Delaney said.

"You must go to the only church in the village. By the lake. The priest there will help you."

"Someone else knows about this?" Natalia said.

"He will know as little as he needs to know. He was not there then. I prevailed upon another priest in that parish to help us. Then I went along with your uncle in the little truck he and Duplessis's man were driving that day. Your uncle and myself only. Duplessis's man we left behind here, to wait. I found a hiding place for their goods and then the other priest and I went away while your uncle did his work. It was very heavy work, he said, and it took him a long time. I cannot tell you what he hid there. But I know where it is hidden."

"And the other priest?" Delaney asked.

"Dead now, *monsieur*. But he never knew more than I told him. He did not know what was hidden in his church or who the men with me that day were. But he is dead now."

"Has anyone ever come to you before us with the password?"

"No, *monsieur*. Never. You are the first."

"How do you know the things are still there?"

Father Lessard regarded Delaney with what looked like pity.

"Because they were entrusted to a priest, *monsieur*," he said.

"How will we get these things then?" Natalia asked.

"There is a new priest there now, Natalia. A young man. I will tell him to help you."

"Does he know there is something in his church?"

"No. It is well hidden."

"And he will let us go in there? He'll help us on this?"

"Yes, Natalia."

"Why would he do that?"

"Because I will ask him," Father Lessard said. "I will tell him what needs to be done."

"We must go today," Natalia said.

"I will call him for you. He will be expecting you. But it is a long drive on poor roads."

"And he will let us into his church, to search for something, and take it out with us?" Delaney asked again.

"Yes," said Father Lessard. "Yes. Have faith, *monsieur*."

They wanted to leave immediately, but Father Lessard seemed unwilling to end his involvement in this great secret so quickly. He asked them about themselves, and more about Stanislaw and Zbigniew. They told him as little as they could. Delaney became very anxious to go, and eventually the old priest saw he could keep them no longer.

He walked with them back into the main church.

"Perhaps you could tell me what becomes of all this," he said.

"Yes," Natalia said.

"If we can," Delaney said.

"It was something I kept with me for so many years, you see. And now there is a natural curiosity. To know that it has ended well."

Still the priest did not want to let them go.

"Are you married?" he asked them.

"No, Father," Natalia said.

"Perhaps, if you marry, you could come here to do it. I could marry you as I did your uncle and his wife."

"Perhaps," Natalia said.

"Your uncle would have liked that, I think. He liked this church very much."

"Yes," Natalia said. Delaney said nothing. He very much doubted things would turn out just that way.

Father Lessard had shaken their hands gravely at the door to his church, before turning suddenly to walk back into the dimness. They waited in the chilly vestibule for a moment, adjusting gloves and scarves. Through the doors, Delaney suddenly saw an olive-green-and-yellow *Sûreté de Québec* police car parked not far from the Mercedes. A uniformed officer was peering inside. Then he went back to the police car and began to use the radio.

"Police," Delaney said.

Natalia saw the car.

"Maybe it's not connected," she said.

"Of course it's connected," Delaney said. "We'll have to get out of here."

"How?"

"We'll just go. Walk with me from the direction of those stores."

They took a side path, and then walked along the slippery sidewalk in front of the church with the lunchtime crowd of skiers and shoppers. Delaney had keys at the ready. When they reached the car he quickly went to the driver's side and opened it. He pulled up the electric lock for Natalia's door and she got in.

He had the engine started and the Mercedes in reverse before the policeman had time to get out of his car. The cruiser was in the way of the heavy traffic and he had trouble getting out on the street side.

"*Hé, là, arrêtez! Arrêtez là, vous deux,*" the officer said in the *joual* accents of rural Quebec. "*Un instant, mes amis.*"

Delaney backed out fast. Cars slithered dangerously to a stop on the icy road. The policeman was shouting louder now, but Delaney was on the other side and roaring off in the opposite direction. The heavy old Mercedes was good on slippery roads. In the rear-view mirror he saw the policeman leaning into his car for the radio. A chase today was apparently not to this officer's taste. That was to be left for others, it seemed.

Father Lessard was still not convinced that he had made a mistake, but the worm of moral doubt had begun to eat away at his insides.

It had been a most intense day and it had left him morally and physically fatigued. Not long after the two young people had left, an hour afterward perhaps, the church secretary had rushed into his rooms with the news that the police were outside, that there was commotion. He had walked to the main doors and seen uniformed policemen arguing on the street with some other men in suits. Cars were blocking the way. A small crowd stood and watched, despite the cold.

Then the men and the police had come up the neatly shovelled pathway to the door of the church itself. They wished to speak to him urgently, they said. The Quebec police, and the men in suits, all of whom spoke French with accents not Quebecois. The anglophone, the leader of the group, was in a terrible rage. He had shouted at the uniformed police in the street and gestured wildly at them as he yelled. Father Lessard could not hear what the dispute was about. Now this same man was raising his voice to him, in his church, his own church. Who were the two people who had come out of the church when a policeman was looking at their car? Where had they come from? What had they wanted? Where were they now?

Father Lessard had had to warn this young anglophone — from Ottawa, or so he had said as he showed official identification of some sort — that, diplomats or not, if they were indeed what they all claimed to be, none of them would be allowed to shout in the church. The anglophone calmed himself. He said something was probably hidden in the church, that a search would have to be conducted immediately. But Father Lessard knew this should not be allowed to be done. This was still a Catholic church in Quebec, despite any changes over the years in the society outside, and he was not one who would allow secular people, particularly impolite anglophone Protestants from Ottawa, to do as they pleased. Even though he had nothing whatever to hide.

And so he had told them, all of them. Particularly, he had thought, as they made no mention of passwords. The Quebec police stood silently by, hoping not to be pulled into such a fundamental debate between an old priest in his church and the apparatus of various states.

But then the worm of doubt had been made to gnaw at Father Lessard's insides. The tall man who spoke French like a Parisian said nothing much at all. But the other two, dark heavy men who spoke yet another sort of French, seemed more menacing somehow, even though they spoke much more calmly and quietly than the young one. They did not look like diplomats, but they were, they insisted, Vatican envoys. They showed papers, they offered to call the Vatican right from his own church, there, that day, to prove to him how grave a matter he had become involved in.

Father Lessard's heart began to pound as he remembered it. Surely, he had not made a moral error? Surely, he had been correct to release his secret information to those two young people with the password? The anxiety of it began to make him sweat, made his face redden, and made him feel ill.

They had threatened him with grave consequences if he did not cooperate. The Bishop would be called, immediately. The Pope's own advisers. Anyone necessary would be called if he did not cooperate. And they wanted an answer immediately. He had searched all their faces, wanted a chance to ponder this alone, to pray for guidance, to be left alone. They would not grant him this, he knew.

So he had decided, eventually, that it was his duty, to the Vatican, to name the place where the two young people had gone. To say simply that they were looking for something there. Not to tell these diplomats about hidden goods, or locations. Not to tell them of passwords and Poles and Duplessis's man. Just to name the place where the two others had gone and hope that *bon Dieu seigneur* would intervene on the side of the just.

Father Daniel Emile Hippolyte Lessard had done his duty as best he could in uncertain times. He had betrayed no secrets. His church had not been violated, the rough men had gone, and only one policeman was now left inside. There was peace again, of a kind. He sat in one of the pews near the candles that flickered before statues of saints and rested himself after the trials of that day. He would discuss this, some of this, with the Bishop at the earliest possible moment.

He had done his duty as best be could. He had been relieved of one burden but now had quite another. The worm of moral doubt gnawed incessantly at his insides.

Chapter 17

Their most immediate concern was to avoid being stopped by the provincial police before they made it to Saint-Jean-de-Mantha. Most of the way would be on back roads, probably snow covered and with little traffic. But to get to the right road they would have to take the Laurentian Autoroute for a short while, from Saint-Sauveur to Saint-Jérôme and then on through Saint-Félix-de-Valois. Most of the Laurentian towns were named after saints, Delaney thought ruefully as he drove south on the highway to the turnoff he needed, and today's route would take them through much of Quebec Catholicism's hagiography.

Natalia pored over maps from the glove compartment even though he had assured her he knew the way. She, like Delaney, often looked behind them and over to the lanes on the other side of the continuous mound of dirty snow that divided the highway. He was careful to keep to the speed limit, despite their desire to rush onward to the last stop on this journey and to complete this complex task of theirs. How exactly to end it, how it might be allowed to end, Delaney could not say.

"I hope Father Lessard calls the other priest for

us like he said he would," Natalia said.

"I think he will," Delaney said.

"I hope the other priest will cooperate."

"He should."

"I hope we can find those things."

"Me too. And find a way to get them out of there. Father Lessard said your uncle had some heavy work to do back then."

This silenced her. She sat stiffly, nursing her various hopes until they reached Saint-Jérôme. Then she seemed to relax as they turned east onto Route 158. Delaney relaxed a little too. Now they were off the main highway used by Montrealers heading for the ski hills and on a secondary road used mainly by the farmers who had neither the taste nor the time for skiing. The white fields were featureless except for the odd stretch of wood-and-wire fence, grey-black against the whiteness, or the leafless maple trees, or the aging farm buildings that stood like islands in a sea of snow.

The car was warm, running well. It felt safe inside. Natalia looked out the window for a long time, saying nothing. Then she said suddenly: "I realize now that I haven't been dreaming at all lately. It has only just occurred to me now."

"Neither have I," Delaney said.

He had started to enjoy, in Europe, playing her therapist games with a morning's stock of dreams. Now there were none.

"We have been completely extraverted since we left Como," she said. "Completely outer-directed."

"Does that always have to be quite such a bad thing?"

"Yes, I think so," she said.

"Where's the harm?"

"Things can creep up on you," she said. "From the unconscious. If you don't pay attention."

Delaney was someone whose energies for years had been neither inner- nor outer-directed. He had simply been a paid observer of the directed energies of others, writing down observations from the sidelines in his reporter's notebook. This had all changed, of course, after he met Natalia. But for today he thought it wise to remain very much outer-directed. He left Natalia to her introversion, and drove.

Hilferty no longer knew where to direct his mounting anxiety. He was sick to death of this whole disastrous operation. He really was. It had been a disaster from start to finish. He was trying, as he drove fast down the Autoroute in his oversized government automobile, to understand just where it had started to go so badly off the rails.

You could pick any number of points on this one, he realized. Not watching those first two Polish agents closely enough after they hit Montreal, for example. That was probably the first mistake in the series. That gave them an opening to go after the old man, and then the shit had very quickly started to hit the fan. Then they had stupidly let those same two guys take out the old priest in Lachine. Asleep at the switch again. And the next mistake, maybe the biggest, though God knows he would never admit this to Smithson and Rawson, was probably approaching Delaney in Montreal. Getting him involved at all. That had also been a very, very bad move. In retrospect.

Hilferty looked over to where Stoufflet was sitting on the passenger side of the car. This guy was another mistake. How did CSIS allow itself to always get saddled with all of this inter-agency bullshit anyway? The diplomatic niceties, the give-and-take for services rendered overseas. First the French, in this one anyway. Now the fucking Vatican. God knows who else he'd have to shepherd around this godforsaken province next.

He looked in the rear-view mirror. The Vatican bastards were keeping up all right. He resisted the urge to speed up, to lose them on the slippery highway, and to finish this up the way he wanted to finish it up. But they were along for this ride and there was not a damn thing he could do about it. For services rendered. He did not at all buy into the argument that when a friendly security service helped CSIS out in an operation they should then be allowed to land right in the thick of it when things went back over to home turf. They were now on his ass, breathing down his goddamn neck, and everything was going to hell.

He did not like their style, any of these Vatican guys. He had not liked it when their crowd sidelined him in Rome, allowed the Poles to get heavy, way too heavy, with the girl. He had wanted to step in, but it was not his turf, they said they wanted to wait and watch, and they sidelined him. That could have turned very bad. They could quite easily have had two dead Canadians on their hands back there, rather than two dead Poles. Things could have gone much worse. But then he had owed them. They had cleaned up the little mess that Delaney left them, and CSIS owed them.

So here were these Vatican guys with him right now, riding around Quebec like tourists. Observers. Diplomatic niceties for him to worry about as this thing slid further and further off the rails. In his most paranoid moments, Hilferty wondered if they were really Vatican at all or just another couple of freelancers who had somehow gotten wind of this thing. Their credentials looked to be in order, but credentials weren't worth a pinch of shit these days anyway.

This whole mess comes from having a god-damned Polish Pope, he thought suddenly. His people then feel impelled to watch over their boy in Warsaw, watch his every goddamn move. And that's what comes from having a former electrician, for Christ's sake, running the show in Warsaw in the first place. When a country bumpkin Polish electrician surrounds himself with thugs and carpetbaggers and spooks and then figures out he's got to start playing hardball to win the next election. When someone starts to get interested in some far-fetched story an old guy has to tell in Montreal and then figures there might be something in it for their side.

But then it's impossible for the dumb bastards to tell who's on first anymore, with spooks and crooks falling over themselves in Warsaw at the moment, so Walesa, or somebody else over there, goes crying to Rome for help. That's when things start to get ugly, Hilferty thought. When you lose control of these situations — allow yourself to lose control. It's impossible to tell who the good guys are after that. Who's working for whom. Who's doing what on whose behalf. In Warsaw, or Rome, or, for that matter, Montreal.

It would be hard to convince anyone that the good guys in this thing would have wanted, for example, to take out that crazy reporter O'Keefe back down in Saint-Jean-sur-Richelieu, as the two Vatican guys had obviously wanted to do. They could barely hold themselves back. Smithson and Rawson had both sounded like they were going to have strokes when he tried to tell them how it had unfolded at the farmhouse. Rawson was so steamed that he was on his way to meet them at the church in Saint-Jean-de-Mantha at this very minute. And our man Rawson did not like straying very far from Ottawa anymore unless he absolutely had to. Especially in winter. Taking over the operation from here on in, he had said. Bringing in back-up, he said. And handling the recalcitrant Delaney himself.

The Saint-Jean-sur-Richelieu incident had been, Hilferty admitted this, a very bad fuck-up indeed.

He could see why his masters in Ottawa were scrambling. But who would have guessed that this guy O'Keefe, a reporter, not an agent, would be armed to the teeth in there and start blasting away at them with a shotgun? With his wife and kid around, for Christ's sake. And now jumping up and down in custody somewhere, making all sorts of threats and allegations. That's not how these things were supposed to work. Especially in Canada. And especially, these days, on Quebec turf. Smithson and Rawson were going to have to do some very fancy explaining to those separatist bastards down in Quebec City.

Hilferty turned onto Route 158. No idea, really, how far ahead Delaney and the girl might be and still a long cold drive ahead. He looked in his rear-view mirror. These guys, on the other hand, were still all too close. Ferramo driving; looking jet-lagged, in need of a shave, grim. And Tremonti, the really rough one, with the dead eyes. He was the problem, Hilferty knew. He'd be the one to watch from here on in. He had been the one to seriously want to take out that crazy reporter bastard back in Saint-Jean. Too quick to go for his weapon. No worries about turf, about who'd clean up after him. Just wanted to blow the guy away and worry about the consequences later. Lucky things didn't turn out worse than they had.

He'd bear more watching, that one would, Hilferty thought. Both of them would. Thugs. With Vatican authority. Maybe.

Stoufflet was complaining again about how

much he wanted *un petit café*. The fucking French simply cannot function without their coffee, Hilferty thought. But there was no way he was going to stop for coffee just when this thing was coming to a head. No way in the world. Anyway, they were in the middle of nowhere now. Rural Quebec at its windswept best. Fields for miles on either side and not a house or a restaurant in sight. Hardly the place to stop for a coffee.

He simply could not believe it when the Italians suddenly flashed the lights on their big rented Ford, flashed them and flashed them and motioned for Hilferty to pull over. He shook his head at them in the rear-view mirror, but they flashed their lights again and honked the horn. Surely they weren't desperate for coffee too.

He pulled over. It was very quiet, and cold.

"*Qu'est-ce qui ce passe?*" Stoufflet asked.

"I don't fucking know," Hilferty said. "They want us to pull over."

"*Mais, merde. Il y a rien ici. Rien.* Why do they stop here?"

Things became clearer as Hilferty rolled down his window, letting in a great gasp of freezing air. Ferramo and Tremonti were walking toward his car. They both had their guns out. Glocks. Wicked-looking guns, Glocks were. Hilferty had never liked them. But by the time he had fully understood why they had their guns out it was too late, far too late. The operation was as far off the rails for Hilferty as it was ever going to be.

Ferramo came around to the passenger door, and fired three fast shots into Stoufflet through the window. Shards of glass exploded over everything. The Frenchman's body shuddered and he was suddenly very bloody and very dead. Hilferty let out a yell and tried to get out of the car on his side. Tremonti kicked the door shut again, and killed him with two shots to the head. The noise died away quickly. There was nowhere for it to go.

It had started to snow gently when Delaney pulled up to the church. There was already a white dusting on surfaces previously cleared. The sun was a bright grey circle through leaden clouds. There were no other cars in the parking lot and the church was on a quiet curved wooded road a long way outside the village they had driven through. A small frozen lake lay smooth and white behind the churchyard. There was no one to be seen or heard.

Delaney wanted to leave the car on the road somewhere away from the church so they wouldn't draw attention to themselves. But he suspected they would need the car close by to load things into if they were lucky enough to find whatever it was that had driven them this far. Or perhaps to get away quickly if necessary. He hoped it wouldn't be necessary. Natalia stood quietly beside him while he chose a few items from the trunk. He knew her well enough by now to understand that the more anxious and frightened she became, the deeper and longer were her silences. Snow began to gather steadily on her hair and shoulders.

He resisted the urge to bring in the shotgun. The Browning was already in his parka, had been there all day. But he did take the shotgun out of its case and lean down to load three shells into the chamber. This appeared to have no effect on Natalia: she apparently expected this behaviour now from the people around her. He put O'Keefe's flashlight in his parka as well. The Bushmills and the Gideon Bible he left where they were, for emergencies of another kind. As he walked with Natalia up to the front doors of yet another Quebec Catholic church, his coat pockets felt suitably laden down with equipment for this last, possibly dangerous excursion.

This afternoon's priest was not at all cut from the same cloth as Father Lessard. Father Carpentier was young, perhaps the same age as Lessard would have been when he was marrying Polish expatriates back in the 1950s. And Father Carpentier was an exceedingly frail, nervous young man. He seemed to shiver in his black priest's suit — no clerical robes for this generation of priests, at least not on a weekday afternoon — and he peered at them through a tiny pair of round spectacles. His head was already balding badly, and the entire effect was of some underfed and highly strung domestic animal. Still, he did not turn them away.

"Father Lessard told me you would be coming,"

Father Carpentier said as he closed the church doors behind them. His was a much smaller church than the one in Saint-Sauveur. And it had little of the carved decoration and dramatic lighting of Father Lessard's. But it was nonetheless a substantial stone structure with a high vaulted ceiling and the requisite images of saints lining the side walls.

"And you know why we are here, Father?" Delaney asked.

"As much as Father Lessard thought he should tell me," the priest said.

"Will you help us?" Natalia asked.

"I will not hinder you, *madame*," he said. "That is as much as I can do."

"Thank-you," said Natalia.

"You know there has been something hidden in this church for many years?" Delaney said. "Something we now have to get?"

Delaney realized as he spoke that probably this young priest was not even born until after Premier Duplessis had prevailed on priests and nuns to hide Polish treasures around the province.

"I was startled to learn of this today for the first time, *monsieur*."

"Are you angry about this?" Natalia asked.

A psychologist's question. Father Carpentier looked at her sharply.

"I am not happy about it, *madame*," he said.

"Well, after today it will be over and we won't interfere with your church again," she said.

"That would be best, *madame*. If it is possible."

They stood uncomfortably together in the underheated church for a moment. Delaney was unsure how much to tell this young man, how much needed to be told before they would be allowed to begin rummaging around in his church. But Father Carpentier was eager enough to end this thing that he decided for them.

"Father Lessard tells me that what you need to find is in the cellar, *monsieur*," the young priest said. "He said you must look carefully at the nave end of the cellar, in the large armoire that is there. He said you would be able to find what you're looking for there."

"In an armoire?" Delaney said.

He felt that this was a very weak hiding place for something as valuable as what they expected to find. Or perhaps a hiding place for something very small.

"That is what he said."

"All right," Delaney said. "Maybe it would be best if we looked for these things without you."

Father Carpentier had clearly not intended involving himself any further than his priestly allegiances required.

"That is what I would prefer, too, *monsieur*," he said.

"We may be some time," Delaney said.

"I have work that must be done in here, *monsieur*. And in the *presbytère* also, if you take a very long time."

"Fine," Delaney said.

Father Carpentier led them to a door just to the

right of the front entrance. He opened it and turned on a light switch. A set of aging wooden stairs disappeared into the musty gloom.

"*Voilà*," Carpentier said. "Down that way. Walk directly to the back."

The priest said nothing else and hurried away. Delaney looked at Natalia. He had expected much more resistance, more suspicion, than this.

"He's frightened," she said.

"He has reason to be," Delaney said. "Let's hurry up."

They went carefully down the worn steps. They found they needed no flashlight. A row of light bulbs had been set in the rafters of the old stone cellar and the weak yellow glow was enough for them to see. An occasional high small window also let in some pale winter light. Dust swam in shafts wherever light penetrated. Bits and pieces of furniture and some old pews lay around near the stairs. There were some trunks and crates further in, but for the most part the cellar was empty. It ran the length of the church and from where they stood the back wall where they were headed was in deep shadow. They walked that way.

At the back, past a smaller enclosed furnace room that smelled sharply of heating oil, was a stout wooden door secured with a piece of timber fitted into two iron brackets. Delaney was certain this would lead up some stairs to the back of the church or to the outside. And there was a giant old armoire against the back wall just as Father Carpentier had said there would be. It stood almost eight feet tall and very wide, clearly designed for such spaces and not for the small farmhouses in the region. It appeared to be made of hard Quebec maple. There was carved lattice in the door panels.

Natalia opened one of the doors. There were some folded pieces of aging vestments on a shelf inside; dusty, neglected, ruined. A small rack held some equally dusty bottles of wine, for Communions that had never been celebrated. In a battered cardboard box were some bits and pieces of ecclesiastical paraphernalia, apparently out of fashion: brass candlesticks, red glass lanterns, and bits of candle end. A very large stack of mouldy prayer books took up another section. But there was little else.

They rummaged through these items, both suspecting that they would not find what they sought sitting on open shelves. Delaney shone the flashlight on the wooden panels at the back. There, behind the wine rack, he found the first clear indication that they were in the right place. Someone, years before, had scrawled in what had probably been bright yellow chalk or grease pencil the word "Mazovia." An arrow pointed to the left. It was very faded now.

"It's here," Delaney said.

"Oh please," Natalia said. "Show me."

He moved aside and shone his light in for her to see.

"Mazovia," she said. "It's here."

"Somewhere here," Delaney said.

"My uncle must have written that himself, all those years ago," she said.

"I would say so," Delaney said.

He looked closely in the corner of the armoire indicated by the arrow and then all around the inside again. There was nothing of interest.

"The priest said it was inside," Natalia said.

"There's nothing interesting in it. Those vestments are worthless."

"But that's what the priest said. In the armoire."

Delaney went around to the left side. He looked at the outside, and peered behind it with the light. The armoire was pushed close up against the wall. He tried to pull it away, but it was too heavy. They stood pondering the problem.

"The arrow indicates left," Natalia said.

"Nothing there."

"Perhaps we have to move it left, push it over to the left," she said.

"Let's see if it moves sideways then."

They both went to the right side of the armoire and Delaney gave it a push. Even with all of his weight it would not budge. Natalia came beside him and they pushed together. With the weight of both of their bodies the massive piece moved slightly, making a loud squealing sound as the old wood scraped the uneven stone floor after decades in the same place.

"Yes," said Natalia.

They put their bodies into the work and the

armoire slid by inches to the left, groaning ancient wooden groans as it did. Then Natalia let out a cry. Set in the wall behind the piece was a small iron door, about half a person's height.

"Yes," she said quietly.

They worked harder and finally got the armoire clear of this small door's frame. Someone had scrawled "Mazovia" on this as well. They did not bother to speak now. Delaney pulled the tubular iron latch out of its slot and pushed at the low door with his foot. It moved inward with a loud series of creaks.

"Francis," Natalia said. "Francis."

Delaney crouched in this secret opening and peered inside with the flashlight.

"It looks like an old coal room," he said. "It looks like there's some bits of coal left in there, a small pile toward the back."

"We have to go in," Natalia said.

"Yes," Delaney said. He took off his parka and put it on an old crate. The Browning made a thud as it hit the wooden planks.

"You wait out here for a bit. I'll call out to you if I find something."

"I want to come in too," she said. "I'm coming in too."

She pulled off her bulky down overcoat and they stood together, quickly chilled in the damp air.

"We'll have to be fast," Delaney said.

They both squeezed through the low opening. On the other side was a filthy room clearly used in years gone by to store coal. They could both stand up, but Delaney had to lower his head when he passed under rafters. A narrow iron handcart with cracked wooden handles lay on its side near the door. A small iron ladder rose up on one wall toward what would probably have been in the past a narrow opening for coal deliveries. That opening had been securely and permanently boarded up with thick planks. A small pile of coal still lay underneath the ladder.

But to the left, away from the coal, sat what looked to be a wooden pallet covered with a greasy tarpaulin. They approached it, both knowing that this, at last, had to be what they had been seeking. Natalia reached onto the tarpaulin and pulled off what appeared to be an old pennant. It was tattered and stained, but intact. It showed a checkerboard pattern with four large red-and-white squares. Rectangles in the same colours surrounded these along the edges.

"It's the Mazovia Squadron's insignia," Natalia said. "Zbigniew showed me something like this in his photos in Paris. They used to paint it on the side of their planes. My uncle would have had to be the one to leave this here. The only one possible."

"Yes," Delaney said.

The weight of the story, and of the years and the lives involved in this story, made them both subdued, respectful. They stood for a moment and then pulled off the cover together.

Even after it has sat unattended for decades, even in dusty places like the one they were now in, even in the narrow beam of a flashlight, gold glows like nothing else in the world. The bars of Polish gold had been neatly arranged in a small stack on the pallet: forty-eight in all. None of the bars gave the slightest sign of having been hidden away for thirty-six years. They were all as shiny and breathtaking that afternoon as they would have been when Stanislaw Janovski had carefully stacked them there in 1959. Natalia and Delaney rubbed their hands over the bars' buttery surfaces, as everyone who sees gold in large quantities instinctively does.

"Unbelievable," Delaney said at last. "Unbelievable."

"I can't believe this," Natalia said. "All this gold, for all these years. Down here."

"It was a good hiding place after all," Delaney said.

"Yes," she said.

"This is worth a fortune," Delaney said. "Do you realize what something like this is worth?"

"To my uncle and his people it was worth more than money," Natalia said.

"But it was to be used eventually," he said. "Surely they would have been planning to use it after the war for something. Or they would never have shipped it to Canada at all."

"They never had the chance. When the Communists took over they no longer had a country to bring it home to."

"But to fight the Communists then," Delaney said.

"They never had the chance. Remember what Zbigniew said. There were factions, disagreements, after the war. How would Stanislaw have known how best to use it? Or who would be the best to use it?"

"But to just leave it here for all those years."

"He was waiting for the right moment," Natalia said. "He was a very patient man."

"He never got his moment."

"He chose the wrong moment, Francis," she said.

They stood silent in the dust and gloom. The bars of gold glowed dimly.

"Now he has his moment," Natalia said eventually.

"Possibly," Delaney said. "You're going to have to decide what to do with this now."

"I know that," she said. "I'll do what my uncle would have wanted done."

"That's going to be a difficult thing to decide."

"I know that," she said.

"And it's going to be difficult to get these out of here," Delaney said. "We can't just toss them in my car. They're too heavy, for one thing. We're going to have to come back with a truck."

He walked around to the far side of the pallet and saw a small case pushed up alongside a row of the gold bars.

"There's something else here," he said.

"Really?"

Natalia hurried over to where he was. They both

sat on the edge of the pallet as she examined it. It was a leather-covered rectangular case about the size and shape of an automobile battery, with a handle on the lid and two latches.

"Open it," he said.

There was no lock. The latches were corroded and stiff but they opened. Inside, something was wrapped in purple velvet. Natalia unwrapped it. Inside the bundle was more gold: a magnificent chalice with embossed religious scenes and with pearls set around the edge.

"Unbelievable," Delaney said.

"It's fantastic," Natalia said. "I should have remembered we would find something else. Stanislaw's letters said he had taken something else to hide. Something religious."

She turned this Grail around in her hands.

"I knew we would find something like this," she said. "I dreamed it."

She looked up at him, flushed now.

"Bring it with you," Delaney said. "But we have to get out of here. We'll have to come back for the rest after we get organized. We should get out of here."

They threw the tarpaulin over the gold again and squeezed out of the coal room into the main part of the cellar. They were chilled and put their coats back on immediately. For a few anxious moments it seemed that the armoire would refuse to budge back into its original position. But after they pushed and strained for several minutes it groaned back into place. Delaney reached inside and rubbed off what remained of the "Mazovia" inscription. He slid the wine rack back into place.

"We really will have to come back here right away," he said. "I don't know how long it will be before someone gets to Father Lessard or to our friend Carpentier upstairs. We'll have to come back as soon as we can."

"Tomorrow," Natalia said. "No later. We can get a truck somewhere near here."

They were both grimy from the coal room. Natalia's face was streaked with dust. She carried the chalice and the rolled-up Mazovia pennant under her arm.

"Let's see if we can leave without saying any good-byes to young Carpentier, shall we?" Delaney said. "Leave him guessing, in case someone else comes?"

"I'm not sure that's a good idea," Natalia said. "What if he thinks the stuff is gone and sends people down here too? We should tell him to keep all of this to himself."

As they climbed the stairs back up to the church Delaney still wasn't sure how to deal with the priest. But when he opened the door and saw the two burly strangers in suits talking to Father Carpentier at the front near the altar he knew that he would not have to decide. He quietly closed the door and pushed Natalia back down the stairs.

"What is it? What's wrong?" Natalia said.

"There's a couple of guys out there with

Carpentier. God knows who they are. But we'll have to go out another way."

They raced across the uneven stone floor of the cellar to the back once again and Delaney tugged at the oak beam that braced the exit door there. It opened onto a narrow flight of stairs that appeared to head up to an outside door.

"If that door up there is not locked from the outside, we're clear," he said.

"The car," Natalia said.

She was clutching her precious Grail case as if to never let it go. The pennant she had now pushed into a pocket of her overcoat.

"We'll get to it," he said.

The door at the top of the stairs was braced from the inside with a wooden beam, but this came away easily. The sudden grey light from the overcast sky blinded them for a moment after the door opened. It had stopped snowing.

"Natalia, we have to watch our step now, OK?" Delaney said. "I have no idea who those guys are talking to the priest but we've got to assume the very worst on this now. We'll go to the car, fast, and just leave. We can figure out later when to come back. But we have to be quick."

They had to pick their way through the deep snow that had gathered throughout the winter under the eaves of the church. When they turned the corner at the front, Delaney saw the other car.

"Fuck," he said. "They've parked us in."

A large white Ford had been parked hard against

the back of the Mercedes. They would not be able to back up and drive out.

"We'll leave the car," he said. "We'll go into the village and wait it out there somewhere."

"Without the car?" Natalia said.

"We have no choice. Let me get something out of the back first."

"Francis, no. Let's just go."

"No. Just give me a second. Then we'll cut across the lake to the village."

He darted out into the small parking lot while Natalia waited under the eaves at the side of the church. There was nothing about the Ford that told him anything about who the men were inside. Probably a rental car. It did not look at all like an unmarked police vehicle. The engine still ticked steadily as it cooled down: it had not been there for long. He opened the trunk of the Mercedes and got out the shotgun. He put some extra shells in his parka, and then quietly closed the trunk again.

It was hard-going through the heavy snow to the lakeshore, but the ice on the small lake itself had been swept reasonably clear by the winds. Only a thin layer of new snow from the afternoon's light fall lay on it. The walking would be easier there. They set out in silence, single file, for the dense grove of maple and birch and pines on the other side. The village was some distance beyond that.

Close to the shore near the church someone had cleared space for a small skating rink The skate blades of local children had left complex designs on the ice inside the rink's snowbank boundaries. No one was skating today, however. Delaney watched Natalia walking purposefully in front of him. In the failing light he felt a strong intuition building that at some point in all of this he had made a grave and fundamental error in judgment. The shotgun he carried gave him no comfort.

Chapter 18

They were almost at the opposite shore of the lake when Delaney looked back and saw in the distance the small figure of a man standing at the back door of the church. He was clearly straining to see who was walking across the ice. Delaney did not feel any fear — just the certainty that now things would move very quickly. Or simply end. From across the ice he heard a brief shout and saw the man disappear back inside the church. Natalia heard the shout too, and looked back.

"They've seen us," Delaney said. "One of them anyway."

"Who is it, do you think?"

"Not police, Natalia," he said.

They ran now, and then had to scramble over a high snowbank to get off the ice. It was deeply silent in the woods. It gave them the illusion of safety. They quickly made their plan.

It had taken them about five minutes to get into the cover of the trees from the time their unknown foe had seen them in the distance. Delaney knew their biggest threat would come if the men in the church decided to take their car around the lake toward the village, to be there as he and Natalia came out of the woods. He very much doubted they would set out across the lake. Surely, Delaney reasoned, such men would not risk exposing themselves on the open lake, or to ambush in the trees, or to getting lost or bogged in snow.

But for him and Natalia to now risk going back out in the open on the lake themselves and head toward the church on the assumption that the men, both of them, had driven away in their car was a gamble he knew they could not take. The only thing to do was carry on through the woods to the village and hope that the possibility of witnesses there would stop their pursuers from any overt aggression.

Natalia was breathless from their run. Her face was flushed from the exertion and the cold. Delaney very much wanted to simply get her out of all this and into some place warm and secure. She did not say anything as she stood trying to catch her breath. Delaney's heart began to ache with the intense connection he felt to this young woman standing with him amongst the snow-laden trees. He supposed some would call that feeling love. He saw no need to name it.

"We'll just have to make it to the village, that's all," he said. "Are you all right?"

"Yes, I think so," she said.

"Let's go."

Delaney pulled at the action on O'Keefe's shotgun and pumped a shell into the chamber. The hard mechanical sound was wrong for the peaceful setting. It intruded, warned.

They found a path of sorts, with the snow packed by locals cruising the woods on snowmobiles. The walking was difficult but not impossible and Delaney knew such a path would eventually have to come out on a road or in the village itself. They walked for a while in silence. There was nothing they could say.

It was hard, slow going. Natalia was behind him now. Delaney watched the path ahead of him intently, listened intently for any sound not muffled by the snow.

When they suddenly saw the man they did not know was named Ferramo coming around a turn in the path ahead, all three of them stopped for a millisecond in their tracks. In that millisecond before the man fired, Delaney was able to push Natalia roughly off the path and down into the deep snow beside it. She fell heavily, and cried out as she was hit. Delaney fell too, but managed to flounder around in the snow to a sitting position and clumsily fire off a blast from the shotgun. He pulled the action and fired again, and then again, at the firing figure approaching.

The noise was deafening. Delaney's ears rang and his shoulder ached from where the gunstock had slammed into it. Melting snow streamed from his face. His three shots were gone. The gunman, if he was still alive, would have a clear run now. But there was silence.

Delaney got up on his knees and saw the man lying on his back in a circle of crimson snow. He looked over to where Natalia lay wounded. She was not dead. She was simply lying prone, as an animal does when hopelessly cornered. A small circle of red also stained the snow near her.

"Natalia," he called out.

"I'm all right," she said, but still not moving. Her face was in the snow as if she was unwilling to leave this chill blanket. "He's hurt my side."

Delaney moved to where Natalia lay. She was limp and didn't seem aware that she was lying in deep snow instead of on a bed. Her eyes stared at him, dark and wide.

"Natalia, are you OK?" he asked.

"Yes, Francis. I think so."

"Where did it get you?"

"In my hip I think. Near there. A little above maybe. It's sore all around there."

He rolled her over and looked. She cried out in pain as she moved. There was a sticky stain in the padded cloth of her coat on the left side just at the waist. Delaney was grateful that if she had to be hit it would be somewhere like that. But he knew there would be bad pain if it were a bone wound, and blood lost.

"Poor dear Natalia," he said softly.

He tried to pull up her coat to have a better look but she cried out again. Perhaps best not to try to pull down her jeans in the cold to examine the wound, he thought. It looked like she had been hit somewhere in the hip or the pelvis, or in the fleshy place below the lowest rib. The bleeding had increased as he moved her.

He felt a wave of panic and regret, like he had when things got dangerous for her in Europe.

"We've got to get you out of here," he said.

"Yes," she said.

"Come. Let's get you up," he said.

Delaney tried to get her to a standing position. She cried out again and again as she moved. Once she was up she tried to hobble along with him holding her, but then she fell to her knees, sweating and moaning.

"I think I might faint, Francis," she said. She had gone very pale. "It hurts badly. I think I might have to be sick."

Delaney tried to stay calm. He tried to heave her onto his shoulders but his feet sank farther into the snow with the weight. He stopped when she cried out again.

"Please, Francis. It hurts too much," she said. "I feel like I'm going to faint."

Tears streamed down her cheeks from the pain and the fear. Delaney knew he could not walk far in the snow with her on his shoulders in any case.

He put her back onto the deeper snow at the side of the path where she had first fallen. There was a lot more blood coming through her coat now. With a bullet wound, it was obviously best to leave her lying comfortably on this snowy bed. Natalia seemed content with this as well. Snow gathered on her eyelashes and exaggerated the movement of her eyelids as she blinked at him.

"I've never been shot before," she said quietly. "It's starting to feel very stiff and strange down there now."

"He may have broken a bone," Delaney said, trying not to let her hear any alarm in his voice. He knew he had to get help right away. The thought of having to leave here alone, even for a few minutes, made his heart sink. But he could not simply sit here with her either. There was too much blood coming and she was likely to go into shock at any time.

Delaney did not tell her the immediate danger was that the other man could come along the path to follow the sound of firing and try to find his partner. He suspected the man would eventually decide to trace his partner's steps along the pathway from the village. So another encounter was possible on that path if Delaney walked toward the village for help. If the second man had not stayed behind at the church.

Delaney quickly reloaded the shotgun.

"I feel quite faint now, Francis," Natalia said quietly. "I'm dizzy."

She was very pale now, looking a little bit as she had after her ordeal in the apartment in Rome. Delaney pulled off his parka and put it over her. Two layers of down; she would not freeze. He arranged her scarf under her head as a pillow. His mind raced for solutions, safe solutions, but he could think of nothing except going for help. Best, he said to himself again and again, if he quickly brought help here rather than try to carry her or drag her, if that were possible at all, and have her lose even more blood.

He elevated her left leg slightly with broken branches and this seemed to make her more comfortable. The wound was still bleeding through the coat, but he was confident that if he got someone in to see to it soon she would be all right.

"I'm going to get the police," he said. "You can't come with me like that. You've got to lie still so you don't lose too much blood."

"You're going to go?" she said.

"I don't want to go, Natalia," he said softly. "But there's no other way."

Delaney sounded much more confident than he actually felt, but he thought that this was the wisest course.

"You're going to get the police in this now?" she said.

"There's no other way."

"Will there be any in a town like that?"

"I don't know. I'll get someone. I won't be long at all. You'll be all right. I promise."

"Don't let them take the chalice," she said.

"I won't."

He pushed with his foot at the leather case where it had fallen in the deep snow, and he submerged it farther.

"It'll be fine there," he said.

He knelt beside her.

"Look, Natalia," he said, "I've got to hurry up now and get someone in here with a snowmobile. It's not far. Will you be all right?"

"Yes, Francis. Will you?"

"Yes."

"Will you be cold like that?" she asked.

"No."

"Where's the other man, do you think?" she asked.

"I think he waited back at the church, in case we went back that way," Delaney said.

That sounded much more convincing than it should. It was impossible to say just where the other man might be. Back at the church? Waiting on the village side of the woods with the car? Delaney felt quite strongly that if the man were to come he would come from the village side, because he would be unlikely to now set out across the open lake alone and risk being fired upon. If he had stayed at the church at all.

Delaney did not allow himself to dwell on the possibility that he could be wrong on any of this. Now, more than any other time, he needed to make a choice, to take action. Someone else needed him to do that. There was no longer the luxury of journalistic observation. There had not been that luxury for him for a long time in this thing, he thought.

"I've got to get someone in here," Delaney said again. "We've got no choice. You're bleeding badly."

"All right, Francis," Natalia said. "Try not to be very long."

"I won't be long," he said. "The village didn't seem all that far from the church. I can be there and back in fifteen minutes or so, I'd say. Maybe twenty.

That's not long."

His heart ached terribly in his chest.

"I'm leaving you the small gun," he said. "If someone comes, you'll have to shoot him. You know that, don't you?"

"Yes," Natalia said.

"Have you ever fired a pistol before?"

"No," she said.

Delaney placed the Browning on some pine branches near her right hand. He put her hand on it so she would know it was there.

"No one will come," Delaney said. "I'm sure the other guy is waiting back at the church with the priest. They wouldn't have wanted to leave the priest alone."

He kissed Natalia's wet cheek quickly and got up. He suspected she would sleep.

"I've got to go," he said. "I'll be right back. Try not to move."

"I'll be OK," she said. "It's very restful here."

They looked silently at each other for a moment — she, lying on her snow bed, and he, standing beside her with a shotgun.

"I've got to go," Delaney said.

"I know," she said. "You go."

"I love you, Natalia," he said suddenly. The words sounded wonderful in the silent woods. He felt no fear about what the words meant, no unease at the implications, no dread of entanglement.

"I love you too, Francis," Natalia said. That sounded wonderful in the silent woods as well.

"I'll be back in a few minutes," Delaney said.

There was no more time to lose. Delaney began trying to control his breathing and his racing heart, to concentrate on the matter at hand.

He went back out onto the path and stopped beside the body of the man he had killed. The wounds from the heavy-gauge shotgun were horrific. There was a great deal of blood. Delaney reached inside the dead man's overcoat for a clue as to who he might have been.

A quick look inside the wallet that he found showed him various things Italian, not Polish: passport, driver's licence, credit cards. He put the wallet into his own pocket, to examine carefully later. Then he threw the dead man's very large and very modern pistol far off into the woods. He took a last look at Natalia lying quietly, bundled up in coats, and he left her, walking fast.

Natalia had worked for many years with dreams, her own and the dreams of others, and she did not fear them. Jungians welcomed dreams, trusted them, and acted on their hints and allusions. So, because this afternoon had been very much like a dream, Natalia was not afraid. She was simply dreaming, and she expected the meaning of the dream to become clear as she pondered it. She had that faith. She turned the afternoon's dreamings around and around in her mind as she lay warm and comfortable on soft cushions of snow. She wondered: *What is archetypal about all of this?*

The black leafless branches above her spread intricate patterns against the dull grey sky and she studied them for secret signs.

She saw how it all had started but not yet how it was to end. She was all of the figures in all of the dreams and she saw things from all perspectives at once. She was her Uncle Stanislaw flying sorties over Germany with his comrade Zbigniew. She spirited secret things away from Europe and into Quebec. She felt Stanislaw's sorrow when the wife he loved so much had had to die. She felt that intensely. She was Zbigniew making small lunches alone in his apartment off rue de Belleville. She saw the pathos in that. She saw herself running through Europe with Francis, dear Francis. She saw them running together in Paris, Rome, and Como. She was skating with Francis, and then with Emma Jung, on Beaver Lake in Montreal. Mrs. Jung was very pleased the Grail had been found. Their skate blades left portentous inscriptions on the ice. Natalia saw the wonder in that.

Then all of their pursuers were running after them, singly and in a group all at the same time — running and running after her and Delaney everywhere they tried to hide. Their pursuers meant them only harm, the purest harm. The Shadow archetype, clearly. But part of life too, she thought as she lay in the snow. Something to be feared only if not accepted as part of life too. Natalia had that faith.

Of course she had dreamed all this before, or most of it. She had just not seen with such clarity how the many parts could begin to fit together. She felt no fear, no sadness.

But then there was sudden intense pain in her side. It intruded sharply on her dreamings. Her head felt light and the branches of the trees over her seemed now to sway too fast. Her feet began to feel cold. She wished in her dream that Francis would come back, wished that he had not gone at all. She imagined him hurrying through the silent woods. Hurrying because he loved her. She could imagine the intense concentration on his face as he walked. She could hear the crunch of his footsteps on the snow.

The footsteps stopped suddenly. They were now close by. But Natalia knew when she turned her head to see that it would not be Francis beside her. The snow felt cold when it touched her left cheek after she turned. She lay with her face on this freezing pillow to see how the waking dream would end. The shadow man in the dark overcoat who stood there was a stranger. He had come from the direction of the lake and the church. Not from where Francis had gone. So Francis, she knew, was safe. The man came closer. He was all of their pursuers at once and she had suspected all of them would eventually come.

There was intense fear now. And sadness. All the fearful images of all the past days and weeks began to well up in her mind in one last overwhelming sequence. She put her gloved hands over her eyes and forehead to block these nightmare images out, to force them back to the place where they were from. This was too much. Even for a psychologist. She wanted to rest now. She interlaced her fingers on the top of her head and pressed down hard to stop the mass of images from tumbling out.

Delaney knew immediately when he heard the far-off gunshot that Natalia was dead. The blood ran suddenly ice cold in his veins. He was almost at the village when he heard it: one shot, a handgun, far away. He had met no one along the way, and this, he now knew, was a very bad sign, the worst of signs. He hesitated only a moment before starting to run back the way he had come. He hoped, he dared to dream, that he was wrong, but he knew as he ran clumsily along the snowy path that it was over.

He started to cry as he ran. The emotions were intense, raw, exposed. He cried and he shouted Natalia's name and hurled curses as he ran. When he got there he was overheated, panting, with hot rivulets of sweat streaming under his shirt and sweater. Snowflakes had started to fall again gently. The body of the man he had killed was now lightly covered with snow. The blood on the snow around the body was frozen into a granular light red patch.

Delaney did not stop there. He ran to where

Natalia lay, much as she lay when he had so rashly left her there only a short while ago.

The snow all around her was trampled now with footprints. She lay on her back as he had left her, with her head tilted to the left. Her hands were interlocked over her head, as if to protect it from the shot she had known was coming. But the bullet had smashed through her hands, and now her hair and dead fingers were a sticky mass of blood. Delaney fell to his knees; nausea and numbness gripped him. His shotgun fell useless on the snow.

It was a good and private place for mourning. The woods were intensely silent. The falling snow made no sound. He knelt with her for a long time while tears burned slow freezing lines down his cheeks. When the tears eventually stopped, the numbness began to increase. He felt a great circle of emptiness spreading out from the centre of his guts. He was no stranger to numbness, had known it well throughout his life. He had ceased being numb for a time; he had forgotten or escaped it these past weeks with Natalia, but he hoped it would now come back. It would be welcome.

Eventually, he got to his feet. He had no taste anymore for clues or searches, but he felt compelled to look around in the snow nonetheless. At least as a witness to what had been done. He did not look at Natalia or at her wound. One look was all he would need for a lifetime.

There was nothing around her that told him exactly how it had been. Her gun, his gun, lay a short distance away. He left it there. The leather chalice case was gone. He did not want it anyway. The Mazovia Squadron pennant lay all but buried in the snow, one edge fluttering in the chill air. He did not retrieve it. He saw footprints leading in every direction: his own, hers, her killer's. He did not wish to run and chase. He felt no immediate desire for vengeance. There was no longer any reason for action or haste or violence. Perhaps that would come again later. Perhaps not.

He cried again for a long while, standing on the darkening path. When he turned to look again, Natalia was covered with a thin clean layer of snow. That was a good thing. He could not see her face anymore or her hideously wounded head. The guns were covered too. The snow in an overlong Quebec winter covers a multitude of sins.

The whine of engines ended this first period of mourning. It came from the direction of the village. The sound grew louder, closer, but he waited without fear. Soon an olive-green-and-yellow *Sûreté de Québec* snowmobile bounced into sight, and then another. Two uniformed SQ officers in big coats sat astride them. They wore goggles and black fur hats. When the first policeman saw Delaney and the body of a man lying across the path he raised his hand and motioned for his partner to stop behind him. Both of them drew pistols and crouched behind their machines.

"*OK, là, les mains sur la tête!*" one of the policemen shouted.

Delaney doubted very much they would shoot if he refused to put his hands on his head. He simply stood and stared. Slowly the policemen stood up, both of their guns still pointed at this staring, unarmed, coatless man as they tried to make sense of what they had found.

They brought the broken amateur spy back to the church parking lot, carrying on along the path to the frozen lake and then across it. Delaney was on the back of the lead snowmobile, watched over by the policeman who followed on the one behind. The police had touched nothing they found lying in the snow. But they had muttered often to each other in French as they began to realize exactly what they had discovered. They had spoken tersely into walkie-talkies, but asked few questions as they searched Delaney for weapons, handcuffed him, and helped him climb onto one of their machines for the ride back.

There were many cars in the parking lot now: SQ cruisers, unmarked cars, his own Mercedes. There was no sign of the large white Ford. The man nominally in charge seemed to be one uniformed, ruddy-faced, and apparently very unhappy member of the *Sûreté de Québec*. He wore an oversized green nylon parka and giant rubber boots with thick blue-felt liners showing at the tops. A small droplet of crystal-clear mucus sat poised to fall from the end of his nose as he listened to the report from the two officers who had brought Delaney in.

The man actually in charge, Delaney soon discovered, was someone else. This one wore a very urban wool topcoat of midnight blue and only small rubber protectors pulled over his brown wing-tip shoes. He had removed his fine brown leather gloves and placed them in a coat pocket. This man listened gravely as the police sergeant briefed him, in turn, on what had apparently been discovered in the woods. He then closely examined the contents of the two wallets that had been taken from Delaney.

The city man rubbed his hand over his close-cropped, salt-and-pepper hair. He considered Delaney for a long time from afar, and he stared at him intently before he and the senior police officer came over.

"*Je pense qu'avec celui ci, c'est préférable si on pose les questions en anglais,*" he said to the policeman in perfect Ottawa civil servant's French. "*Je pense qu'avec celui ci, c'est préférable, si vous êtes d'accord.*"

The man in the blue topcoat looked politely over at the policeman to see if there could possibly be any political objection to the use of the English language in this freezing parking lot somewhere in the wilds of Quebec.

"And you of course would prefer that too, wouldn't you, Mr. Delaney?" he said in civil servant's English, delivered with a thin smile.

"It makes no difference to me one way or the other," Delaney said.

"Would it make a difference to you if we asked Sergeant Morier here to remove those handcuffs and get you a jacket? You can't be very comfortable."

"Whatever you like," Delaney told him.

The request was made in French to Morier, who called one of his snowmobile patrol over to take off the handcuffs and give Delaney a policeman's parka from the trunk of one of the cars. Delaney put it on. He had been shivering from the sweat that had cooled on his skin.

The man in charge saw fit to introduce himself formally as this was done.

"I am Jonathan W. Rawson. I'm with CSIS, as you may have already deduced. This gentleman is Sergeant Raoul Morier, *Sûreté de Québec*. Sergeant Morier has consented to assist us with our investigations while we are in the province of Quebec today. That is very kind of him."

Morier listened with a slight scowl. Rawson nodded slightly, diplomatically, in Morier's direction.

"I have told Sergeant Morier that you are known to us at CSIS and that all may not be quite as it seems here," he said. "That's why we thought there was no need for handcuffs."

Rawson waited for some sign from Delaney about how things might best be played. But this smooth CSIS gamesman was intruding on Delaney's numbness, intruding on his grief. Delaney did not reply.

"I must say, Mr. Delaney," Rawson continued, "that we seem to have what my people in Ottawa like to call a very delicate situation here this afternoon."

Delaney still gave him no opening.

"They tell me there are two bodies over·there in the woods," Rawson said. "One of them is a young woman, they tell me. I have to assume that would be Natalia Janovski. Is that correct?"

"You know who that is in there," Delaney said, angry now. "Both of them."

"Why would you assume that?"

"It's obvious who they both are," Delaney said. "If you've been tracking this operation."

"I would not assume too much, Delaney," Rawson said. "That may in fact be what's led you and some others into this little situation this afternoon."

"It is far more than a little situation, my friend," Delaney said.

"I'm extremely sorry about the girl," Rawson said. "Sincerely sorry."

Rawson blinked rapidly in a brief civil servant's display of empathy.

"Fuck you," Delaney said.

Morier now took a renewed interest in the conversation.

"Who is the other person in the woods, Delaney? Who would you say that is?" Rawson asked, his period of mourning now over.

"You've got his papers over there. With mine."

"Papers can be quite easily faked these days, Delaney. Who would you say is lying dead in those woods besides Ms. Janovski?"

"He's a Vatican agent, probably," Delaney said.

"Or if he's not, he's learned something awfully important from Vatican people and he came over here to follow up. He's dead because he tried to kill us."

"Did he kill Ms. Janovski?"

"No, his partner did. Who probably just left here in the big white Ford that was parked up against my car."

Rawson looked quickly over at Morier and then back at Delaney.

"Sergeant Morier, would you mind if I had a word privately with our operative here?" Rawson said. "Just for a moment?"

Morier seemed relieved. He nodded and walked over to an unmarked car, where he sat down in relative comfort and warmth.

"I'm nobody's operative, Rawson," Delaney said.

"That's not how I understand it," Rawson said.

"Well, you've got it wrong. Hilferty had that wrong from the start."

"I'm sorry to say that Hilferty is dead."

Rawson waited to see what effect this news would have.

"If he's dead that's because he was out of his league," Delaney said. "I don't give a damn about Hilferty."

"That is a very hard thing to say about someone you worked with so closely on this, Delaney."

"I wasn't working closely with anyone," Delaney said.

"Well then, we're going to have to sort all of this out very, very quickly," Rawson said. "Just who was working for whom and your own involvement, and so forth. Because, as I hardly need to remind you, we have two bodies in the woods across that lake, plus one of my agents dead a few kilometres down the road, and a French agent lying beside him. We have a whole raft of very unhappy and suspicious SQ officers and some very unhappy people over in France. We're going to have to sort out people's allegiances very quickly here, Delaney, or it could get even more complicated than it presently is. If you see what I mean."

"You mean you've got to decide how to save your ass in this fiasco," Delaney said.

"Yours is the one very much on the line just now, I'm afraid," Rawson said. "There is a world of difference to those people standing over there near those cars if we have a CSIS operation gone wrong and an operative offside, as opposed to simply having a journalist wandering around the backwoods of Quebec carrying guns."

"And what about Vatican agents carrying guns and killing Canadians on Canadian soil?" Delaney said.

"Will that be your position, Delaney? Vatican? I think we're going to be calling it rogue elements from Polish State Security. From where we sit."

"That would be convenient," Delaney said in disgust.

"Well, yes, it would. Sometimes, if we're very lucky, a certain scenario can be more helpful than others in matters of diplomacy and international affairs. You've been around long enough to know that as well as I do."

"Helpful but not true."

"We're going to play it the way we see it, Delaney."

"More convenient for you if it's rogue Poles, and . . . let's see how you'll play it, Communist rogue Poles to boot, than if it's friendly agents, so-called, from the Vatican. Is that how you're going to play it?"

"We are going to play it the way we see it," Rawson said again. "In Canada's best interests. At least for public consumption. Other aspects of this of course we'll have to deal with a lot more discreetly. If you're right about who that dead man is in there. But we will deal with all aspects of this, have no fear of that."

"In the best interests of your pathetic little security service," Delaney said. "And in the interest of future relations with the Vatican. And maybe even for a nice little outcome in the Polish election. Walesa's people will be very grateful to the government of Canada for some fresh dirt on the Communist side about now, wouldn't they? The Vatican will be too. You get an awful lot just by keeping the lid on an inconvenient little killing or two."

"We've lost one of our own people in this, Delaney," Rawson said. "Remember that. On what as far as I can gather here this afternoon has been nothing more than a wild goose chase of some kind."

Delaney didn't try to explain what he himself had lost, with Natalia dead. Nor did he try to guess how much Rawson might actually know about what had been going on.

"I would think losing one of your own agents would be enough to outweigh any diplomatic niceties in this, Rawson," Delaney said. "Depending on who killed him."

"I'm not sure what you mean by that, Delaney."

"Really? That guy lying dead out there tried to kill Natalia and me. And his partner killed Natalia. I suppose it would be terribly inconvenient, diplomatically inconvenient, if we were to discover that one of those guys also killed your man Hilferty."

"You're naïve, Delaney," Rawson said. "For a journalist of your reputation. To think that anything like that would ever get dealt with publicly. Even if it turned out to be true."

They stood contemplating each other's options.

"You can come onside or not, Delaney," Rawson said finally. "It's as you wish. Either you're an operative, or perhaps we would now just call you an informant, a bad one, an amateur who fouled up badly on our behalf, or you're a journalist. But very much a freelancer. As in having no visible means of CSIS support. The outcome in your case will be very different, as you can imagine."

"The outcome will be very different in your case, too, Rawson, if the real story gets out about who's killing whom in this. Which country's agents are operating where. And about some new operational procedures I've observed among certain CSIS agents lately."

"Oh, I don't think you'll be writing any stories about this one, Delaney," Rawson said. "I'm betting that when you've thought it over very carefully this is one you'll decide to help us keep off the record, as you people like to say. One you'll decide to let us handle. When you see what you're risking."

Rawson stood and waited for Delaney to respond. Light snow fell steadily. It gathered on their shoulders. Police officers moved around the parking lot. Radios crackled from the open doors of cars parked here and there. All of the talk and the activity had distracted Delaney. But he now began to think again of Natalia lying under a blanket of snow out in the woods.

He thought suddenly of what had been stolen from her that afternoon. He wondered where the gold chalice she had paid for so dearly might be now. He thought also of all the bars of gold still likely lying in the cellar of the old stone church. He wondered how much longer that secret could last. He wondered whether the young priest, or the old priest in another church a long drive away, would now be at all inclined to make that secret last.

Delaney realized that he wanted very much for it to last. He wanted those bars of gold to be Natalia's monument. Until he could decide what she would

have wanted done and until he could make sure that
the right thing was, eventually, done.

Chapter 19

Delaney back in Montreal, standing quietly near another lake. This one not frozen. It is Beaver Lake on Mount Royal, where he and Natalia once etched infinity signs with their skates.

He came here often now, ever since things had settled a little. It was spring. In Montreal in April the sun is still weak, but strong enough to melt snow and soften ice and give people a hint of what is to come.

As he walked away from the lake, Delaney smelled the rank thawing earth and watched workmen clearing away the last of the snow from sidewalks and terraces in the park. He took in deep bracing drafts of rich spring air as he watched, and loosened his scarf and unbuttoned his coat. His plane ticket to Warsaw, newly purchased that afternoon, was tucked in an inside pocket of that coat, close to his heart.

It was almost time to leave this city again. But Delaney had wanted a last look at what was now his favourite place. He had wanted a last moment to think of Natalia and frozen lakes and infinity signs before setting out to do what must be done.

Delaney had been arrested, of course, for form's sake. He had not minded the long ride from Saint-Jean-de-Mantha to Montreal in the back of a big *Sûreté de Québec* car. It gave him time to rest and think. The two police officers assigned to bring him back said nothing at all to him and little to each other. The silent ride after the events in the woods near the church was a blessing.

They took him to Parthenais Detention Centre for questioning. But CSIS provided him with a lawyer, a sharp young Quebecois who knew precisely what needed to be said. This young man, solemnly on behalf of his masters in Ottawa, gave Delaney the wise, worldly, cynical advice that was required and sat blinking behind gold spectacles as his client was interviewed by the police again and again.

In the end, the version for the police of what had happened in the woods that afternoon sounded very much like the truth. A young woman had been killed. One of her assailants had been killed by CSIS operative Francis Delaney; the other was nowhere to be found. Clearly, it had been a matter of self-defence, of life and death. Life for Delaney; death for Natalia. The police seemed satisfied with this explanation. CSIS had also put words into appropriate ears, had made the right noises at high levels about agents and informants and the Official Secrets Act, and that had satisfied some others in Quebec. Delaney was to remain available to help various investigators in their work, should he be required. He was to be available for a coroner's inquest. He was to cooperate in every way. And that, for the moment, was that.

In some ways, it was all too simple. A part of Delaney wanted more drama, more complications, and more conflict. A part of him wanted to make a scene, to shock, to shout out that Natalia had been wrongly, foully, coldly murdered and that he would not stand for this, would call down justice from the heavens, would bring everyone down around him in a grand theatrical catharsis of rage and retribution.

But he did not make such a scene, at least not for the Quebec police. He sat quietly with his lawyer and did what he was told until they said, eventually, that he could go. He went along with this because he knew that what needed to be done required far more than staging scenes of impotent rage, and he was willing to wait. As Stanislaw Janovski had known how to wait. As Natalia would have wanted him to wait.

There were other interviews to be endured. Delaney was summoned to Ottawa for debriefings with Rawson and a man called Smithson and some other grim-faced CSIS types. They seemed to think he owed them something now that they had helped him with the police. They expected him to be grateful, to cooperate as best he could. They had no doubt after they helped him that Delaney would be their man, as Hilferty once assured them he had the potential to be.

They pretended to bring him into their confidence as much as they possibly could, sitting all together in secret briefings in secret Ottawa offices. And Delaney pretended to bring them into his. There was an elaborate charade of traded information, reconstructed scenarios, conspiracy theories. Occasionally, they even helped each other with their various agendas.

The main CSIS agenda was to find out which agents had been operating on Canadian soil and why. Delaney saw no reason now to hide from them most of what had happened in Quebec, or for that matter in Paris and Rome. They seemed to know most of it anyway. They hungrily lapped up his new information, however, about what had been hidden in the cellar of the old church. A golden chalice, he told them, inlaid with pearls. Catholic Church treasure from the war. Hidden in an old armoire all those years and sought so urgently by competing teams of Polish and Vatican agents, rogue or otherwise. The chalice missing once again. Likely now somewhere in Rome, or en route from Rome to a Polish church where it once belonged. Imagine that.

They were happy to imagine parts of that. But they claimed they could still not buy Delaney's theory of Vatican involvement in the murders of Natalia and Hilferty. They would look into it, of course, but they could not buy such a theory. Poles, they said. Rogue Poles. Not Vatican. Delaney, however, insisted that this was incorrect. Polish agents for Stanislaw's murder; yes, he agreed. For the priest in Lachine who had been Stanislaw's friend; yes,

Polish agents. Quite possibly rogue Polish agents. But not for Natalia and Hilferty. No, he said. That was another matter. And further, Delaney insisted, he believed Vatican agents had sat back and watched the kidnapping and mistreatment of Natalia in Rome, if indeed they had not been directly behind whatever Polish faction carried it out. These were his theories and he wanted it to appear he was doing his best to convince his Ottawa interrogators that his theories were correct.

Delaney's agenda was for them to see that he believed these things with all his journalist's heart, because for him not to insist would be seen as something out of character and reason for suspicion. So he stuck to his position, his theories, his accusations, as they expected he would do. He showed outrage at their obstinacy, as they expected him to do. He played his part to the hilt, as they played theirs, and in the end their exchange of information was all very earnest and civilized and off the record and incomplete.

Delaney knew they would never reveal to him who they thought was responsible for Natalia's death, if indeed they did know, and that they would never reveal any suspicions they might have had about the extent of Vatican involvement in the whole affair. As Rawson had explicitly told him that last afternoon near the church: such things are best dealt with in far less public ways. For Delaney, all that was fine. He would find out for himself and needed no CSIS confirmation. He had decided to leave for another time, however, the issue of exactly what he would do to those responsible if ever he found them.

Delaney also knew that CSIS would never share with him any accurate information about whether the Polish side, the Polish sides, were still in the game. Or whether some among the various Polish players had now decided the game was lost and that the treasure all sides had been seeking was beyond reach. Delaney's CSIS handlers would only say to him that, yes, continued covert Polish activity must always be considered a possibility. One must be watchful, of course. They would keep him informed. Of course.

He had asked them about such things, not because he expected the truth, but because his handlers would have wondered why he did not ask. He knew he would be very much on his own in this when he continued it, and he expected no help from CSIS. This task, he knew, was now his alone to carry out.

The CSIS men had feigned outrage of their own that Hilferty had given Delaney a gun, that Hilferty's surveillance methods had been irregular, that he had gone far beyond his mandate, that he had put the good name of Canada's security service at risk at home and overseas. For them not to be outraged would under other circumstances have raised suspicions in a journalist's heart. They knew this very well. So, they said piously, if Hilferty had not been killed he would have had some explaining to do about his procedures. This is not the way things are normally done in the Canadian Security Intelligence Service, they said, and Delaney should have no illusions about that. None.

Delaney had no illusions. He simply wanted them to relax, to think that he was chastened, heartbroken, glad to be done with it and, above all, willing to remain silent. He wanted them to harbour no suspicion that the story was still not fully told, that perhaps something else lay hidden in an old Quebec church, that Delaney had decided to get it to the right people in Poland once he could decide who the right people actually were. He wanted his supposed handlers to harbour no suspicion that once that first job was finished he would set about finding who had killed Natalia and that there would be much more to this saga yet.

And so he signed their little oaths of secrecy and their other scraps of legalese, and he agreed that this was no matter for the media. He gave them no reason at all for unease. And they seemed, as far as he was able to determine, content. A terribly nasty complex business, they said. Such troubled times we live in. Thank-you for your help, they said, but your part in this is finished. Leave it now to the professionals and the diplomats. If only because, they ever so politely warned, the legal consequences, the career consequences, the various other consequences for not doing so would be severe.

There had been the funeral to get through. This was

a scene much more difficult to play.

They buried Natalia in Côte des Neiges Cemetery, near her uncle. Gustavo, the Chilean refugee social-worker soccer-player ladies' man, had been helpful with the arrangements. As had some of Natalia's other colleagues from work.

They stood apart from him during the service, leaving him alone. A few of them stole looks in his direction, wondering about this lover Natalia had never told any of them about. Delaney had no idea what they knew about the circumstances of her death or even who had told them she was dead. But they never asked him what had happened, never pried.

CSIS sent two men who watched from a distance near their car. They nodded at Delaney but he did not nod back. The CSIS men studied the small group of mourners for a while and then they left. Delaney very much doubted there were any other agents present. But you could never really tell. He understood that now.

O'Keefe had wanted to come along to give Delaney moral support. O'Keefe had offered support in any number of ways after he was told that Natalia had been killed. But Delaney decided he would not involve his friend in any of this anymore. O'Keefe had been dragged far enough into danger and difficulty already. So Delaney told him very little about what had happened in Saint-Jean-de-Mantha, but promised to tell him more as soon as he possibly could and then declined the offer of company at the funeral. O'Keefe was friend enough and experienced enough to simply accept that and stand clear.

It was a grand spring day, full of sun. There was still a little snow among the headstones but the roads and walkways in the cemetery were dry. The ground was thawing, and when the coffin was lowered into the grave there was some loose moist earth available for those who wanted to throw it in. Delaney threw none in. He stood silently among strangers and thought about Natalia and their time together and what he had lost. But he was not one to grieve in public. There would be plenty of other private time for grieving and for guilt.

Gustavo did the public grieving for them. Gustavo cried great Latin American cries of grief for all of them, his shoulders and his ponytail heaving as he cried, tears streaming down his lined and pockmarked cheeks. After it was over, Gustavo came to Delaney and hugged him roughly and said over and over: *Lo siento, amigo, lo siento. I'm sorry. She was a good woman.* Some of the others came to shake Delaney's hand but didn't seem to know quite what to say. They shook his hand and wiped their tears and said they were sorry and they went away.

Gustavo wanted Delaney to come back to the apartment afterward. He had been the keeper of the keys and he thought Delaney would want a last look around before he began to get rid of Natalia's things. She had truly had no family except Stanislaw, just as she had said. Her work friends would share up her possessions, Gustavo said. Delaney should also take what he wanted.

Against his better judgment, Delaney went. He had not been there since before he and Natalia went to Paris. Nothing at all had changed. Gustavo stood quietly while Delaney had a last look.

"Take something, *amigo*," Gustavo said. "To remember her by. She was your lady."

"No, I have what I need," Delaney said. "I have some things already. *Gracias*."

He had her suitcase and a few other items that were in his car on the day she was killed. The police had returned them to him after he was released. Passport. Commonplace book. Rosary. Those things would do to remember her by if he could ever bring himself to look at any of them again.

Delaney and Gustavo stood awkwardly together in the warm stillness of the apartment. Delaney had a sense that Gustavo was about to ask what had really happened. But he didn't.

"*Lo siento, amigo*," Gustavo said. "*Mucho*."

Delaney had to go.

He was amazed once again at the utter reliability of certain priests.

Delaney decided he would go again to Saint-Sauveur to talk to Father Daniel Emile Hippolyte Lessard, perhaps for the last time. He very much needed to know what Father Lessard knew and what the old priest, and his younger *confrère* at the other church, might now be willing to keep secret.

Delaney waited for some days after his Ottawa debriefings and after the funeral before he went. He made it clear to any who might be watching or listening that he was simply trying to get his affairs in order and return to his life as a journalist. He made the appropriate phone calls to editors, publishers, colleagues, contacts. He rested. He spent a lot of time alone. Anyone watching or listening would be convinced, Delaney hoped, that he was slowly easing himself back into his work after going through what he simply told people had been some serious personal troubles.

So he waited and he watched and eventually he made his way again to Saint-Sauveur. One day he rode the Montreal subway to a main transfer point, changed trains, changed again, and darted this way and that in crowds until he was sure he was not being followed. Then he took another subway train to the bus terminal and rode a Greyhound up the Laurentian Autoroute to Father Lessard's church.

Even there, Delaney had been careful. After the bus dropped him off he stood for a long time on rue Principale, studying traffic and pedestrians and parked cars until he was confident there were no watchers, nothing out of the ordinary. Then he walked quickly across the street and let himself into a side door of the church.

Father Lessard was in his yellow office at the back, where Delaney and Natalia had first spoken with him. When Delaney put his head in through the open door and knocked on the frame, the priest looked up from some papers and then stood up right away. He was wearing black trousers and a black shirt with a clerical collar.

"*Mon Dieu, seigneur,*" the priest said.

"Sorry to startle you, Father," Delaney said. "We need to talk."

"Yes, my friend, we do," Father Lessard said. "But I didn't know if you would come."

Father Lessard closed the door and motioned to Delaney to take a seat. They talked for a long time.

Delaney saw no reason now to hide very much at all from this old priest. But he was surprised at how much Father Lessard already seemed to know. He knew, for example, about Natalia's death. The police and young Father Carpentier and various other players had told him what happened in the woods that day; that there had been shooting, that Delaney had been taken away, that bodies had later been taken away.

The priest knew that Delaney and Natalia had gone into the cellar of the other church and that they had exited suddenly and left their car behind. He knew that there had been two men in the other church that day and that they had been gruff in their questioning of Father Carpentier. The old priest knew most of what had happened, but Delaney needed much more from him than that.

"Some men came here afterwards, with police," Father Lessard said. "They all asked me what it was you wanted that day. They wanted to know who you both were and what I had told you."

"What did you tell them?" Delaney asked.

"I told them the truth," Father Lessard said. "I saw no reason not to. I told them about the Polish man from so long ago. I told them he had hidden something in the church as part of some secret wartime business with the government and with Duplessis. I told them I had told you where to find it because you had a password, because that had been my solemn task."

"You told them," Delaney said.

"Yes, my friend. I told them. But I did so because I knew more than they thought I knew."

"What do you mean?"

"Father Carpentier told me that you and the young lady had been only a short while in the cellar of his church before you went out across the lake toward the village. He said you left your car behind and then there was that unfortunate business in the woods. So I knew that either you had not found what it was you were looking for or you had found it and it was still where it had been hidden."

"How would you know that?" Delaney asked.

"Because on that day when I went with the Polish man in his truck it took him a very long time to unload whatever it was he was hiding. He said it was very heavy and he would need some time. You could not have taken it away so easily. And Father Carpentier has given me no indication that anything was taken away after you were there."

"But he didn't know what it was," Delaney said.

"No, he didn't," Father Lessard said. "He still

doesn't. And he has given me no indication since that day that he knows anything about the small room behind the armoire. He is a good priest. A young one, but good. He would have told me all he knew."

"Do you think the things are still there?" Delaney asked.

"Yes, I do," the priest said. "Father Carpentier would know if all those people with their questions had found something large and heavy and taken it away."

And some of those people with their questions think that what we were after was stolen from us that day in any case, Delaney thought. *Because that is what I have told them.*

Delaney did not tell Father Lessard about the gold. The priest had never said he wanted to know exactly what was hidden and Delaney thought it best to keep that secret still. But he told him about the chalice. And he told him about who he thought had taken it and who he thought might have killed Natalia and others to get it. Whether under official orders or not.

Father Lessard did not seem perturbed by the thought that Vatican agents or former agents or rogue agents or anyone else might be willing to do such things. He had been a priest too long for that.

"Monsieur Delaney," Father Lessard said quietly, "I don't know if you are correct in this. I can tell you nothing about who murdered your friend or who murdered the others. Or who may have taken the chalice away. I am sorry those things happened. But I can also tell you that nothing in the human heart surprises me anymore, and nothing in the Catholic Church, I am sorry to say, surprises me anymore. It is a very worldly church. I will not try to deceive you in this."

"So you'll help me keep the other things hidden?" Delaney asked. "You'll help make sure the right thing gets done?"

"I have been trying to do that in this matter since 1959, Monsieur Delaney," Father Lessard said. "I gave my word."

Delaney told the priest a little more about Stanislaw Janovski and his wish that what was hidden in the church would one day be returned to the appropriate people and used for the right purposes in Poland. Delaney told him that he wanted to find out who those people might be and decide what Stanislaw, and now Natalia, would have wanted done.

Delaney told him these things partly because he felt the old priest deserved to know at least a little more about what he had become involved in. But also because he needed someone else to know the story, or most of it, in case something happened to him and he failed to see it through. Father Lessard was his only possible ally now and could well end up the last person in the world to know these secrets. Father Lessard was a priest clearly accustomed to such burdens.

When all that business was done, they talked for

a long time about other things: loss and grief and guilt and rage and the desire for revenge. This was a priest accustomed to such burdens as well. Father Lessard had been the one to steer the conversation in that direction and Delaney had not resisted very much. But it surprised Delaney, once they began, how very much he needed something like this. Confession, if not absolution.

Afterward, Father Lessard saw him out. They walked through the empty echoing church together, saying nothing. There were no other sinners seeking assistance that day. Delaney shook the old priest's hand at the door.

"Thank-you, Father," he said.

"Thank-you for telling me about these things," Father Lessard said.

"I'll have to come back again," Delaney said. "At least one more time. I'll have to get back into the other church eventually."

"I understand that," the priest said.

"It may be a while," Delaney said.

"Yes," Father Lessard said. "It will not be an easy thing for you to decide who are the deserving ones in this."

"I know that," Delaney said. "But I have to try."

"Yes," the priest said. "You will have to try."

Before leaving for Poland, Francis Delaney dreamed this:

He is with Natalia. They are in an apartment together.

445

It is his apartment and her apartment at the same time. Each place has taken on some characteristics from the other and they have become one new living space. It is spare and spartan like his former home, and full and mysterious like hers, all at the same time. Some of his things are on shelves and walls, and some of hers. He feels safe and comfortable there.

He and Natalia exchange gifts. He gives her a small silver vial. It contains his tears — now a powerful elixir. She gives him a handsome volume of bound blank pages, embossed on the cover with mandalas and stars. "Yours now," Natalia says. He knows he will fill it. He knows this is a good thing.

Delaney stood alone in his quiet apartment, looking appreciatively around as he always did before leaving on a long trip or a new assignment. It was still his personal style of meditation. But there were differences now.

In the past he had used this place as a sanctuary removed from complexity and entanglements. In the past he had ventured out from here to make his journalist's observations, to observe the actions of others. It would still be a sanctuary, but this time he would venture out to observe and then to make choices, take sides, become involved in a story in ways he had never done before.

He knew, as he had always known, that action is a most dangerous thing. He knew that he now had many crowded hours ahead of him in distant cities. But this time any action he took would be for love and memory and responsibility — for Natalia — and that would make it different.

He was still not absolutely sure how he would proceed. He would start by flying to Warsaw and using all his skills and experience to try to make sense of what was happening there and who might be deserving. He had an intuition that in the end no decision might be possible, no immediate resolution possible. The time, he realized, might still not be right. To finally resolve Stanislaw Janovski's dilemma, he realized he too might simply have to wait.

He did not know Poland well, so he would be on unfamiliar ground. He knew he would be watched by the various sides if they found out he was in the country. As he would be in Rome, when he eventually travelled there. He would have to tread very carefully indeed. In this, as in so much of what he had done in the past, his biggest risk as well as his best weapon would be the fear among the players of a journalist telling all. But what his adversaries could not know was that Delaney very much doubted he would ever write a story about any of this. That sort of thing didn't matter to him anymore. Because for once, for the first time, this story had become his own story.

Mystery Shipment of Gold Arrives in Polish Port

GDANSK, March 6, 1996 (Newswire) – Polish officials were still baffled on Wednesday by the arrival at a Gdansk customs warehouse of four small wooden crates containing 48 gold bars worth an estimated US$8 million.

The sturdy, purpose-built crates arrived in Gdansk early Monday on a container ship from Canada, accompanied by documents indicating they contained "personal effects" destined for the museum at historic Wawel Castle in Krakow, in southern Poland.

The Curator of the State Art Collection at Wawel Castle, Tadeusz Cygnarowski, travelled to Gdansk yesterday from Krakow after receiving word from Polish customs officials that the crates had arrived and gold bars had been discovered inside.

Cygnarowski said he had in recent days received documents in the mail concerning the mysterious shipment, including bills of lading and an unsigned letter, but until being contacted by Polish customs authorities on Monday had thought they were a hoax.

Cygnarowski said the bills of lading indicated the crates had been shipped from Montreal in late January by someone acting "on behalf of" one Stanislaw Janovski.

The unsigned letter indicated that Janovski was one of the Polish officials who had been in charge of the famous shipment of Polish art treasures sent to Canada for safekeeping at the outbreak of World War II. It was thought all the art treasures had been returned to Poland in two lots in 1959 and 1961 and that the major players in the saga were now dead.

"The letter said Mr. Janovski

had died last year in Canada and it was his wish that the gold in these crates be returned to Wawel Castle," Cygnarowski told reporters at an impromptu news conference at Gdansk docks.

"Mr. Janovski apparently wished for the proceeds of the disposal of this gold to be used to locate and retrieve any pieces from the State Art Collection that were lost or stolen during the war, so they can be returned to the collection," Cygnarowski said. "He also wished that the money be used for the permanent upkeep of the national art treasures, to improve security and exhibition arrangements at Wawel Castle if required, and possibly to expand the collection in future."

"The letter indicated that Janovski did not want the money to be used for so-called 'political purposes,'" Cygnarowski said.

Adding to the mystery, Cygnarowski told reporters that the unsigned letter also indicated that he, as Curator, should "as a matter of urgency" attempt to locate a precious gold chalice, inlaid with pearls and possibly dating from the 16th Century, which was part of the original shipment to Canada and subsequently lost.

"The letter indicated that the missing chalice might now be sitting unclaimed in an unexhibited collection at the Vatican Museum in Rome," Cygnarowski said.

"We have no record of such a chalice being part of the original shipment of goods to Canada," Cygnarowski said, "but they were very chaotic times and I cannot rule out the possibility that my predecessors at Wawel Castle might have failed to include such an item on bills of lading in 1939."

He said he would make inquiries immediately among Vatican curatorial officials about the missing item.

Asked if the 48 bars of gold formed part of the original shipment to Canada, Cygnarowski said: "There is no doubt in my mind that this gold is the rightful property of the State Art Collection at Wawel. It is my firm intention to use it as the last custodian intended it to be used."

For the moment, the gold is to remain impounded at the Gdansk docks, customs officials said.

Cygnarowski said he had "no idea whatsoever" who might have sent the gold to Poland on behalf of Stanislaw Janovski some 35 years after the last shipment of treasures back from Canada.

A spokesman for the Canadian Embassy in Warsaw, who did not wish to be identified, said the Canadian government would make inquiries in Canada about Stanislaw Janovski if officially requested to do so by Polish authorities.

"No request has been made at this time," the embassy spokesman said.

Shipments by sea of small lots of personal effects are not normally subject to customs inspection before leaving Canada, the embassy spokesman said. It is the responsibility of customs officials in the country to which the goods are being shipped to inspect the contents when they arrive and that is what happened in this case, he said.

Political observers and Western diplomats here, who did not wish to be identified, said that they expected the gold would likely be allowed to remain in the possession of

Wawel Castle museum. The political situation in Poland is still in flux after the narrow defeat in the November 1995 presidential elections of Lech Walesa by the candidate of the former Communists, Aleksander Kwasniewski.

There was no immediate comment from President Kwasniewski's office, or former president Walesa, on the mysterious gold shipment. The Vatican press office in Warsaw did not return reporters' telephone calls on Wednesday afternoon.

Execution-style Murder in Downtown Rome

ROME, Italy, March 14, 1996 (Newswire) – Police in Rome said on Thursday they had no clues as to who was behind an execution-style shooting of a man in broad daylight in a street not far from St. Peter's Square.

The dead man has been identified by police as Vincente Pino Tremonti, aged 36. He was shot three times in the upper body at close range by an unidentified assailant in Via Candia, police said.

Tremonti was found lying beside his car at 2:40 p.m. (1240 GMT) by a local resident. He was pronounced dead at the scene by ambulance workers.

The street was deserted in the quiet time after the lunch hour and police say no eyewitnesses have come forward with a description of the gunman.

One restaurateur in the Via Candia said he heard what he thought was an automobile backfiring as he was cleaning up after lunch, but he saw nothing.

One senior police investigator said privately that Tremonti may have been a former member of the powerful Vatican security service. That report could not be independently confirmed.

Vatican officials refused comment on the killing, referring all inquiries to the Rome police.

LEADING REPORTER CALLS IT QUITS

by Fraser J. Harrelson, *Tribune* Media Writer
April 23, 1996

MONTREAL — One of Canada's leading investigative journalists, Montreal's own Francis Delaney, is leaving his post as a senior feature writer at *Forum* magazine to take an extended sabbatical and consider other career options, the *Tribune* has learned.

A senior editor at *Forum* yesterday confirmed the rumour that had been circulating among media watchers since last week. When contacted subsequently, Delaney, who is 44, said he wanted to take "at least a couple of years" away from journalism after a career which sent him on difficult assignments to many of the world's trouble spots.

He has spent much of the last year on various assignments in Europe, including coverage of the November 1995 presidential elections in Poland. He has only recently returned from another European trip.

In addition to his reporting work over the years, Delaney has written two well-received books on political topics.

Delaney refused to say whether he intended to return to the media after his sabbatical. He said his immediate goal was to take a sailboat journey through the Caribbean islands and "forget about everything for a while."

He has purchased a 30-foot sailboat, which he will take delivery of next month in Key West, Florida. Delaney said he had named the boat *Natalia*.